The Night He Disappeared

A J WILLS

Cherry Tree Publishing

The Night He Disappeared

Copyright © A J Wills / Cherry Tree Publishing 2025

All rights reserved. No part of this publication may be reproduced, stored in a retrieval system, or transmitted, in any form or by any other means, without the prior written permission of the author, nor be otherwise circulated in any form of binding or cover other than that in which it is published and without a similar condition being imposed on the purchaser.

This book is a work of fiction. Any resemblance to actual persons, living or dead is purely coincidental.

**Transcript from the podcast, *Fallen Hero*.
Interview with eyewitness, Tammy Whitmore**

It wasn't until I saw my legs, or what was left of them, that I realised how badly I was hurt. I kept staring at them, not really believing what I was seeing. And I reached for Teddy behind me where he was lying on the sidewalk, his body all crumpled up, and I says, Teddy, you okay? But he didn't say nothing. I kept crying his name and I really thought he was dead.

And as I'm lying there, crying and yelling, I see this figure come through the smoke, so calm, like he was there to help, you know?

And I says to Teddy, Hey Teddy, it's going to be okay. There's an angel come to help us.

And in that moment, I felt nothing but peace. I honestly thought he was a gift from god.

But I couldn't have been any more wrong.

I didn't know who he was back then, but I can tell you he was definitely no angel.

Chapter 1

PIPPA
February 14, 2024

A champagne cork pops like a gunshot in a church. A woman squeals and I almost drop my phone.

'Will you put that damn thing away?' Nathan scowls across the table as the heady buzz of chatter resumes, filling the restaurant until I can barely hear myself think.

I flip my phone over and place it face down on the pristine, snowy-white tablecloth, my fingers twitching.

'Sorry, what were you saying?'

'Let's play a game.'

'What kind of game?'

'Word association.' Nathan's grin shows off the perfect set of teeth he bought himself as a present in Turkey before we met. They're almost as white as the tablecloth, giving him the luminescence of a Hollywood star.

'Are you sure?' Although he has a determined competitive streak, Nathan's never shown much interest in playing games before. The one and only time I talked him into playing Scrabble, I beat him so resoundingly that he sulked for the rest of the evening and most of the next day.

'I'll say a word and you have to say the first thing that comes into your head.'

'Psychologist.'

'What?'

'It's the first word that came into my head.'

'Don't be flippant.'

'Sorry.'

'Ready?' He leans across the table, his dark eyes twinkling. He's up to something. I can read him like a book. 'Roses.'

'Manure.'

Nathan frowns. 'Red.'

'Blood.'

'Pippa! Be serious.'

'I *am* being serious. It's the first word I thought of.'

'Valentine's Day.'

'Massacre.'

'You can't say massacre.' His chin dips onto his chest.

'Why not?'

He slumps back in his chair, his brow hooding his eyes. He folds his arms and stares at the plate he's virtually licked clean, silently brooding. We rarely eat meat these days, but Nathan chose for us both and ordered the duck confit as it's supposed to be a special occasion, although it was too rich for my taste. Too fatty. And it's now sitting heavily on my stomach, bloating my abdomen. I should have had the salad.

I know what Nathan's doing, but he's trying too hard. It feels forced. Like bringing me to this fancy French restaurant by the river packed with couples quaffing champagne and whispering words of devotion to each other just because someone in a marketing department arbitrarily picked today as the day we all should be declaring our undying love for each other. And paying a fortune for the privilege. It's not us.

I'd have been happy with a night in front of the TV and a bowl of chocolate-dipped strawberries. That would have been a treat.

Would Nathan notice if I slipped my phone into my lap and checked my Instagram? There's every chance my video views might have smashed through a hundred thousand by now. That would be something as I only posted it this afternoon.

It was only a simple message to my followers on Valentine's to remember that the most important love in their lives is themselves, but it's really taking off. It's the closest thing I've ever had to a post going viral.

Don't wait for someone to bring you flowers. Go out and bloom on your own terms. **#empoweredwomen #strongnotskinny.**

But before I have the chance, Nathan pushes his chair back. The screech of legs scraping across the floor cuts through the noisy chatter. With a soppy, lop-sided grin, he edges around the table and drops to one knee.

'Pippa Ravenscroft,' he says, taking my hand.

A rash of heat prickles across my chest and creeps up my neck. 'Nathan, what are you doing?' I hiss.

'Would you do me the enormous honour...'

Oh, god. This can't be happening.

A hush descends across the restaurant as, one by one, people swivel in their seats, falling silent to watch. At the next table, a woman points her phone at us, filming.

I want to shrivel up and die.

'...of being my wife?'

Nathan's free hand snakes into his jacket, pulls out a small velvet box and thumbs it open. He wafts it under my nose. An enormous diamond set into a delicate white-gold band sparkles under the low lights.

It's a joke. It has to be. We've never even discussed marriage. It's too soon. Too much. My throat tightens and like a child who thinks they're invisible to the world if they remain rigid, I freeze.

'Pippa, will you marry me?'

The restaurant snatches its collective breath while a waiter saunters towards our table with a grin a mile wide, carrying a bottle of champagne in a silver ice bucket and the biggest bunch of red roses I've ever seen.

Every eye is on us, waiting for me to burst into tears, clutch my chest, and choke on my words as I tell Nathan that of course I'll marry him, like we're in a trashy romance.

My heart thumps. My cheeks burn. If only the polished terracotta floor would open up and swallow me whole.

I roll my eyes to the ceiling, stalling, trying desperately to find the words to save us both from inevitable humiliation. A red light blinks on a fist-sized CCTV camera on the wall. It makes it even worse to think someone might be sitting at a bank of screens recording the moment.

'Nathan... I...'

The way he's looking at me, so full of hope and expectation with his shirt taut across his muscular chest and puckering open at the neck, offering a tantalising glimpse of smooth, tanned skin... it'll break his heart. And I know Nathan. He'll totally overreact.

'Is that a yes?'

'Can we talk about it? In private?' I whisper, leaning closer.

His smile fades and his eyes mist with confusion. Slowly, he lowers the ring box and glances around the restaurant. A nervous titter spreads through the room.

'What's there to talk about?' He shakes his head, bemused.

'Please, get up.'

'I don't understand. Are you saying no?'

The waiter with the champagne and roses shuffles on the spot. I shoot him a tight-lipped smile of apology as Nathan stands and slips the ring back into his pocket. People turn away and quietly resume their meals, deflated. It's as if I've taken a giant pin and burst the good cheer in the room. As if I don't feel bad enough.

Nathan finally lets go of my hand and returns to his chair with his head down, defeated.

'I thought it's what you wanted. I've gone to so much trouble.'

'I know, but I had no idea you were going to propose.'

The waiter coughs discreetly. 'Would you like me to —?'

'Just take them away,' Nathan snaps. He waves angrily at the poor man. It's a shame. They were beautiful flowers. I hope they don't end up in the bin.

I tap my phone with my fingers.

'Well, this is embarrassing.' Nathan drops his napkin into his lap and smooths it flat.

When I reach across the table for his hand, he pulls it away. 'It was a lovely gesture. So thoughtful and I can see how much planning you've put into it, but don't you think we should have discussed it first?'

'I thought you loved me?'

'Of course I do, but getting married is such a big deal and we're both still young.'

'I'm thirty-two next year. My parents were married and had kids by the time they were twenty-six.'

'It was different for them.'

'What's the problem? I'm not enough for you, is that it?'

'Don't be silly.'

'What is it, then? I'm all ears.' His tone's changed. It's sour. Bitter.

I spin my phone around with one finger, a distraction from Nathan's penetrating gaze.

'I have so much on with work. You know that. It's all I can think about right now.'

'Will you leave that bloody phone alone?' he shouts, slapping his hand on the table. 'This is important. I'd like your full attention for once, if it's not too much trouble.'

I curl my hand into my lap.

'Honestly, Pippa, you spend more time checking your engagement and replying to comments than you do talking to me. I swear you don't listen to half of what I say.'

I catch the eye of the woman who was filming us at the next table. She glances away, embarrassed.

'I'm sorry. You're right. I shouldn't have had my phone out.' I slip it into my bag, which is hanging off the back of the chair, out of sight and temptation.

'I thought what we had meant something. But maybe I was the only one who's serious about us.'

'You're blowing it all out of proportion. You know I love you.'

'Do you?'

'Of course.'

'I should have known better. It's always been your followers first and me second.'

'Now you're being ridiculous.'

'I thought what *we* had was real.'

'Don't make me choose between you and my work. That's not fair.'

'Work?' Nathan snorts. 'All you do all day is cavort around in front of a camera telling insecure women how to live their lives.'

His words sting like a thousand pin pricks. I've worked so hard to build up my following and make a career out of what started as a hobby. A sideline. I thought he was proud of what I've achieved. I stare at him, open-mouthed.

He sighs and his shoulders droop, his whole body deflating. 'I didn't mean that.'

I've had a suspicion for a while that he's jealous of my success, especially since the following on my Instagram page surpassed three-quarters of a million, and my TikTok presence continues to grow daily, driving fans towards my YouTube videos and paid subscriptions, which is earning me more than a comfortable living. Maybe it's male pride. Maybe he doesn't like the fact that I'm earning more than he does at his crappy insurance sales job.

A waiter sidles up to our table to clear away our plates. We both fall silent. 'Would you like to see the dessert menu?'

'Just the bill,' Nathan says.

It would have been nice if he'd checked with me, but anyway, I've lost my appetite.

The waiter returns with a leather wallet and slides it in front of Nathan with an archaic presumption that grates, but I bite my tongue. I don't want to be at the centre of another scene.

'Let me pay.' I reach for the bill, but Nathan snatches the wallet away.

'My treat,' he says, less than enthusiastically.

'You paid last time.'

'I can afford to take you out for a meal on Valentine's Day,' he snaps.

It's not worth another argument.

Nathan drops his credit card onto the wallet without even checking the bill and leans across the table.

'So,' he says, 'where does this leave us? Is this your way of telling me you want to break up?'

I draw in a deep breath. I wouldn't have chosen tonight to have this conversation, but since he's forced the issue, I guess it's time I told him the truth.

Chapter 2

I thought we were fine. That we were having fun and enjoying life. Why spoil it? We've only been together eleven months, and the truth is, I don't know how I feel about getting married. I'm not someone who's spent her teenage years fantasising about dresses and flowers, horse-drawn carriages and candlelit churches. It's not that I'm against the principle of marriage. It's just not on my agenda.

'Well?' Nathan arches an eyebrow.

Before I have the chance to answer, the waiter returns with a card reader and a simpering smile.

'I trust everything was to your satisfaction this evening?'

'It was fine,' Nathan and I bark at the same time.

'Of course I don't want to split up,' I say when the waiter withdraws.

Nathan's my rock. My everything. Although I wish he wouldn't be so sensitive.

'But you don't want to marry me?'

I sigh. 'Can we talk about it?'

'What's there to talk about? Either you do or you don't.'

He jumps to his feet, pulls on his coat, and before I can gather myself, storms out.

'Nathan, hang on!' But he's already gone. I have no desire to hang around either after tonight's fiasco, but he could at least wait for me.

As I attempt to pull on my own coat, my chair tumbles backwards, crashing to the floor and attracting more unwanted attention. The waiter who brought the flowers and champagne to our table comes rushing to my aid, but it's a bit late. My humiliation is complete. My cheeks burn as everyone stares. The waiter rights the chair, helps me on with my coat and hands me my bag.

I need air. It's so hot in here. With a nod of thanks, I charge for the door.

'Mademoiselle!'

What now?

I glance over my shoulder. The waiter waves my phone in the air. 'This is yours, I think?' He comes rushing over with it.

It must have spilled out of my bag when I knocked the chair over. I clutch it gratefully to my chest. I'd have been a hot mess if I'd lost it. Even though everything on it should be backed up, I'd have been worried sick if I thought it had been stolen and someone was able to access my life. My bank account. My social media accounts.

'Thank you so much.'

'You're welcome.' The waiter places a hand on my upper arm. 'And I hope you and your boyfriend can work things out.'

He means it genuinely. I can see it in his eyes and in his touch. I don't know what to say. I mumble an inadequate thanks and glance back at our table. I didn't enjoy the meal, but the staff were wonderful. Attentive without being intrusive, gliding between the tables like choreographed shadows, although I bet Nathan didn't add a tip to the bill.

I pull out a ten-pound note from my purse and press it into the waiter's hand. 'Thank you.'

And then I'm outside, racing to catch Nathan. He's ambling along the promenade overlooking the river with his hands shoved deep into the pockets of his charcoal-grey overcoat, his neck pulled in and his shoulders hunched against the biting chill of the February night. Ahead, Tower Bridge straddles the Thames like a sentinel, so brightly lit you could probably see it from space.

'Nathan!' He doesn't slow down or look back, pretending not to hear me.

I slip a hand through his arm and squeeze his solid bicep.

'I'm sorry, okay? Please, can we start again and pretend I didn't spoil a lovely evening?'

'It was all planned. It was going to be perfect,' he grumbles.

'I wasn't expecting you to propose.'

'I thought it would be romantic. Don't you want to build a life together?'

With a sigh, I pull up the faux fur-trimmed hood of my quilted puffer jacket and arch my shoulders against the penetrating chill.

'I'm not ready, Nate. To marry you or anyone else. We're both still so young.'

'Not that young.'

'What's the rush?'

'It's what people do when they love each other. But hey, I guess nothing's allowed to derail the Pippa Ravenscroft brand.'

'What's that supposed to mean?'

'Sometimes I feel like I don't even exist. You've never even acknowledged me to your followers, have you?' Nathan stops suddenly and turns to face me. 'It's as if you're embarrassed by me.'

'That's not true!'

He raises an eyebrow. 'Isn't it? So why do I feel like your dirty little secret?'

I don't know where this has come from. I've always been careful about how much personal information I post and try to respect the boundaries between my public and personal life. There are too many oddballs and weirdos out there online to take the risk. I thought I was protecting us both by keeping Nathan out of the spotlight, but I guess he sees it differently.

'I didn't realise you felt like that.'

He shrugs and breathes out heavily through his nose. 'I miss how things were. We used to be so close, but now it feels as though there's not much time for us. You're always so busy.'

'That's not fair.'

I devote every spare minute to Nathan. We train together most mornings and he spends almost every weekend at my flat. We regularly meet for lunch or dinner and grab coffee when we can. We take long walks in Richmond Park or in the Surrey Hills. In fact, there's not much I do on my own since we met. But creating compelling digital content and building my business takes time and effort. It's a never-ending grind, like being stuck on an endless treadmill. I'm a slave to the algorithmic gods, trying to remain relevant and current while making my voice stand out in a crowded market.

'You know what I mean. Your followers always come first, don't they?'

He walks on, head down, hunched over. I have to jog to catch up with him.

'I'll try harder,' I promise.

'I'm worried you're going to burn yourself out. Of course, if we were married, you wouldn't need to work.'

'Are you kidding? I don't want to be a housewife relying on someone to support me.'

'All I'm saying is that you don't need to kill yourself.'

'I'm not.'

'So why am I always in competition for your time?'

'I didn't realise you were.'

We cut through a narrow brick archway onto a cobbled street that runs through a row of Victorian riverside warehouses converted into shops and cafes, battling against a tide of strolling couples. Lord knows what they must think of me and Nathan, marching along boot-faced.

Those heady, intoxicating, first few months when everything was new and exciting between us, and we were constantly hungry for each other, seem a distant memory. Somewhere along the way, as our lives have become meshed together, novelty has given way to familiarity, but we'll get through this.

I'll find a way to make it right so that Nathan sees how much he means to me.

We turn off the cobbled street and climb two flights of stone steps onto Tower Bridge, where the buzz of traffic is noticeably louder and thick crowds of people are crammed onto the narrow pavement.

As we turn under an arching grey stone abutment, I grab Nathan's arm. I can't stand the bad atmosphere between us.

'I don't want to fight. Please, can we be friends again?'

'Who's fighting?'

A man in a hurry inadvertently catches my shoulder and knocks me off balance. Nathan catches me and we stare intently into each other's eyes.

'I don't want to lose you, Nathan.'

He wets his lips and gives a slight shake of his head. 'What are you trying to tell me? Should I propose again?'

'No, that's not what I'm saying.'

Nathan's gaze falls.

'But that doesn't mean I want to break up either. I've never mentioned you in my posts only because I wanted to keep you to myself. You understand, don't you?'

'You're not ashamed of me?'

'Why would I be ashamed of you, you big goon?' I punch his arm playfully. He reacts like I've stabbed him, wincing in mock pain before his face cracks into an amused smile.

'As long as I'm your—'

But the high-pitched grind of an engine, a vehicle travelling too fast, cuts him off mid-sentence. A white van hurtles past, weaving through the traffic at reckless speed, heading onto the bridge. It bobbles on its axles, a cloud of black smoke belching from its exhaust. Heads turn, eyes drawn. Everyone watching in disbelief. It's like viewing a video playing at double speed. Everything's happening too fast. Too quickly.

Car horns blare with censorious irritation. A taxi skids across the road with a screech of brakes and a bus driver coming in the opposition direction stares through his windscreen, eyes wide with alarm.

'What the hell?' Nathan mutters, his hand fishing for mine.

The van bounces off metal railings that separate the traffic from the pedestrians with an ear-splitting screech before veering around a dark-coloured saloon, straddling the centre line, and cutting through a narrow gap in front of an approaching truck.

The van is out of control, the driver either drunk or high on drugs, the vehicle's taillights streaking through the night. People walking across the bridge come to a halt, shocked, while a flicker of unease creeps into my chest. I tug at Nathan's hand, the urge to run coming from somewhere deep inside, a primal survival instinct, even before the blast rips the air apart with a thunderous roar as if the world is being wrenched in two and we're thrown clean off our feet like we've been smacked in the chest with a sledgehammer and dumped onto the ground under a cloud of smoke and debris.

Chapter 3

My body's pinned to the ground under its own weight, a sack of muscle and bone, while a chill from the freezing flagstones seeps through my coat. My mind's a fog, everything hurts and when I try to swallow, my throat's dry. A buzz like a thousand angry hornets trapped in a barrel rings in my ears and there's a dull throb at the back of my head.

It's as if my consciousness is cocooned deep inside a fluffy part of my brain. Not awake but not asleep either, while my body feels like an alien extension of my being. A toxic cocktail, like burning plastic or rubber tyres tossed onto a flaming bonfire, claws at the back of my throat, the smell so intense it draws me to the surface.

'Pippa?'

I peel open my eyes and stare into Nathan's face as it swims in and out of focus. His hand curls around mine and I squeeze his cold fingers.

Why's he standing over me, looking at me like that?

An image flashes across my mind, so transient it's gone no sooner than it appears. A van travelling too fast and out of control. An explosion. The air being forced from my lungs and punching me to the ground.

'You're alive. Thank god.'

He looks different. Uncharacteristically dishevelled, his face grey, his eyes darker and blacker than I remember.

'What happened?'

He helps me to sit. I rub the back of my head, tender where I must have hit it when I fell, and check my fingers for blood. Nathan stares right through me as if his mind is elsewhere.

I glance over his shoulder along the length of the bridge where mangled vehicles, charred and twisted, are strewn across the road among chunks of stone and pockets of fire. People are lying unmoving. Others stagger around, dazed, and the air is thick with smoke and dust, curling in tendrils towards the sky. And yet somehow, the bridge is still being illuminated like a giant, ravaged Christmas tree.

A cough catches deep in my lungs and I double over with tears in my eyes and spittle dribbling from my mouth. The buzzing in my ears quietens, but it's replaced by the blare of car alarms and horns, the rumble and crackle of fire, and worst of all, people screaming. Gut-twisting howls of terror and pain like nothing I've ever heard before. Sounds dredged up from the pits of hell.

'Are you hurt?' Nathan asks.

'I don't think so. You?'

He pulls me up by my hand and I stand swaying like a newborn calf.

'I'm fine.' But he doesn't sound it. There's a tremor in his voice. A quiver of uncertainty and fear.

'What the hell happened?'

Nathan shakes his head, puffs out his cheeks and runs a hand through his hair, dislodging clouds of dust and dirt. He brushes it off the shoulders and sleeves of his coat.

'Some kind of explosion, I think. I don't know.'

An explosion? We could have been killed. If we'd left the restaurant thirty seconds earlier, or hadn't stopped to talk at the top of the stairwell...

I throw myself at Nathan, burying my head into his muscular chest and sinking into his warmth. I squeeze him so tightly, my arms begin to ache. He lightly grips the back of my head and, as I close my eyes, there is nothing but the two of us. We stand holding each other for what feels like an eternity, suspended in time, until he eventually peels himself away and holds me at arm's length, checking me over.

I take another glance along the bridge, hardly able to comprehend what I'm seeing. The iconic towers, famous across the world, are partially obscured by thick, swirling plumes of smoke and there's debris and chaos everywhere. Shattered glass. Twisted metal. Lumps of tarmac gouged out of the road. A vehicle on its side. A bus that's come to a halt skewed across both lanes.

A woman lurches towards us with blood streaming from her head, her face and clothes whitewashed with dust. Her eyes are two blinking onyx orbs, like ghostly holes cut in a sheet. I'm not sure she even notices us as she staggers past, cutting a lost and lonely figure.

'Come and sit.' Nathan encourages me towards the top of the stone steps we climbed moments ago. 'Do you have your phone?'

'My phone?'

'To call the police.'

He settles me in the corner of the stairwell, sitting me with my back against the cold, hard wall so I'm blinkered and can't see the bridge. My only view is the worn steps that fade into the gloom.

'Pippa!' Nathan shouts.

I gaze up at him, my head floating. 'Mmm?'

'Your phone? Call the police. Tell them what's happened.'

'Right.' Hunched up with my coat rucked around my waist, I struggle to reach into my pocket, but eventually tease my phone out with my fingers.

Nathan watches as I make the call, eyes never still, darting left and right, his body twitchy with nerves.

The call handler sounds hassled. She asks for my location and whether I'm hurt, tells me that help is on the way, and then she's gone. I guess they've been overwhelmed by calls.

I drop my phone in my lap. All I want to do is go home and forget everything. Pretend none of this is real.

'Wait here,' Nathan says.

'Why? Where are you going?'

'I'm going to see if there's anything I can do to help.'

'You can't leave me!'

'I'll only be a few minutes. Don't move. I'll be back in a bit.' He strips off his coat and drapes it over my arm. 'Look after that for me. And don't go anywhere, okay?'

'Don't leave,' I beg. I can't face the thought of being left alone or of Nathan putting himself in danger. What if there are more explosions? 'It's not safe.'

'I can't stand here and do nothing.' He leans over and plants a kiss on top of my head.

I grip his hand. 'Please.'

'Pip, I have to.'

'If you leave, I'll never forgive you.' It's a churlish, selfish thing to say, but I don't want him to get hurt.

He pulls his hand free, offers me a grim smile, and walks away. And in a blink, he's gone.

I stare at the empty space he's left and shiver. How could he walk away and leave me? I need him. Fiery bubbles of anger rise in my chest. What does he think he's playing at?

This is classic Nathan, always trying to prove himself. To be the guy who can push himself further than anyone else in the gym. Lift heavier. Run faster. I should have known he'd try to play the hero. And what am I supposed to do? Just sit here and wait?

I bury my head in my hands and scrape my fingernails across my scalp. I'm being a bitch. There are people injured and dying and he's only trying to do the right thing. I should be proud of him for being so selfless, not wallowing in petty resentment. I know what he's thinking, that it might help with his attempts to join the police. The Met have already turned him down once, but he's determined to reapply and being able to show he can act on his own initiative in a stressful and confusing situation is bound to count in his favour.

A shirtless man, his bloodied jeans in tatters, red and blue football tattoos on full display, ambles past, eyes fixed ahead, feet shuffling. I ought to check if he's okay. I could put Nathan's coat around his shoulders and offer to let him use my phone to call a loved one, but instead I sit frozen on the ground, staring as he disappears from view. The emergency services will be here any moment. It's best to leave it to the professionals and, anyway, it's not as if he's noticeably injured.

The cold seeps into my bones as seconds pass like minutes. I shuffle on my bottom to glance around the top of the stairwell, praying that Nathan's heading back. But there's no sign of him. He's been gone at least ten minutes now and I need him back.

I'll call him.

I press my phone to my ear and wait a few moments for it to connect.

A vibration rattles against my thigh in short, rhythmic bursts. It's coming from the pocket of Nathan's coat. My heart plummets as I pull out his phone, its screen lit up.

Pippa calling

What kind of idiot doesn't take his phone with him?

I end the call with an angry prod of my finger and scream in frustration. If I wait here much longer, I'll freeze to death. It's already much colder than when we left the restaurant. I pull my legs up to my chest, wrap my arms around them, and rest my chin on my knees, my teeth chattering. I need to do something to take my mind off Nathan and to keep warm. Realistically, there's only one thing I can do.

I clamber to my feet, my legs stiff and my muscles cold, and drape Nathan's coat over the wall. I run a hand over my hair, flattening it down and brushing out dust and fragments of debris. I wouldn't normally dream of appearing on camera if I didn't look flawless, but I came within a whisker of dying tonight. I think my followers will cut me some slack if I'm not looking my best.

In the distance, the first sirens wail pitifully, announcing their imminent arrival. The cavalry on a charge. I open my Instagram account, frame myself with the bridge in the background, and begin a live broadcast.

'Hey, everyone.' I force a smile, conscious that I'm badly lit. Usually, I work from a script I've written well in advance, so I know exactly what I'm going to say, but tonight I'll have to talk off the cuff. 'As you can see behind me, there has been some kind of explosion tonight in central London. It's chaos here. Lots of people have been hurt. And I mean, really badly hurt.'

Without a tripod, it's impossible to hold the phone steady, especially as my arm is shaking, but I've been presented with the unique advantage of having a front-row seat to the sad events of the evening and it's only right that I document what I'm seeing and spread the news.

'Tower Bridge has been damaged and I can see a number of fires still burning. A bus has come to a halt across the road and at least one car is on its side.' I swing the camera around, panning from left to right, attempting to show the full extent of the scene, although the camera doesn't really capture the true horror.

'I was about to cross the bridge when I was caught in the blast,' I add, 'but I'm okay. I was lucky, although if I'd been here a moment earlier, it might have been a different story. It's too soon to know the cause at this stage, but it's brought the whole area to a complete standstill on what was a busy night here in London, full of people out celebrating Valentine's.'

Could it have been a bomb? It hadn't occurred to me before, but it's entirely possible. It happened right after that white van raced onto the bridge and crashed, so there's every chance it's connected, but I don't want to start unfounded rumours. With such a large fan base, I'm keenly aware of my responsibilities.

A few hearts pop onto the screen and fade away, while the number of people watching rapidly ticks up, along with messages of shock and disbelief.

'It's utterly terrifying to see something like this first hand. After all, you don't expect anything like it to happen in the city where you live. A city you love. There are people running everywhere. Injured and bloodied. It's hard to put into words how I'm feeling about it at the moment. I guess I'm a bit numb. No one seems to know what's going on. You can probably hear the sirens in the background, so I think the emergency services will be here at any moment. I'm trying to stay calm, but you know, it's... hard.' My voice cracks and I glance down at my feet to gather myself.

'From where I'm standing, I can see debris everywhere. Glass, masonry and bits of... things I can't even begin to describe. Things you never want to see. The truth is, I don't know what to do. I've never felt more powerless. I'm just... I'm just praying everyone makes it out of this alive. And I guess my message to you all tonight is to stay safe wherever you are. Hug the people you love. You never know what's around the corner.'

Another small explosion on the far side of the bridge causes a collective scream. Maybe a fuel tank blowing up. Or another bomb. I duck behind the wall with my free hand covering the back of my head. Oh, god, please don't let Nathan be hurt.

I hold the phone up to my face again, still crouching.

'I don't know what that was. Another small blast. Hopefully, nothing significant. I'll check in again when I know more, but until I see you next time, please be kind to each other. And pray for everyone caught up in this awful tragedy. It's all we can do.'

As I finish my broadcast, the first police cars come screaming into view, battling through the traffic backed up on the approach to the bridge behind me, washing the street in a hypnotic, pulsing blue glow.

Officers spill out of the emergency vehicles, hurrying in all directions like bees tearing out of a hive, running plastic tape across the road and ushering people to safety.

Instinctively, I start to film on my phone. After all, while I'm concentrating on filming, I'm not worrying about Nathan.

'Madam, I need you to step back.'

I peer at a young female officer striding towards me.

'It's not safe. Please move,' she says firmly. She looks me up and down, her face softening when she sees I'm covered in dust. 'Are you injured?'

I shake my head, my bottom lip quivering.

'Then please, let us get on with our jobs.'

'I can't. I'm waiting for my boyfriend.'

She smiles sympathetically. 'You can't stay here. I need you back behind the cordon.' She points to a length of police tape strung between two lampposts and stretched across the width of the road, around fifty metres down the street.

'What about Nathan?'

'I'm sure we'll find him. Why don't you come with me and you can give me a description of him? Don't worry, we'll get him back to you.'

Chapter 4

It's well past midnight and I've not heard from Nathan in almost three hours. I understand the police are busy, but I wish someone would take me seriously. They've told me they'll let me know if they have any information, but nobody's told me anything yet. Nathan can't have just vanished. He must be somewhere.

If only he hadn't run off without his phone, we could be safely back at home by now. Instead, I'm still at Southwark Police Station, waiting to be interviewed for a second time. I've already given them a statement and told them everything I know, but for some reason they want to talk to me again.

It's been crazy in here all night. Plain-clothes officers with anxious expressions have been running around on their phones. Witnesses have come and gone. Uniformed patrols have been in and out. I wish someone would just tell me what the hell is happening. They did at least confirm that it was a bomb that caused the explosion and they're treating it as a terrorist incident. That's such a neutral word. Not an attack. Not a bombing. But an incident.

When they first brought me in, I was taken to a quiet rest area on the first floor, where I sat with a friendly female officer. I told her in as much detail as I could remember exactly what I saw while she scribbled notes on a pad of paper, and when we were finished, she promised to see what she could find out about Nathan. She thought he'd probably been taken to another station in the city to give a statement like me, but I've heard nothing since and they won't let me leave. I get the distinct impression they've been caught wrong-footed and now they're in panic mode.

I'm checking the clock on my phone for the millionth time, on the verge of walking out and becoming increasingly irritated that they've left me hanging around, when the female officer who interviewed me earlier approaches with an apologetic smile.

'Any news on Nathan?' I jump to my feet, expecting her to tell me they've found him and he's on his way over.

'Not yet, sorry. But I'm sure he'll turn up. They usually do, sooner or later.'

'I know there's a lot going on tonight, but you *are* looking for him, aren't you?'

The brief hesitation before she answers tells me everything I feared. 'We're doing our best. In the meantime, we do have a few more questions for you, if you'd like to come with me.'

'I'm not sure there's anything more I can add.'

'You never know.'

I sigh, but if this is what it takes to get out of here, then let's get it over with. The sooner they're done with me, the sooner I can get back to finding Nathan. What's the betting he's back at his flat by now, pacing the floor, waiting for me to call and wondering where I am?

The officer leads me down a long corridor and into a spartan interview room where the air conditioning has been set too low. It's freezing. I pull up a chair in front of a table and drop my bag and Nathan's coat on the floor, my bones weary with exhaustion.

Less than a minute later, two officers in dark suits sweep into the room with an energy that disturbs the air. They announce themselves so hurriedly I barely catch their names, let alone their ranks. McClennan and Butcher, I think they said. They're from the anti-terror unit, which makes me sit up a little straighter.

McClennan drops a file on the table and they take seats opposite me in perfect synchronicity, even pulling in their chairs at the exact same time, like a pair of well-rehearsed figure skaters.

'I'm not sure there's anything more I can tell you,' I say, folding my arms across my chest, which I'm aware looks defensive, but it really is cold in here.

'Let's go through it anyway. Talk us through your evening, if you wouldn't mind,' McClennan says, taking the lead while Butcher sits forward, studying me with an unnervingly steely eye.

I glance up at a camera mounted high on the wall, a red light blinking. I assume that means the interview's being recorded, although they've not said so. Don't they need to warn me?

'Where do you want me to start?'

'You'd been at a restaurant close to Tower Bridge. Is that right?' McClennan is almost freakishly tall and thin, like he's been stretched out on a rack, with hollow cheeks and a hook nose. He's wearing the weary expression of a man carrying a heavy cross of responsibility on his shoulders.

'Yes, with my boyfriend.'

'Nathan Pierce?' McClennan flicks open the file on the desk. He glances up, eyebrows raised, and chews his lower lip, his nose twitching like a rabbit sniffing danger. 'How long have you known Mr Pierce?'

'We've been dating for about a year.'

'How did you meet?'

'We go to the same gym, but I don't really understand what that has to do with anything. Have you found him yet?'

'What time did you leave the restaurant?'

'I don't know. Nine. Maybe nine-thirty.'

'Which is it? Nine or nine-thirty?'

I don't like his tone, as if he's accusing me. 'I don't remember.'

'And how did Mr Pierce seem? Anything unusual about his behaviour?' McClennan sits back and folds his arms, mirroring me.

I slip my hands into my lap.

Of course Nathan was behaving unusually. He was building up to propose and I turned him down in front of everyone. Not that it's any of their business. I shrug. 'No, he was fine. I'm sorry, but why are you asking about Nathan? I thought you wanted to know what I saw?'

'Was there anything unusual about Mr Pierce's behaviour tonight, in your opinion, Ms Ravenscroft?' McClennan repeats, his tone becoming increasingly aggressive.

I laugh. What sort of question is that? It's almost as if they think Nathan might be a suspect. 'Why? You can't seriously think Nathan had anything to do with the attack? That's ridiculous.'

Neither man so much as smiles. They continue to stare at me, challenging me to answer. This is the stuff of nightmares. It's positively Orwellian. How could they think for a second that Nathan was involved in something so heinous? Are they really that clueless?

'I'd remind you that we're investigating an incredibly serious attack that's caused multiple fatalities and left many more seriously injured. All we're trying to do is get to the truth.'

'I'm telling you the truth. It's crazy to even think that Nathan could have been involved. What possible reason would he have?'

The two men exchange a look. 'Tell us about the white van,' McClennan says.

'It was a white van, like a thousand others on any given day in this city. I wouldn't have even noticed it if it hadn't been travelling so fast.'

'How fast?'

'Too fast, like the driver was in a real hurry. I thought he might be drunk.'

'Because he was driving erratically?'

'Yes.'

'What did he look like? Did you see him?'

'Like I said, he was travelling fast. He went past in a flash.'

'Did he have anyone with him?'

'I don't know.'

'You said in your earlier statement that Nathan abandoned you shortly after the bomb detonated,' McClennan says.

'He didn't abandon me.'

'But he left you alone to tend to the victims? Or at least, that's what he told you?'

I can't deny it. It's what happened, but I hate the way he's framing it, making it sound like Nathan's guilty of something.

'He wanted to see if he could do anything to help before the emergency services arrived, yes.'

'Did you see where he went?'

'No.'

'It's strange that after spending a romantic meal together you simply let him wander off on his own into what was clearly a highly dangerous situation.' McClennan taps his finger on the cardboard folder.

'What's strange about it? He could see people were badly injured and he wanted to help. It's in his nature.'

'He's done this kind of thing before, has he?'

'Well, no, not exactly. But he's joining the police. He wants to give something back.'

'That's interesting you should mention that. Are you aware he failed the online assessment for the Met?'

The two men raise their eyebrows in unison, waiting for my reaction.

'He's never been good at written tests. He's more practically minded.'

'It was the behavioural questionnaire he failed.'

'I don't know what that means.'

'It means he wasn't considered to be a suitable candidate. He didn't have the requisite mental aptitude.'

I'm not sure what point he's trying to make. 'He's going to resit it and I'll make sure he's better prepared next time.'

'He's had his heart set on becoming a police officer for a while, has he?'

'Yeah, I think so.'

'The rejection must have hit him hard.'

'That depends on your perspective. He was disappointed, of course, but he's so bloody-minded, he was determined to apply again and prove them wrong. I think he'd make an excellent police officer,' I say.

'Not bitter about the rejection at all?'

It was a big deal for Nathan at the time as he's been desperate to hand in his notice on his boring nine-to-five desk job for months. When he found out he'd not made it through the initial selection process, he had a bit of tantrum and sulked for a few days, but he picked himself up and vowed he was going to prove they'd made a big mistake and that they were wrong about him.

I shake my head. 'Initially, maybe, but he quickly moved on.'

'So where is he?'

'That's what I'd like to know.'

'Don't you think it's strange that he just vanished?'

'Of course I do. I thought you were supposed to be out looking for him.'

'You've tried calling him, have you?' McClennan asks.

Seriously? Do they think I'm that stupid? 'He left his phone in his coat with me.'

The men share another glance. 'He didn't have his coat? It's freezing tonight.'

Why are they twisting everything I say? 'I guess he didn't want to get it dirty. It's not a crime, is it?'

'Can we see his phone? Do you still have it with you?'

I reach down into my bag where I put it for safe-keeping, but pause, my fingers on the catch.

If they seriously suspect Nathan was involved in the bomb attack, which is frankly insane, I'm not sure I should hand over his mobile. And given how they've twisted everything I've said so far, I don't trust them. What if they use it to incriminate him? I ought to talk to a lawyer before I do anything.

'Actually, unless you have a warrant, I don't think I can let you see it.'

McClennan leans over the table, coming so close I can smell stale coffee on his breath. 'The thing is, Ms Ravenscroft, everyone we know was on the bridge at the time of the blast has been accounted for. Everyone except your boyfriend. I'd like to know what he was doing and where he's gone.'

'You and me both,' I growl. 'Have you tried his flat? He has a place in Clapham. He probably went home when he couldn't find me.'

McClennan nods. 'We sent a patrol to check it out. Anywhere else he might have gone?'

'My flat in Camden? He'd planned to stay over tonight.'

'Address?' Butcher asks, speaking for the first time.

He writes it down in his notebook as I dictate the details, then he gets up and leaves.

'If there's anything you're not telling me, now would be a good time,' McClennan says as the door swings closed.

'Like what?'

'Like your boyfriend's involvement in tonight's drama.'

'I've told you! He's not involved. All he was doing was trying to help the victims.'

'Okay.'

'You don't believe me, do you?'

'What makes you think that?'

My head slumps onto my chest. I don't know what else to say. I know he's clutching at straws, but it doesn't make it any easier. We both want an explanation for Nathan's disappearance, but we're not going to find one sitting in a police station going around in circles.

McClennan draws a deep breath and lets it out slowly. 'Why were you filming the scene?'

'What?'

'When the first officers arrived, they said you were filming on your phone. Why?'

He can't be serious. 'What, is it a crime to film in public now?'

'It's just a question. Why are you being so defensive?'

'If you really want to know, I was broadcasting on my Instagram page. There's no law against that the last time I checked,' I answer sharply. It's probably not too clever losing my temper with an anti-terror officer, but I'm tired and I just want to get out of here.

'It's a bit insensitive. There were people injured and dying. Did you really think that was appropriate to share with a wider audience?'

'I- I just thought people had a right to know what was going on.' It never even occurred to me it might be considered improper. Maybe he has a point, but I can't remember showing any of the victims.

'What's this Instagram page of yours called?'

'*PippaRavenscrofthealth*. All one word. Capital P, capital R.'

He writes it down in a notebook and underlines it. 'What else did you film?'

'Nothing.'

'Mind if I take a look at your phone?' He holds out a hand across the table.

'Actually, I do.'

'Why? What do you have to hide?'

'Look, I came in willingly to give a statement and you're treating me like some sort of criminal.'

'We're investigating a serious terrorist attack. Everyone's a suspect until we can rule them out.'

'So I *am* a suspect? In which case, I'd like a lawyer before I answer any more questions.'

'A lawyer? Only guilty people hide behind lawyers. And I thought you said you were here to tell me the truth.'

He's fishing, trying to rile me and trip me up, and I'm so tired I'm liable to say something I might regret. I'm not saying another word.

'I want a lawyer. I can give you a number or I can make the call myself.'

'It's late. It might take a while and I don't want to keep you here longer than absolutely necessary.'

'Let me get this straight. Are you denying me access to legal representation?' I glare at McClennan through narrowed eyes.

'Of course not.' His jaw tightens. 'I'm just making you aware that if we involve the lawyers, it's going to draw things out. But if that's what you really want?'

An hour later, I'm in the back of a taxi with my sister, Sam, heading home.

I didn't want to call her and give her the excuse to come and rescue me, but for all I knew, those detectives might have kept questioning me for hours when I should be looking for Nathan.

Sam grips my hand and squeezes it tightly. She sitting so stiffly, I can tell she's still fuming.

'You should have called me the moment they said they wanted to question you,' she says.

'I didn't know they were treating me as a suspect.'

'The way they've behaved is appalling. Unforgivable. I'll be speaking to the commissioner's office in the morning, don't you worry.'

'Don't, Sam. Please? Just leave it.'

She's always been like this, acting like she's my mother because she's a few years older than me. She behaves like I can't look after myself, although on this occasion it's useful to have a criminal barrister as a sister.

I glance out of the window, staring through the condensation frosting on the glass at all the lights illuminating the buildings across the city. Nathan's in trouble. I can feel it. He wouldn't just disappear.

Worry gnaws at my innards, but there could be plenty of reasons that might explain why he's vanished. Maybe he's stayed with one of the victims to comfort them in hospital. Or what if he's in shock and has taken himself off for a drink to decompress?

'Are you sure you don't want to stay at ours tonight? The guest bed is made up and the kids would love to see you.'

I shake my head. I want to go home. 'I need to find Nathan.'

'I'm sure he's fine.'

'Are you? Why?'

Sam blanches at my sharp tone. She's never liked Nathan. She's made no secret that she thinks he's cocky and self-centred. She's said as much to my face. She'd rather I was dating someone with greater ambitions and prospects. But I love him. He's good for me. And he makes me happy.

'He'll turn up,' Sam says. 'There's bound to be a reasonable explanation.'

'I hope so.'

So why do I have this niggling fear at the back of my mind that something bad has happened to him? Why do I keep imagining that he's dead?

Transcript from the podcast, *Fallen Hero*. Interview with PC Tariq Ahmed, Metropolitan Police

I was one of the first responders on the scene. What we found was utter carnage, like a disaster movie. At that stage, no one knew for sure that it was a bomb, but the thought went through my head. Not that that was important. What was important was getting people off that bridge to safety.

A few people were just sitting staring into space, all covered in blood and dust. They were the lucky ones, I guess. You get used to seeing all sorts of injuries in my job, but this... it was different. I couldn't do anything for the ones that were most seriously hurt, so I concentrated on helping those who could walk to get as far away from danger as possible.

I wish I could have done more for the others, but... you know, I did what I could. Of course, there was a lot of confusion. People wanted to know what had happened, but at that point, we didn't even know ourselves.

Do I remember a civilian helping with first aid before the ambulances arrived? Truthfully, no. I reckon we'd have seen him if he'd been there. And nobody ever mentioned him. So no, I couldn't say for sure that he was there.

Chapter 5

PIPPA
February 15, 2024

I'd hoped that by some miracle Nathan might be waiting for me on the doorstep, overjoyed to find me safe, but there's no one at the flat. It's empty and desolate and for the first time this evening, I find myself truly alone. It hits me like a sucker punch.

The heating went off hours ago, and a damp chill skulks in the air. I hang Nathan's coat on a hook next to mine, smooth it out the way he always does, making sure the arms are hanging straight, and heel off my shoes.

My body aches with exhaustion, but what's the point of going to bed? I'll never sleep while Nathan is missing. Instead, I collapse on the sofa and stare at the wall as my mind replays the horrors of the night over and over on a loop in my head. The screams. The honking of car alarms and horns.

The blood. The panic. The fear. And the lingering stench of smoke. I sniff my sleeve and wrinkle my nose. My dress reeks of it. An unwanted reminder that's seeped into my clothes and hair. I ought to shower and change, but I can't bring myself to move, my limbs as heavy as blocks of concrete, my nerves numb.

I should never have let Nathan go off. I should have fought harder to make him stay and see sense. I should have begged him instead of losing my temper and issuing him with an ultimatum he was always going to ignore.

If you leave, I'll never forgive you.

What an awful thing to say. If something terrible has happened to him, if I never see him again, how can I live with myself knowing those were my last words to him? Not *I love you*. But *I'll never forgive you*.

If Sam was here, she'd tell me to stop beating myself up and point out that I was only trying to protect Nathan. The problem is, Nathan has always thought he's invincible. He never thinks anything bad could happen to him. But he's not Superman. What if he fell into the river? Or dived in to save someone? The currents in the Thames are notoriously strong. Almost certainly he would have been swept away, although at this time of year, he's just as likely to have died from hypothermia as he is to have drowned.

I squeeze my eyes shut and pinch the top of my nose, trying to banish all the negative thoughts flooding my mind. Until there's any firm news, I need to stay positive. It's much more likely that Nathan's been picked up by the police and he's being questioned, the same as I was. Until there's any solid information, there's no point catastrophising.

The silence in the flat hangs like freezing fog. It's too quiet. Too empty. I grab the remote and flick on the TV. The BBC is running rolling news on its main channel, with the London bomb blast predictably dominating coverage.

A reporter looks down the barrel of a camera, while over her shoulder the smouldering bridge is lit up in the darkness by a bank of powerful spotlights that have been brought in by the emergency services and which reveal a handful of white tents, presumably put up to preserve the scene. Or maybe to protect the forensics teams from the elements or simply to stop prying eyes. A rolling ticker tape scrolls along the bottom of the screen with the latest headlines.

Twelve people confirmed dead.

At least 22 people being treated in hospital for their injuries.

Far-right group claims responsibility for attack.

Twelve people dead? My stomach roils with nausea. How many of them were out celebrating Valentine's, like me and Nathan? It's awful.

The shot of the reporter cuts away to an interview with the Prime Minister standing outside 10 Downing Street, his face ashen under blinding TV lights. He looks stunned and not quite as well turned out as I'm used to seeing him. He offers his condolences to the families of the dead and injured and vows that no stone will be left unturned in bringing the perpetrators to justice.

A presenter in the studio, his familiar face sombre, picks up off the back of the interview.

'It's believed the bomb was packed into the back of a van which was driven onto Tower Bridge at high speed before being detonated at around nine thirty this evening,' he says. 'Tourists and couples celebrating Valentine's Day are thought to be among those killed and injured. Tonight, engineers have begun assessing the structural integrity of the bridge which it's believed will remain closed for several days while investigations and repairs are carried out.'

It never occurred to me that the attackers might have been trying to destroy the bridge. That would have been some statement. It's one of the most iconic architectural structures in London, a city famed for its landmarks. Not that it's of any consequence to me. Not while Nathan remains missing.

I check my phone again in the vain hope that I've missed a call from him, that he's found his way to safety and borrowed someone's mobile. But there are no missed calls. No unread texts or WhatsApp messages. It's as if he's been beamed up by aliens. I swipe open my photos and flick through all the pictures of us together, pausing on my favourite, the selfie we took in Dorset on a long weekend away last October, when we stayed in a sweet little thatched cottage in West Chaldon, near the coast, and spent our days hiking and exploring. We both look so happy, blonde wisps of hair flying loose around my face and Nathan's smile so broad and so full of joy it melts my heart. Behind us stands the natural rock arch at Durdle Door, silhouetted against a cloudless sky and a pumpkin-coloured sun plunging below the horizon.

Nathan planned the trip as a surprise. He chose the cottage because it had no phone or broadband coverage, and he wanted me to switch off for a few days. It was so thoughtful, and it did us both the power of good. I didn't have to think about anything. He planned our walks, cooked every night, and even built in some time every day for us to meditate together so we could align our goals. It definitely drew us closer and made me realise how lucky I am to have him in my life.

If anything's happened to him, I don't know what I'll do.

I catch myself as my thoughts turn dark again. What's the use of wallowing in self-pity? To distract myself, I check Instagram.

I've not been on it since I hosted the live broadcast on the bridge earlier and I'm staggered by the number of messages waiting to be read. Most of them are kind outpourings of love and good wishes which bring a smile to my face. Maybe I'm not as alone as I thought. All these strangers around the world rooting for me, sending positive vibes, have an unexpected calming effect.

I start to answer a few of the comments, but it could take me the rest of the night to get through them individually, especially as they're still coming thick and fast. I should post an update, like I promised. People deserve to know I'm home and safe.

If anything, I look worse than before as I hold my phone up and stare into the camera lens. My hair's lank, my eyes tired and my make-up really could do with a touch-up, although I'm sure people will understand after everything I've been through this evening.

I relax my mouth and gently blow air through my lips as I snap a dozen images. None of them are great. As well as looking like I've not slept for a week, the lighting's awful and my face is washed out, but that's what filters are for and after playing around with a few settings, I finally manage to digitally inject a little colour into my cheeks and some plump into my lips. With a few clicks, I look several years younger.

Finally happy with the result, I post the best photo with the caption:

In a world full of uncertainty, the only thing we can control is how we rise to meet the challenge.

Thanks for all the messages. I'm safe and back home now. My thoughts and prayers are with the families of all those who've lost their lives in the Tower Bridge attack this evening. #PrayForLondon #LondonStrong

When the post is successfully uploaded, I switch off my phone and come to a decision. I can't sit here for the rest of the night waiting for Nathan to get in contact. He's out there somewhere and I need to find him. That's not going to happen sitting on my sofa. I need to get out there and look for him.

I order an Uber and twelve minutes later I'm on my way to Clapham.

Chapter 6

Nathan's apartment on Lyham Street is on the top floor of a Victorian terraced house, a short walk from Clapham Common. It's hardly a palace, but it's modern and when he bought it a few years ago, it had been recently renovated.

I squint up at a Velux window in the roof, trying to work out if there's a light on inside. There's a faint glow, but nothing conclusive. I push open a squeaky, wrought-iron gate and march up to the front door. My thumb hovers over a panel of buzzers. I press the top button down for a second or two and stand back, not sure why Nathan never gave me a key, but I suppose we don't often spend time at his place.

No one answers. No one comes to the door, but I hadn't really expected Nathan to be here. If he'd made it home, surely he would have tried to contact me? My only other hope is that he's being held by the police and subjected to the same accusatory questions I faced, although they could at least have had the decency to let me know and put my mind at rest. I just can't think where else he'd be.

I contemplate heading back to Tower Bridge and asking around to see if anyone has seen him, but where would I start? And I doubt I'd get anywhere near the bridge now it's been sealed off by the emergency services. It would be a pointless exercise.

With no clear idea of what to do next, I amble down the street in a daze with the freezing air numbing my face and frosting the cars parked on either side of the road in a thin sheen of ice. I hunch my shoulders and bury my hands in the pockets of my coat.

When I reach a junction where an intermittent procession of vehicles flashes past, my mind's blank, tiredness and the cold taking their toll as I struggle to find my bearings and work out how to find the nearest Tube station. And anyway, I don't even know where to go next, so I slump on the pavement with my back against the plate-glass window of a bathroom showroom. Without Nathan, I'm lost. I don't know what to do or what to think.

'Oi, oi! Who's this?'

I glance up and my insides shrivel. A group of lads, clinging to each other and swaying drunkenly, while singing out of tune like they're at a football match on a Saturday afternoon, are heading my way.

'Alright, darling. Whatcha doing?'

They crowd around me, a huddle of jeans and trainers and stale cigarette smoke.

'You all on your own? Lookin' for some company?' one says with a smirk.

The others laugh, a pack of dogs surrounding a wounded fawn. I look up and shoot them a condescending thin-lipped smile. They can't be much older than eighteen or nineteen, still awkwardly spotty, their youthful insecurities forgotten at the bottom of a pint glass.

The youngest-looking of the group, a boy with floppy blond hair and eyelashes so pale they're virtually invisible, plonks himself on the pavement next to me and drapes an arm casually around my shoulder.

I'm momentarily paralysed by fear, the blaze of a distant memory resurfacing from the depths of the dark box in my mind where I've kept it hidden. His touch is as unwelcome as being stung by a cattle prod.

I shrug him off and recoil from his toxic, boozy breath.

'What about a little kiss?' he asks, puckering his lips suggestively.

'That's your best line? Wow, did you rehearse that or make it up on the cuff? Either way, it's tragic.'

The boy jolts like he's been punched. 'There's no need to be rude.'

'What are you going to do? Run off and tell your mum?'

He jumps up, his face clouding as his friends laugh at him.

'Go on, run along. It's way past your bedtime anyway,' I add. 'You don't want to be late for school tomorrow.'

The boy opens his mouth to say something back, but either changes his mind or can't think what to say, and clamps it shut again.

'Let's get out of here,' he says, storming off across the road with his mates tagging along behind, still chuckling.

I shiver as I watch them go, not quite so full of swagger now. My pulse gradually slows. They would never have dared to speak to me like that if I'd been with Nathan. I doubt they'd even have risked looking at me. He's a big man and can be quite intimidating if you don't know him.

To make myself feel better, I pull out my phone and check my Instagram messages. Predictably, my latest update is garnering a further outpouring of love and respect. A warm glow spreads from my core to the tips of my fingers as I scan through some of the lovely comments.

We were all so worried about you! Stay strong, queen

Your strength inspires me every day. So happy to know you're okay

Take all the time you need to recover — you've got an army of supporters behind you

So much love and kindness from people I don't even know. The universe sending me good vibes and reminding me I'm not dealing with this on my own.

I should stop scrolling, but I can't. Every message is a reminder I have a virtual family who care about me.

And then I find a series of less welcome messages. Nasty, unpleasant comments from trolls. Bitter, twisted, spiteful, anonymous haters who don't have anything nice to say. It's not the first time I've been targeted, and usually I can shrug them off, but tonight their remarks cut like a rusty razor.

You really don't have any limits you won't sink to, do you? Sickening.

Of course you'd turn a bombing into an Insta post . Why am I not surprised?

Wow, way to make it all about you. Classy.

Using a tragedy for likes? Seriously?

Another so-called influencer profiting off tragedy. Gross. Your family must be so proud.

How can people be so cruel? If they had any idea what I was going through, perhaps they'd be a little more sympathetic. But they don't know anything about Nathan or that he could be dead for all I know. What pathetic, meaningless lives they must all live to be so horrible to a stranger. My mother always used to say, if you don't have anything nice to say, don't say anything at all. But everyone has a keyboard these days and it's too easy to be mean. I doubt any of them would have the guts to say anything to my face.

I shudder as the cold settles in my bones. There's no point hanging around a chilly street corner feeling sorry for myself, catching pneumonia, but I can't just wander the streets aimlessly. And I can't face returning to my flat. I thought I'd wanted to be alone, but without Nathan, it feels so depressingly empty. So, although it's late, I book another Uber and ask the driver to take me to Hampstead.

Chapter 7

Sam's husband, Alex, welcomes me with a beaming smile. He throws his arms around me and I return his embrace awkwardly, patting his back, conscious he's only wearing pyjamas and a stripy towelling dressing gown hanging off one shoulder. He doesn't seem in the slightest bit surprised to see me even though it's the early hours of the morning.

'Sorry, did I wake you?'

He waves his hand dismissively. 'It's fine.'

I step into their grand hall with its stylish chequerboard black and white tiled floor and tastefully panelled taupe walls. It's a proper grown-up house, like I imagine I might own one day, if I ever win the lottery. It must be worth several million, particularly as it's in one of the most desirable postcodes in London.

'I know it's late but —'

'Sam told me what happened.' His voice is honeyed with concern. 'We were watching it on the news. Absolutely awful. Sounds like you were lucky not to have been injured.' He speaks with a posh-boy public school drawl, flattening and elongating his vowels with an accent that screams entitlement and money, both of which he possesses in abundance.

I hadn't thought of myself as being lucky, but I suppose I am. The worst that happened was that I laddered my tights when I was thrown to the ground and had a ringing in my ears for a short time after the blast. Other than that, I'm fine. Physically, at least.

'Nathan's missing,' I blurt out. 'And I don't know what to do.'

For a moment, I fear Alex is about to sweep me up into another hug, until my sister's voice calls from the top of the stairs.

'Darling, who is it?'

Her bare legs and feet appear as she gingerly descends, craning her neck, with her mobile phone clutched in one hand as if she's expecting to find a band of masked intruders storming the house.

'It's your sister.'

'Pippa?' Sam rushes down the stairs, eyes wide with concern. 'What's happened?'

'Nothing. I just need a place to crash.'

'I thought you wanted to stay at your flat?'

I shrug. 'I couldn't face being on my own tonight after all. Is that okay?'

'Of course. I didn't like the idea of you being on your own in that flat tonight anyway. Any news on Nathan?'

'I've just come from his place, but there's no one there. I still haven't heard a word from him.'

'Oh, honey.' Unlike Alex, she doesn't try to hug me. Sam's never been a hugger. 'I'm sure there's a logical explanation. He's probably been caught up in something and has been delayed getting home.'

'But he was supposed to be coming home with me! What if something's happened to him?'

'Come and have a drink. Alex, where are your manners?'

Alex snaps to attention. 'Sorry. Whisky? Brandy?'

'I think I'd rather just go to bed, if that's alright?'

'Absolutely.' Sam nods enthusiastically. 'You must be exhausted. Look at you. We can talk tomorrow. The guest room's all made up.'

She leads me upstairs and shows me into one of the rooms at the back of the house, as if I've never stayed over before.

'There are clean towels in the en suite. Otherwise, you know where everything is. Help yourself.' She's the consummate host.

I stand at the end of the king-sized double bed and wait for her to leave. She wishes me goodnight and as she pulls the door closed, a wave of exhaustion almost barrels me off my feet. With my last ounce of energy, I slip off my dress and climb into bed in my underwear, sinking into luxuriously thick pillows. It's not exactly how I imagined this evening was going to pan out.

But my mind's still too busy to sleep. I lie in the darkness staring at the ceiling replaying the events of the night and the horrors I witnessed, although I guess I must have eventually dropped off as I'm jolted awake by the door bursting open with a loud thud that almost causes my heart to burst out of my chest. Freddie and Isabella, my nephew and niece, charge into the room and jump onto the bed, screaming with delight.

I push the hair out of my eyes and force a smile, pretending to be happy to see them.

'Aunty Pippa! Aunty Pippa!' Isabella squeals, jumping up and down on the end of the bed. 'Will you come and play with me in my room?'

'No, play with me!' Freddie demands, tugging my hand under the duvet.

A second later, Sam barges in like someone's put a firecracker up her arse.

'Freddie! Isabella!' she screams, the hiss of her words like steam escaping from a pressure cooker. 'Leave Aunty Pippa alone. She's trying to sleep.'

She snatches the children by their wrists and drags them off the bed.

'I'm so sorry, Pip. I said to leave you alone. Go back to sleep.'

'It's fine. I was awake anyway,' I lie.

'Alex stupidly told them you were here and they were so excited to see you. Don't rush to get up. I'll keep the little horrors out of your hair.'

She yanks the children out of the room and swings the door closed. I'm plunged back into darkness, but there's no point chasing sleep again with so much adrenaline chasing around my veins.

I check my phone, more in hope than expectation. It's almost seven thirty, but I have no missed calls. No messages or voicemails. Nothing from Nathan at all. By contrast, I have hundreds of new messages and comments on Instagram, although I'd trade every single one of them for just one word from Nathan to let me know he's safe.

A long, hot shower makes me feel marginally better, although I can still smell smoke, as if it's ingrained in my skin and under my nails, no matter how hard I scrub. I borrow a pair of Sam's designer blue bootcut jeans that I find hanging up in the wardrobe and match them with a pink T-shirt that smells of her perfume and a chunky navy blue sweater, before heading downstairs where I can hear the family having breakfast.

Alex is at the table with his head buried in his phone alongside the children, who are squabbling over a soft toy, while Sam is buttering toast on the kitchen worktop. They all glance up at the same time as I walk in and hover in the doorway, pulling at the cuffs of my borrowed sweater.

Alex lowers his phone. 'Morning! Feeling any better?'

'A little.'

'Anything from Nathan?' Sam holds a buttery knife suspended in mid-air.

I shake my head, a hollowness aching in my chest. One text message. One quick call to tell me he's okay. It's all I need. And then I can stop worrying.

'Come and have something to eat. You must be starving.' Sam points to the table, encouraging me to take a seat.

I pull up a chair next to Isabella, who has a picture book open on a page showing a princess staring along a winding road towards an ominous mountain in the distance, a fire-breathing dragon soaring in the sky above. The book is covered in greasy fingerprints. I put my mobile on the table, face up in case by some miracle Nathan calls or texts.

'I'm going to be late,' Alex announces, jumping up as Sam hands me a glass of orange juice. 'Catch you later, Pip.'

He kisses Sam briefly on the cheek, plants kisses on the kids' heads, and hurries out, snatching his jacket from the back of his chair.

'Day off?' I nod at Sam's clothes, her tailored cream trousers and olive-coloured cashmere sweater a little casual for the office.

'I don't have to be in court today, so I've told chambers I'm taking the day off to be with you.'

'You didn't need to do that.'

'I don't think you should be left alone, Pip.'

'Honestly, I'm fine.'

'You don't look fine.'

'I'm worried, that's all. What if Nathan —'

'Freddie! Stop that and eat your breakfast,' Sam screams across the room. While Sam's attention was distracted, he tried to steal his sister's book. 'Sorry, what was that?'

'It's unlike Nathan not to call. He's not even messaged.'

'He's a big boy. I'm sure he can look after himself.'

'So where is he?'

'Freddie, I'm not going to tell you again. Give Issy her book back. Now!' Sam storms across the room and snatches Isabella's book from her son, who instantly bursts into tears. 'Hurry up, you're going to be late for school. Sophia's going to be here any minute and you know she won't stand for any of your nonsense.'

'You'd think he'd have tried to call, wouldn't you?' I say.

'Who?'

'Nathan.'

'I thought you had his phone?'

'He could have borrowed a phone. It's London, not the Outback.'

'Maybe he tried and couldn't get through.'

'I'm going to be like Aunty Pippa when I grow up,' Isabella announces, wiping her hands on her pleated school skirt.

Sam rolls her eyes at me. 'It's her latest thing. She wants to be an influencer, like you.' She says *influencer* like she's tasting her own earwax.

'It's social media, not an OnlyFans page.'

'Yeah, whatever. She needs to work hard at school and get a proper job, don't you, darling?' she says to her daughter.

'What's wrong with her following her dreams? You should be encouraging her if that's what she wants to do. It beats a dead-end job slaving away in an office for forty years.'

Sam's mouth curls up with barely concealed disgust. 'She needs to concentrate on working towards a proper career. Not following a pipe dream.'

'A pipe dream?'

'Oh, Pip, I'm sure you're very good at what you do, but it's not a career, is it? It's fine for the time being, but it's not going to last forever.'

'Why not? What's wrong with what I do? I enjoy it and I'm good at it. We can't all be hotshot lawyers.'

'I'm not having a go, Pip. Really, I'm not.' She plucks a stray crumb from her sweater. 'I just want Isabella to understand that if she works hard at school, she can do anything she wants.'

'Or she could do something she loves, work for herself and dictate her own hours.'

'You mean pulling ridiculous poses for the camera and chasing comments and likes all day?'

I finish my juice and place the glass carefully back on the table as I count silently to ten in my head. I don't have the energy for this. 'I think I might go and lie down again for a bit.'

'Of course. Go and rest. Just shout if you need anything. And you know you're welcome to stay as long as you want. You want anything to eat?'

'No. Thanks.' I'm sure my smile doesn't even flirt with my eyes.

I push my chair back and stand at the exact moment my phone buzzes with an incoming call. Unknown caller. Sam and I both freeze, staring at each other across the room.

'Nathan,' we announce in unison.

Chapter 8

I snatch up the phone. 'Nathan? Where are you?'

There's a long delay on the line. A weighted pause.

'Are you hurt?'

I can hear him breathing, so why isn't he saying anything? Sam leans over the kitchen worktop, glowering at me. I turn my back to her and shove a finger in my ear.

'Pippa, it's James.' The voice is familiar, but it takes a few seconds for my brain to catch up.

'James?'

'Sorry to call out of the blue, but I was wondering how you are.'

James Whitaker? It's been years since we last spoke. I'm surprised he still has my number.

'I— I've been better.' I rub my forehead with my thumb and forefinger. 'Sorry, I was expecting someone else.'

'Is it a bad time?'

Sam stares at me with wide, curious eyes. 'Who is it?' she mouths.

I waggle a finger, push my chair back and step out into the hall. I could do without an audience while I'm talking to my ex-boyfriend.

'No, it's fine.'

'I saw the video you posted from Tower Bridge. You seemed pretty shaken up. I know it's been a long time, but I was worried about you.'

'Eight years.'

'What?'

'It's been eight years since we broke up.'

'Yeah, I guess it must be.' He laughs. 'Seems like yesterday.'

Not to me. It feels like a different life. So much has changed since James and I were together. So much has happened.

'The thing is, I'm waiting for a call.' I don't want to be rude, but what if Nathan's trying to get through and the line's engaged?

'I couldn't believe it when I saw you'd been caught up in the bombing. It's all over the news. I just wanted to check you were okay.'

'It was a bit scary, but I'm fine, thanks.'

'That's really good to know.'

'Was there anything else?'

'Look, I know we've not spoken in a while, but I still... you know?'

'Yeah, thank you. Like I said, I'm okay.'

'And I wanted to make sure...'

'Honestly, I'm fine.'

'You're sure?'

I sit on the stairs and hold my head in my hand. I need to clear the line, but it's surprisingly comforting to hear James's voice after all these years. Things could have been so different if we'd met at a different time in our lives. We might even still be together. But I was too young for a serious relationship. My scars were too raw. I know it broke James's heart when I called it off, but it was the right thing to do, even though everyone said I was crazy. They all loved James.

'I'm staying with my sister for a few days. She's looking after me.'

'Samantha?' He draws air in through his teeth. 'And how's that going? Do you need rescuing yet?'

'Stop it.' I smirk. He used to find it funny when I vented about my sister. He knows all too well how easily she winds me up, treating me like she's my mother and always putting me down. 'It's not that bad.'

'No?'

'Come on, she's my sister.'

The letterbox rattles and a stack of post lands on the doormat with a thud.

'If you say so. Anyway, I was wondering if you fancied meeting up for a coffee? I mean, if you're not busy and it's not too weird.'

'Coffee?'

'Or an almond milk chai latte, if you prefer?'

I hesitate for a beat, momentarily thrown. It's been almost a decade since I last saw James and out of the blue he's asking me out for a coffee? I never expected that. Should I tell him about Nathan? Probably, but I don't want to make this any more awkward than it already is.

'I don't —'

'I thought you could use some company, that's all. But if you prefer, you could always spend the day being patronised by your sister. It's entirely up to you.'

'Stop it.' A grin spreads across my lips, even though I have no right to be smiling while Nathan is missing.

'I have the day off, that's all, so I thought it might be fun.'

Fun? 'Look, James, I appreciate the offer, but —' I have important things to do, like finding my missing boyfriend. I can't be going out for coffee with my ex.

'No, I understand. As long as you're not alone today.'

'It's good to hear from you, though. I really appreciate the call.'

'Well, take care of yourself, Pippa.'

When he hangs up, I stay sitting on the stairs for a moment or two, staring at my phone. I was a naïve twenty-one-year-old when we began dating. Too young. Too damaged. He wanted to move more quickly than I was ready for, and everything became too intense. I panicked and bailed. I'm not sure I ever properly explained to him why I dumped him. I just ditched him and ran. I imagined he'd never forgiven me, but he's obviously been following me on social media, and what's more, kept hold of my number. Should I be flattered? Or is it a bit creepy?

'Who was that?'

Sam's voice makes me jump. How long has she been standing at the kitchen door, listening?

'No one.'

'It wasn't Nathan?'

'Do you remember James? I went out with him for a while a few years ago.'

Sam leans against the wall with her arms folded and arches an eyebrow. 'Why's he sniffing around all of a sudden?'

'He's not sniffing around. He's concerned about me. He saw my Insta post last night and wanted to check I was okay.'

'Is that right?'

'Why do you have to be so suspicious of everyone? At least he cares.'

'Actually, I liked him. I never understood why you dumped him.'

Freddie comes flying out of the kitchen, skids across the hall floor in his socks, and charges up the stairs, knocking me out of the way.

'How many times? Don't run,' Sam screams after him. 'Go and clean your teeth. Sophia will be here any minute. You too, Issy. Come on, hurry up.'

Isabella appears from the kitchen with her nose stuck in her book and no sense of urgency.

Sam rolls her eyes at me. 'You're going to be late for school if you don't hurry up. Why is it like this every morning?'

'Can Aunty Pippa take us to school today?'

'No, she's busy. Sophia's going to take you.'

'I could take them if...' I start to say, but Sam holds up her hand, cutting me short.

'It's what I pay the childminder for. You and I have more important things to worry about, like finding Nathan.'

There's no point arguing with her. There's a reason she's such a successful lawyer.

'In that case, I might head back to bed for an hour. I didn't get much sleep last night.'

I sink into the soft pillows and pull the duvet up to my neck, but sleep remains elusive. My mind's in a spin thinking about James and what prompted him to call out of the blue, and worrying that it's been nearly twelve hours now that Nathan's been missing. I listen to the sound of the children getting ready for school. Sophia comes and goes, the front door slams shut, and the house falls silent.

I check my phone once more in case I've missed a message from Nathan, more now in hope than expectation. As much as I'm trying not to imagine the worst, it's hard. There has to be an explanation as to why he's not been in touch or returned home, and I can't think of many that involve him being alive and well.

On top of everything else, I'm worried about James's motives for contacting me. I should have told him about Nathan and made it clear I'm in a committed relationship. The last thing I need right now is for him to get the wrong idea. Guilt burns in my chest, but it's not as if I've done anything wrong.

I spend the next hour tossing and turning, chasing sleep, but eventually give up when a knock at the front door echoes through the house. I hear the door click open, Sam's voice, and a muted one-sided conversation.

'Pippa!' Sam yells.

'What?'

'There's someone here to see you.'

What? No one knows I'm here.

'Who?'

She's obviously not going to tell me, so with a huff, I roll my legs off the bed and smooth down my hair.

'I was trying to sleep,' I grumble as I trudge down the stairs.

It takes a second or two to comprehend what's happening as I stare at the man standing in the hall.

'I'll leave you two alone.' Sam floats off towards the kitchen with a wink.

I stare at the visitor in disbelief. 'James? What the hell are you doing here?'

Chapter 9

James and I sit on a wooden bench wrapped up in our coats, staring at a skyline punctuated by towering office blocks and skeletal construction cranes. I've always loved this spot in Hampstead Heath with its picture-perfect view of the city, although today it's not the skyline that occupies my thoughts.

'I should have deleted your number, but...' James clasps his hands and rests his elbows on his thighs, unable to look me in the eye. 'Anyway, you're looking well.'

I run a hand through my hair. I'm not exactly looking my best. James, on the other hand, has definitely improved with age. He was always tall, but he's much broader across the shoulders and chest now with the kind of natural muscle that doesn't rely on lifting weights and downing protein shakes, unlike Nathan whose carefully honed physique has been sculpted and crafted by a relentlessly strict routine in the gym. And while Nathan spends more time in the bathroom than me with his exfoliators, toners, serums and moisturisers, James has a wild, thick hipster beard and rough, weathered features like a lumberjack used to working outside in all seasons.

'I'm surprised you saw my post,' I say.

'Why? I've been following you for a long time.'

'You're not exactly my target audience.'

'I've enjoyed watching your following grow. It's impressive. I guess it makes you kind of famous.'

I shrug. I've never been comfortable with compliments. 'I'm still a minnow compared to other content creators. What about you? Did you ever open that chain of gyms?'

'Not exactly. I work at a community gym for troubled kids.'

'That's amazing.'

'The idea is that we get them off the streets and try to keep them out of trouble. It's not what I imagined I'd be doing with my life, but it has its rewards.'

'I'm impressed.' What a way to make a girl feel inadequate. I like to think my content has had a positive impact on women and their health, but it's not exactly helping underprivileged teenagers.

'I thought you were going to be working with the rich and famous? That's what you always said.'

'Did I?' I chuckle, but he's right. I'd long followed a dream of working with glamorous businesswomen and celebrities as a personal trainer, but it's funny how dreams change. I started using social media to promote myself, but the content I was producing took off in a totally unexpected way and it wasn't long before I was making more money from social media than through any direct training. 'How did you end up working with kids?'

'I drifted for a while, floating from one office job to another. I even ended up working for the government for a while, before this job at a gym opening in Haringey came up. Officially, I'm now a community outreach coordinator. Sounds worthy, doesn't it?'

'Not at all.'

An old woman totters unsteadily along the path towards us, cane in one hand and bulging shopping bag in the other, grey wisps of hair peeking out from under a rust-coloured knitted hat.

James strokes his beard. 'I can't believe it's been eight years.'

'I can't believe you kept my number.'

'I'd always hoped one day we could be friends.'

Frankly, I'm amazed he wants anything to do with me at all after the terse break-up text message I sent him all those years ago and can still remember word for word.

Sorry, James, things aren't working out. I think it's best if we went our separate ways.

What an awful way to tell someone you're dumping them. I didn't even have the grace to pick up the phone and talk to him. And yet here he is, back in my life and not a bitter bone in his body.

We met years ago on a fitness training course when we both held ambitions of becoming personal trainers and found common ground in poking fun at the course leader, an intense woman who probably had good cause to sue her plastic surgeon. Her head looked as if it had been artificially inflated, and she had plumped-up, pouting lips, stretched eyes and a frozen, emotionless expression.

I hadn't been looking for romance, but after the final weekend session, James asked me out, and I was flattered and couldn't think of a reason to say no. For our first date, he took me for a stroll along the Southbank, pointing out all his favourite architecture. St Paul's Cathedral. Somerset House. The Tate Modern. And we ended up in Gabriel's Wharf drinking hot chocolate until the staff wanted to close for the evening and threw us out.

He was my first serious boyfriend and we dated for around four months until it became clear he was looking for something more serious than I was ready to commit to. I sent the text in a blind panic, never expecting to hear from him again.

'Are you still in Bethnal Green?' he asks.

'Camden. I have a place not far from the market. It's only a one-bedroom flat, but it's perfect for me.'

'Oh,' James says, surprised. 'You don't live with your boyfriend?'

'How do you know I have a boyfriend?'

'Lucky guess. Is it serious?'

A second wave of guilt hits me. What am I doing here with James while I should be out looking for Nathan? This is so wrong. He'd be furious if he found out I was meeting up with my ex. Nathan can be so possessive over silly things like that.

'Not really,' I lie. At least I didn't think so until Nathan surprised me by popping the big question last night.

'Sorry, it's none of my business.'

'Actually,' I say, glancing down at my hands as I pick nervously at my fingernails, 'I was with him last night on the bridge. But he's gone missing.'

James frowns. 'What do you mean?'

'He went off to help, to see if there was anything he could do for the people who'd been injured. He was supposed to come back to find me, but he never did and I've no idea what's happened to him.' Tears bubble in my eyes as my throat tightens.

'Have you reported him missing?'

I shake my head. 'The police aren't interested. They were more concerned with trying to pin the blame for the bomb on us.'

'What?'

'Because he'd disappeared and I was there filming, they thought we must have been somehow involved, which is just crazy.'

'He can't have just disappeared,' James says.

'Exactly. But something's happened to him. I keep worrying that maybe he fell in the river and drowned. I can't think of any other rational explanation.'

James sniffs and wipes a hand across his nose. 'I wouldn't rush to any hasty conclusions. It's not been twenty-four hours yet. I'm sure there's a perfectly innocent explanation and he'll turn up when he's ready.'

'You think?'

'You can't write him off yet. What about friends or family? Has anyone else heard from him?'

'He has a brother, Ryan, but that's it. He doesn't have many friends. He's too busy.'

'Okay,' James says, nodding to himself. 'And have you spoken to Ryan?'

Everything in the last twelve hours has been so dizzying, so disorientating, I hadn't thought about

Ryan, although I don't know why Nathan would reach out to his brother rather than me. But James is right. It's worth a shot.

'I didn't think about that,' I say, feeling stupid.

'Why don't you give him a call?'

'I don't have his number.'

I've only met Ryan a couple of times, although I know he lives in Hackney. Nathan took me to a party at his apartment not long after we started dating, although it's not a fond memory. Nathan hit the booze hard, mixing tequila shots and bottles of lager until he was too drunk to stand and it was a struggle to get him into an Uber home. We had to leave the windows open because I was so worried he was going to vomit.

'Do you know where he works? Maybe that's a way to reach him.'

'No, hang on a minute. I might have his mobile after all,' I say, diving into my bag for my phone.

I remember now, Ryan added me to a WhatsApp group he'd set up when he was planning the party, which he'd organised for his girlfriend at the time. An awful woman called Bethany. Or was it Bridget? No, it was Bianca. That's right. She was all mouth, big boobs and long legs. If the group still exists, Ryan's contact details should be accessible.

To my amazement, the group hasn't been deleted and under group info, there are twelve people listed, with Ryan's name and number at the top as an admin. Bingo.

'I've got it.'

James cups his bare hands over his mouth and blows into them. 'Go on, then. Call him.'

I steel myself. Will Ryan even remember who I am? It's not as though Nathan's particularly close to his brother and we only met that once.

The call rings six times before cutting to voicemail.

'He's not answering,' I hiss.

'Leave a message.'

'Hey, Ryan, it's Pippa. Nathan's partner. I was wondering if you'd heard from Nathan at all? He's... he's gone missing and I'm really worried.' I decide not to freak him out by telling him we were caught up in the explosion on Tower Bridge. 'Maybe if he's been in touch, you could let me know? I've not seen him since last night when he took me out for dinner. Anyway, that's all. Call me back as soon as you can. Thanks.'

I hang up, deflated.

'So I guess now we wait,' James says. 'Did you fancy grabbing that coffee? I'm frozen.'

'No, I have a better idea.'

'Okay.'

'I think I can remember where Ryan lives. He's in Hackney. I'm going to go round there and see if he's in. I've got nothing else to do.'

'Sounds like a good plan. Want some company?' James asks. 'I don't have anything else to do either.'

'Sure, if that's how you really want to spend your day.'

Transcript from the podcast, *Fallen Hero*. Interview with Leila Singh, Senior Account Director, Crestline Insurance Group

Nathan was a popular employee. Everyone got on well with him. He was good at his job, too. I always used to say he could charm the stars out of the sky, the kind of guy you'd want batting on your side. He was what I call one of life's winners.

That's why I was so disappointed when he said he wanted to leave to join the police, although I guess it made sense. If Nathan wasn't in the office, he was at the gym or out running around the park. Always training. Always pushing himself physically. I can see why he thought the police would suit him.

So no, I wasn't surprised when I heard that he'd wanted to help those poor people on the bridge, even though he was putting himself in danger. It was an incredibly brave and selfless thing to do.

I still can't explain why no one in the office noticed he wasn't at his desk the day after the attack. He hardly ever took time off sick, and he was religiously at work by eight at the latest. You could set your clock by him. I was away at a conference and I suppose everyone else thought he had meetings.

It's embarrassing though. I hope if something ever happened to me and I didn't turn up for work, someone would notice and ask questions. It makes you wonder how much we all notice what's going on around us outside our own little bubble, doesn't it?

Chapter 10

JAMES
February 15, 2024

We jump on a train at Hampstead Heath station and take seats in a half-empty carriage that smells of greasy burgers and chips.

'Are you sure you don't have somewhere you need to be?' Pippa asks, her eyes straying to the window as we pull away. The train creaks and wheezes as it picks up speed and rocks us gently from side to side.

'No, I'm yours for the day.'

I took a big risk. There was every chance Pippa could have flipped out when I turned up at her sister's house unannounced, but I'm glad I did. She's matured so much from the naïve twenty-one-year-old I used to know. She's flourished. Become far more confident. Far more self-possessed. Her boyfriend is a lucky guy. I hope he appreciates her - if he's still alive. But if Pippa's right and he's fallen into the river, I don't rate his chances. People always underestimate the strength of the tides on the Thames. They can overpower even the strongest swimmer. And if Nathan did fall from the bridge, he almost certainly wouldn't have survived.

It's obvious she's still in shock, although she's more composed than she appeared in the video she posted from the bridge right after the bomb went off, when she was pale and dead-eyed, her voice quivering and her hair dusted with ash. A hare caught in the blinding beam of a courser's lamp. But as we sat and chatted in the park, her gaze was vacant and unfocused and she couldn't stop fidgeting, constantly twisting her rings, tapping her knees with her fingers and picking at her nails. Then there was the way she sat, perched on the edge of the bench, nervously coiled and jumpy. I guess you can't blame her.

'There's something I ought to tell you,' Pippa says, still staring out of the window as the train rattles over an uneven section of track and our shoulders bump. 'I wasn't completely honest with you earlier. You asked if my relationship with Nathan was serious.'

'Okay.'

Pippa chews her lip and scratches the fabric of her jeans with a fingernail. 'Last night, before the bomb, Nathan took me to a posh restaurant for dinner and proposed.'

I swallow my surprise. 'On Valentine's? That's romantic. Congratulations.'

'He did the whole thing of getting down on one knee with a diamond solitaire in front of the entire restaurant, but I turned him down.'

'That's brave.'

'Is it? He put me on the spot, and I didn't want to say yes just because that's what you're supposed to do.' Pippa finally turns her gaze to me, her face twisted in distress. 'We've only been together less than a year. We've never even talked about marriage.'

'How did he take it?'

'Badly.'

The train slows as it approaches Gospel Oak. The doors hiss open and a gaggle of young women with talons for nails and extravagant hair extensions hop on board, brushing past with shopping bags and thick coats.

'Actually, he stormed out of the restaurant,' Pippa continues. 'It was awful.'

'Right.' I nod. 'That makes sense. It's why you feel so guilty that something might have happened to him?'

'We were arguing when the bomb went off. He was angry with me and accused me of neglecting him because of my job.'

'Ouch.'

'And when he said he was leaving me to go and help the victims, I told him that if he abandoned me, I'd never forgive him. And that was the last thing I said to him.' She bangs her head against the window, her eyes screwed tightly shut. 'Sorry, I don't know why I'm telling you all this.'

'It's fine. I won't breathe a word to a soul.'

'If something has happened to him and those were my last words to him, how am I supposed to live with myself?'

'Let's concentrate on finding him, shall we?' I grab her hand and give it a friendly squeeze. 'We're going to get to the bottom of it, alright?' I stop short of reassuring her that we're going to find Nathan. I'd hate to give her false hope, but there has to be a logical explanation for his disappearance. I just hope for Pippa's sake that it doesn't end with her having to identify a body in a morgue.

'I feel bad that I've dragged you into my mess.'

'You haven't dragged me into anything. I offered, remember?'

She gives me a half-smile. 'Won't the kids at the gym be missing you today?'

'I gave myself the day off.'

Pippa sits up straight and tucks a blonde wisp of hair behind her ear. 'I bet you're really good with them. I'd never have the patience.'

'I'm sure you'd be great.'

'No, seriously, I'd have no idea. Teenagers terrify me.'

'They're okay. And it can be pretty rewarding, knowing that if they weren't with us, they'd probably all be out on the streets in gangs, carrying knives and dealing drugs. There was this one kid, he was only fifteen, who nearly died after being stabbed. By some miracle, the blade missed his heart by millimetres. He came to us when he'd recovered and we showed him there was more to life than gangs and knives, and he's completely turned his life around. I like to think he's still alive because of our intervention.'

'That's some story.'

'It's true.'

'Aren't you worried about them bringing knives to the gym?' Pippa asks.

'Sometimes you have to take the leap, embrace the uncertainty.'

She glowers at me. 'That sounds familiar.'

'It should. It's one of yours. "You can't wait for the perfect moment because life will always throw curveballs. Sometimes, you have to take the leap, embrace the uncertainty…"'

She grins. '"And remember, failing is just proof that you're trying," we chorus together.

'You really have been watching my videos.' Pippa's eyes sparkle with delight.

'A few of them.'

'That's so sweet.'

'You're really talented, Pippa. Never forget that. I'm glad you found your calling.'

It takes Pippa a moment or two to orient herself when we hop off the train at Hackney Central station and find ourselves in a bustling, dirty street lined with nail salons, takeaways and off-licences, where stationary traffic spews out filthy fumes.

'I remember Nathan made us walk to the party from the station,' she says, tapping her phone against her bottom teeth as she glances up and down the road. 'This way,' she announces, marching off.

After a twenty-minute fast march through the centre of Hackney, cutting through a spacious park, we arrive in Albion Drive. Pippa brushes her fingers over a street sign and studies a row of handsome Georgian terraces.

'This is it,' she says. 'I'm sure of it.'

I trail behind as she ambles along, scanning the houses on either side of the tree-lined street. She stops suddenly, pointing to a handsome Georgian-style building with fancy neoclassical dentils over the windows and a short flight of steps leading up to a glossy black door.

'Here! I'm certain. I remember there was a girl right there, leaning against the wall, arguing with a guy. They were Ryan's friends, I think. God knows what he'd done wrong, but she was screaming at him at the top of her voice and making such a racket, I was sure one of the neighbours was going to call the police. Just as well they didn't, given what was being passed around inside.'

'Drugs?'

Pippa glances at me as if I'm stupid. 'No, a gun.'

She says it so casually, it's as if it's no big deal. Maybe I misheard. I catch her by the elbow as she's about to skip up the steps to the door. 'A gun?'

'You know, a handgun. A pistol. I don't know what you call it.'

'Where did it come from?'

She pulls her arm free and scowls at me. 'I don't know. I think it was Ryan's. All the lads were passing it around and posing with it like they were John Wick. It was pathetic.'

She scampers up the steps to the door and presses a buzzer.

I follow and stand at her side, clasping my hands over my stomach, trying to look relaxed. I'm a big guy and my size can make some people nervous, but I'm not here to intimidate Ryan.

'What if he's not in?' Pippa jigs on the balls of her feet, a fizzing ball of nerves.

'Then we'll come back later. Or we could push a note through the door.'

But Pippa's worries are unfounded. The door creaks open and a short, dark-haired, unshaven man with a crooked nose appears. 'Yes?' he raises an eyebrow, glancing between us.

'Ryan, it's me, Pippa. We met at your party last year? Nathan's girlfriend?'

Ryan leans on the door, one hand in the pocket of his trousers, trying too hard to appear casual. He has the look of a used-car salesman about him, superficially charming, but as slippery as an eel. A full head of hair oiled back and his shirt crumpled, like he'd dressed up for a night out and is still in the same clothes the next morning.

'Pippa?' He plays with her name, drawing it out syllable by syllable as if trying to remember. 'Yes, of course. How are you?'

He glances only briefly at me, eyeing me up and down. I don't give him the satisfaction of introducing myself. Let him wonder.

'Have you heard from Nathan?' Pippa asks.

Ryan frowns. 'No, why? Is everything okay?'

'Didn't you get my message?'

'What message?'

'Nathan's missing. I've not seen him since last night. I was hoping he might have been in touch.'

Ryan gives a slight shake of his head. 'Nope. Not heard anything.'

Pippa sighs and tells him how they'd been caught up in the Tower Bridge bombing, narrowly avoiding being injured.

'He had this crazy idea that he could help give first aid,' she says. 'But that was the last I saw of him.'

Ryan runs a hand over his chin. I can't work out whether his stubble is supposed to be fashionably designer or he just hasn't bothered to shave.

'I've not heard from him in a few weeks. In fact, I can't remember the last time we spoke. Have you tried his mobile?'

'He left his phone with me, so I don't have any way of getting hold of him.'

'What about his flat? He's probably at home,' Ryan says.

'No, I've tried that. He's not called *you*, has he?'

Ryan pulls a phone out of his trouser pocket, checks it briefly, and shakes his head. 'Nope.'

'I don't understand. Where is he?'

'I'm sure he'll turn up. You know what he's like,' Ryan says. He doesn't sound concerned. 'But I'll tell you what. Leave me your number and if I hear anything, I'll let you know.'

'Thank you. I'm going out of my mind with worry.'

I'm surprised she doesn't tell Ryan that Nathan proposed. It's important context, but I guess she has her reasons and it's not my place to say anything. I'm here to support her and that's it. She doesn't need me sticking my size elevens in.

Pippa gives Ryan her number and apologises for bothering him.

'Not a problem,' he says with a greasy smile. 'I'll let you know the second I hear anything, but,' he glances back inside the house, 'I really need to go. I'm due on a call at any minute.'

He shuts the door in our faces, leaving us standing on the doorstep shivering in the cold, and none the wiser about Nathan.

'Are you okay?' I put a hand on Pippa's arm as she wilts.

It's understandable that she's disappointed. She came so full of hope, but now she's back to square one.

She pulls away from me, hurries down the steps and marches off down the road without waiting.

'Pippa, hold up.'

When I catch up with her halfway down the street, she stops and spins around on her heels, her eyes narrowed and her lips pursed. 'Did you think that was weird?'

'What was weird?'

'Ryan's reaction. I told him we'd been caught up in the bombing and now his brother's missing and he didn't seem concerned in the slightest. He was more worried about getting back to his call.'

'Has Nathan ever done anything like this before?'

'What, go missing? No, never.'

'So what did Ryan mean when he said you know what he's like?'

'I've no idea, but something's not right. And I don't know about you, but I didn't believe a word Ryan said.'

Chapter 11

PIPPA
February 20, 2024

I've not seen or heard from Nathan in six days and yet not a minute has passed when I've not thought about him and wondered whether he's alive or dead. I'm back in my flat now, my days spent monitoring the TV and news websites, hoping for a crumb of information that might lead me to finding out what happened to him, but so far there's been nothing at all.

Although I'm grateful to Sam for taking me in, after a few days I couldn't spend another minute with her and her constant fussing, treating me like I'm a child. I didn't even have any spare clothes and I'm used to having my own space, so it made sense I came home. She was disappointed I didn't want to stay longer, but we would have killed each other if I'd stayed.

The official death toll from the bombing has now risen to fifteen, and another thirty-four people have needed hospital treatment, many with what the media are calling life-changing injuries, whatever that means. The loss of limbs or facial disfiguration, I guess.

Everyone who was killed has been named, their photographs widely used by the media in bulletins, newspapers and online stories. Each face now so familiar. Each name forever tied to the tragedy. Sadly, many of those killed were foreign tourists, including a family of four from Tampa in Florida, who had only arrived in Britain the night before, ahead of a three-week tour of Europe, and a German couple in their fifties who'd been taking photos on the bridge close to where the bomb detonated.

Other fatalities included a couple in their early thirties who'd been due to marry in the summer, out celebrating Valentine's like Nathan and me. Two Australian backpackers in their early twenties, a thirty-six-year-old woman who ran a small boutique shop in the city, an Italian exchange student who'd been out visiting friends, a primary school teacher from Devon, spending time in London with her sister, and a young cycle courier with a pizza delivery that never made it.

And, of course, the bomber himself. The man I'd seen driving onto the bridge at high speed in a van I now know was packed with explosives intended to kill and maim. They say Jack Reeves was twenty-seven, originally from Birmingham, and that he was radicalised after becoming involved with the outlawed far-right group, the *Patriots of the Isles*, that claimed responsibility for the bombing in the hours after the attack.

No one's mourned his death.

Police have carried out dozens of raids at houses and warehouses across the country and have so far arrested ten men with links to the organisation. They're promising there'll be more raids and more arrests, and eventually all those involved will be brought to justice for their roles in planning and coordinating the attack. Not that it's much consolation to the families of the bereaved. Nor is it going to help me find Nathan.

I've watched so much coverage on the TV, scoured so many online articles in the search for answers, but I'm no closer to the truth. He's not returned home. His office hasn't heard from him. And he's not made contact with his brother. It's looking increasingly likely that he's dead and that it's only a matter of time before his body is found. At least that would give me closure and I could think about how to move on with my life.

For now, I still have so many questions, like what happened in those minutes after he left me, when he strode bravely into the epicentre of hell without a single thought for his own safety? Who did he speak to? What did he do? Where did he go?

I've called all the hospitals in London but no one has any record of treating him, and I pester the police daily, but every time it's the same. Someone takes my details, promises to look into it, and never phones back. I understand they're stretched, but I can't understand why no one's taking Nathan's disappearance seriously.

The only consolation is that those counter-terrorism officers who questioned me so aggressively on the night of the attack haven't been in touch again since Sam made an official complaint about the way I was treated. Although I've not heard officially, now they know more about the bomber and his motivations, they've ruled me and Nathan out of their enquiries.

James has tried calling a few times, but I've ignored his messages. It was good of him to reach out, and I enjoyed seeing him again, but I don't need his help or his pity. I need to find Nathan. What I don't need is to be hanging out with my ex.

Up until now, I've been reluctant to turn to my followers for help, or even reveal what really happened the night I was caught up in the blast. I've been too worried about opening myself up to abuse from the keyboard crackpots and weirdos who stalk the darkest recesses of the internet. But with a following of three-quarters of a million on Instagram alone, I've come to a decision.

Last night, as I lay in bed listening to the late-night drunks passing under my window, I decided I'm going to tell my followers about Nathan and his mysterious disappearance, even though it means admitting I've been in a secret relationship for the last year.

The face that stares back at me in the bathroom mirror is almost unrecognisable. I've not slept much since Nathan disappeared, running on a combination of adrenaline and green tea, and it's taking its toll. My eyes are puffy, ringed with dark circles, and I have an outbreak of spots on my forehead and chin. I never usually get spots.

A dab of concealer does a reasonable job on the blemishes, but there's no covering up how tired I look. My skin's grey and my eyes lack any sparkle.

I compensate by tying my hair in a ponytail, adding a bold flick of eyeliner and a smear of pink lipstick.

I set my phone on a tripod inside a ring light in front of the window in the lounge and frame myself with my head and shoulders prominently in the shot. Closer than I'd shoot when I'm recording a fitness video, but this is different. It needs to be intimate.

I hit record, force a smile and take a deep breath.

'Hey, everyone, I wanted to take a moment to talk today about something extremely personal.' I pause for a beat, staring directly at the tiny lens as if I'm looking my best friend in the eye. 'As you know, last week I was caught up in the London terror attack on Tower Bridge. First of all, I wanted to let you know that I'm absolutely fine, but there's something I didn't tell you about that night...'

I hesitate, not sure whether to reference Nathan as my romantic partner or simply as a friend, but I've always taught my followers to be true to themselves, so it would be hypocritical if I lied to them.

'I was with my boyfriend, Nathan.'

Speaking his name out loud stirs up a plethora of emotions. I take a moment to compose myself and clear my throat. I'm not looking for pity. I just want help to find him.

'Since the attack on the fourteenth, Nathan has been missing. We became separated in the immediate aftermath of the explosion and I've not heard from him since. He's not returned home, he didn't have his phone with him, and he's failed to turn up at work. What happened to him is a complete mystery. Obviously, it's been a difficult few days, but I'm staying positive because I know he's out there somewhere. I just don't know where, but with your help, I'm certain we can track him down.'

I make a mental note to edit a photo of Nathan into the video. Maybe the one I took a few weeks ago after one of our early morning runs when he didn't realise I was taking his picture. The light was glorious, the rising sun shedding a beautiful amber glow across the park, back-lighting Nathan as he stretched against a bench, muscles popping under a tight, black T-shirt and wearing a casual, unguarded smile that made my heart loop.

'I last saw him heading across the bridge. He wanted to help the survivors. He thought it was his duty, without stopping to consider how dangerous it might be. He was a hero. My hero. But he never came back to me and I'm worried sick. The police haven't been able to help either. They don't seem interested, which is strange, but I'll let you make up your own minds about why that might be.

'Honestly, the last few days have been incredibly tough, but I'm focusing on what matters and that's finding Nathan. I've always believed that inner strength comes from how we face our challenges, and that's what I'm holding onto right now,' I say, ensuring I don't break eye-contact with the camera lens.

'So I'm begging for your help. If anyone has seen or heard anything that might help locate Nathan, please reach out. Drop me a message or leave a comment. You're my family. My team. I know that together we can do this. Let's hold on to hope together. Thank you.'

I stop the recording and check the footage. My ponytail's askew and my smile doesn't reach my eyes, but I can't face reshooting it. So before I change my mind, I edit in the photo of Nathan in the park and upload it to Instagram as a new reel. A minute later it's live. There's nothing more I can do now other than wait.

I flop onto the sofa, switch the TV back on and grab my laptop to continue scouring through social media, looking for new footage of the bombing. It's become my new obsession, hunting for clues in the hours of video that's appeared online. It's extraordinary how much of it has been uploaded, from all different angles and different times, from dashcam footage that captured the exact moment the bomb detonated, to clips taken in the aftermath showing the fires, smoke and devastation.

All the best footage has been picked up by the news channels and shown over and over, including a now-famous clip from a camera in a black cab that shows the white van that was carrying the bomb scything through traffic, crashing through a metal barrier and into the south tower before exploding in a terrifying fireball which lifted the van clean off the ground, tore chunks out of the masonry, ripped up the road and flipped a car travelling in the opposite direction onto its side like it was a toy.

Other footage of the van hurtling towards the bridge was captured by security cameras on commercial buildings along Tower Bridge Road, but I'm more interested in the footage posted by people who were in the area at the time and who filmed the aftermath on their phones. It was a busy evening on Valentine's Day. Hundreds, if not thousands, of people witnessed the attack. Almost all of them had phones, and a large number of them instinctively took them out to film what they were witnessing. Many of them have shared their footage online.

Much of it is too grainy, shot from too far away with trembling hands to be of much use, but I have found one short clip where I think I've identified Nathan, and I can't stop watching it.

It was shot by someone standing on the south side of the bridge, on the opposite side of the road to me and Nathan. It starts a little shakily, initially focusing on the pavement, but accompanied by the soundtrack of people screaming and car alarms going off, which only makes it more haunting. There are fleeting shots of random feet and hands until finally the camera steadies, pointing towards the apocalypse of pluming spires of smoke, what's left of the smouldering white van and a few punch-drunk survivors lost and dazed in the confusion and chaos.

And, briefly, a figure who I'm fairly certain is Nathan, strides purposefully across the bridge. Muscles bulging under his suit jacket, sweeping a curl of jet-black hair off his forehead and smoothing it back in the way I've seen him do a thousand times. Even the way he walks, arms swinging at his side, head swivelling from side to side, is painfully familiar. It's him. I'm sure it is.

He slows as a figure staggers towards him wearing a mask of dust. Blood streams from his head, eyes wide with shock. He steps to one side and lets him pass, staring in horror.

Then the camera pans away, sweeping from left to right and back again as if whoever is filming can't take in the enormity of what they're witnessing and is making a vain attempt to capture everything all at once, but their filming becomes ragged and jerky which makes it hard to make sense of anything.

A few seconds pass. The camera finally steadies, although the phone's on a slight angle, and the figure that I'm sure is Nathan comes into view again. He's further away now and has slowed to an amble. I can't imagine what's going through his head. The horrors he confronted. The suffering. A swell of pride thickens in my chest.

It was such a brave thing to do, never once stopping to consider his own safety, his only concern to help people who couldn't help themselves. I wish I never gave him that ultimatum and made him choose between me and his conscience.

Yet no one's talking about him. Why? He hasn't been featured on the news or in the papers, his story of selfless heroism totally undocumented. Nathan deserves recognition for his actions. An acknowledgement at least of the lives I'm sure he must have saved before the ambulances arrived.

The last shot of Nathan is when he vanishes behind a double-decker bus that's pulled up to a sudden halt and skidded across the road. And that's it. The footage ends, frozen on a blurry shot of what appears to one of the suspension chains looping from the top of one of the towers.

I replay the footage, bringing the screen closer to my face, hoping there's something I've missed the last dozen times I've watched it. A clue that will finally reveal what happened to Nathan that night and why he never came back to me.

But there's nothing. It's the only footage I've found that shows Nathan on the bridge that night, and it tells me nothing about his disappearance that I didn't already know.

Transcript from the podcast, Fallen Hero. Interview with senior news producer, Zara Bukhari

I've covered some big stories for the channel, but I'd never covered anything like I saw on Valentine's night on Tower Bridge. My job was to do the legwork, finding eyewitnesses and victims who'd be willing to talk on camera. I filmed a few interviews on my phone and sent them back to the studio, and then my priority became sourcing footage that captured the moment the bomb went off.

It's the holy grail, what all the news organisations were chasing. Plenty of people had filmed the aftermath on their phones and most of them were all too happy to share it in return for a name check on screen. But it wasn't enough.

Then I got lucky. I started talking to this guy who was standing behind the police cordon, staring at the bridge, raking his hands through his hair. He was an older guy. Maybe late fifties or early sixties. I don't know why I approached him in particular. I was talking to lots of people. His name was Kofi and he told me he'd been driving a black cab in London for almost twenty years and that he'd never seen anything like it.

He'd been a few cars behind the bomber's van and had seen everything. It was lucky he wasn't killed. I asked if by any chance he had any dashcam footage, thinking it was unlikely, but he nodded and pulled a camera out of his pocket which he'd had the sense to grab as he abandoned his cab and fled the scene.

And that was it. The footage the whole world has now seen that shows the precise moment attacker Jack Reeves detonated his bomb in the middle of Tower Bridge and killed fifteen people.

I didn't leave Kofi's side until he was safely back at the studio with his camera. There was no way I was going to risk losing him or letting the footage fall into the hands of another news crew.

Of course we paid for it. I can't tell you how much. That's confidential, but he did pretty well out of it. Let's just say, he's not going to have to worry about picking up fares for a while.

But it was worth every penny. It was syndicated around the world and to this day it's the only footage that's been uncovered that shows the exact moment the bomb detonated. So yeah, it was a good night's work.

Chapter 12

PIPPA
February 24, 2024

An insistent hammering at the front door jars me out of a stupor with a jolt of alarm. I grab the remote and mute the TV, stiffening with anxiety. Who the hell's at the door at this time on a Friday evening? I have no intention of answering it, especially as I'm curled up on the sofa in my pyjamas under my duvet, the TV droning on in the background. I'm only half-watching it. It's a programme about a railway journey through Sri Lanka which was the least offensive show I could find, a distraction to dull the silence and occupy my mind. Otherwise, I'd be sitting here torturing myself about Nathan, imagining his lifeless body floating down the Thames in the dark or being dragged under by the currents. It's all I can seem to think about while there's no news. I thought after ten days they might have at least found his body. But I'm still waiting, clinging on to hope that he's somehow miraculously survived.

It's probably kids mucking about. Or a cold caller who wants to guilt me into donating to a questionable charity. Don't these people have lives to live? If I leave it long enough and keep quiet, maybe they'll go away.

On the screen, a winding train made up of a seemingly never-ending string of carriages painted in vibrant shades of red and blue snakes through rolling hills of emerald-green tea plantations. I've given up watching the news around the clock since the coverage of the bombing was overtaken by other events. The escalating war in Ukraine. Researchers announcing a breakthrough cancer drug. A well-known businessman on trial for historic sexual offences against a string of women. The bombing still features, but it's not headline news anymore.

The hammering at the door starts again. Louder. Don't they know I'm not in the mood to see anyone? I can't even bring myself to work. My only significant contact with the outside world in the last week has been with my Instagram followers who've inundated me with messages since I posted about Nathan's disappearance, although frustratingly it's not produced a single credible sighting or lead worth following up and I'm left in a complete state of limbo, lacking all motivation.

The only real person I've spoken to is Sam, who rings several times a day to check up on me. James has been messaging, attempting to persuade me to meet up again, but I've been making excuses. I know he only wants to help, but I don't want to see him.

Annoyingly, whoever's at my door isn't going away. Maybe it's an emergency. A fire? A neighbour suffering a heart attack? A child choking?

Bang. Bang. Bang.

For pity's sake. Why can't they leave me in peace? I finally cave in, swing my legs off the sofa and head down into the hall.

I flick on the light and attach the security chain before peeling the door open a crack. I'm instantly hit by an Arctic blast.

'Whatever it is, I'm not interested.'

'Pippa, it's me.'

I stare through the narrow gap in disbelief. James is standing on the doorstep wrapped up in a thick, plaid lumberjack coat, a beanie hat pulled down over his ears.

'James? What are you doing here?'

'You weren't answering my messages, so I thought I'd come and check on you.'

'You didn't need to do that.'

'I know. I wanted to.'

I slip off the chain and open the door. James raises an eyebrow as he casts an eye over my dishevelled state. I've not washed my hair in days or changed out of my pyjamas. There didn't seem any point.

'I'm fine. Happy now?'

'Are you eating properly?'

'Yes,' I lie, although the truth is, I've not had much of an appetite.

'Right, well, I have an enormous favour to ask.' He clasps his hands in front of his chest in supplication. 'It's my sister's birthday. I'm supposed to be meeting her with some of her friends for a drink.'

I stare at him blankly.

'They're all lovely, but I don't really know any of them that well. It would be amazing if you'd come and keep me company, just for a few hours.'

'Oh, James, no. Please don't ask.' I back into the shadows, flinching away, which he wrongly interprets as an invitation to step inside.

'It might be fun. Please?' He draws out the syllables of his plea like a child begging to be allowed to stay up for an hour longer.

'I'm not even dressed. And even if I was, I'm not in the mood.'

'When's the last time you left the flat?' He pushes the door closed behind him.

'I don't know. Yesterday?' I head back up the stairs and into the warmth of the lounge. James follows, but doesn't take the hint, even when I collapse on the sofa and turn up the volume on the TV.

'Where did you go?'

'Out.'

'To do what?'

'To pick up some soya milk, not that it's any of your business.'

James lets out a long sigh. 'Look, it's just the pub and we only need to stay for an hour. Please don't make me face Cat's friends on my own.' He flutters his eyelashes and pouts.

'Don't you have anyone else you can ask?'

'Not really. And besides, I want to go with you. It'll do you good. You've been moping around in this flat for too long.'

'Who's moping?'

'One hour, that's all, and then I'll bring you home. I promise.'

'In case you've forgotten, my boyfriend is missing. For all I know, he could be dead. I'm not exactly in the right frame of mind to go out partying.'

'It's just one drink. And at some point you have to move on with your life.'

I glare at him. 'It hasn't even been two weeks.'

'I know, but do you think Nathan would want to see you like this?' James waves a hand around the room. 'Wasting your life?'

'I'm not wasting it. Anyway, I think I might have found someone who remembers seeing Nathan the night he disappeared.' I lean over the side of the sofa, grab my laptop and navigate to an online news article I found earlier when I was looking for new footage. 'One of the survivors has described seeing a man in a dark suit wandering around the bridge shortly after the bomb went off. I mean, the rest of the article's nonsense. Typical tabloid conspiracy theory stuff, speculating that it was someone working for the government and questioning why he was on the scene so quickly. They seem to be suggesting there was some kind of collusion with the bomber. Anyway, that's not the point. The man they saw was obviously Nathan. He's the man in the suit.'

'Right.' James's eyes narrow. 'And the significance is?'

'Isn't it obvious?'

'Explain it to me.'

'Well, if this woman saw Nathan, maybe she saw what happened to him. I thought if I could track her down and talk to her —'

'Right, that's it. You're coming out and I'm not taking no for an answer. You're driving yourself mad locked up in this tiny flat. Go and get some clothes on.'

He snatches the laptop out of my hands, flips it closed, and puts it out of my reach on the dining table by the window. Then he stands with his arms crossed over his chest, staring at me.

'No, I can't.'

He continues to stare without saying a word.

'James!'

He glances at his watch. 'You've got precisely two minutes and then I'm dragging you out whether you're ready or not.'

'You're insufferable.'

'And you'll thank me later. Clock's ticking.'

'What are people going to think if they see me out?'

'They'll think you're brave and strong. No one's going to judge you, Pippa.'

The credits on the railway programme start to roll over a shot of a train snaking precariously over a brick viaduct in a lush, green jungle.

'Fine,' I huff.

'Fine, you're coming?'

'One drink and that's it.' I wave a finger in warning. 'I mean it.'

Chapter 13

The Crown and Compass is in the trendy area of Shoreditch, less than two miles from Tower Bridge. James promised it would be a quiet drink, but the pub's so busy, there are already several groups of people who have spilled outside clasping pints of beer and glasses of wine, even though it's a chilly February evening. We have to squeeze our way inside, the fuggy, sweaty pub crowded with a mixture of city workers who've stopped off on their way home and early evening revellers warming up for a night out.

'I'm not sure about this.' I grab the back of James's jacket, terrified of losing him among a sea of strangers.

'What?' he shouts over the din.

'I don't think I should have come.'

'You'll enjoy it once you've had a drink.'

James's sister has secured a table in a back room. I gratefully slide onto a bench seat, nodding a wordless greeting to everyone. Eight pairs of eyes turn on me at once, staring at me in judgement. I cast my gaze down. I knew this was a bad idea.

'Everyone, this is my friend, Pippa. Be nice to her, okay?' James says.

It's a rude shock to be in company again after being cocooned inside and not seeing anyone for so long.

I raise a hand and give a self-conscious wave. 'Sorry for gatecrashing the party.'

If any of them recognise me from Instagram, they don't say anything. There's no flicker of uncertainty in their eyes or unexpected double-takes, which is simultaneously a relief and a disappointment. Over time, I've become used to the knowing glances of strangers in the street. It's an occupational hazard when you have such a big following. I've even been approached for my autograph a few times. The first time it happened, I was so flustered I've no idea what I wrote on the poor girl's bare arm that she'd held up to me with a nervous smile. These days I'm better prepared. I like to add a message of hope along with my squiggle of a signature. *Chase the light, even on your darkest days* is one of my favourites. But tonight, I'm happy to be anonymous. Just James's friend. It also means I don't have to spend the evening talking about how I was caught up in the terror attack or how my boyfriend mysteriously disappeared, especially as I don't know any of these people.

I can tell instantly that James and his sister are related. They share the same kindly eyes and lopsided smile, Cat's calm, reassuring presence a mirror of James's quiet strength and stoicism. I didn't meet her when James and I were together, but he talked about her so much and so fondly, I feel as if I know her. Wasn't she hoping to become a documentary filmmaker? I must ask if her dreams ever became a reality.

'Glass of wine?' James asks.

I nod. I don't usually drink because it affects my sleep and I'm awful if I don't get a solid eight hours. Nor do I like how it dulls my mind. But this evening, in the company of strangers, a large glass of Dutch courage is in order.

Cat reaches across the table and lays her hand on top of mine. 'How are you?' she asks, a shock of tight curls falling to one side as she cocks her head.

James must have told her about Nathan.

I shoot her a tight smile, determined to not let the kindness of a stranger choke me. 'I'm okay, thanks.'

'I'm glad you could come.'

'James didn't give me much choice.'

Cat rolls her eyes. 'He's been so worried about you. I take it there's been no news?'

'Not yet.'

She takes the time to introduce me properly to each and every one of her friends. They seem nice and show genuine interest when I tell them what I do for a living.

'I've never met a real-life influencer before,' one of the women says, squealing with delight. 'Do you actually make a living from it, or is it just a hobby?'

I'm saved from her questions when James returns with a pint of stout and a glass of white wine. He scoots along the bench seat, squashing me into the corner against the wall, and slides the wine glass under my nose.

'Nathan hates stout,' I say. 'He thinks it's like drinking tar.'

'More of a lager man, is he?' James raises his eyebrows, hinting at some innuendo which goes straight over my head.

'He wouldn't like this pub much, either. Far too many people, not that we often go to the pub. We don't really drink.'

'A glass of wine might help take your mind off Nathan for a while.'

Is that what I want? To forget about Nathan for an hour or two? If only he could see me now, out at a pub with a glass of wine, enjoying myself while I should be looking for him. He'd be horrified.

'I prefer to keep a clear head.' I run a finger around the bowl of my glass, drawing a line through a frost of condensation. It's really hot in here. Oppressively warm. I peel off my thick sweater and shove it behind my back.

'You need to learn to let yourself go.'

'You mean get drunk and say a bunch of things I'll regret tomorrow?'

'No, but you could do with lightening up. This obsession with finding Nathan isn't healthy.'

'That's easy for you to say. Did you know that almost eighty per cent of missing adults are found within twenty-four hours, but only three per cent go missing for more than a week?' I take a long sip of wine, savouring the alcohol as it hits my empty stomach.

'All I'm saying is —'

'It's been ten days and I don't have the first clue what's happened to him. The police aren't interested. Even Ryan's been conspicuously quiet. I sometimes wonder if I'm the only one who cares that he's vanished.'

'I thought we were here to relax? Not to talk about Nathan all evening. Look, I can't imagine how hard it's been on you, but you need to start thinking about you.' James finishes his pint and bangs the glass on the table.

'You think he's dead, don't you?'

'I don't know. Come on, drink up. I'll get you another.'

He points to my glass and I shake my head. 'I'm fine.'

'One more. They're only small glasses.'

I suppose one more small glass of wine can't hurt, especially as I already feel calmer, the alcohol working its magic. 'Okay, but that's it. No more after that. I don't want a hangover in the morning.'

But when James returns, it's with a bigger glass than my first. He shrugs. 'They've run out of small ones.'

'Are you trying to get me drunk?'

James's mouth falls open, his eyes wide with horror. 'No, of course not. Don't drink it if you don't want to.'

'I'm only teasing. It's fine.'

In fact, it's more than fine. My limbs feel as light as air and my fingers are tingling. I glance across the table at one of Cat's friends. She's telling a story about her boss who accidentally bleached his hair orange. She has the whole table, me included, doubled up with laughter.

Two drinks turn into three. And then four, until I'm no longer worried about getting home or having a hangover in the morning. Nathan barely enters my thoughts.

When someone suggests shots, I shout with delight, much to James's amusement. He's promptly dispatched to the bar and comes back with a tray of shot glasses filled with clear, viscous liquid which might be vodka or tequila or something else entirely. After a quick toast to the birthday girl, we down them in one. I wince as the alcohol burns my throat.

Tequila.

Yuck! I don't even like it. Never have. It leaves a nasty, bitter taste in my mouth and sends my head spinning. But I'm drunk and I'm having a great time. Isn't it funny how the best nights often come about when you don't plan them? And to think I was only going to stay for one. Cat's friends are amazing and funny. Strong, independent women. I'm so glad James persuaded me to come, although from his long face, he's not having such a great time.

'I need the bathroom. Let me out,' I say.

He slides out of my way, and catches me as I stumble, the extent of my drunkenness apparent when I attempt to stand. The room spins and my head flips.

'Woah, careful.' His grip on my arm is reassuringly firm.

I take a second to steady myself and as an afterthought, throw my arms around James, pulling him into a hug. 'You were right. This is exactly what I needed. Your sister and her friends are amazing.'

'Did you want to get going soon?' His eyes are glassy, his face even more handsome than I remembered. 'I know I promised we'd only stay for one.'

'Don't be a party-pooper.' I prod him in the chest and sway backwards, rocking on the balls of my feet as I catch my balance. 'Maybe one more itsy-bitsy, teeny-weeny drinkie?'

He laughs. 'I think you've probably had enough.'

'I'll be the judge of that. I've had an incredibly trying few weeks, you know.' I pout like a sulky teenager. 'I deserve to let my hair down.'

'You're right. Just let me know when you're ready and I'll make sure you get home in one piece.'

'Yes, sir!' I slur, pressing a two-fingered salute to my forehead.

The pub's even busier than when we arrived, and threading my way to the ladies is a nightmare. I have to jostle and shove my way through small gaps, but it's a Friday evening and everyone's in such a good mood. Even when I stand on someone's toes, nobody seems to mind. A cheery smile and an apology go a long way. After all, we're all here to have a good time and let our worries and woes go for a few hours.

It's quieter in the ladies bathroom. As the door swings shut behind me, the deafening roar of drunken chatter and laughter is muted to a quiet rumble.

I cling to the basin with my ears ringing, staring into the mirror with bloodshot eyes and wild, untamed blonde hair plastered to my forehead. I brush a couple of strands out of my eyes with the back of my hand and grin. After the stress I've been under in the last ten days, it's as if someone's released a safety valve and let all the pressure out.

I'd usually avoid getting drunk and losing control, but tonight it's liberating. Tonight, I don't have to worry about being Pippa Ravenscroft, fitness guru. Women's advocate. Content creator. Influencer. Tonight, I'm just me. And it feels good. Really good. Even if I'll regret it in the morning.

I rinse my face with cold water and run my fingers through my hair, putting a little volume back into the limp mess. I probably shouldn't have any more to drink. What I should do is ask for a glass of water and for James to take me home. But where's the fun in that?

Two young women barrel in, laughing so hysterically it puts a broad grin on my face. I catch the door as it clatters against the wall, and stumble back into the bar, staring left and right, trying to work out where James and his sister are sitting.

I stand on tiptoes to see over the sea of heads, mildly amused that I've managed to get myself lost going to the toilet. How embarrassing.

A chill breeze strikes my cheek. I glance across the bar as a handful of men pulling on coats walk out of the pub. The door clatters closed behind them, but it's not the door shutting that causes my heart to lurch or my breath to catch in my throat. It's the sight of a familiar figure across the room. The back of a head I know so well. Broad shoulders as recognisable as my own hands. A swagger and poise as distinct as a fingerprint.

'Nathan?' I gasp.

It can't be. It's impossible. My mind and the wine are playing tricks on me, conjuring him up in my imagination. After all, why would Nathan be in a pub in Shoreditch on a busy Friday evening when he's been missing for two weeks? I shake my head, squeeze my eyes shut and open them again, expecting the mirage to have vanished. A puff of smoke blown away on a strong breeze.

But he's still there, no more than ten metres away, sinking into the crowd.

'Nathan!' I yell, my voice lost in the noisy hubbub.

He glances over his shoulder in my direction, and I know with absolute certainly it's him. It's Nathan. I don't know where he's been or what's happened to him, but one thing's for sure, he's very much alive.

Chapter 14

In an instant, I'm as sober as a nun. A middle-aged man in an expensive business suit stumbles into me, knocking me off balance. He catches me by the arm, slopping his pint over the floor, and apologises for being a clown. When I look back across the bar, Nathan has vanished.

'Are you okay?' the man in the business suit asks. 'Let me buy you a drink to say sorry.' He leers at me, swaying from side to side like a sapling in the wind.

I push him out of the way and dive across the room, trying to part the sea of hot, sweaty bodies, but nobody's in a hurry to move.

'Nathan!'

Over the din, I hear the door open and rattle shut. Was that him leaving? I can't let him disappear. Not again.

I switch direction, aiming for the exit, pushing and shoving through groups of drinkers who are blissfully ignorant of my desperation. At the door, I bowl through a group of four women tottering in on high heels, ignoring their abuse and dirty looks. The only thing on my mind is catching Nathan.

I fall out into the street, a blast of icy February air sucking the air from my lungs.

'Nathan!' I scream.

It might be a cold evening, but the area is humming with people drifting in and out of restaurants, pubs, cocktail bars and clubs. Among them, somewhere, is Nathan. I scan up and down the street, looking for his familiar loping walk, but it's hopeless.

A couple wrapped up in thick coats and scarves stare at me like I've lost my mind as I stand in my T-shirt, hollering Nathan's name.

'Pippa, what's going on?' James's hand on my back makes me jump.

'I saw Nathan.'

'Where?'

'In the pub.'

'Are you sure?'

'Yes! I'm positive. But now he's gone again.'

'It's freezing out here. Why don't you come back inside?' James tries to shepherd me back into the pub, but I shrug his hand off.

Doesn't he understand? Or maybe he doesn't believe me. I absolutely did not imagine it.

Left or right? It's a fifty-fifty decision. I turn right and sprint down the road, my feet pounding along the pavement like I'm flying, swerving around bemused groups of people. So many people. Where have they all come from?

'Nathan!'

My chest tightens as I labour for breath and eventually, with my thighs burning, I'm brought to a stop at a junction with an intersecting street. I know I didn't imagine it. As impossible and unfathomable as it seems, I saw Nathan. I know I did.

I bend double, catching my breath. Those tequila shots really weren't a good idea. My head rolls and my stomach somersaults.

James races up to me, breathing hard. 'Pippa, what are you doing?'

'Leave me alone.'

'Please, come back to the pub.'

I straighten up and stand tall. 'He's here. I saw him.'

'Okay,' he says, but I can tell he's not convinced. He thinks I'm seeing things. Going crazy. Maybe I am.

'Don't you understand? It means he's alive.'

'Pippa, you're going to freeze to —'

I double over, a flush of nausea catching me by surprise, and vomit all over James's shoes. He rubs my back as I continue to retch, emptying my stomach until there's nothing left but bitter bile and a hopeless hollowness in my core.

'I think it's time we got you home, don't you?'

Chapter 15

PIPPA
February 25, 2024

My brain hammers at the inside of my skull as if it's making a bid for freedom, my mouth's desert-dry and my stomach is tender with nausea. Why did I drink so much? I want to curl up and die.

I roll onto my back, kick off the duvet, and gaze at a moth stuck to the ceiling. No wonder I'm so hot, my body drenched in alcohol-tinged sweat. I'm still in my jeans and T-shirt from last night. Too drunk to even undress before bed. Ugh, what a crazy evening.

Snatches of memory come back to me, but most of the night, especially the latter half, is hazy. Was it really Nathan I saw across the crowded bar, slinking away into the night? Or maybe it was just someone who looked like him, my imagination deceived by my desperation, fooling me into thinking it was him.

After all, why would he be in a pub in Shoreditch on a Friday night when I haven't seen or heard from him in almost two weeks? It doesn't make any sense, although it doesn't mean it isn't true. I looked into his eyes. That wasn't a trick of the light. It was him. I'm certain of it.

Another memory flashes into my mind, of running down the street, chasing him, and of James catching up, not believing a word I was telling him. Then, throwing up all over his shoes. How embarrassing. I don't remember much after that, other than a vague recollection of climbing into the back of an Uber and falling asleep on James's shoulder. I don't recall getting home or how I made it into bed.

I fling out an arm, locate my phone on the bedside cabinet, and bring it close to my face. I open the camera app and inspect the wreck that's my face. It's even worse than I thought. Bloodshot, puffy eyes, pale skin and a fresh crop of spots on my chin. Mascara streaks down my cheeks in dirty rivulets and scarecrow hair is plastered to my forehead. I could easily blame James for dragging me out, but no one forced me to down those tequila shots, the thought of which brings on another bout of nausea, and actually, until I saw Nathan, I was having fun. James's sister and her friends couldn't have been more welcoming. It's been a long time since I've laughed so much or spent time in the company of friends.

When I check my Instagram messages, I find yet more comments from strangers offering sympathy and concern. A few more directing unnecessary hatred towards me, but nothing from anyone who's seen Nathan or who has any tangible information about what's happened to him, other than the odd speculative theory.

It means the only lead remains my possible sighting of him in the Crown and Compass last night. I knew instantly it was Nathan, from the shape of his shoulders, the way his head was cocked slightly to one side, and his glossy, dark hair swept casually back. And then he turned, only for a split second, and I looked into his eyes. Cold and determined, with a hint of nervousness that I'd never seen before. He's always been so confident and self-assured. I've never known him to be nervous about anything.

Was it him? It had to be.

But the more I concentrate on recalling that moment, freeze-framing it in my mind, the more indistinct the memory becomes, like trying to snatch a handful of smoke out of the air. James certainly doesn't believe me, although it's understandable. It's some coincidence that Nathan happened to be in the same pub at the same time, but it doesn't mean it didn't happen. If only there was a way I could prove it. That I'm not going mad or making it up.

But how do I do that?

Unless...

Surely the pub has CCTV cameras? Everywhere has them these days, don't they? Is it possible they captured an image of Nathan in the bar? My heart flutters with a surge of excitement.

I throw my legs out of bed and stand too quickly, almost collapsing as my head spins and my stomach rolls. I need some water before I do anything or go anywhere.

With gritty eyes and wobbly legs, I shuffle out of my room and into the kitchen, catching the faint smell of vomit on my clothes. A horrible reminder of the evils of alcohol. As I peel off my T-shirt and toss it in the direction of the washing machine, the sofa creaks and someone groans. I squeal with shock and jump backwards, covering my body with my arms.

'Who's there?' I call out, my voice trembling. I grab a carving knife from the draining board and hold it up with a stiff arm.

A head pops up. A thick, bushy beard. Bleary, kindly eyes.

'Morning,' James says, yawning. 'How are you feeling?'

'James! What are you doing here?' I drop the knife and wrap both arms around my body, conscious of the eyeful he's getting.

He blinks twice, finally notices I'm standing in just my bra, and turns away, holding his hand theatrically over his eyes. 'Sorry, I didn't realise you weren't dressed.'

'Why are you sleeping on my sofa?'

'I didn't want to leave you last night. You were a bit of a mess. How's the hangover?'

'Not great. It feels like there's an army marching through my head. You shouldn't have made me drink so much.'

'Me?' James stands and pulls on his shirt, wearing only a pair of tight boxer shorts that sculpt his tight arse. I should look away instead of leering, but it's a fine sight for my sore eyes this morning. 'I didn't force you to do anything. You're a grown woman.'

'Well, anyway. I still blame you.'

'You had fun though, didn't you?' He yanks on a pair of jeans and buckles up his belt.

'Actually, I did. Your sister's nice. I'm sorry about your shoes.'

James shrugs. 'It's fine. I was more worried that you spent most of the night jabbering on about having seen Nathan.'

'I did.'

James stares at me blankly.

'It was one hundred per cent him,' I add.

'Pippa —'

'You still don't believe me, do you?'

'Look, we'd all been drinking —'

'I didn't imagine it. He was there in that pub. I saw him with my own eyes in the bar. He looked straight at me. And then he walked out.'

'Okay, assuming you're right, and it's a big assumption, what the hell was he doing in the Crown and Compass last night when he's been missing for the last two weeks?'

'That's exactly what I want to find out.'

'Pippa, it's really not helpful torturing yourself like this.'

'Why won't you believe me?'

'It's not that I don't believe you...'

'But?'

'Isn't it possible that your mind was playing tricks on you? You've hardly slept in days and you'd had a lot to drink...'

'I know what I saw and I'm going to prove it.'

Chapter 16

The window is smoked with dust and grime. I stand on tiptoes, shade my eyes against my reflection with my hand, and peer in. It's too early for the Crown and Compass to be open, but there's a skinny teenager with pockmarked skin and a faded, threadbare T-shirt behind the bar, cleaning glasses.

I tap on the window and wave. 'Can you let me in?'

He raises his wrist and points to his watch.

'I need to speak to the manager. It's important.'

The guy gives me an exaggerated shrug, but I'm not leaving until I've checked their CCTV footage, assuming there is any.

'Two minutes. Please?'

Eventually, he slides out from behind the bar and walks to the door.

'We're not open for another hour,' he says, studying me through a narrow gap.

I whip off my sunglasses, put them on my head, pull my shoulders back and fix him with a cold, hard stare. 'I'm trying to find a missing man. I have reason to believe he was here last night. I was hoping I could take a look at your CCTV.'

He stares at me, opening the door a fraction wider. 'What man?'

'His name's Nathan Pierce. He disappeared two weeks ago after the Tower Bridge bombing, but he was spotted at the bar last night.'

'I don't know anything about that. You'll need to speak to my manager. Can you come back later?' He attempts to close the door, but I've already put my foot over the threshold.

'I'm afraid it can't wait. I need to see your CCTV now. It's urgent.'

His eyes dart sideways, caught in indecision. 'I'm not sure...'

'Look, I shouldn't really be telling you this, but this man is vulnerable and could be in danger. I need to find him as a matter of utmost urgency.'

The guy's head tilts to one side as he studies me, taking in my long, black coat, grey cashmere scarf and skintight jeans. 'Are you the police?'

'What's your name?'

'Matt.'

'Matt, I don't have time to waste. Let me see the footage and I'll be gone. Five minutes of your time, that's all.'

'I'm not really allowed to —'

'I'm sure you'd hate it if something bad happened to him. You wouldn't want that on your conscience, would you? And right now, every second counts.'

He glances over his shoulder into the empty pub. 'My manager will be here at lunchtime. It's best if you speak to him.'

'That's another two hours, Matt.' I reach out and touch his arm lightly with my leather-gloved hand. 'I don't want to get you into trouble, but if there's any way you could do this for me, I'd forever be grateful. It'll be our little secret.'

Matt bites his lip, his gaze falling to the ground.

'Nobody needs to know I've even been here.' I raise my eyebrows, flutter my eyelashes and smile.

'I suppose I could let you have a quick look.'

'That's so sweet of you.'

'But nobody can find out, okay?'

'Nobody needs to know apart from you and me.'

Matt leads me up a staircase behind the bar and into a small office at the back of the building where an ancient-looking computer and monitor take up most of the space on a battered metal desk. Matt pulls up a chair that's worn through to the foam and taps at a keyboard. The monitor sparks into life and a black-and-white image appears of the deserted bar below, distorted by a wide-angled lens.

'What time do you think this guy was here?'

'Around ten, I think, but maybe you could check from a little earlier in the evening?'

Matt clicks open a folder and locates a file. An image of the bar appears from the same angle as the live shot, but this time it's crowded with people. He scrubs forward as I watch a timer in the top right-hand corner. It creates a fascinating time lapse of the ebb and flow of people coming and going all day.

'Play it from there.' The timestamp shows seven fifty-three in the evening.

I lean forwards and stare at the pub entrance in the top left of the image. People filing in. Easing through the crowds. Queuing at the bar. Three members of staff working with quiet efficiency, serving dozens of drinks.

'This what you're looking for?' Matt asks, pushing his chair back to give me a better look.

'Can you speed it up?'

'Double speed?'

'Perfect.'

At eight-twelve, according to the timestamp, James walks into the bar, easy to spot in his beanie hat, thick beard and checked lumberjack coat. Behind him, I'm clutching his coat-tails, glancing around like a frightened mouse.

'That's me and my friend.' I point to the screen.

Matt nods.

People continue to come and go, a constant wash of customers rotating through the bar. James and I disappear out of view, heading for the back room where Cat was waiting with her friends.

'Is this the only view of the bar?'

'There are three other cameras, but you don't need to see all of them, do you?' He glances at me with a pained expression. 'I'm supposed to opening up.'

'Let's see. Can you scroll forward to nine-thirty?'

The bar becomes busier and busier. I catch a glimpse of James several times returning to the bar for more drinks, but so far no sign of Nathan.

When the timestamp hits nine-thirty, Matt stops scrolling and lets the footage play at double speed again. I keep my eyes on the door, gripping the edge of the desk, not daring to blink.

The minutes tick past, the time heading rapidly towards ten.

And then, at precisely seven minutes to the hour, a figure I recognise comes into view.

'Stop it there!'

Matt hits the pause button, but the frozen image of the man who's caught my attention is so blurred it's impossible to tell whether it's Nathan or not.

'Play it at normal speed.'

Matt clicks the mouse. The pub comes to life again, the wash of people at the bar less pronounced at regular speed. I lean in close to the monitor until I can almost make out the individual pixels.

Is it Nathan? It could be. He has the same build. The same shape. But lost in a crowd, it's not as clear as I'd hoped, his face blurry and indistinct.

'I think that might be him. Are there any different angles we could check?'

Matt rubs a hand across his jaw, pulls up the folder of video files, and selects another. The footage that blinks onto the screen is shot looking back towards the bar. But it's no better. All I can see is the back of the man's head. It could be Nathan, but it's hardly definitive proof. I tap my fingers on the desk and sigh, disappointed.

Matt glances at his watch. 'Is it him or not?'

I shake my head, glad the painkillers are finally taking effect. 'I'm not sure.'

'There's one more camera that might have picked him up.' Matt clicks on another video file and opens up footage from a third camera, which is directed towards the entrance to the toilets. 'We've had some trouble with people doing drugs,' he explains.

He fast-forwards the video until the timestamp hits ten, then presses play.

I stare at the screen with my eyes stinging, scanning every face.

'I was thinking if your man used the bathroom, you might get a better look at his face from this angle.'

He's right. The camera is positioned lower and with a light shining down from directly above, people's faces are perfectly lit as they approach.

Time races on. So many people. So many faces. It's almost impossible to maintain concentration.

'There!' I slam my hand on the table, hardly able to believe what I think I've just seen. 'Roll it back a few seconds.'

A gaggle of drunken women stagger backwards, catching their spilt drinks. Behind them, a staff member jumps up from behind the bar. But my interest is in the man coming into vision from the toilets.

'Pause it there.'

This time, the man's face is perfectly captured, his eyes glancing sideways, his shirt unbuttoned at the chest. And there's absolutely no mistaking who it is.

'That him?' Matt asks.

I shake my head. 'No.'

'Oh.'
'But it's the next best thing.'

Chapter 17

The bus pulls away, and my head vibrates against the cold window. From the top floor of the double-decker, I have a good view of the street below, but I hardly register the hordes of shoppers, tourists or bike couriers darting around with their oversized-boxes strapped to their backs. My mind is lost in a fog of confusion, my body numb with shock.

I'm surprised I didn't spot Ryan last night, but I suppose we were in the back room and out of the way for most of the evening. Kim Kardashian could have walked in and I probably wouldn't have noticed.

Matt and I re-examined the footage from the camera above the bar, and it was definitely him. At exactly nine fifty-three and eighteen seconds, Ryan strode into the pub with another man I'm now certain was Nathan. He had his head held high and was swinging his shoulders while Nathan hung back, glancing around anxiously.

It's the proof I've been desperately seeking that Nathan is alive, but also evidence that Ryan lied to me. That they've both been deceiving me. But why? Is it their idea of a sick joke? Are they having a good laugh behind my back? I can't understand why they would put me through such agony. Ryan knew how worried I was about Nathan and yet he lied to my face and has continued to lie, feigning concern, even through a series of WhatsApp messages we've exchanged. He and Nathan even had the gall to go out drinking together.

Part of me thinks I should walk away and forget I ever met Nathan. If this is his way of punishing me for turning him down when he proposed, I'm better off without him. But it's not that easy to move on and forget, especially when my mind's burning with questions. Like, when exactly did he plan his disappearance? And if he wanted to end the relationship, why didn't he say something? Moments before he vanished, he was desperate for my assurance that I didn't want to break up, so when did he change his mind? And is he really that cruel that he wanted me to think he was dead? To put me through the agony of not knowing whether I was going to get a phone call at any moment to tell me his body had been found?

I still don't know where Nathan's hiding, but if there's one person who has the answers, it's Ryan. I want to know exactly when he found out that Nathan wasn't dead, or if he was in on it all along.

I jump off the bus at Haggerston Station and march towards Ryan's flat, determined to read him the riot act, rehearsing what I'm going to say as I walk, which is going to start with me calling him a lying scumbag.

I know exactly where I'm going this time. Ryan's flat is about three-quarters of the way along Albion Drive, opposite a house with paint-flaking windows and two old bikes chained up to the fence in an unkempt front garden. If he's not in, I'll wait. I'm not leaving until I have answers.

Up ahead, I spot a man in running shorts and a T-shirt, standing on the pavement prodding his phone, but it's only as I draw closer that I realise it's Ryan.

I yell his name, but he doesn't hear me as he slots his phone into a strap on his arm and jogs off in the opposite direction.

'Wait! I need to talk to you about Nathan!'

It's hard to run in heeled ankle boots, although I give it my best shot, clip-clopping behind him with my coat flapping until he dodges behind a black van parked on the road, disappears around a corner and vanishes from sight. I pull up, breathing heavily, stamp my foot and let out a growl of frustration.

He can't have gone far and I'm sure he'll be back soon, so I turn around, head back to his flat and take a seat on the steps outside, pulling the collar of my coat up against the cold. I'll wait. I have all the time in the world and I don't care what the neighbours think.

This whole thing is beyond crazy. Did Ryan and Nathan honestly think they could pull the wool over my eyes and I'd simply accept Nathan had vanished and move on with my life? After Nathan proposed in the restaurant, I thought I'd smoothed things over. If he was still feeling aggrieved, why didn't he talk to me instead of putting on this ridiculous charade, pretending he's dead? I've never stood up to Nathan. That's not the kind of woman my mother brought me up to be. I've always thought it was more important to maintain a harmonious relationship than to get dragged into petty bickering, like some couples who seem to do nothing but grouse and gripe at each other. But I've had enough of playing nicely. When I see him again, he's going to get it both barrels for putting me through the mill so callously. How dare he treat me like this?

On the opposite pavement, a man strides past with his head down, engrossed in his phone, his long herringbone coat buttoned up to his chin and a leather satchel slung across his shoulder. I'm not sure he even notices me sitting on the steps watching him. Even if he had, the chances are he'd ignore me. It's typical city mentality. Avoid eye-contact. Never smile at a stranger. Keep your head down and don't open yourself up to becoming a victim. It's sad really.

It's a peaceful street in a pleasant residential area. Not as nice as my part of Camden with its vibrant market, trendy coffee shops and chilled vibes, but I can see the appeal. I bet you get more for your money here, too. Ryan's flat was certainly spacious, from what I remember, with a big garden at the back, a kitchen extension, and two bedrooms.

Two bedrooms?

A thought wheedles into my brain as unwelcome as a snake slithering through a hole in the ceiling. What if Nathan's been hiding here with his brother all this time and that's why I've not been able to find him? If Nathan wanted to lie low, of course he'd come here.

I remove my sunglasses and rest them on my head, turning to study the house and its imposing door, the gloss-black paint offset by a stately brass letter box and matching knocker. What if Nathan's in there right now, watching me? After all, where else would he be? They've not seen him at work for days and I've checked his flat several times. His neighbours said he hadn't been back there since the attack on Tower Bridge.

In a second, I'm on my feet and hammering at the knocker, the weighty clunk of metal on metal echoing down the street. What if Nathan answers? It'll be like confronting his ghost. Over the last two weeks, I've pretty much become resigned to the fact that he's dead. No wonder my mouth's so dry. I wipe my sweaty palms on the backs of my legs and listen for the creak of footsteps inside. The click of a latch.

I knock again and poke my fingers through the letter box, peering inside, but it doesn't look as if anyone's home. There are three pairs of shoes lined up neatly in the hall, and coats and jackets hanging from three pegs, but none of them belong to Nathan.

'Nathan!' I shout. 'It's me, Pippa. I know you're in there.'

The only window at the front of the house is so high off the ground, it's impossible to reach to see inside, but I remember from the party that there are patio doors at the back that open out from the kitchen-diner into the garden. I shouldn't be snooping, but if Nathan is hiding in Ryan's flat while pretending to be missing, I have a right to know.

With a quick glance up and down the street, I let myself through a wooden gate at the side of the house and creep past a rusting gas barbecue and a bicycle leaning against the wall under a faded rainproof black cover. The side alley leads directly into the back garden and a long, narrow strip of lawn that's overgrown and in desperate need of mowing. I climb onto a raised patio area with a table and four chairs that have seen better days, rusted by the weather, and step cautiously up to a set of sliding glass doors, conscious of a dozen windows in neighbouring properties that overlook the back of the house, fearful I'll be spotted and mistaken for a burglar.

I put my face to the glass and squint into the unlit room, familiar from Ryan's party, when the kitchen counter was heaving with cans of beer and bottles of wine and spirits. A rectangular table is covered in paperwork, a laptop computer and a couple of mugs, as if someone has been using it as a desk, but otherwise the kitchen is clean and tidy. An everyday image of home life. Nothing at all to suggest that Nathan is living here. No sign of any of his belongings or his clothes.

I thump the glass with my palm. 'Nathan? Are you in there?'

But if he's not living here or in his own apartment, then where is he hiding? Maybe he's holed up in a hotel or an Airbnb. But how's he affording that? And for how long? Until he thinks I've given up looking and moved on? None of this adds up. There must be a missing piece of the jigsaw I'm not seeing.

I slip back down the side alley, pull the wooden gate closed, and sit back on the steps to wait for Ryan. I'll just have to make sure he tells me the truth.

While I wait, I check my phone and discover several missed calls from James, who'd wanted to come with me to view the CCTV, but I thought I'd have a better chance of persuading the pub to let me see it on my own. I bet he's calling to check up on me, as if I can't look after myself without a man in my life. He's behaving like we're best friends, not an ex I haven't seen in nearly ten years. It's weird, and a little suffocating. I'll call him later and give him an update. I have more important things on my mind right now.

'Pippa? What are you doing here?' Ryan peels out an earbud, sweat pouring from his brow and his breathing laboured.

I jump up, startled. I hadn't seen or heard him coming. 'Where is he?'

'Who?'

'Don't play dumb with me, Ryan.'

'What are you talking about?' He wipes an arm across his forehead, his hair glistening with sweat.

'You know damn well what I'm talking about. Where's Nathan? I saw you together in the pub last night.'

Ryan's face freezes like he's overdosed on Botox. 'Don't be ridiculous. What pub?'

'The Crown and Compass. And don't try denying it. I've checked the CCTV this morning. What's going on?' I cross my arms and stare at him, daring him to lie to me again.

Ryan's mouth opens and closes like a floundering fish. 'Have you been spying on me?'

'I think I deserve the truth, don't you?'

'You're out of your mind,' he says, gathering his composure. 'You've been under enormous stress. You're not thinking straight. Go home. Get some rest and let's pretend this didn't happen.'

'Don't patronise me. Is he here?'

'I told you, I've not seen him in weeks.'

'So you won't mind if I come in and take a look?' I trot up the steps ahead of him and stand by his shiny black front door.

'Pippa...'

'Open it.'

He puts a hand on my arm and looks at me from under his brow. 'Would you like me to call you an Uber?' he asks, his tone condescending.

'Prove he's not inside and I'll go.'

We square up to each other like two boxers in a ring, waiting for the first punch to land. Then Ryan leans into me and puts his lips to my ear.

'Walk away, Pippa. You don't know what you're getting yourself involved in.'

'What?'

'I mean it. Forget about Nathan.'

I put a hand to my chest. 'Are you threatening me?'

'I'm giving you some friendly advice. He's gone. Move on with your life,' he says.

Why do I feel like I've been parachuted into a foreign country where I don't understand the language and nothing makes any sense? He's talking in riddles.

'What do you mean, he's gone? If you know where he is, you have to tell me. Please, Ryan, I'm going out of my mind.'

'Listen to me, Pippa. Go home.'

'Just tell me where he is!' I scream, finally losing it.

'I can't.'

'You know Nathan asked me to marry him, just before the bombing? He got down on one knee in front of the entire restaurant and told me how much he loved me.'

'And you rejected him.' Ryan glances into the street and I instinctively follow his gaze. A young couple with a dog and a pushchair slow as they walk past, staring at us, their attention drawn by all the shouting.

The woman stops at the bottom of the steps. 'Is everything okay?'

'It's fine.' At least it will be when Ryan starts telling me the truth. 'Just a misunderstanding.'

'Sure?'

'Yes, thank you.'

The woman shoots me an uncertain smile and walks off towards the park, but while I'm distracted, Ryan darts past me. I'm too slow. He's already stepping inside, pulling the key from the lock. I throw myself at the door as it closes in my face.

'Ryan, let me in!' I yell.

He peers at me through a narrow gap. 'Stay safe, Pippa. And don't contact me again,' he says.

He shoves the door closed, knocking me backwards.

'Ryan! Where's Nathan?' I beg, hammering the door with my fists. 'I just want to know what's happened to him.'

Chapter 18

Ryan's picked the wrong woman to mess with. If he thinks I'm going to walk away and forget about Nathan, he's a moron. I'll find out what's happened to him if it kills me. And if he's in some kind of trouble, we'll fix it. But they can't just shut me out and expect me to give up on Nathan like an obedient child. It's time to mobilise some help.

I keep my sunglasses pulled down over my eyes to hide the bags and the puffiness, hold my phone at arm's length and hit record, framing my head and shoulders as I walk along the street towards the Underground.

'Hey, everyone. Sorry I've not been around as much as I'd like in recent days, but I'm still dealing with the fallout of the bombing and trying to find my partner, Nathan. Firstly, I wanted to say a massive thank you to everyone who's sent messages, and yes, I'm doing okay. Some days are harder than others, and that's alright. Like I always tell you, we can't control what happens to us, but we can choose how to respond. Today, I'm choosing strength, but I need your help.

'Nathan is still missing, but - and I know this is going to sound crazy - I now have proof that he's alive, and that he's being sheltered by his brother, Ryan. I confronted Ryan this morning, but he denied everything. He says he's not seen Nathan, although I know that's not true, and now I don't know what to do for the best. How do I find Nathan and work out what's going on? Any good ideas? Let me know in the comments, because honestly, I'm absolutely at a loss. Thanks, guys. Love you loads. And stay strong.'

I finish with a forced smile and end the recording. When I watch it back, the sound's not great, the wind distorting the microphone, but it's good enough. It might not be my most polished performance, but it's raw and it's honest. I add a filter to give my skin a youthful glow and post it.

It seemed like a no-brainer to appeal to my followers for ideas, but recording the video is also surprisingly cathartic. It feels good to get it all off my chest and share what I've been going through with my tribe.

While I wait for Instagram to work its magic, I find a quiet coffee shop overlooking Regent's Canal and order a matcha latte. I sit at a table outside with my nose and cheeks burning with the cold, still reeling from my encounter with Ryan. What was all that about, forgetting Nathan and moving on with my life? Threatening me and telling me I wasn't safe? He has no idea who he's dealing with if he thinks I can be fobbed off so easily.

A waiter brings my drink to the table with a nod and a polite smile as a narrow boat slides silently past, cutting through the water with the grace of a swan. I snatch up my phone, unable to hold off checking Instagram any longer. The suggestions are already pouring in thick and fast. Some sensible. Others less so.

You should definitely go to the police and let them handle it.

Are you okay? Maybe take a step away and think about your mental health. This sounds really scary.

Have you thought about hiring a private investigator? They can find out things the police can't.

You should totally break into Ryan's house and find out what he's hiding. Check his computer. His phone. Everything!

What about speaking to a psychic? You might think it's a crazy idea but honestly it works.

Follow Ryan. Spy on him. It won't take long for him to lead you to Nathan.

Go to the press with your story. That's what I'd do.

I'm not going to the police or speaking to the press as I'm not sure either of them would take me seriously. I can't afford a private investigator and I'm not spending money on a psychic. The sensible suggestion is to stake out the flat and keep a close eye on Ryan. If Nathan is inside, he'll have to come out eventually. He can't stay holed up forever. If he's not, the chances are Ryan could unwittingly lead me to him. But how do I maintain round-the-clock surveillance on Ryan and his flat? It's a shame I don't have a car. Otherwise, I could park in the street and observe from a distance. But I don't even drive. I never saw much point in learning.

If only I knew someone with a car who wouldn't mind helping me out for a few days. The obvious person is James. He's been desperate to help. I bet he wouldn't mind, although I'm not sure if he owns a car. What the hell. There's no harm in asking.

James answers my call on the second ring, sounding breathless.

'Do you have a car?'

'Yes. Why?'

'Can you drive over to Hackney and meet me?'

'What, now?'

'Yeah, I think I've found Nathan.'

'Seriously? Where?'

'Staying with Ryan at his flat.'

'So why do you need me?'

'I'll explain when you get here, but I need you to drive.'

'I'm kind of busy, Pippa.'

'I wouldn't ask if it wasn't important.'

'Have you spoken to Ryan?'

I sigh. 'Can you just come?'

'I'll have to see if I can juggle things around. Give me half an hour.'

'You're an angel.'

'Yeah, when you want something.'

'I'm at a coffee shop by the canal. I'll drop you a pin.'

James hangs up abruptly. He didn't sound too happy, but I have no one else to ask. Sam and Alex will be at work, and I've lost touch with most of my friends.

But I'm sure he'll be fine. After all, he's my only hope.

Chapter 19

JAMES
February 25, 2024

I slip my phone into my pocket and clap my hands. 'Right, listen up, everyone. I don't remember saying we're done. Give me ten more.'

It's amazing how quickly you lose the kids' attention when you're distracted for a moment. I had ten of them diligently banging out a dozen press-ups until Pippa rang. Now they're all mucking about, playing the fool and chatting.

They respond with a collective groan and a few catcalls.

'You want to get in the ring and spar? You need to do the warm-up first. Same every week.'

One by one, the kids get back into their positions on the gym's dusty floor and, with varying degrees of athleticism, start knocking out more press-ups. I walk up and down the line, watching for the cheats.

The ones with their backsides sticking up in the air or not getting their noses low enough into the dirt.

'Dina, don't scrimp. I want to see you go all the way down.' She might be the only girl in the group, but she's far from the weakest. When she puts on a pair of gloves and climbs into the ring, she's as tough as the boys, if not more so. I guess that's what comes from growing up with three older brothers. She doesn't take shit from anyone, no matter how much bigger they are.

'I am,' she whines.

I place my boot on the small of her back and ease her further towards the floor. 'That's better. Now you're working.'

Daryl, a skinny teenager with crooked teeth, a three-inch scar on his cheek and a permanent scowl, is the last to finish his reps.

'Okay, flip over. On your backs. Give me ten sit-ups.'

Another groan, but marginally less resistance this time.

'Remember, it's all about showing up and putting in the work, whether you feel like it or not. That's what's going to make you strong. Come on, who's going to finish first?'

I count backwards from ten. '...three, two and one. And you're done. Well done. Great work. Now go get gloved up.'

As they disappear into the changing rooms, I stick my head around the office door. 'Hey, Carl. Can you oversee the rest of the session for me? Something's come up.'

He rolls his eyes and lifts his feet off the desk.

'What's the emergency this time?'

I chew my lip, toying with my phone. 'Pippa.'

'Again? Is it true you two used to date a while back?'

'Long time ago. Water under the bridge.'

'If you say so. You go and rescue your damsel in distress. We'll cope without you.' His grin is so wide, I can see his shiny gold incisor.

'I appreciate it. Be back later.'

Pippa's sitting at a table outside the cafe by the canal, where she said she'd be, her cheeks rosy with cold.

'You took your time,' she says.

'I was busy. Anyway, what's the urgency?' I pull up a chair and scan a laminated menu as a waiter wanders over to the table.

'We don't have time for that. We need to get going,' she says, snatching the menu out of my hands. 'Did you bring your car?'

The waiter wanders away again.

I nod. 'But we're not going anywhere until you tell me what's going on.'

'I'm pretty sure Nathan's holed up with his brother, but I need to prove it.' She tells me about the CCTV at the pub and confronting Ryan at his flat.

'Okay. So what's the plan?'

'I want to stake out Ryan's place.' I laugh and she glowers at me. 'What's so funny? We can park outside his flat and watch who comes and goes.'

'Is that even legal?'

'No law against watching.'

'Okay.'

'What? You don't think it's a good idea?' she says. 'I need answers and I thought you wanted to help?'

'I'm not sure this is the way.'

'Do you have any better ideas?'

'I could try talking to Ryan to see what he has to say for himself?'

Pippa takes a deep breath and stares into her empty mug as if the answers to all her questions might be lurking in the foamy residue at the bottom. 'I tried that. He threatened me.'

'He did what?'

'He said I should forget about Nathan for my own safety and that I didn't know what I was getting myself involved in.'

'What's that supposed to mean?'

'He was trying to warn me off, but I have no idea why.'

I push my chair back and stand. 'Right, I'm going to talk to him.'

'Hang on. You're not going to do anything stupid, are you?'

'I'm just going to have a quiet word.'

Pippa's eyes narrow and for a moment I think she's going to try to talk me out of it. 'You remember his address?'

'I think so. Stay here. I won't be long.'

The houses along Albion Drive all look alike. The majority of them are big Georgian properties constructed from pale London stock bricks and I spend ten minutes walking up and down before I identify Ryan's flat. But as soon as I see it, I remember the front door. Plain black. Glossy paint. Like the famous door at 10 Downing Street.

I jog up the steps, knock, and stand back with my hands casually in my jacket pockets as the sun breaks through the clouds and showers me in a glow that does nothing to ward off the chill in the air.

Ryan answers the door with a hint of annoyance. He raises an eyebrow and looks me up and down, slouching casually. 'Yeah?'

'I'm James. Pippa's friend? We spoke a week or so ago when she was looking for Nathan.'

Ryan stiffens. He's no less oily than I remember. The kind of guy whose ambition outreaches his ability, who'll be stuck in the same dead-end job for twenty years complaining about how he's been overlooked for promotion time and time again, arrogance and laziness conspiring against him. He still hasn't shaved, and his hair's wet like he's fresh out of the shower, dressed casually in a faded black Rolling Stones T-shirt, the one with the lips and the tongue, and a pair of fleece jogging bottoms. 'I already told her I've not seen him.'

'She saw you with him at the pub.'

Ryan shakes his head. 'She's mistaken. It wasn't me.'

'Look, she's worried about him, that's all. She can't understand why he's taken off and vanished from her life. She thought he was dead. She's in a real mess. If I could just have a quick word with —'

'Look, mate, I've told you already. I've not seen Nathan. I've not heard from him in weeks. Months.

The truth is, we don't really keep in touch. We don't get on that well.'

'Oh?'

Ryan relaxes and leans against the doorframe with his arms crossed. 'We're not exactly close.'

I stare into his eyes, looking for evidence of a lie. He's either a bloody good poker player or he's telling the truth.

'Pippa's convinced she saw you both in the Crown and Compass last night.'

'I don't even know where that is.'

'And Nathan's not phoned or messaged in the last two weeks?'

'No.'

'Aren't you worried about him?' I ask.

'Like I said, we're not close. If he's gone to ground, I'm sure he has his reasons.'

Even so, you'd think he'd show some concern that his brother's vanished.

And now I don't know who to believe. Pippa's adamant she's seen Nathan and Ryan at the pub, and is convinced the CCTV proves it, but Ryan's telling me an entirely different story. Where does the truth end and the lies begin?

Is Pippa chasing ghosts? It wouldn't be entirely surprising if she's imagined it all, her brain's way of coping. After all, why would Nathan fabricate his own disappearance?

'Pippa's convinced that Nathan's staying with you in the flat.'

Ryan scoffs. 'Yeah, right. Whatever.'

'And that you threatened her.'

Ryan's eyes open wide with surprise. 'Threatened her? Why would I do that?'

'You told her to forget about Nathan for her own safety. Why would you say that?'

'I didn't. I promise I've not seen Nathan in weeks and he's certainly not here.' Ryan puts his hand over his heart. 'If you don't believe me, you're more than welcome to check.' He steps into the hall and holds out his arm, inviting me in.

It's tempting. Maybe if I tell Pippa I've had a look around the flat and found nothing, she'd come to her senses, but it feels a bit weird nosing around a stranger's home and tantamount to admitting I don't believe him. I don't like Ryan much, but I don't think he's lying to me.

'Nathan?' I call out, without any real conviction.

'Come in and take a look,' Ryan urges me. 'I've got nothing to hide.'

I stare into the hall, listening for movement. 'You're alright. I believe you.'

'Are you sure?'

'I'm good. Thanks all the same and I'm sorry to have bothered you. You will let Pippa know if you hear from him, though?'

'You have my word.'

He closes the door with a resounding thud, and I trudge back down the steps onto the street, not sure what I'm going to tell Pippa. I can hardly say I think she's losing her mind and she probably could benefit from some professional help. Someone to talk to, who can help her process her grief, especially as she doesn't seem to have any real friends to chat with.

She's pacing up and down the canal, chewing her nails, when I return.

'How did it go? What did Ryan say?' she fires at me as I approach.

'Nathan's not there.'

She freezes, her eyes roaming across my face as if she's trying to work out the hidden meaning behind my words.

'He told you that, did he? Then he's lying.'

'I don't think so.'

'How can you be so sure?' The words spit from her mouth like venom.

'He invited me in to look around for myself.'

Pippa shakes her head as if I've betrayed her. 'You went into the flat?'

'Not exactly, but he wouldn't have invited me in if he had anything to hide, would he?'

She huffs. 'I can't believe this. He lied to you and you swallowed every word.'

'Pippa —'

'I thought you wanted to help me.'

'Maybe it's time you spoke to someone, you know, to help you process how you're feeling.'

'What?'

'A professional. Someone who understands what you're going through.'

'I'm not crazy, James. I saw the two of them together at the pub. They were on the security footage as clear as day.'

'And you're a hundred per cent sure it was them?'

'Yes!'

'Or did you see what you wanted to see?'

Pippa opens her mouth wide and clamps it shut again. 'I know what I saw,' she says, her laser-like gaze burning through me. 'Are you going to help me stake Ryan's place out or not?'

I take a deep breath. 'Nathan's not there. I'm going to take you home and you're going to rest. Then we're going to the police. We're going to tell them everything that's happened, and we're going to leave it with them.'

'They don't care. I've tried.'

'Then we'll try again. But we're not pestering Ryan any more. We're going to leave him alone to get on with his life in peace.'

Chapter 20

PIPPA
February 25, 2024

I take the train home. James offered to drive me back, but I want to be on my own. I don't want to spend another minute with him when he doesn't believe a word I've told him. I thought he was on my side, but the way he was talking, it's as if he thinks I'm going crazy, chasing shadows that don't exist. But I know what I saw in the Crown and Compass, and the CCTV proved it beyond any doubt. Ryan is sheltering his brother, while they're trying to fool me into thinking Nathan's dead, and I have absolutely no idea why. I need answers, not a psychiatrist.

What am I even doing wasting my time? If Nathan doesn't want to be found, if he doesn't want to be with me, why should I bother looking for him? I should let him go and get on with my life.

If only it was that straightforward.

If I've done something wrong, something so terrible he had no other option other than to disappear to escape from me, I have to know. I'm still struggling to believe it was because I turned down his marriage proposal. That would be so pathetically vindictive and childish I'd be better off without him anyway. But what other reason could there be?

I need a distraction, so flip open my laptop on the dining table and go through my routine of searches for anything new about the Tower Bridge attack. After all, I still don't know what happened to Nathan after he abandoned me and I'd like to know. I can usually lose myself for hours down various rabbit holes, following threads on forums and social media, and cross-checking facts against some of the fiction and ludicrous conspiracy theories that have surfaced about the bombing. I know I shouldn't read it, but I can't help myself.

It's terrifying how many people seem to believe there was some kind of government cover-up, even though there's not a jot of evidence of any such thing. The theory gaining most traction is that the attack had nothing to do with the far-right, or the *Patriots of the Isles*, who've claimed responsibility, but that it was orchestrated by the state itself, in coalition with a new world order of a powerful global elite, and that the bombing was intended to hasten the introduction of social surveillance measures to strip people of their civil liberties and establish total control over the population.

It would be funny if it wasn't so scary, especially when you watch how quickly these baseless opinions from a network of anonymous self-appointed keyboard analysts and commentators take hold and become fact in some people's minds.

As far as I can tell, it's a problem generated by a vacuum of silence created by the intelligence services and the police who've failed to keep the public informed about their investigations. People want answers, and when they're not forthcoming, they make it up.

Another speculative theory doing the rounds is that the security services were aware of the bomb plot and even had agents embedded with the *Patriots of the Isles*, but failed to intervene to stop the bomb being detonated. It seems crazy to me, but people are willing to believe it, and when this kind of nonsense is out of the box, it's almost impossible to keep a lid on it, especially when it catches the attention of the algorithms that amplify the message.

Social media and forums aren't my only source of information. I still keep across everything the mainstream media publishes and have news alerts set up for all sorts of trigger words, like *Tower Bridge*, *London attack*, *London bombing*, and *Patriots of the Isles*. Alerts to three new articles in my email inbox catch my eye. I click them open and read them in turn. There's another profile piece on the bomber, Jack Reeves, and an article about an MP who's calling for spending to be diverted to the security services to prevent another attack. But the third article is of much greater interest to me.

It's a rare interview with a bomb survivor who's not previously spoken, as far as I can tell. An electrician called Dan Boaten was travelling across the bridge in his van when the bomb went off. He lost control of his vehicle, crashed into another car and collided with a safety barrier. He was trapped for fifty minutes before the emergency services were able to cut him out.

His is typical of the stories from the survivors I've read, full of harrowing details, loss, anger and regret. But what interests me in this account is a mention of a stranger in a suit he says he saw hunting through the wreckage and debris, stopping to speak to survivors.

It sounds suspiciously like it could be Nathan.

He was well-dressed in a suit and open-neck shirt, as if he'd come straight from the office or dinner. I thought he was another victim, but while everyone else was covered in dust and blood, there wasn't a scratch on him. He came over to my van and asked if I needed help. I told him I couldn't feel my legs. He squeezed my hand and told me help was on the way. I don't know who he was, but he gave me hope and the determination to hang on. I'm so grateful for his kindness.

The interview brings an unexpected tear to my eye. I make a note of the man's name. If I can track him down and talk to him myself, maybe he holds the key to finally unlocking the mystery of what happened to Nathan that night.

I stretch my arms above my head and yawn, my eyes stinging, and glance out of the window through the slated blinds. It's already dark. In the cold and wet, everything is grey and desolate. Nobody's out on a night like this. Or if they are, they're all taking refuge in the restaurants, bars and clubs. Is that what Nathan's doing tonight? Rebuilding his life without me?

In the shadows, under one of the street lights a short distance down the road, a figure stands half-hidden behind a car, dressed in a construction worker's luminous jacket, a cigarette smouldering in one hand. I crack open two slats of the blind to see better. The figure turns his head and stares right back at me. I recoil, the blind snapping with a loud crack.

When I look again, the figure has gone, the street deserted. I shudder. It's probably nothing, my imagination working overtime, but I had the impression he was watching my flat. But that's crazy. Reading too many conspiracy stories has made me paranoid. Why would anyone be watching me?

I never used to be like this. I'm supposed to be a strong, fearless woman. What kind of role model am I when I'm jumping at my own shadow?

I need to get a grip.

But then a knock at the door echoes through the flat, shattering the silence, and sends my heart rate soaring through the roof.

Chapter 21

The hair on the back of my neck prickles and my gut twists. It's not even that late, but I'm not expecting anyone and after seeing that man outside, staring up at the window, I'm a bag of nerves. It's ridiculous.

I clutch my phone to my chest and creep down the stairs into the hall.

'Hello?' I holler through the door.

'Pip, it's me,' a familiar voice replies. 'Can you let me in? I'm getting soaked.'

My shoulders sag. With a sigh of relief, I peel open the door.

'What are you doing here?'

My brother, Daniel, finishes his cigarette, blows out a stream of grey smoke and grinds the stub out on the ground with his battered work boots, their steel toecaps exposed under scuffed and ripped leather. Rain runs off his luminous yellow coat in rivulets and pools at his feet.

I glance up and down the street. 'Quickly. Come inside.'

Daniel shoots me a look of surprise as I usher him in and hurriedly shut and bolt the door behind him. 'Ashamed someone might see me?'

'Of course not. Don't be silly.'

He shrugs off his coat, wet hair plastered to his head. He's shockingly skeletal, the outline of his skull visible beneath tightly drawn pale skin, like it's been days since he's had a decent meal. His eyes are glassy and haunted and his stubble is thick and uneven.

He looks awful. Far worse than when I last saw him, which was what, four, maybe six, weeks ago?

'How are you?' I ask, with a deliberately light tone.

'Yeah, not bad.'

I pull back sharply as he leans in for a hug, his noxious breath spiked pungently with alcohol, and instead plant a chaste kiss on his cheek. 'You're soaking wet,' I laugh.

'It's raining,' he points out.

He heels off his boots and stands in a pair of dirty socks with his big toes poking through large holes, like the grotesque heads of a pair of conger eels hiding in the rocks.

'Are you hungry? Can I get you something to eat?'

Daniel follows me upstairs. 'Nah, I'm okay, cheers.'

'When did you last eat a proper meal?'

He shrugs. A baggy jumper that doesn't look as though it's been washed in years hangs off his shoulders. 'I'll grab a McDonald's later.'

We both know he doesn't have the money for burgers, otherwise he wouldn't be here.

'I have a leftover veggie chilli in the fridge. Why don't I heat that up for you?'

'Don't go to any trouble, honestly.'

'You need to eat.'

Ten minutes later, he's sitting at the table shovelling reheated chilli into his mouth like he's in an all-you-can-eat competition while I watch with growing unease. The food puts some colour back into his cheeks, the meal stalling the moment we'll dance around the real reason he's here. As if I can't guess.

'Everything good with you?' he asks, wiping his mouth on the sleeve of his grubby jumper, which stinks of stale cigarette smoke and sweat.

Where do I start?

'You heard about the bomb on Tr Bridge?'

'Awful,' he says with a grimace. He runs a finger around the inside of his bowl and licks it clean. His fingernails are black with dirt.

'I was on the bridge with Nathan when it happened.'

Daniel freezes with his finger in his mouth.

'If we'd been a minute earlier, we'd probably be dead.'

'I had no idea. Are you okay?'

My throat closes up with a catch of emotion. 'Not really. Nathan's gone missing.'

Daniel stares at me in disbelief. 'What do you mean, gone missing?'

'He's vanished. He went to help the victims. He was supposed to come back and get me, but he never did.'

'Jeez. Do you think...?'

'I don't know. I don't think so. It's complicated.' Daniel needs to understand he's not the only one with problems. We're all going through our own personal hell.

'I'm sorry, Pip. I had no idea.'

He continues licking the bowl until there's no trace of sauce left.

'What are you doing here, Daniel?' I study his emaciated face and the deep lines that mark his weather-beaten, leathery skin. He's aged several years in the few weeks since I last saw him.

He fidgets and plucks at the back of his hand, pulling the near-translucent skin into a peak and letting it go again. 'I was in the area. Thought I'd stop by and see how you are.'

I can always tell when my brother is lying. He can't look me in the eye or keep still. Sometimes he jiggles his leg up and down so fast, it's like watching a jackhammer.

'How much this time?' I fold my hands in my lap, guilt knotting my stomach. I shouldn't be cross with him. It's not his fault he's like this. If anyone's to blame, it's me, and I live with that guilt every single day.

Daniel scratches his head. 'Things have been a bit rough. You know I don't like to ask.'

'How much?'

'They've laid me off, Pip, and it's not easy finding a new job. There's not the work out there, but the thing is, my rent's due and I don't have the cash.'

'You've lost your job?'

'It was crap pay anyway.'

'But it was a job, Daniel. What are you going to do?' The last time he was here, he said he'd been taken on for a construction project building thousands of new homes in Barking.

He finally looks me in the eye. 'I've been looking around, but there's not much call for labourers. Something will turn up, but I was wondering, you know, in the meantime, if maybe... you know, just to tide me over?'

'How much this time?'

He flinches. 'I'm trying my best, Pip. I don't like coming here to borrow money.' *Borrow?* That's a joke. 'But maybe if you could spare a couple of hundred? Just to keep the wolf from the door. I'll pay you back as soon as I can. You know I'm good for it.'

How many times have I heard that? The only time I ever see him these days is when he wants something, money usually, and we play this game where he thinks I don't know what's really going on. But I can't keep doing this. I have enough of my own spinning plates. It's not the rent he needs money for, but we go through this charade every time and he always comes back for more, no matter how many times he promises he's going to get clean.

'I'm not giving you money for drugs.'

Daniel screws his face up in horror. 'Why do you always think the worst of me? Please, Pip, you know I've been clean for months.' He nibbles at a dirty fingernail, his leg jogging up and down ferociously under the table.

'Clean?'

'I am. I promise.'

But his bloodshot eyes and gaunt, drawn face tell a different tale. Every time he shows up, I pray it's going to be different. That he's finally turned his life around.

'We all have problems, Dan.'

He springs out of his chair, knocking it flying, and hammers a fist on the table, his nostrils flaring. 'I don't ask for much. What's a couple of hundred to you anyway?' he snarls. 'You've got your cosy life here, and your job. It's alright for you, isn't it?'

'Daniel, don't. You're scaring me.'

'I've got nothing.'

I take a deep breath, centring myself. We've been here too many times. 'You need help. Real help, not more money. I love you. You're my brother, but I can't keep doing this.' I can't be his crutch forever.

He stands, panting, glowering at me with fire in his eyes. His gaze falls on the table and the bowl he's licked clean. He snatches it up and hurls it across the room. I squeal as it smashes against the wall and splinters into a dozen jagged pieces.

'Fine. You've made your point. You've got better things to spend your money on. Don't worry about me, I'll figure something out.'

He storms out of the room and thuds down the stairs while I stand with my arms wrapped around my body, shaking. The front door crashes open and slams shut.

My legs give way and I collapse to the floor, trembling. If I thought money could fix him, I'd give him every penny I own. But it can't. Money can't save him.

I crawl across the floor, reach for my phone on the table, and call Sam.

'What is it? Is it Nathan?' she asks, her voice tight with concern.

'It's Daniel.'

She pauses for a beat. 'Is he there?'

'He wanted money again, but I couldn't do it, Sam. He lost his temper and I thought he was going to… He's gone now. I didn't give him anything, but I don't know if I did the right thing.'

'Of course you did. He's not your responsibility. You have enough on your plate.'

'So why do I feel so bad?'

'Pippa, you don't owe him anything. You did the right thing.'

'He said he's lost his job. And he looked awful, like he hadn't been eating. It wouldn't surprise me if he's been sleeping rough. And I turned him away.'

'Listen to me. You did the right thing,' she repeats. 'You know if you'd given him money, he'd have only jacked it into his arm.'

'He looked… he looked like death.'

In the background, Isabella screams. Alex yells with the fury of a parent on the verge of being tipped over the edge.

'Sorry, Pip. It's all kicking off here. The kids are playing up and, as usual, Alex has no idea how to cope. Do you want me to come over?'

'No, I'm fine. You go. Sounds like you're needed.'

'Alright. I'll call you in the morning, yeah?'

'I shouldn't have called. Sorry, I was just feeling a bit emotional. You go back to the kids. Love you.'

I hang up, drop the phone between my knees, and take a deep breath, repeating a mantra to myself.

Breathe in strength, breathe out weakness.
Breathe in strength, breathe out weakness.

Slowly, my heart rate starts to drop as I embrace the warm glow of calm that settles over my mind.

I'm not responsible for my brother's life.
I'm strong and brave and I can handle this.

I breathe in through my nose, hold it for a few seconds and let it out through my mouth, sinking into a bubble of tranquillity, until another knock at the door shatters the moment.

My heart rate spikes again, and I snatch a breath.

Daniel.

Back again, no doubt full of faux regret and abject apologies for losing his temper and yelling at me. It's the drugs. They make him so volatile, but I'm not going to be bullied. I'm not giving him money, not until he can prove he's clean.

I storm down the stairs into the hall, ready for his lies and excuses, determined not to fold.

I crack open the door. 'I've told you, I can't —'

But it's not Daniel.

'I need to talk to you. Do you have a moment?' Nathan's brother, Ryan, has a black baseball cap pulled down low over his eyes, his hands buried deep in the pockets of his rain-soaked coat. He glances over his shoulder nervously.

He's the last person I expected to show up on my doorstep. As if tonight could get any stranger.

'Sure,' I mumble. 'Come in. Is it about Nathan?'

'We can't talk here,' he says, his voice low. 'Grab a coat. Let's go for a walk.'

Transcript from the podcast, Fallen Hero. Interview with Pippa's brother, Daniel Ravenscroft

I only met the guy the once, but you get a feel about someone in that first moment, don't you? And I got a bad feeling about him right away. I didn't like the way he talked down to me, like I was beneath him. And no, I don't think he was good enough for Pippa. But it's not the point, is it? I should have been there for her, but I let her down when she really needed me. And that's what I regret most.

Every day still feels like a fight, but I'm getting there. I'm finally winning, taking it one day at a time. After seven months, I can actually see a future for myself. Who knows, a family of my own? Kids? My own house? A big part of the battle to get clean has been facing some things I buried in the past for too long, confronting what happened to Pippa and facing up to my own demons.

We'd both locked it away. Never talked about it. Never dealt with it. Never told anyone what happened that night, but people need to know the truth because it's an important part of who she is. It changed her. It changed us both.

There was this guy, Jago. I don't know where he is now and I don't want to know, but we used to hang out. I must have been about seventeen. He was older and lived in a caravan in the woods, working odd jobs on one of the local farms. He had this thick mop of curly black hair and these hazel eyes that seemed to dare you to look away. I was mesmerised by his wildness. He acted like the rules weren't meant for someone like him and he didn't care what anyone thought.

He made me feel like I was someone worthy. We drank beer and smoked cigarettes together, and he told me all these crazy stories about his life. Probably none of them were true, but I was hooked.

I should never have introduced him to Pippa. I should have seen the risk, but like me, she was enthralled by his charm and his looks. She was only fifteen, and I don't think she'd ever had a boyfriend before. Of course, Jago loved the attention. He made her feel special. You could see it in her eyes, but I was too wrapped up to realise where it was heading.

That night was humid and sticky, one of those nights where the air is so heavy it makes you forget yourself. Pippa caught me sneaking out of the house and begged me to let her come, too. She'd been to Jago's caravan before, but never after dark, and she was so insistent, I couldn't say no.

We sat around a fire Jago had built in a clearing, drinking beer and smoking roll-ups, but with Pippa there, he didn't have much time for me. She was hanging on his every word and you could see he was loving it. Making her laugh, treating her like she was the most important person in his life.

When we ran out of beer, he told me to run into town and fetch some more. I didn't want to go. It was a long walk there and back, but he had this way of making you do things you didn't want to do, like you owed him. So I went. And I left Pippa alone with him.

It was obvious something was wrong the moment I returned. The atmosphere had changed. Pippa was sitting by the fire, staring into the flames, her arms wrapped tightly around herself. Her eyes were wet and glassy and the sleeve of her T-shirt was torn. Jago grabbed the beer like nothing had happened. He had this look in his eyes — cold, smug, like he was daring me to say something. But I didn't. I didn't say a word.

I should have said something. Done something, but I froze. And I let him get away with it. We walked home in silence, but something inside Pippa had shattered. I don't know exactly what he did to her, but I can guess. She was never the same again. It broke her and left a deep, ugly scar.

She's had a few boyfriends since, but nothing serious. At least not until Nathan. But it was obvious he wasn't right for her. I couldn't tell you what she saw in him. It's easy to say in hindsight, but I never trusted him. I certainly couldn't imagine them ever getting together if it hadn't been for Jago, which is why I don't think I'll ever get over the guilt.

Chapter 22

PIPPA
February 25, 2024

It's a struggle to keep up with Ryan, especially as my umbrella keeps catching in the breeze. Eventually, I admit defeat and collapse it. It's only a bit of rain.

I've no idea where he's leading me as he strides past the police station, the big supermarket and over the canal. He only slows down once he turns into a narrow, cobbled street and glances back over his shoulder to check I'm still with him.

'Keep up,' he orders.

'What's this about? Is it Nathan?'

Ahead, a dingy tunnel under a bridge carrying a network of railway lines looms. It's dark and deserted. The kind of place you'd take someone to murder them, out of sight of any nosy neighbours or passing vehicles.

I keep a few paces behind him, watching him warily, ready to scream and make a run for it. But he's too quick for me. He turns suddenly, snatches my wrist, and pulls me violently into the tunnel and out of the rain.

'Who was that man?' he hisses.

The question catches me by surprise and stills the scream building in my chest. 'What man?'

The tunnel smells of stale urine and lost hope.

'The man who was at your flat earlier.'

I shake my head, confused. There was no man in my flat.

He pulls me nearer, until our faces are dangerously close. So close I can see every individual hair of stubble on his chin and the threads of veins in the whites of his eyes. Rivulets of sweat and rain from his hair run down his cheeks, and he's breathing heavily, his breath sour.

'I was watching. You let a man in. Florescent jacket. Dirty trousers. Who was he?'

'Oh, you mean my brother, Daniel?'

Ryan's eyes narrow as he studies my face. 'What did he want?'

I snatch back my wrist and clasp it to my chest. 'Money. Not that it's any of your business.'

Ryan glances over his shoulder, his body twitchy and tightly wound up, then over the top of my head, down the street. Finally, his eyes return to mine.

'What the hell's going on, Ryan? You've dragged me out of the house in the middle of the night in the rain. What's got into you? You're acting really weird. Is it Nathan? Have you heard from him?'

'Do you trust him?'

'Who?'

'Your brother.'

'There's no need to raise your voice. His name's Daniel and of course I trust him. Now, you'd better tell me what's going on or I'm turning around and going home.'

I cross my arms over my chest, not prepared to be intimidated, but Ryan shoves me against the wall and looms over me, pressing his hands against the filthy, blackened brickwork either side of my head.

'There's something you need to know.' He takes another glance up and down the tunnel. 'About Nathan.'

I gasp. 'What?'

'He's alive.'

'But you said —'

'I lied. I was trying to protect you.'

I shake my head in disbelief. 'Can I see him?'

Ryan bites his lip. 'It's too dangerous.'

'Too dangerous? Why?'

Out of nowhere, a teenager on a BMX bike with no lights comes hurtling down the tunnel, rattling over the cobblestones. Ryan waits until the boy shoots past and disappears.

'Can I trust you to keep your mouth shut?' he asks.

'About what?'

'If you say a word to anyone, you'll not only be putting Nathan's life at risk, but yours, too.'

'Now you're frightening me.'

'Can I trust you?'

'For Christ's sake, just tell me what's going on, Ryan.'

'Nathan saw something he wasn't supposed to see. On the bridge, after the bomb.'

Ryan pushes himself off the wall and takes a step back, giving me space to breathe. He strokes his chin and turns in a tight circle, his shoulders hunched.

'Seriously, Pippa, you mustn't breathe a word of this to anyone, okay? There was a van with blacked-out windows that arrived within minutes of the bomb going off. Nathan saw it pull up close to where he was helping a woman who was bleeding badly.'

'What does that have —'

'Shut up and listen,' Ryan snaps. 'Nathan said as it pulled up, all its doors flew open and these men in dark clothes jumped out like they were looking for something or someone. Nathan thought they must be undercover cops, but all they did was drag this one guy out of a car, unconscious, and threw him in the back of the van.'

I frown, unable to square what Nathan's telling with all the reports and eyewitness accounts I've read. No one has ever mentioned a van turning up or men in dark clothing spilling out and dragging people off.

'Nathan saw it all, but I don't think he was supposed to,' Ryan says. 'One of the guys spotted him and yelled at him to get down on the floor with his hands on the back of his head. Nathan was scared witless. And that's when he realised who they really were.'

I stare at Ryan blankly.

'British intelligence,' he says, as if I'm stupid.

I smirk. He can't be serious. But Ryan's face remains stern and unflinching.

'He saw too much.'

'What are you trying to say, that Nathan witnessed some kind of government cover-up?' I chuckle at the thought. It turns out Ryan's no better than those crazy conspiracy theorists online.

'That's exactly what I'm saying. We think the guy they picked up must have been undercover and had probably infiltrated the terrorist cell who tried to blow up the bridge. Our guess is that his job was to have stopped the bomb.'

'That's crazy.' I study his face, waiting for Ryan to crack up with laughter and tell me how gullible I am.

'Is it?'

A train trundles overhead with a threatening rumble like thunder that shakes the ground under our feet.

'You can't expect me to believe that.'

'I don't care what you believe. I'm telling you what happened and why Nathan had to disappear. He panicked, and in the chaos, he was able to slip away. He dived under a stranded bus and played dead until whoever they were lost interest and drove off,' Ryan says.

Headlights at the end of the alley glint through the gloom, momentarily illuminating us. Ryan freezes, squinting into the distance as a car approaches, its tyres hissing on the wet road. Ryan pushes me into the shadows and flattens me against the wall. The lights go out and the thrum of the engine falls silent. A car door opens and slams shut. Ryan peers down the road and sighs, his body relaxing.

'And afterwards? Why didn't he come back to find me, like he promised?' I ask. Nothing about what Ryan's told me sounds remotely plausible.

'He waited until the police and ambulances turned up, then used the diversion to sneak away. He was too scared to go home or contact you. He didn't want to put you in danger.'

'So he turned up at your flat?'

Ryan runs his hands through his sodden hair and scratches his head, still twitchy. Still glancing up and down the tunnel as if he's expecting a SWAT team to come storming down the road at any moment with weapons raised.

'Only later, when he was certain he wasn't being tailed. He was a real mess, Pippa. I didn't believe him at first either. It sounds insane, doesn't it? But I know Nathan. He's telling the truth, and he's scared.'

'I don't know, Ryan. It doesn't sound —'

'Fine. Don't believe me. I thought you wanted the truth?'

I arch an eyebrow. 'That's all I want.'

We hold each other's gaze for what feels like an eternity, until Ryan sighs and turns away, like he's come to a big decision.

'Alright, I wasn't going to tell you this,' he says, 'but it might help you understand how serious this is.'

'I'm all ears.'

Ryan frowns. 'The next day, I went to Nathan's flat to pick up some bits for him, but they'd already been there.'

'Who?'

He shrugs. 'MI5? British intelligence? Who knows. All I know is that the place had been turned over. Drawers tipped out. Clothes strewn across the floor.'

'Could have been burglars.'

'You think? There was something else. One of the smoke alarms was hanging half open like it had been tampered with. I found a camera inside. Only a small one. About the size of my thumbnail.'

'Which would mean they know who he is and where he lives,' I point out.

'Exactly. My guess is they picked him up on a security camera and identified him using facial recognition software. The thing is, Pippa, if they know it was Nathan, how long do you think it's going to take them to come after you or me?'

I flinch. 'Me? But why?'

'These people aren't mucking about. If I'm right and the government knew about that bomb before it was detonated, it's going to make the Watergate scandal look like a fairy tale. They can't risk it leaking. It means they have to silence Nathan.'

Silence him? What the hell does that mean? 'I want to see him,' I say.

'Absolutely not. I can't put you in that kind of danger.'

'It's a bit late for that. If you really wanted to protect me, you wouldn't have said anything.'

Ryan sucks the air through his teeth. 'You forced my hand. You wouldn't leave it alone, would you? We only decided to tell you because Nathan was worried about you and wants you to know he's safe.'

'I really need to see him.'

'I don't know, Pippa.'

'Please?'

'Look, I can't promise anything, but I'll see what I can do, okay? Leave it with me. But in the meantime, watch your back. I'm serious. Keep your eyes peeled for anything suspicious and don't answer your door to anyone you don't know. Don't speak to anyone. Don't go anywhere. Don't put anything on social media. Just wait for my call, alright?'

My head's buzzing. This is such a surreal conversation.

'Okay.'

'Good.' Ryan gives me a thin-lipped smile. 'Go home. Stay safe. Don't try to contact me.'

And then he's gone, skulking off into the shadows with his shoulders hunched and his head down, leaving me standing alone in the dark wondering what the hell just happened.

Chapter 23

The lonely walk back to my flat is the longest of my life. In every shadow and every window, dark figures lurk. Every passing car causes me to snatch my breath and unseen eyes watch my every step. I know it's all in my head, but Ryan's filled it with nonsense about secret agents and government cover-ups and my nerves believe every word he said.

Finally, when I'm back on my street, I dive into my bag for my house keys, my pace hastening, desperate for the sanctity of my flat, where I can lock and bolt myself in.

I scamper up the steps with my key poised between my fingers, but the door's partially open letting out all the warm air. My stomach lurches. I'm certain I closed it when I left.

'Hello?' I push the door and peer into the dark hall. 'Who's there?'

My hand snakes into my pocket, searching for my phone to call the police, before I remember Ryan's warning.

Don't speak to anyone. Don't go anywhere.

I step inside and close the door, wincing as the latch clicks shut.

'Is there anyone here?'

I shoulder off my coat and bag, hang them up, and creep up the stairs, my heart beating a frantic rhythm.

A rowdy group of Saturday-night drunks passes by outside, but inside my flat, the only sound is the rush of blood in my ears.

I step into the lounge and let my fingers crawl across the wall, searching for the switch. The room floods with light, but nothing's out of place. There are no masked intruders ripping the TV off the wall or slipping my laptop into a sack, although it's not burglars I'm worried about.

Ryan's filled my head with crazy stories about government conspiracies, hidden cameras and faceless spies, but it's far more likely that in my surprise at seeing Ryan at my door, I forgot to lock up properly. And yet, why do I have this sense that someone's been in the flat while I was out? It's like the air's been disturbed, the atmosphere altered by the presence of a stranger.

Don't be so stupid, Pippa. Of course no one's been here.

I'm tired and hungover. It's been a long day, full of surprises, revelations and stress. The best thing is to get a good night's sleep and I'm sure everything will be clearer in the morning.

But as I shoulder open my bedroom door, any hope I had of a peaceful night catching up on sleep is instantly chased away. My clothes are strewn across the bed and the floor, the wardrobe doors flung open. Skirts, dresses, blouses and trousers scattered as if they've been ripped off their hangers in a fit of anger. But worse, all the drawers in my dresser have been turned out. Tights, bras, knickers, vests and socks left in heaps on the floor, while my duvet hangs off the bed, my pillows tossed aside.

My blood runs like ice through my veins. When Ryan said Nathan's flat had been turned over, is this what he meant? Have the same people broken in while I was out and ransacked my home? But what could they possibly have been looking for? And it's such an intimate intrusion. They've been through my underwear, for pity's sake. It's too much. Too crazy. I can't believe this is happening to me.

I can't bear to look at it. I slam the door shut with tears bubbling in my eyes. My home has been defiled. My privacy plundered. And for what? All because of what Nathan might have seen in the moments after that bomb? It's the stuff of nightmares, like being caught up in a spy movie where I don't know who to trust or what to do. I can't even call the police, because for all I know, they're involved in this. Right from the start, they've been suspicious. Those two anti-terror officers who questioned me on the night of the bombing were convinced Nathan and I had something to do with the attack and as good as accused me of being complicit.

Trembling, I stagger back into the lounge and collapse on the sofa with my phone in my lap and tears dripping from my chin. Should I call Sam? She'd know what to do. But if I call her, I'd have to tell her everything and Ryan was explicit.

Don't speak to anyone.

In which case, there's only one person I can call.

To my surprise, Ryan picks up almost immediately, but not with the warmth I'd expected. 'I told you not to ring,' he hisses.

'I didn't know what else to do,' I sob.

'Alright, calm down. What's happened?' Ryan's tone softens.

'They've been in my flat. They've turned my bedroom upside down and been through all my things.'

Ryan sighs. 'This is what I was worried about. I'm sorry, Pippa. I should never have come to see you. They must have followed me. Are you okay?'

'Not really. I'm scared, Ryan. I don't know what to do.'

'Is your door locked and bolted?'

'I did it as soon as I came in.'

'Good. You should be safe for now. I'm sure they only did it to scare you,' he says. 'Is there anywhere you can go? Somewhere you can stay tonight?'

'I guess I could try my sister, Sam.'

'Alright. Make some excuse about needing to see her, but don't say anything to her about Nathan or what I told you. Understand?'

'Okay.'

'I mean it, Pippa. Anything you say to her is going to put your sister and her family in danger, too.'

'I won't. I promise.'

'Good. I've got to go. I'll be in touch soon. Stay safe.'

And with that, he's gone. At least he's letting me see Sam. Even if I can't tell her the truth, I'll feel happier sleeping at her house tonight. I'm tempted to jump straight into an Uber and head over there right now, but I ought to call first to check she and Alex are in, especially as it's a Saturday night.

Her number rings and rings, but she doesn't answer. It's odd. It's not like her. It cuts to voicemail, so I try again. As I wait for the call to connect, I cross the room to the window and peer out of the blinds.

Is that someone in a car opposite? A vehicle I don't recognise? It's not one of the neighbours' cars. This is awful. I can't stand it. I need to get out of here.

When Sam eventually answers, she sounds flustered, as if she was in the middle of something and I've interrupted.

'I'm having a bad night, Sam. Any chance I could stay at yours tonight?'

'Why? What's happened?'

Why always the big inquisition? Why can't she just say yes?

'Nothing really. It's just I could use some company. I'm going stir-crazy here on my own.'

'Of course. Come and spend a few days with us if you're not coping.'

'I didn't say I wasn't coping,' I say through gritted teeth.

'Don't worry, I'll look after you. You just get yourself over here. Want me to send Alex to pick you up? The guest room's all made up from last time.'

I want to scream at her to stop fussing and treating me like a baby.

'I can make my own way there.'

'Will you take an Uber? Put it on my account. I don't like the idea of you getting on the Tube at this time of night.'

'I can manage, Sam.'

'Please, take a cab. I'll pay for it.'

'You know what, I think I've changed my mind. I'll be okay here on my own after all.'

'Don't be silly. You know we have plenty of room and Freddie and Isabella love having you to stay.'

'I know, but it's late. I don't know what I was thinking. I was being silly. I'll speak to you later.'

'Pip —'

I hang up before she can utter another word. I know she means well, but I'd rather stay here and take my chances than spend the next few days being mollycoddled by my older sister. And besides, I can't keep running to her at every hint of trouble. I'm a grown woman. I have to learn to stand on my own two feet. It's what I tell my followers every day. So why is it so hard to take my own advice?

Whoever was in the flat has been and gone. I doubt they're coming back. And if they're watching the place, so what? I don't have any secrets. I don't even know where Nathan's hiding.

My mind made up, and feeling marginally braver, I sneak into my bedroom, snatch my duvet and a couple of pillows and make up a bed on the sofa. I'm sure things will look much better in the morning.

Chapter 24

My phone buzzing leeches into my dreams and yanks me awake like an enormous fist dragging me up by the collar through a sea of molasses. I roll over and crack open one eye in the darkness, forgetting for a second that I'm sleeping on the sofa. Who's calling at this time of night?

I flail around the floor to locate my mobile, bring it close to my face, and squint at the screen.

Unknown caller.

'Hello?' My voice is thick and gruff with sleep.

But there's no one there. Only the hollowness of a dead line. Probably someone who's mis-dialled. 'Who's this?'

When there's still no answer, I end the call and as the phone slips from my hand, I drift back into the embrace of sleep under my warm duvet.

When my phone rings again a few moments later, I snap awake with my heart racing. Two calls in quick succession in the middle of the night aren't a coincidence. There must be an emergency.

'Who's there?' I prop myself on my elbow with the phone clamped tightly against my ear. Catastrophic thoughts flood my brain. Has something happened to Freddie or Isabella? Mum and Dad? What else could be so urgent? I check the screen, my eyes gritty with tiredness. It's almost four in the morning. Unknown caller again. 'Sam? Is that you?'

Nothing other than an echoing silence. I hold my breath, but there's only my own pulse, heavy and rapid, in my ear.

'Nathan?'

I can't imagine he'd risk calling, and even if he did, why ring at four in the morning and say nothing? More likely, it's a troll who's somehow found my number and thinks they can easily intimidate me. Normally, I'd shrug it off, but since Ryan's revelations about Nathan and finding my flat broken into last night, I'm not so blasé. And what if the call is connected to all this craziness? What if it's the same people who ransacked my bedroom trying to scare me?

'I don't know what you want, but just leave me alone, okay?' I raise my voice, just short of shouting, and hang up.

I pull my knees up to my chest with my heart galloping hard and fast, any chance I had of falling back to sleep gone.

Twenty minutes later, when my phone rings for a third time, I'm paralysed with fear. It's another unknown caller. Do I answer it? Switch off my phone? No, I refuse to be cowed in my own home.

'What do you want?' I mumble, holding the phone lightly to my ear as if whoever is calling might try to crawl down the line and grab me.

Nothing but silence. But there is someone there. I can't hear them, but I can sense their creeping, menacing presence. Finally, I catch a distinctive rasp of breath that grows steadily louder until it sounds as if they're holding the phone too close to their mouth.

'Say something, you coward.'

A shiver runs down the length of my body and prickles the hairs on the back of my neck. I wish Nathan was here. That I wasn't on my own, utterly isolated in this lonely flat.

The line clicks dead, and I drop the phone like it's a hot stone.

Is this what it's going to be like from now on? A constant barrage of silent calls? Strangers breaking into my flat? Always being watched? Never sure of my safety? It's psychological warfare. I can't think of any other name for it.

Panic tightens my chest and squeezes my lungs. I try to meditate, concentrating on slowing my breath, focusing on the rise and fall of my chest, the weight of my limbs, my body pressing into the sofa, but it doesn't help. I can't control the relentless grip of fear and anxiety. I need a distraction.

With the duvet wrapped around my shoulders, I switch off my phone, drag myself to the table by the window and flip open my laptop. It's been a while since I last checked my Instagram feed and it seems like a good way of taking my mind off the threatening calls.

Predictably, there are hundreds of unread messages and comments. This strange connection with strangers has been such a comfort in the last couple of weeks, but as I glance through my latest notifications, something's off. Most of the comments don't make any sense.

I can't believe you're leaving us Hope you're okay and come back soon — we need you!

Gutted to hear this, Pippa, but can't wait to see what you'll do next. Take care of you!

Noooo! Don't disappear on us! Your channel has helped me through so much. I really hope everything's okay.

Totally respect your need for a break! You've given so much to us, now's the time to focus on yourself. Much love, Pip!

Since when am I taking a break? I know I've not been posting as often as I'd like recently, but I've never threatened to abandon social media. Why would I? It's my lifeblood.

Confused, I scroll back through my feed.

And there it is.

A post I've never seen before and which I certainly didn't write, accompanied by a selfie I took in Regent's Park a couple of years ago after a morning run when the sun was shining and it caught my face at a flattering angle. I'm glowing, my cheeks rosy and my hair blonder than I can ever remember. But I didn't write the caption.

Hey, everyone - I wanted to let you know that I'm going to be taking a break for a while. Need to find some headspace with everything that's been going on in my life. Who knows when I'll be back. Take good care of yourselves and stay strong. X

It kind of sounds like the sort of message I'd post. It even sounds like my voice. But there's no way I wrote it. And I'm definitely not quitting.

A panicked flush of heat washes across my chest and rises up my throat.

Someone's hacked my account. There's no other explanation. And it doesn't take a genius to work out who's behind it after the break-in and a night of silent calls. Just another tactic to intimidate and scare me. And it's working. I've never felt so unsafe, so violated. I don't even know who these people are or what they want from me, but I refuse to let them defeat me or destroy the business I've worked so hard to build from scratch.

I immediately delete the rogue post and change all my passwords, but the damage has already been done. The post has been liked by hundreds of people and has probably been seen by thousands more. I'll have to put out a clarification. I rush into the bathroom, splash my face with cold water, run a brush through my hair and apply some eyeliner, mascara, concealer and a nude lipstick. Then I steel myself and head into my bedroom, trying to ignore the carnage of my clothes scattered across the bed and floor and the fact that someone's been snooping through my things, and grab the nearest items to hand. A fitted sports crop top and a pair of leggings. I pull the door closed on the mess, dress quickly in the hall, and head back into the lounge.

With my hair tied into a ponytail, I set up my home studio, adjusting the position of the plants and the books on the shelves in the background. It's all completely unnecessary, but going through the familiar routine puts me in a better frame of mind, like an athlete going through a pre-race ritual. I switch on a pair of ring lamps and the fairy lights in a glass bottle on the floor, set my phone on the tripod and hit record.

'Hey, everyone, you may have seen a post on my channel earlier that claimed I was taking a break, but I just wanted to let you know that I'm not going anywhere. It looks as if I've been hacked.' I grimace. No point worrying people with the truth, whatever that is. Let them speculate. 'Anyway, everything's back to normal now. Thanks for all the messages, and I hope to have some good news soon about my search for Nathan. I've had word that he's alive, and he's well. But that's all I can tell you at the moment.' I take a second to compose myself. 'It's kind of a complicated situation right now. But anyway, hope you're all staying strong and living healthy. Love and peace to you all.'

I end the recording and watch it back. I look pale and drawn and the camera's tilted fractionally off centre, but it's the audio that makes it unusable. For some reason, the microphone has picked up a distorted buzz, like static interference. I never normally have any issues, but I'll have to record it again.

This time, I push my phone further back towards the window, the early morning daylight catching my face and making me look less haggard. The result is marginally better and the audio clean. I hit upload, and while I wait for it to process, make myself a matcha tea to settle my nerves and collapse back on the sofa.

Last night, everything Ryan told me about why Nathan had disappeared and gone into hiding seemed so far-fetched and fantastical, the idea that he was being hunted by the security services for what he might have seen after the bombing utterly unbelievable. But now? Maybe he was telling the truth. How else do I explain the silent calls, the break-in and my Insta account being hacked? It's too much of a coincidence. I should have swallowed my pride and stayed with Sam last night, but how can I drag her and her family into this, whatever it is, in good conscience?

I stare at the ceiling as the walls of the flat close in and I experience a weird sensation of standing at the edge of a dark, bottomless hole, tottering to keep my balance. One misstep and I'll fall.

My eyes drift across a rough patch of plaster, greying and discoloured, towards the ugly lampshade I inherited when I moved in and which I really must replace, towards a blinking red light coming from the smoke alarm that I've not noticed before. Maybe it's always been there, but didn't Ryan mention he'd found a camera hidden in a smoke alarm in Nathan's flat?

Goosebumps pucker my arms. Since I returned to the flat last night, I've had the sense I'm being watched. I thought I was being paranoid, but what if they didn't only ransack my room but installed spy cameras around the flat to keep an eye on me?

I jump up, almost spilling my tea, and drag a chair from the dining table across the room. I've never had much of a head for heights and even standing a few feet off the floor with my head angled towards the ceiling, my legs turn to jelly. I reach up and unclip the yellowing plastic housing. Inside, a rectangular battery is attached to a circuit board via several thin wires of different colours, but thankfully there's no obvious evidence of a camera. I allow myself to smile at the absurdity of what I'm doing, standing on a chair in the middle of the room looking for hidden cameras. What's happening to me?

My calves tighten as the chair wobbles and I have to grab the back of it to catch my balance. But when I reach up again to close the housing, I spot something that chills my blood. A thick black disc, no bigger than my thumbnail, has been attached to the inside of the plastic that I hadn't initially noticed. It looks new, incongruous against the yellowing housing. I pick it off and stare into what looks suspiciously like a tiny camera lens, a beady black eye glowering at me.

I drop it like it's burnt my fingers and snatch my hand back with alarm. The disc bounces on the carpet and rolls under the sofa where, frankly, it can stay.

Seriously, this cannot be happening. Has someone been watching me the entire time I've been home? While I was sleeping? Recording my Instagram video? It can't be legal, but what can I do? I don't trust the police and no one else is going to help me. Cold fingers of fear skip down my spine. What if there are other cameras? I glance around the room, into all the dark corners. I can't stand it. There's no way I can stay here if there's any chance I'm being spied on. I have to get out.

I stumble off the chair, almost turning my ankle, and hop into my bedroom to grab a jumper. Suddenly, my ransacked room is the least of my worries.

I fly down the stairs, pull on a pair of boots, snatch a coat from a hook on the wall, and hurry out.

The chill in the air hits me like a slap in the face. It's a beautiful, clear morning with a russet sunrise that suggests a sunny day ahead. The tightness in my chest eases and I breathe deeply, sucking the cold, clean air into my lungs.

I've no idea where to go, but I can't spend another minute in the flat. I need to clear my head and get my thoughts straight. I need to work out what the hell I'm going to do.

I pull my collar up and, with my head down, march along the street. It's too early for most people to be up and out, and yet I still can't shake the creeping sensation that eyes are on me. That I'm being watched and monitored.

When a hand grabs me from behind, snatching my elbow and spinning me around, my heart almost gives up with fright. I scream in alarm, my whole body tensing in expectation.

'Where are you going so early?' he asks.

Chapter 25

JAMES
February 26, 2024

Pippa's scream echoes down the street, piercing the early morning silence.

'Hey, it's only me.' I raise my hands, palms out, as she backs away, looking as if she's lining up to throw a punch. 'I didn't mean to startle you.'

'James? You scared the living daylights out of me.' She presses the heel of her hand into her sternum like she's suffering from a particularly uncomfortable bout of indigestion.

'You're up early. Where are you going?' I ask.

'Out.'

'Everything okay? It's a bit early for a walk.'

She looks me up and down. 'What are you doing here?'

'I saw your video. I was worried. You really think you've been hacked?'

She glances at her feet, her body softening. 'I've sorted it. It's fine.' She can't stand still, fidgeting like a junkie desperate for a fix.

'Pippa?'

'I said it's fine,' she snaps, before abruptly turning and walking off.

'Wait!'

'Just leave me alone.'

It's not the welcome I'd hoped for, especially as I dropped everything to come over. I was worried. That video, posted early this morning, was unsettling. She had a haunted look about her even though she was trying to appear jaunty, making light of her account being compromised. Almost manic. Her voice wavering. Scared. Something else has happened that she's not telling me.

It takes half a dozen long strides to catch up with her as she marches on. 'What is it? Is it Nathan? Have you heard something?'

'Please, I just want to be on my own.'

'Let me buy you a coffee.'

'I don't drink coffee.'

'A fruit smoothie, then. Let's just get out of the cold and we can talk.'

'I don't want to talk. I just want to be left alone.' There's a desperation in her voice. I've never seen her look so vulnerable.

'They've not found... his body, have they?' I ask.

'What? No.'

'So what is it? Please, Pippa, don't shut me out.'

She stops suddenly and stares up at me with damp, red-rimmed eyes. 'He's alive,' she whispers. 'Nathan is alive.'

I should never have insisted on dragging her to the pub. Ever since that night, she's been fixated on this notion that Nathan has staged his own death and started a new life without her. I'm no psychologist, but it doesn't take Freud to work out it's her brain's way of coping with the grief. If Nathan's not dead, it spares her the pain of dealing with her loss.

I shake my head, not sure what to say. 'Pippa, you're going to have to —'

'No, listen to me.' She glances up and down the street. 'You don't understand. I talked to Ryan last night. He's been helping to hide Nathan.'

'When? I told you to keep away from him.'

'He came to my flat last night.'

An alarm goes off inside my head. 'I don't understand. Why?'

Pippa looks around again, chewing her bottom lip. 'We can't talk here,' she whispers. 'Let's find somewhere quiet.'

She runs off like a squirrel with a plump, ripe acorn.

'Pippa!'

But she doesn't stop. Or look back. She puts her head down and marches on, elbows pumping. What nonsense has Ryan been filling her head with now? She leads me down Camden High Street, through Pratt Street, and eventually slows down as she turns into a small, secluded park. She sits on a bench overlooking a stone memorial cross, her knees together, her legs jiggling up and down, and waits for me to join her.

'Are you going to tell me what's going on?' I shrink into my coat to keep warm. Although a weak sun is rising, there's no warmth in its rays.

'You can't breathe a word of this to anyone.' Her voice remains low and breathy, like she's sharing a tantalising snippet of gossip.

'Okay.'

'I mean it, James. This is serious.'

'Yeah, okay, I won't say anything to anyone. What is it?'

'It's about the bombing.' She checks over her shoulder, her eyes scanning left and right. 'Nathan found out there's been a cover-up.'

I laugh. 'What?'

She glowers at me. 'I'm serious.'

'Come on, Pippa.' She's the last person on earth I thought I'd ever hear peddling conspiracy theories. 'Can you hear yourself?'

'It's the truth. I know it sounds... mad, but it's possible an MI5 agent was embedded with the terrorists. I think he was supposed to stop the bomb. Nathan saw him.'

I twist sideways to study her face, half expecting her to crack a smile. To point at me and laugh for being so naïve. Instead, she chews on a fingernail, her legs continuing to jig up and down. She's deadly serious.

'He saw this van and all these men who turned up right after the explosion. We think they might have been —'

'We?'

'Ryan and me. Don't you get it? It makes perfect sense.'

'What does?'

She sighs with frustration. 'That they were working for British intelligence or counter-terrorism or something.'

I sit up straighter. She actually believes what she's saying, even though it's wildly implausible.

'You're saying there was an institutional cover-up?'

'I don't know what to believe, but yes, it kind of makes sense, and it explains why Nathan disappeared.'

'Does it?'

Pippa sighs again, like she's talking to an educationally stunted child who needs everything spelled out in black and white. 'He had to go into hiding, otherwise they were going to arrest him.'

'Right. Because he saw these men?' I ask, incredulous she's even entertaining this nonsense.

'And now they're watching me.'

'MI5?'

'I don't know. Yeah, maybe.'

'Pippa —'

'I know how it sounds. You think I'm crazy, don't you, but I found a hidden camera in my smoke alarm. How do you explain that?'

'Okay,' I say, drawing out the word. It's worse than I thought. She's sleep-deprived, emotionally vulnerable and under so much stress, it's no wonder she's susceptible to Ryan's delusions. 'And how did they manage to get into your flat?'

'They broke in while I was out with Ryan. They've been through all my things and turned out my drawers. I couldn't stay there a minute longer, knowing they might be watching me.'

'You had a break-in? When? Last night?'

She nods.

'Was anything taken?'

'I don't think so.'

'But you've reported it?'

'Of course I haven't. How can I? I can't trust the police. They're all in it together,' she says with absolute conviction. 'You don't believe me, do you?'

'It's quite a story.'

'Why would I lie?'

'I don't think you're lying. I think you believe every word, but that doesn't mean it's true.'

Her jaw tightens and she draws her lips into a thin line. 'I spent the night answering my phone to silent calls, my flat was broken into and they've hacked my Instagram account.' She raises an eyebrow, challenging me to contradict her. 'How much more proof do I need?'

Her hand flies to her head and she scratches her scalp furiously as she squeezes her eyes shut.

'So where's Nathan?'

'I don't know. Ryan wouldn't tell me, but I've said I want to see him.'

'And in the meantime? Where are you going to go?'

Pippa shrugs.

'I don't have much room, but you could always stay at my place for a few days. You can have my bed,' I add hurriedly. I don't want her getting the wrong idea. 'I'll sleep on the couch. It might help —'

But before I can finish my sentence, Pippa's attention is grabbed by her phone buzzing in her pocket. She pulls it out and stares at the screen. Then she wets her lips, glances at me, and opens her eyes wide with surprise.

'It's Nathan,' she gasps.

Chapter 26

PIPPA
February 26, 2024

Nathan spoke precisely twelve words. A code only I could decipher. While it was a relief to hear his voice, he didn't apologise for the hell he's put me through, ask me how I was coping, or even explain where he's been. It's a call that's left me with mixed emotions, but maybe he'll be more open when he finally turns up.

'Meet me tonight at eight where we went on our second date,' he said, with the deadpan tones of an AI robot.

I knew instantly where he meant. The Regent's Canal towpath, near the Pirates' Castle in Camden, a boating and outdoor activities centre in a brown-brick, castellated building that's supposed to look like an actual castle.

I'm back there again now, loitering nervously, watching for anyone who looks suspiciously as if they've followed me. If my flat has been under surveillance, there's every chance they've been tracking my movements too, and the last thing I want is to unwittingly lead them straight to Nathan after everything he's been through to avoid detection.

Being back reminds me of our first proper date, which went much better than I'd expected. I'd not been on many dates since James and I broke up, and I was out of practice and not sure what to expect. I remember being incredibly nervous, but I didn't need to worry. Nathan was the perfect gentleman. He took me to a quirky bar in Soho with a cosy, speakeasy vibe, leather seats and vintage posters on the walls. He introduced me to Manhattan cocktails and told me all about the amazing things he'd done in his life and all the incredible places he'd visited. He was so charming, so attentive, I didn't even have to look at the menu as he ordered for us both. It was perfect.

Afterwards, he walked me to the station and lingered, no doubt hoping I'd invite him back to my place, and when I didn't, delivered a theatrical kiss on the back of my hand, his stubble rough against my skin, and withdrew with an ostentatious bow. It was silly, but it made me laugh and when he suggested meeting the next day, how could I refuse? I was already itching to see him again.

I spent ages choosing the right outfit, my favourite powder-pink cashmere crew-neck sweater and straight-legged jeans with the camel coat I wore to death last winter. Tonight, my primary concern is keeping warm and anonymous rather than appearing alluring and glamorous. I have the hood of my fleece pulled up over my head and a scarf wrapped around my nose and mouth, while avoiding eye contact with anyone.

I've been waiting for almost fifteen minutes and it's so cold I can't feel my toes anymore. I stamp my feet and bow my head as a middle-aged man with wild hair, baggy, stained trousers and a clanking carrier bag full of glass bottles shuffles past, casting a curious look my way. It doesn't feel the safest place to be on my own at night, but hopefully Nathan will be here soon.

Another five minutes pass. How long do I leave it before giving up and accepting he's not coming? He's not called or sent a message, so where is he? I hope he's not been spooked and bailed out on me.

'Hello, Pippa.' His voice from behind startles me.

I spin around and suddenly we're face to face. I'm looking into his eyes and it's as if everything is back to as it was before the attack and Nathan's Lord Lucan vanishing act.

'Jeez, Nathan. You nearly gave me a heart attack.'

But everything isn't back to normal. For a start, he looks awful. His hair, usually so fashionably tousled, is a ragged mess, his stubble has become a rough beard that doesn't suit him, and his eyes are bloodshot and restless, darting around furtively. It doesn't look as if he's slept in days. I know the feeling.

'Are you okay?' He steps forwards, pulling his hands out of his pockets as if he's about to hug me, but when he notices me standing stiffly, he hesitates, uncertain.

It's a moment I've been dreaming about for the last twelve days, when we're finally reunited and Nathan tells me how sorry he is and we sweep each other up and hold each other tightly.

Except, now he's here, standing in front of me with that silly lop-sided grin, I don't know how I feel.

Does he have any idea of the stress he's put me through? How many sleepless nights I've endured, tortured by thoughts of his bloated body washed up on a tidal beach out by the old tobacco docks? I was convinced he was dead, and that at any moment I would get a phone call from the police with the bad news. The last two weeks have been an utter nightmare. He could have picked up the phone and called or dropped me a text to at least let me know he was alive, instead of letting me think the worst. It was cruel and it was selfish. How can I ever forgive him?

'I've been worried sick.' I cross my arms over my chest and turn away.

'I know. I'm sorry.'

'If you'd just let me know you were okay.'

'I wanted to. I really did, but...' He glances along the length of the towpath.

'You have no idea what you put me through.'

'It's not been easy on me either, you know, Pip. I didn't want to put you in danger.'

'So you abandoned me and let me imagine the worst? I was waiting for the call to tell me they'd found your body. It's not fair, Nathan. You can't do that to people,' I cry, thumping him in the chest with clenched fists, my violence springing from a dark place.

He parries my blows until my fury's spent.

'Feel better?'

I grunt and step away, panting. 'How could you?'

'I know you're angry, but I didn't want you dragged into this mess.'

I sweep a few stray strands of hair from my eyes and let my breath come back under control. 'So what changed? Why now?'

'You want to walk? I'm getting cold.'

He puts a hand on the small of my back and shepherds me along the path. We stroll in silence for a few moments, past the red, blue and green long boats moored up for the night, where the canal is flanked by expensive flats and apartments that overlook the water. Nathan reaches for my hand, but I snatch it away. I'm not ready. Not yet.

'You know, I saw some terrible things,' he says. 'People who'd been horribly disfigured and really badly injured. And bodies, too. Lots of them. The ones who were beyond help. I still hear the screaming in the middle of the night. It was awful, Pip. You have no idea.'

'You shouldn't have left me. I told you not to go.'

'I had to do something. You understand that, right?'

Do I? Did he need to leave me to put himself in danger? And what was he actually able to do for anyone, anyway? It's a question that's niggled at the back of my mind for a while. Did he act out of a genuine desire to help or because of how it would look?

We cross the canal over a narrow bridge that brings us out by a lock next to the night market.

'I didn't know where to start,' he says. 'There were so many people and they all needed help. It was overwhelming.'

'You could have been killed.'

'What was I supposed to do?' he snaps. 'Stand back and watch while people were dying?'

'No, of course not.'

'Although I wonder now, if I could turn back time, whether I'd do it again.'

'Ryan told me what you saw.'

'He told you about the van?'

I nod. 'And the man they picked up. Who do you think they were?'

'I'm guessing secret services. MI5, I would imagine.'

'You really think they would have arrested you? You hadn't done anything.'

Nathan shrugs. 'I saw too much, that's all they care about. I wasn't going to take any chances. If I'd let them arrest me, I might never have seen you again. I had to run. It's all I could do.'

It still seems so extraordinary. And yet, there's a tremor in Nathan's voice, a catch of fear. He's scared, and someone like Nathan doesn't scare easily.

'I wish you had let me know what was going on. I was out of my mind with worry.'

'I couldn't, Pip. You understand that, don't you? It was dangerous and I didn't want to drag you into it. But it's been hell. I couldn't stop thinking about you.'

'I thought you were dead.'

Nathan lowers his gaze, ashamed. 'I'm sorry. But I was only trying to protect you.'

'It's a bit late for that. They broke into my flat last night and ransacked my bedroom.'

'They did what?' Nathan's eyes widen in alarm as he runs a hand over his scraggy beard.

'And I found a camera hidden in the smoke alarm.'

'Shit.'

'It gets worse. All last night, someone kept calling my mobile but when I answered, there was no one there. And this morning, I discovered they'd hacked my Instagram page.'

'I should never have let Ryan reach out to you. I should have tried harder to keep you safe.'

'Don't be silly. It was driving me crazy thinking you might be dead.'

'I suppose they were bound to come looking for you in the end, when they couldn't find me.'

'Where have you been hiding?' I ask. 'Have you been staying with Ryan?'

'Probably best you don't know.'

We continue walking past another lock where the canal opens into a wide basin.

'Is it worth trying to talk to them and explain?' I ask.

'Who?'

'These people who are looking for you. You could give them a reassurance that you won't tell anyone what you saw. You could offer to sign the Official Secrets Act. I could get Sam to put out some feelers. I'm sure she'd know what —'

'No.' Nathan grabs my arm and drags me into the shadows, pressing me against a dirty brick wall. 'I'm not going to hand myself in, if that's what you think.'

'So what are you going to do?' I shrink away, the mad look in Nathan's eye filling me with dread.

He lets me go and steps towards the edge of the canal, his shoulders slumped in defeat. I've never seen him like this before. Part of the attraction has always been his calm, cool confidence. Nothing ever fazed him. No challenge was too big. Even when he was knocked back for a job by the police, he took it on the chin and became even more determined to make the grade next time. I guess all that's in jeopardy now, too.

I place a gentle hand on his shoulder. 'It's going to be okay, Nate. We'll work it out.'

He shakes his head. 'I can't stay in London. It's too dangerous. I have to get out of the city. Somewhere they can't find me, where I can lie low for a while.'

'You're leaving?'

He turns around slowly, takes both of my hands, and stares into my eyes. 'Come with me, Pip.'

'What? I can't.'

'Of course you can. There's nothing tying you to London. I want us to be together and build a new life.'

'But... where would we go?'

'I don't know. We'll figure it out.'

'I can't just leave.'

'Why not? What's stopping you?'

'Nathan...'

'Come on, it'll be an adventure.'

'At least let me think about it.'

'There's no time. They could be watching us right now. If we're going to do this, we need to go tonight.'

'Tonight?' I gasp.

'Trust me, Pippa. When have I ever let you down?'

'It's not that, it's —'

'I can't guarantee your safety if you stay. They'll come for you, like they're coming for me. And don't think the police will help you either.'

I stagger backwards like a punch-drunk boxer, pulling free of Nathan's hands. I can't leave my home to start a new life with Nathan god knows where. 'It's such a big decision.'

'Let me look after you and I promise I won't let them get to you. Just think, we can finally be together. The two of us. No more running. No more hiding. We could have an amazing future ahead of us.'

'But we'd always be in hiding.'

'They'll forget about us in time. It won't be forever. I know it's a lot to take on board, but I think this could be good for us. A chance for a new start. But you need to decide quickly. Are you coming with me or not?'

Chapter 27

One lousy hour. That's all Nathan's given me. It's hardly enough time to pack for a weekend away, let alone start a new life. In a total blur, I shove two weeks' worth of clean underwear into the rucksack I bought several years ago when I planned to go travelling around Asia, before my friend, Katie, got cold feet and pulled out, and pack a sensible selection of warm clothes on top. Jeans and thick sweaters, socks, thermal tops and a set of gym wear and trainers. I'd take more, but I'm already struggling to lift the bag, and I haven't even packed any toiletries or cosmetics yet. But how do you pack light when you're upending your life and moving on?

I have too many things. Stuff I don't use and don't need most of the time, like my favourite pair of running shoes that have more holes in them than a Swiss cheese. A stack of journals filled with fitness goals from years gone by that I shoved under the bed in a cardboard box and forgot about. A broken microphone from when I first started vlogging. My first yoga mat. Clothes I no longer wear. Jewellery my mother gave me that I've always hated. But I don't have time to clear the flat. It'll be the letting agent's problem, not mine. At least it's one way to get rid of the clutter.

Nathan's been sketchy on the details of where we're heading or even where we'll sleep tonight, but I trust he has a plan and I'm more than happy not to spend another night like last night in the flat. It's like going on holiday, except I have no idea of the destination and it's unlikely we'll ever come back. It's exciting. Thrilling. And totally terrifying. It's a fresh start at life. How many people get that opportunity out of the blue?

It's just after eleven when Nathan turns up at the door, his cap pulled down low over his eyes and a bulging, black, military-style rucksack strapped to his back. He glances furtively down the street and slips inside.

'Ready?' he asks, studying my rucksack which is so full I barely managed to do up the straps.

I take a deep breath. 'I think so. Where are we going?'

'You'll find out soon enough.'

'Intriguing.' I smile, but Nathan's expression remains stony, deep worry lines furrowing his brow.

'I'll just message Sam to let her know I'm going to be out of contact for a while and then we can get going.'

But as I pull my mobile out of the back pocket of my jeans, Nathan swipes it out of my hands.

'Are you fucking kidding me?' he snarls, eyes blazing. 'How stupid are you? Did you hear a single word I said earlier? We need to vanish. Nobody can know where we are, including your interfering bloody sister.'

'But —'

'I can't believe you were even thinking about bringing your phone. Are you completely out of your mind?'

It never occurred to me it would be a problem. I need my phone to post content, especially as I'm leaving my laptop behind as it's far too heavy to carry.

'I can't live without my phone.'

'You know they can trace it, don't you? You might as well wave a big red flag above your head announcing where you are.'

He shoulders off his rucksack and it lands on the floor with a thud that suggests it's even heavier than mine.

'What if I keep it turned off?' I absolutely cannot be without my phone.

Nathan shakes his head. 'Do you want to come with me or not?'

'Of course.'

He storms up the stairs and into the kitchen where he removes the SIM card from the phone and tosses it into the sink with the handset.

I stare at it longingly, but there's nothing I can do. I don't want to put us in danger, and I have to trust that Nathan knows best.

'Where's your purse?' he asks.

'In my rucksack.'

'Bring it to me.'

'Why?'

'Just do it.'

Nathan's on edge. I know better than to argue with him when he's in this mood, so I head back downstairs, fetch my purse and hand it to him without question.

He unzips it and pulls out all my debit and credit cards.

'You won't be needing these either.' He flips open the kitchen bin and throws them away. 'We'll be using cash from now.'

'But I don't have any cash.' Who does? I can't remember the last time I paid for anything with notes or coins.

'I have plenty. Don't worry about it.'

'But you can't pay for everything.'

'We'll work it out. But like your phone, if you use a card, they'll be able to track us down. Trust me, okay?'

It doesn't seem as if I have any choice.

Ten minutes later, we're on a bus into central London, travelling past all the famous sights. Leicester Square, around Trafalgar Square and down Whitehall towards the Houses of Parliament. I wonder if or when I'll see any of them again.

When we jump off near Victoria railway station, I imagine we're getting a train somewhere. I'd predicted that Nathan would want to head north, maybe even into the wilds of Scotland, but the only trains from Victoria run south. So it's no surprise when he marches right past the entrance and we head along Buckingham Palace Road to the coach station instead, struggling under the weight of our luggage.

'Are we getting another bus?'

'If they're still running at this time of night.'

When we reach the station entrance, Nathan pulls me to one side and dumps his rucksack on the ground. He bends over, rummages through it and pulls out a dark mop that looks like a dead animal.

'Here, put this on,' he says, handing it to me.

Curious, I shake it out. It's a bloody wig. He doesn't seriously expect me to wear that, does he?

'Are you joking? I'm not putting that on.'

'You'll do as I say,' he growls. 'The station's full of cameras.'

It smells rank, like it's been shoved at the bottom of a damp drawer for a long time and been used by a family of rodents as a toilet.

'It's filthy.'

'Just until we're on the coach.'

'And then I can take it off?'

'Hurry up, Pippa.' Nathan glances anxiously at his watch. 'We don't have all night.'

'Fine.' I flatten my hair and pull the wig over my head, tucking loose strands under the itchy cap. I must look ridiculous.

Nathan stands in front of me, eyeing up my new look. He makes a few adjustments, tugging the wig down on one side and then the other. Finally, he brushes his fingers through its coarse, dark hair and nods his approval. 'I never imagined you as a brunette before.'

'Don't get used to it.'

Inside the station, it quickly becomes clear that we're not going anywhere tonight. A bank of departure boards reveals we've missed the last bus and the next one isn't until six tomorrow morning.

'Great,' I moan. 'What now?'

Nathan scratches the back of his neck. 'Shut up and let me think,' he snaps.

We're going to have to check into a hotel. Fortunately, there's an abundance of accommodation in this part of London, so I'm sure we can find a cheap room. It's not the end of the world.

'We'll have to wait until the morning,' Nathan says.

'Here?' I glance around the draughty station and the rows of uncomfortable-looking metal benches.

'No, not here. It's too risky.'

If I'd been allowed to bring my phone, I could have found a cheap hotel room in less than a minute, but I guess we'll have to go knocking on doors instead. 'Let's find a hotel and grab a few hours' sleep.'

'We can't afford a hotel, Pip. We need to watch our pennies, plus they'll want our details and I don't want to leave a trail.'

I stare at him, not sure whether he's joking. 'We can't sleep on the streets.'

He shrugs. 'Why not? I'll find us somewhere cosy, out of the wind.'

'Nathan, no. I'm not sleeping in a doorway. At least let's find an all-night cafe where we can hang out.'

This is descending into a farce. I'd been so excited about the adventure ahead, but if I thought it involved sleeping on the street, even for one night, I'd have thought twice. I understand we need to be careful, but Nathan's taking it to extremes.

'It's my fault. I should have checked the coach times,' he says. It's a rare admission of culpability. 'I thought there was one after midnight.'

If we'd been able to check our phones, we'd have known before we arrived and wouldn't be stuck in this stupid situation, stranded in the middle of central London. But I'm not going to risk pointing that out to Nathan, not while he's so grumpy. It would be asking for trouble.

'Let's find a hotel. It's one night, that's all. And even if they do manage to track us, by the time they work out where we are, we'll be long gone.'

Nathan sighs and takes my hand. 'I'm not putting you in danger again. Neither of us really knows what we're dealing with. These are powerful people and they're worried about what we know. We have to be on our toes and keep one step ahead. If we check into a hotel, it's asking for trouble.'

I shiver as the cold seeps into my bones. On the other side of a glass panel, a cleaner sweeps the empty coach bays. It's one night. A few hours of discomfort and then we'll be on our way. The alternative is telling Nathan I've changed my mind and I'm heading home. I'd probably never see him again. He might as well be dead.

'We can't stay here,' he says. 'It's too exposed.'

'Where do you want to go?'

'We'll find somewhere. It's only for a few hours. We'll be back by six and on our way out of here by breakfast.'

'I don't know, Nathan.'

'Pip, don't argue. I'm not in the mood.'

Chapter 28

JAMES
February 27, 2024

It's a perfect day for an early morning run, although try telling that to the kids who've turned up at the park bleary eyed before school this morning. I jog back through the group, urging them to run faster. To pick up their feet. Push themselves and work harder. It's only a mile. It's not exactly a marathon, but it's not the distance that counts.

Clayton, a small kid with a big mouth, who lives with his ageing grandmother in a high-rise tower block, is flagging.

'Keep working, Clayton. You're doing a great job.'

His skinny body is lost inside an oversized, counterfeit football shirt, his head lolling from side to side as he tries to keep up with the stronger, faster, fitter kids.

'I can't,' he pants, slowing.

'Don't you dare give up on me.'

Clayton pulls up anyway, swinging his arms like pendulums, tears of anger and frustration moistening his eyes.

'I'm too slow. I'm never going to beat any of them,' he says, watching the group disappear around the top edge of the park.

'It's not about winning. It's about keeping going when the going gets tough.'

He kicks the ground, pouting. 'I can't.'

'Only losers quit. You've heard that before, right? You've done the hard bit. You turned up on time and made a commitment to be here. That's more than most kids your age would do.'

It always amazes me how many of the kids, all from chaotic, dysfunctional backgrounds, roll up at the gym in the morning before school, especially on a Monday when it's cold and dark. Before they found us, most of them would have struggled to get out of bed before midday, let alone do any form of physical exercise or make it to school. That's the kind of difference the project has made. They're learning self-discipline and paving the way for a future that doesn't involve prison, when most of them had been written off as no-hopers or troublemakers. We're steering them away from the gangs and the extremists by showing them their potential and what they can achieve if they put their minds to it.

They all know the deal. It's why they've dragged themselves out of bed to be here. If they want to spar in the ring later and do all the fun stuff, they have to commit to at least two early-morning runs a week. Not so difficult when the mornings are warm and light in the summer, but it requires a whole different level of commitment in the depths of winter.

'My knees hurt,' Clayton says.

'We'll take it slowly. Come on, I'll run with you.'

He shakes his head, defiant, and wanders off, turning his back on me.

'Clayton! Don't run away.'

'What's the point?' he yells.

'The point is you turned up and you're going to finish the run. We'll do it together, okay?'

'I don't want to.'

'So you're going to give up? Just like that?'

'Yeah.'

I jog after him, across the damp grass, and walk at his side. 'Look, I get it. I used to feel the same way when I was younger. I felt like all the other kids were stronger and faster than me and I hated it. I didn't think I was good enough, but you know what? It's okay to feel weak and to be vulnerable.

It's part of getting stronger. You think Mike Tyson was always the toughest boy in his neighbourhood? Of course he wasn't. He used to get bullied because he was so shy.'

'The boxer Mike Tyson?'

'I know, hard to believe, right? But he didn't give up, and that's the bravest thing he could do. To keep going when life gets tough. You think Mike Tyson would have been heavyweight champion of the world if he'd quit?'

'I guess not.'

'So, are we going to finish this run?'

Clayton shrugs, his head rolling to one side.

'Come on, I'll race you.' I turn and head back to the path, breaking into a slow trot.

When I glance back, Clayton's face has lit up with an excited smile. He races after me and shoots past, giggling.

I jog a few feet behind him all the way back to the gym and let him outsprint me to the finish line, where the rest of the kids are standing with hands on their hips, panting, or flat out on the floor, catching their breath.

'Loser!' Clayton cries.

'Beat me fair and square. Well done.'

While the kids disappear inside to change, I check my phone. Nothing from Pippa even though she promised to let me know how things went with Nathan last night.

I wasn't happy about her going alone to the canal to meet him, but she accused me of fussing when I suggested going with her as a chaperone. After all, it was only a couple of years ago that a homeless guy was beaten to death not far from where they'd arranged to meet. But Pippa said she didn't want to spook Nathan.

Not that I'm worried. I know Nathan walked Pippa to her door and she made it home safely. I'm more surprised that neither of them spotted me. At six-foot-four, I'm not exactly inconspicuous. And yet I was able to tail them and keep them in full view the whole time, even though Nathan supposedly thinks he's being hunted by MI5 to silence him, which would be laughable if he hadn't brainwashed Pippa into believing it, too. If he was that concerned, I would have expected him to have been more vigilant.

I'm surprised Pippa has been so gullible, but I saw in her eyes when we chatted in the park yesterday that she believed every word Ryan and Nathan have fed her, regardless of how preposterous it sounds. Does she really believe a surveillance team would have broken into her flat and turned it over, installed cameras in her smoke alarm and hacked her

Instagram account? If she took a second to step back and think about it, she'd realise Nathan's manipulating her. Constructing a fantastical story that doesn't stand up to any scrutiny.

What I don't understand is why he's doing it. And where's he been for the last two weeks? It's entirely possible he's had some sort of emotional breakdown, maybe triggered by the bombing and what he witnessed. The death. The injuries. The devastation. It must have been horrendous. I've seen the news footage and that was bad enough. I can't imagine how much worse it must have been to have witnessed it first-hand.

Unless there's something else going on that I'm missing? It's certainly an elaborate web of lies he's weaved, convincing enough to have totally sucked Pippa in, and I don't like it. There's something sinister about his motivations and I can't help but worry he's putting Pippa in danger. I just wish I could put my finger on it.

It's still early, but I can't wait any longer. I need to know what Nathan said to her last night, what excuse he gave for abandoning her and letting her believe he was dead. I hope he appreciates what he put her through and the strain it's put on her mental health.

I hit the call button and wait.

It takes a couple of seconds for an automated voice to kick in and announce the number I'm calling is unavailable.

That's weird. I try the number again but get the same troubling message.

Something's wrong. Why would Pippa's phone be unavailable? I rack my brain but can't think of any good reason that alleviates the swelling nub of anxiety in my chest. She always keeps her phone on.

'Everything okay?' My colleague, Carl, appears at the door. 'Kids have a good run?'

'Yeah, not bad. Listen, I know I still owe you for the last time, but can you take the session for me this morning?'

'Problem?'

I roll my eyes. 'It's Pippa. Something's up.'

It's all I need to say.

'Go. Hurry,' Carl says.

Major signalling problems mean it takes more than twice as long to make the journey to Camden by Tube. Not that there's anything I can do about it. Everyone's facing the same headache. I try calling an Uber, but the rest of London seems to have had the same idea. It's like hunting for the wreck of the

Titanic with just a snorkel and flippers. Near impossible. I have little choice other than to wait on the crowded platform with all the morning commuters, everyone stressed and grumpy.

It's mid-morning when I finally roll up at Pippa's flat. I've tried calling her mobile several times during the course of the morning, but the number remains stubbornly unavailable.

Her blinds are open but there are no lights on. I hammer at the door and wait, hoping it's nothing. That there's a simple explanation for why I can't get through, and it has nothing whatsoever to do with Nathan.

When there's no answer, I knock again. Maybe she's gone shopping. Or filming a new video. Or even meeting up with Nathan again now they've been reunited. But I can't shift the knot of worry that's settled in my stomach. A sense that something's wrong.

An adjacent door peels open and a middle-aged woman with bright red hair and a colourful, yellow dress leans out.

'If you're looking for Pippa, she went out late last night and I don't think she came back,' she says, eyeing me warily.

'Right. What time was that?'

'Late. She woke me up with all the doors banging. She should have more respect for people sleeping, especially on a Sunday night.'

'Did you notice if she was with someone?'

'Sounded like it.' The woman tuts, rolls her eyes, and disappears back inside.

Nathan. It has to be. But where's he taken her?

In desperation, I try Pippa's mobile once again, but I still can't get through. What do I do now? Maybe she's been in touch with her sister. Hopefully she'll know where she is, and although I don't have Samantha's number, I know she's a lawyer in central London and her married name is Bennett. It's ridiculously easy to find out with a quick Google search that she works in a small chambers in Berkley Square in upmarket Mayfair. I call the number listed and I'm put through to Samantha's haughty-sounding personal assistant.

'I need to speak to Samantha Bennett. It's urgent.'

'I'm afraid Mrs Bennett is in meetings for most of the day. If you'd like to leave a name, I'll pass her a message,' her PA says.

'Do you think you could interrupt her? I really need a quick word.'

'I'll get her to call you as soon as she's free.'

I sigh. There's no chance of getting past the gatekeeper, even when I tell her I'm a friend of Samantha's sister, so I leave my name and number and have to trust she'll pass it on.

But the dismissive tone she takes with me makes me doubt she's grasped the urgency of the situation and I'm convinced my message is going to find its way to the bottom of her bin rather than Samantha's desk. Maybe I'd have more luck if I turned up at the office in person. Berkeley Square is less than thirty minutes away on the Tube, or it would be if the signalling wasn't screwed up. It's probably quicker to walk. It's only two-and-a-half miles.

My mind made up, I head off, skirting around Regent's Park, past the iconic BT Tower, and along fashionable Regent's Street with its swanky shops, restaurants and cafes. It only takes me fifty minutes.

I march up to the entrance of a modern, seven-storey building, through a set of revolving glass doors and into an opulent, marble reception area. A well-groomed man in shirtsleeves and a dark waistcoat looks up from the desk and gives me the once-over. It's hardly any wonder he looks at me suspiciously. I've come straight from the gym, still wearing my tracksuit and trainers.

'I need to speak to Samantha Bennett. It's urgent,' I say with a determined smile, hoping if I'm confident enough, it'll make up for my appearance.

The receptionist returns my smile, but it's stiff and cold.

'Do you have an appointment, sir?'

'No, it's a family matter.'

'I'm afraid if you don't have an appointment —'

'Just call her and tell her it's about her sister, Pippa, okay?'

'As I said, if you don't have an appointment, I'm afraid I can't help, but if you'd like to leave your name and number I'll let her office know —'

'It's urgent,' I hiss, leaning across the counter. 'Tell her Pippa's friend, James, is here and that I need to speak to her urgently. Trust me, she's going to want to hear what I have to say.'

Behind me, air sucks through the revolving doors, and a small group of women, chatting in serious tones, walk into the building. From the corner of my eye, I catch them in their smart business suits and heels heading towards the elevators. They all glance at me, curious about who's raising their voice and causing a scene.

'Yes, sir, I'll make sure that message gets to her,' the receptionist says.

This is a waste of time. He's not going to contact Samantha or let me up to speak to her.

One of the three women presses the elevator call button and they all stand back to wait. A second or two later, the elevator pings and the doors gush open. Without a second thought, I turn and sprint, my trainers squeaking on the shiny tiled floor.

'Excuse me! Sir!' the receptionist shouts. 'You can't go in there!'

I barge into the lift behind the women with a smile of apology and stab repeatedly at the buttons on the wall.

As the doors slide closed, I see the receptionist racing towards me, but he's too late. The doors clank shut and we begin to rise.

I smile to myself. It's too easy.

'Which floor did you want?' I ask, turning to the women who've backed into a corner in a fug of expensive perfume, and come eyeball to eyeball with Pippa's sister.

'James?' she says, her eyes narrowing. 'What are you doing here?'

'Actually, I came to see you. I've been trying to reach you all morning. I think Pippa's in trouble.'

Chapter 29

Samantha's office has thick cream carpet, a leather-topped mahogany desk and floor-to-ceiling windows with views overlooking the square. It's the epitome of plush. I can only imagine how crippling the rent must be, so I guess business is good.

She shuts the door and points me to a comfortable chair in front of the desk while she shrugs off her coat and jacket and hangs them on a stand in the corner.

'What kind of trouble?' she asks.

'You heard Nathan's been found?'

Her eyebrows shoot up. 'Alive?'

'His brother, Ryan, has been sheltering him, and that's where it all gets a bit weird.'

I tell her everything I know, including how Nathan convinced Pippa that he's being hunted by the security services because of what he supposedly saw during the Tower Bridge attack.

'I know it sounds crazy, but Pippa believes every word of it, and now she's disappeared, too. I've been trying her mobile all morning but her number's unobtainable, and she's not at her flat. A neighbour says she heard her leaving with someone late last night.'

'Nathan?'

'I guess so.'

'You're right, it does sound crazy.'

'I'm worried about her, and I didn't know who else to turn to.'

'You did the right thing. Any ideas where she might have gone?' Samantha asks.

'That's what I was hoping you might be able to tell me. I'm worried Nathan's talked her into doing something stupid.'

'Like what?'

'I don't know, but I have a really bad feeling about it. It's like he and Ryan are manipulating her and she's just going along with everything they tell her.'

Samantha snorts. 'I've never warmed to the man, but what can you say? Pippa was smitten, even though I thought he was a bit controlling.'

'To be fair, it could be that Nathan's suffering some sort of nervous breakdown, but I'm still worried about her. For a start, why would she switch off her mobile? You know what she's like with her phone.'

Samantha taps a scarlet fingernail on the desk, lost in thought. 'Let me try,' she says, reaching for her mobile.

Outside, people flow through the square like swarming ants on the hunt for food, a seething mass of random journeys. If I had this office, I wouldn't get much work done, distracted by watching the world go by. But then the thought of being stuck in an office all day, every day, makes my flesh crawl.

'I can't get through either,' Samantha says. 'I'm getting the same message.'

'So what do we do?'

'You really think she's in trouble?'

'She's hardly left the flat since the bombing, but the second Nathan's back on the scene, she vanishes. You know he proposed to her, don't you?'

Samantha's face darkens. 'No. When?'

'Valentine's night. Just before the bomb attack. Sorry, I assumed you knew.'

'No.' She takes a deep breath and lets it out slowly. 'I didn't.'

'She turned him down. She thought it was too soon.'

'Good.' Samantha toys absentmindedly with a thin gold bracelet around her wrist.

'And then Nathan disappeared.'

'You think the two things are connected?' she asks.

'I don't know. Maybe he wanted to punish Pippa. Maybe he wanted her to think he was dead.'

'That's pretty messed up.'

'I don't know. I'm just guessing,' I say. 'You don't like him much, do you?'

Samantha fixes me with a cold, hard stare, the kind of practised look I imagine turns defendants in the dock to jelly. 'No,' she says. 'But I like him even less now.'

'I don't understand how she's been taken in so easily by his lies. Does she really think he's being hunted by MI5 agents?'

'When it comes to Nathan, she doesn't think clearly.' Samantha sucks in her cheeks like she's chewing on a lemon. 'She likes to preach about female empowerment and taking control, but when she's with Nathan, all that goes out of the window. He only has to tell her to jump and she'll apologise for not leaping high enough.'

'So we're agreed, we need to find her?'

Samantha nods, thoughtful for a moment.

'Any ideas where to start?' I ask.

'Do you think we should alert the police?'

'And tell them what? That Pippa's taken off with her boyfriend? I'm not sure they'd take us seriously.'

'No, you're right. What about her social media? How many followers does she have these days? Several thousand, isn't it?'

'Try three-quarters of a million.'

'Wow. Then that's where we start. We ask them to help us find her.' Samantha folds her hands in her lap as if Pippa's as good as found.

'Right. And how do we do that?' It's a great idea, the equivalent of deploying a small digital army. Hundreds of thousands of pairs of eyes across the world, all on the lookout. But how do we access her account? 'I've no idea of her passwords, have you?'

A sly smile creeps across Samantha's face. 'No, but I have a spare key to her flat. Knowing Pippa, she'll have written them all down somewhere. We just have to find them.'

That's her plan? Hunting through Pippa's flat in the hope that she's scribbled down the password to her Instagram account?

Samantha lifts the receiver of the phone on her desk and presses a button.

'Belinda, can you clear my diary for the rest of the day? Something urgent's come up I need to deal with. See if you can move everything back.'

She hangs up the phone and grabs her jacket and coat. At least I have Samantha on my side, I suppose. It's an unexpected partnership.

'Right, are you coming or not?' she asks, heading for the door.

Transcript from the podcast, Fallen Hero. Interview with Pippa's sister, Samantha Bennett

Pippa could have had any job she wanted. She's bright, beautiful and incredibly capable, which I suppose is why I was a little disappointed when she announced she was making this influencing thing a full-time career. I mean, it's not a career really, is it? Not in the regular sense of the word. I thought she could do much better. At one stage, she was talking about setting up her own business as a fitness trainer. Alex and I had even talked about investing in it to help her get it off the ground.

I suppose I wanted something better for her. I was worried she was going to end up just another desperate wannabe trying too hard to make a living out of social media because it was the trendy thing to do. But actually, she had a real talent for it. I shouldn't have been surprised. As I say, she's a capable woman, but big sisters always worry, don't they?

I watched a few of her videos on YouTube and the clips she'd post on Instagram and she was so engaging. She looked great and people were obviously responding to the content. I should have told her how proud I was of her because it takes someone special to create a business from nothing and make a success out of it.

When I found out how many followers she'd built up, I was staggered. I couldn't imagine three-quarters of a million women around the world watching my little sister advocating for healthy minds and bodies. It was crazy. It was as if she'd created her own online self-help community.

And ultimately, it was a brilliant resource we were able to tap into when she went missing. I only wish I could thank everyone individually who cared enough to help us with the search. I can't tell you how immensely grateful I am.

My only regret is in the way things turned out. It was such a tragedy. Such a waste of a life.

Chapter 30

PIPPA
February 27, 2024

Motorway traffic buzzes past in a blur while Nathan snores at my side. He fell asleep the moment the coach set off and is now caught in a repeating loop, his head drooping onto his chest and rolling to one side before he jars awake for a split second and instantly nods off again.

I hunker down, trying to stay anonymous. At least I have a better idea where we're headed. After a cold and uncomfortable night drifting between all-night cafes, shop doorways and briefly the brutal, cavernous concourse at the train station in Victoria before we were thrown out, we returned to the coach station at around five-thirty this morning, where Nathan bought warm croissants and hot chocolate before we jumped on the first bus of the day to Norwich.

Nathan still won't tell me if it's our final destination. He's being so cagey. It's as if he doesn't trust me. Which is crazy. If I didn't trust him, I would never have left London with him.

I don't know how Nathan can sleep. I'm dog-tired but so fraught with nerves, anxious that at any moment we're going to be caught, sleep is a distant aspiration. I look at everyone with suspicion, even the other passengers.

Like the elderly couple on the other side of the aisle, who've not stopped whispering to each other from the moment they took their seats. They must be in their seventies or eighties, but they're acting like teenagers, holding hands in their tweed coats they've refused to take off, even though the coach is comfortably warm. They have the kindly, wrinkled faces of grandparents, but they're behaving as if they're in the first flush of love. It seems unlikely they're MI5, but you never know. I don't trust anyone.

From under the fringe of the ridiculous wig Nathan has insisted I wear for the whole journey, I glance at the seat in front of them. A teenage girl with bright pink hair and long, stripy socks pulled up above her knees below a short, pleated skirt, is nodding along to music from a pair of oversized headphones. It's so loud I keep catching the tinny beat. If the elderly couple are above suspicion because they're too old, surely she's too young to be a cop or a spy?

If there's anyone who's been planted on the coach to keep us under surveillance, it's the guy who took the seat in front of us after giving me a quick, silent once-over. He slung a threadbare rucksack down by his feet and is now slouching with nothing but the back of his faded baseball cap visible above the headrest. There's nothing memorable about him at all. I can't even remember what he was wearing. A pair of old jeans and a donkey jacket? I think he was unshaven, with patchy, dark stubble. Chocolate-brown eyes. It wouldn't surprise me if he turned out to be an undercover agent.

Two hours into the journey, Nathan finally wakes up, stretches and looks up and down the aisle. He takes my hand, rests it on my knee and gives it a reassuring squeeze.

'Where are we?'

'Just past Newmarket.'

'Did you sleep?'

'No.'

Nathan nods and grabs a bottle of water from the wire mesh pocket under the fold-up table by his knees.

'Are you going to tell me where we're going?'

He smiles enigmatically, like he's taking me on a day trip to the coast, rather than dragging me across the country on the run from the authorities. How insane is that? What are we even doing?

'Are we staying in Norwich?' I lower my voice, conscious of people, and particularly the guy in the baseball hat in front, listening.

'Just trust me, will you?' Nathan's grip tightens.

'I'm scared.'

'I'm scared too, but everything's going to work out. You'll see.'

'I'm worried what we're going to do for money.'

'I've got cash.'

'But how much? It's not going to last forever.'

Nathan scowls, a cloud falling across his face. 'I said, everything's going to work out.'

'But you do have a plan, don't you? Because I've just turned my back on everything. My flat. My family. My job.'

'You'd prefer jail, would you?' he hisses.

The seat in front of me creaks as the man in the baseball cap sits up straight and turns his head to look out of the window.

'Of course not, but we can't run forever.'

'Just stop it, Pippa. Just stop your whining.'

'But I just want to know —'

'God, you can be a real pain in the arse when you put your mind to it.' He glowers at me, nostrils flaring. 'I'll work it out. Now stop banging on. You're doing my head in.'

I shrink back into my seat, fold my arms across my chest, and rest my head against the cool glass. We're both tired and emotional, but there's no need to speak to me like that.

We don't talk for the rest of the journey, and when the coach finally pulls into the station at Norwich, Nathan insists we wait until all the other passengers have disembarked before we get off. He keeps his cap pulled down low over his eyes as we collect our rucksacks that have been dumped on the pavement by the driver.

I struggle with the weight of my bag and regret bringing so much when I don't have the strength to lift it onto my back. Nathan doesn't even stop to help. He's already striding off down the street and when I do finally manage to hoist it onto my shoulders, by sitting on the ground and sliding my arms through the straps, it's a battle to catch up with him.

When he spots I'm lagging behind, he turns on me and shouts. 'What are you dawdling for? Hurry up.'

My back twinges and my stomach rumbles. All I've eaten today is a croissant.

'I'm hungry. Can we grab something?' I ask, my energy dipping.

'Seriously? You're thinking about your stomach right now?'

'We've not had anything since first thing.' Usually I avoid eating carbs, but it was a croissant this morning or nothing.

'We'll pick up something later.'

I pull up to stretch my back, sweat dripping down my chest. I need a breather. I drop my rucksack and sit on it like it's a beanbag. 'Give me a minute.'

Nathan turns around with his hands on his hips. 'What are you doing?'

'I just...'

He marches towards me, pulls off his cap and wipes his brow. I'm glad to see he's sweating, too.

'Pip, we're in the middle of a city. There are CCTV cameras everywhere. The sooner we get out of here, the better.'

'I know, but I really need to eat something. Have you felt the weight of my rucksack?'

'And whose fault's that? I told you to pack light.'

Did he? I don't remember. He told me to bring whatever I needed until we could find somewhere to settle down.

'Please?'

He looks up and down the street, a wide road busy with free-flowing traffic.

'You can have a bag of chips,' he says, pointing down the street towards a miserable-looking fish and chip shop alongside an equally unappealing Chinese takeaway.

I shudder. The thought of greasy chips in an oil-soaked paper bag turns my stomach. He couldn't have suggested anything less healthy if he'd tried.

'I'd prefer a veggie wrap.'

Nathan shoots me a withering look. 'It's chips or nothing. But you'll have to hurry. I want to get to the ring road.'

'Why? What's there?'

He sighs as if I'm stupid. 'It's where we're going to hitch a ride to the coast.'

'The coast?'

'You want these chips or not?'

Predictably, the chips are stodgy, greasy, and covered in far too much salt. I force a handful of them down because I'm hungry, but they stick in my throat and form a starchy lump in my stomach. Nathan finishes what I can't manage, screws up the paper bag into a tight ball and tosses it into a waste bin.

'Let's go,' he orders, like we're on a route march.

I struggle again with hitching my rucksack onto my back and waddle to catch up with Nathan, who seems to know exactly where he's going.

'Is it much further?' We've been walking for miles and my shoulders are aching.

'Nearly there.'

When he finally pulls up at a bus stop on the side of a busy road and drops his rucksack, I could cry with relief.

He helps me off with my own bag, adjusts my wig and wipes away tracts of sweat pouring down my face with his thumb. I assume we're going to catch another bus, but Nathan has other ideas.

He guides me to the side of the road and instructs me to stick out my arm to hitch a ride.

'We need a lift to Blakeney,' he says. 'Smile and look sexy. Someone's bound to stop for a pretty face like yours.'

My insides wither and a little part of me dies.

'Oh no, Nathan, I can't,' I cry. I'm not standing on a street corner like a cheap hooker touting for business. 'Can't we get the bus?'

'We need to save our money.'

'But —'

'Stop whining, Pippa, and get on with it, will you? We don't have all day.'

'Where's Blakeney, anyway?'

'I told you. It's by the coast. It's only a little village, but it's perfect. Now, the sooner you get your thumb out, the sooner we'll be on our way.'

He gathers up our bags and hides them behind a nearby tree.

When Nathan persuaded me to come with him, he made it sound so appealing, like we'd be some kind of modern-day Bonnie and Clyde on the run from the law. I was swept up in the romance of it. I never imagined it would be like this. Nathan's not even being nice. He's hardly had a civil word to say to me since we left London. Snappy and irritable. I can't seem to do or say anything right.

He crouches down out of view as I run a finger under the wig and scratch my scalp, chasing an irritating itch. Sod this. If he wants me to hitch a ride, I'm not wearing it. It's pointless, uncomfortable and undignified. And if he dares say anything about it, I'll tell him exactly where he can shove it.

I ram the wig into my pocket, pull my ponytail loose and run my nails through my hair. I shake my head and take a breath of the chill air.

I've never hitched a ride in my life. I've never needed or wanted to. There's nothing glamorous about begging strangers for a lift. It's grubby and desperate, but I suppose that's what we are. Desperate. And in trouble. I need to swallow my pride.

Most of the drivers who fly past don't even look me in the eye. A small number stare, curious, and a few single men in white vans leer at me with the kind of unwanted attention that makes my skin crawl. And for the first hour, not a single motorist shows the slightest interest in pulling over.

Although I'm feeling less self-conscious, I'm beginning to lose hope. My arm's sore and my cheeks ache from smiling. It's a waste of time. If we'd taken a bus or a train, we'd probably be there by now, wherever *there* is.

Nathan pops up from behind the tree as I glance over my shoulder, hoping he'll see the futility of carrying on and call it quits.

But he gives me a thumbs up and a big smile. It's the first time he's smiled at me all day. 'You're doing great. Keep going,' he mouths over the rush of the traffic.

Somewhere in the distance, a siren wails. Living in London, I'm used to the sound of sirens day and night. It's part of city life, like putting up with standing on crowded, stuffy Underground trains to get anywhere in the summer or accepting we have to pay the best part of our monthly income to afford anywhere half decent to rent.

But we're not in London and the siren's wail catches my attention. Chances are it's an ambulance. Or a fire engine. I step back from the road as the wail grows louder, carried on the freezing February air, the vehicle coming closer.

I squint into the distance, looking beyond the oncoming traffic and spot pulsing blue lights. A car heading towards us, at speed.

'Get down!' Nathan yells. He snatches my arm and pulls me violently backwards, towards the tree he's hiding behind.

We stumble, tripping over our rucksacks, and Nathan pulls me inelegantly down onto the ground.

'Stay still!' he hisses in my ear. 'It's the cops.'

Chapter 31

JAMES
February 27, 2024

Samantha plucks a key on a short length of pink ribbon from her bag and, without knocking, lets herself into Pippa's flat.

'Pip,' she calls out. 'Are you home? It's only me.'

I hover on the doorstep. It seems odd to invite myself in while Pippa's not here, as if I'm breaking a taboo. But it can't be trespass if I'm here with her sister, who's let herself in with a key, can it?

Samantha's already halfway up the stairs before she notices I'm not following.

'James, come on,' she beckons. 'What are you doing?'

'Coming.'

I push the door closed and join Samantha in an open-plan lounge-dining area that's instantly recognisable from Pippa's videos. She's even left the tripod and lights that she uses for filming set up by the window.

Samantha and I stand side-by-side for a moment, looking around like we're detectives examining a crime scene. As far as I can see, nothing's out of place. Nothing to indicate Pippa left in a hurry, more like she's popped to the shops and could be home at any moment. There's a laptop on the table. Stacks of books lined up neatly on wooden shelves. A spread of lifestyle magazines fanned out on the coffee table in front of the TV.

'I'll check her bedroom,' Samantha says. 'See if you can find anything useful out here.'

'Like what?'

'I don't know. A notebook or a scrap of paper. Somewhere she's written her passwords.'

I think it's highly unlikely that someone like Pippa would be foolish enough to write down her passwords. She's more likely to have them in her head or in a digital safe on her phone. But we're here now. It's worth checking. But where do I start?

I wander into a small but functional kitchen. The worktops are uncluttered and there are no dirty dishes left lying on the side, but before I start hunting through the cupboards, I spot Pippa's phone in the sink, its sparkly pink case tossed to one side.

Alongside the phone, a tiny SIM card lies dangerously close to the plughole.

I pluck them both out and hold them up to the light spilling through the window. I can almost guarantee this is Nathan's work. I bet he's told her that she can be tracked through her phone and has convinced her to leave it behind.

'Her bedroom's an absolute bomb site. Clothes everywhere. I think you're right, she left in a hurry,' Samantha says, wandering up behind me. 'What's that?'

'Pippa's phone. I found it in the sink, minus the SIM card.'

'Not taking any chances, are they?'

'Wherever they've gone, they don't want to be found, that's for sure. I'd say it's almost certainly Nathan's idea.'

'I told you he was controlling. Find anything else?'

I shake my head. 'No, but this could work to our advantage.'

Samantha scowls. 'How?'

I pull open a drawer, find a fork, use it to tease open the SIM slot and reinstall the SIM, then power up the phone and wait for it to reboot. It only takes a few seconds.

'What are you doing?'

'If we can get into her phone, we don't need to worry about finding her passwords. The chances are, all her passwords for all her apps will be remembered on the device.' I glance at Samantha and grin, buoyed by the opportunity Pippa has inadvertently presented to us.

As the phone completes its power-up cycle, a lock screen pops up, showing an image of two young children wrapped up in woolly hats and scarves, their faces beaming, their noses rosy.

'These your kids?' I ask, showing Samantha.

She peers over my shoulder. 'That's Freddie and Isabella. I didn't know she had that photo on her phone. That's so sweet.'

I swipe up and when the phone doesn't recognise my face, it demands a passcode.

'Any ideas?'

Samantha chews her lip. 'Give it to me.'

She punches in four numbers and passes the phone back again.

'How did you do that so quickly?'

'We've used the same code for years. It's from a cartoon we used to watch when we were kids. One-two-two-one. Don't you remember? From *The Wishing Clock*? Every day when this big old grandfather clock struck twelve twenty-one, the kids could make a wish and it would instantly come true. We thought it was the coolest thing ever and it kind of stuck. It's our lucky number, I suppose.'

I have no idea what she's talking about, but my focus has already moved on, looking for Pippa's Instagram app, conscious it's another violation of her privacy.

'We should check her messages,' Samantha says. 'In case there's anything from Nathan.' She snatches the phone back.

I turn away. It's not my place to snoop through Pippa's messages. It's bad enough that we've broken into her flat.

'No, there's nothing from him since before he disappeared,' she says.

'Right, let's go back to the plan and post an appeal on her Instagram page. Now you're in her phone, you shouldn't need a password.'

'Do you think I should post the message from me?'

'Makes sense. People are more likely to take it seriously if it's come from the family.'

'Okay.' She thinks for a moment or two before her thumbs fly across the screen, typing. 'What about this?'

She holds up the phone to show me. Under a smiling picture of Pippa that I assume she found in her photo album, she's added a caption.

This is Pippa's sister, Sam. Pippa has gone missing, and we're extremely worried about her safety. It's not clear what's happened to her, or if she's in any kind of danger, but we need your help to find her and make sure she's safe. She was last seen at her flat in Camden late on Sunday night, but she's left her phone and laptop behind, which is totally out of character. We're hoping her community of followers can help us by keeping an eye out for her. We think she might be travelling with her boyfriend, Nathan, but we have no way of contacting either of them. Please, if you see her or know where she might be, leave a comment or send a direct message to this account and we'll pick it up. Thank you so much. Sam x

'Perfect.'

'Does it sound okay?'

'It's great. You'd better hold on to her phone and let me know if it turns up anything.'

'Fine. So I guess now we wait.'

I sigh. 'I suppose so.' I'd rather be doing something active to find Pippa. I don't trust Nathan, and I don't think we should sit around waiting for a miracle.

I glance around the flat, looking for any clues we've missed.

'We've done everything we can for now,' Samantha says.

'I guess you're right. There's nothing more we can do for now.'

Chapter 32

PIPPA
February 27, 2024

While we cower behind the tree, the police car hurtles past in a blur, its siren deafening.

'Don't move,' Nathan hissed in my ear as he dragged me back from the road. 'I wouldn't be surprised if every police force in the country has our details by now.'

So this is what it feels like to be a fugitive on the run. Except we've done nothing wrong. All Nathan is guilty of is being in the wrong place at the wrong time. I don't know if I can deal with this constant looking over our shoulders, worried that at any moment we're going to be caught. And then what? Maybe we'd be better off handing ourselves in and taking our chances, especially with a competent lawyer on our side. As far as I can tell, there are no legitimate grounds to detain us or charge us with anything. But how do I persuade Nathan? I've never seen him so scared.

As the wail of the siren fades and the car vanishes into the distance, we pick ourselves up. An unexpected euphoria bubbles up from my stomach and I laugh, the relief bursting the tension like a hot needle piercing a swollen blister.

'You ready to try again?' Nathan asks, his sombre expression instantly sobering me up.

'Try what again?'

'Finding us a ride.'

I groan. I hate standing by the road with my thumb out, begging. It's so cheapening. 'Why this place Blakeney anyway?'

'I know somewhere we can lie low for a while until I figure out what to do next.'

I assume that means he knows of a property in the village where we can stay. Maybe a holiday cottage his family owns. I've heard of Blakeney, but I've no idea how far it is from here. The only time I've ever been to Norfolk was years ago with my family when we stayed on a boat on the Norfolk Broads.

'It's beautiful. You're going to love it.' He nods towards the road and shoves me gently in the back. 'Give it one last big effort.'

Surely a bus wouldn't cost much, but Nathan's being stubborn. He says he doesn't want to spend the money, but I think he's worried someone might recognise us. It's not as if our pictures have been plastered over the news. At least, not yet. With a resigned sigh, I amble back to the bus stop, turn my lips up into a forced smile, and focus on the traffic. After all, I only need to persuade one driver to stop and give us a lift.

Another forty minutes pass. I can hardly feel my toes anymore and my fingers and nose are numb with cold. But it'll be worth it when I'm curled up in front of a roaring fire in a picturesque, thatched cottage, cradling a mug of warm soup, watching the waves roll onto the shore and listening to the seagulls as they wheel around lazily in leaden skies.

I've always been a city girl. I was born and raised in Winchester, before spending three years as a student in Manchester and then moving to London to pursue a career in health and fitness, but I can see the appeal of living a less complicated life at a slower pace in Norfolk. I don't need to be in the city to work. As long as I can connect to the internet, and I have a phone and a laptop, I can work anywhere I fancy. Maybe I'll even start a new channel helping people to disconnect from their busy lives and promoting the benefits of relocating to the country. I could shoot videos on the beach and around the house. Maybe I could concoct some new recipes and talk about the benefits of natural ingredients.

My mind races, my stomach twisting with excitement. In time, maybe Nathan and I could even start a family and I could expand the channel into a resource for new mothers. The opportunities are endless.

I'm so lost in the fantasy of my new life in the country that I don't register that a car has pulled up in the bus bay until the driver winds down her window and beckons me over.

'Where are you heading?' she asks, peering through wire-rimmed glasses that have hazy, smudged lenses.

I lean on the roof and speak to her through the open driver's window. 'Blakeney. Are you going that way, by any chance?'

'I can take you as far as Cromer. Does that help?'

I don't know. I have no idea whether Cromer is close to Blakeney or even if it's in the right direction. I glance back towards the tree, helplessly looking for Nathan. He's already heading towards the road, struggling with our heavy rucksacks.

'This lovely lady says she can take us to Cromer.'

'Oh, I didn't realise there were two of you.' For a moment, I think she's going to change her mind and drive off. My heart sinks.

'Sorry. Would that be okay? This is my boyfriend.'

'Hi,' he says with a cheery smile and a wave.

I can't spend another minute with my arm out, prostituting myself at the side of the road because Nathan's too tight - or too worried - to take the bus. Every cell in my body wills her to let us get in.

The woman climbs out of the car and throws open the boot. 'I don't mind, but there's not much space for your bags, I'm afraid.'

I let out a sigh of relief. She tells us her name is Carolyn, or Carrie for short, and that she's a grandmother with four children, three grandchildren and another on the way. She's a retired schoolteacher and a widow who's on her way home after a morning volunteering at a charity shop in Norwich.

Thankfully, she's more interested in telling us about herself than she is about quizzing us, which saves me from having to lie. I sit back, my body slowly thawing in the warmth of the car, and let her talk. Nathan slinks down low in the back, staying quiet. I don't have the energy to chat, but Carrie seems to be happy filling the time, telling us all about her life.

When she drops us off at a petrol station on the outskirts of Cromer, I offer to pay some money towards fuel. It's the least we can do, although I sense Nathan scowling at me. I know we don't have much cash, but it would have cost a fortune if we'd taken a taxi.

'Don't be silly,' Carries says, waving away my offer. 'I was coming this way anyway. And to be honest, it's nice to have the company.'

The petrol station offers better opportunities for hitching a lift for the final leg of our journey, somewhere we can accost drivers as they're filling up. Instead of hours, it only takes twenty minutes for a courier driver in a white van to agree to give us a lift.

He's the polar opposite of Carrie, an overweight, monosyllabic hulk of a man with a body odour problem, who wears sunglasses, even though the sun's not out, and drives so aggressively that when he finally drops us off just outside the village centre, I'm green with nausea. He's not interested in talking and I spend the entire journey with my hands pressed into the dashboard, bracing myself as he attacks every corner far too fast.

He mounts the pavement as he pulls over and I waste no time jumping out to gulp in deep lungfuls of briny sea air to clear my head and settle my stomach, while Nathan retrieves our rucksacks from the back where they've been stowed amongst piles of packages and parcels.

We follow a sign to the quay, past pretty flint cottages with red-tile roofs and attractive walled gardens and, after all the stress and worry of getting here, my heart lifts. It's a village steeped in history, where every property, every weather-beaten fence post, is a reminder of a simpler time where mornings don't begin with the wail of a siren, but with the gentle lapping of the tide and the rustle of reeds.

'What do you think?' Nathan asks.

'I love it. It's so pretty.'

We cross a road onto a promenade running alongside the quay where a dozen pleasure craft are moored. I can't wait to see the house. Nathan's never mentioned his family owning a second home before, but I'm guessing that's why we've ended up here of all places. To hide in the family bolt-hole until we work out what to do next.

'Is it in the village?' I ask.

'What?'

'The house.'

'Not exactly. It's a little more remote. Somewhere we won't be disturbed. You're going to love it.'

The promenade spills into a large gravel car park which is largely empty, although I imagine it gets busy during the tourist season. In fact, the whole place has the hollow feel of an out-of-season resort. Not quite abandoned, but quiet and undisturbed as if all the residents have either left for the winter or are hunkering down inside in the warm.

'Hungry?' Nathan asks.

'Famished.' All I've eaten today is a croissant and a handful of indigestible chips. What I wouldn't give for a steaming bowl of spiced butternut squash and coconut soup.

Sadly, the village doesn't appear to be at the cutting edge of vegan cuisine. I might have to settle for whatever we can find and suffer for it later.

Nathan sets off towards a mobile food shack on the edge of the car park. As we approach, a young woman behind the counter puts the book she was reading to one side and drags herself to her feet, looking less than impressed at being interrupted. She stands, bored, while Nathan and I study a menu chalked on an A-board.

'Two toasted halloumi sandwiches,' Nathan says.

A please and a thank you wouldn't go amiss. He can be so rude to people sometimes. To counter Nathan's brusqueness, I flash a friendly smile at the woman, who on closer inspection isn't much more than a girl. A flicker of recognition flits across her face. She stares at me for a second or two longer than feels comfortable and for a moment I think she's going to say something. My smile solidifies into a rictus grin. The last thing we need in a small town is someone recognising me. I half expect her to ask for a selfie. It's what most people want and usually I'm more than happy to oblige, but I'm already preparing the lie in my head. If she asks, I'll tell her she's made a mistake and that I've never heard of Pippa Ravencroft. But thankfully she spares me the indignity, either deciding she's mistaken or is too shy to say anything. She returns to sullenly making our sandwiches without a word.

We eat at a picnic table overlooking the quay.

'Are you going to tell me where we're staying?' I ask between mouthfuls.

Nathan points into the distance, across the mudflats, towards the sea. 'Out there.'

At first, I think he's joking. I can't see anything beyond the quay other than windswept salt marshes and a vast expanse of grey sky.

'No, seriously. Where is it? I can't wait to get settled in. I'm dying for a long soak in the bath, although at this point I'd settle for a decent shower. I feel so grubby.'

Nathan smirks. 'I don't know what you're expecting, Pip, but this isn't supposed to be a holiday.'

'No, but —'

'We're supposed to be lying low, remember? It's the perfect hideaway. No one's going to find us out here.'

'It's not your parents' holiday home?'

Nathan frowns, his eyes searching my face. 'My parents' what?'

'I thought...' A strangled sigh escapes my lips. 'It doesn't matter.'

I gaze out across the barren landscape as a brief glimpse of the sun slips behind a bank of dark cloud. Why do I suddenly have a bad feeling about this? No one knows we're here. No one knows I'm with Nathan. I didn't tell anyone I was leaving London. Not even Sam. She's going to be frantic when she realises I'm missing and not answering my phone. I should have left a note and told her not to worry.

'It's an adventure,' Nathan says.

'Hmm?'

'Just you and me. No phones. No family. No stress. We can really reconnect out here. It's going to be so good for us.'

'There is a house, though?' I ask, my dreams of an open fire, a soft sofa and a mug of warming soup fading like a receding tide.

'Of course.'

I finish my sandwich, wipe my fingers on a paper napkin, and take a swig of water. 'I'd like to see it. Is it far from here?'

'We'll need to take a boat.'

'Boat?'

'Otherwise, it's a bit of a long hike.'

'But we don't have a boat.'

Nathan gives me a knowing look. 'That's why we need to wait until after dark.'

Chapter 33

JAMES
February 27, 2025

A snaking train bound for Stratford winds into Camden Road station, its brakes squealing as it slows to a halt, shoving a rush of air in its path. If I hop off at Highbury and Islington, I can pick up the Tube and be back at the gym in thirty minutes, but as I climb on board a half-empty carriage and find a seat by the window etched with indecipherable graffiti, a knot of anxiety tightens in my core. I can't concentrate on anything else while Pippa's missing. I need to find her, but how? I have no idea where she is, or how much trouble she's in, although if she's with Nathan, it's hard not to assume the worst.

He's treated her appallingly, vanishing without trace after the bombing and letting her think he was dead, but she seems to have conveniently forgotten about that and completely bought into his delusions. He's clearly mentally and emotionally unstable, but does that make him dangerous? Maybe. Probably. There's certainly no way of predicting how he might react if he's cornered, and that almost certainly puts Pippa in danger.

If his state of mind is so troubled, there's no knowing what he'll do. The sooner I find them, the better. Posting an appeal asking for sightings was a good idea of Samantha's, but I can't wait around on the off chance someone on Instagram spots them. It could take days, or weeks, if someone spots them at all. But where to start? I have absolutely no idea where they've gone.

The train lurches as it pulls away, wheels and axles clunking and squealing. My eye drifts to a map above the window, which shows all the stops along the line. It's only two stops to my station. After it, Canonbury, Dalston, and then Hackney, where Nathan's brother, Ryan, lives.

The last time I spoke to him, the oily little prick brazenly lied to me, telling me he hadn't seen his brother in weeks, while all the time he was harbouring him. And I believed his lies. I even apologised for bothering him and told Pippa to stay away. How naïve.

The train arrives at Highbury and Islington. The carriage doors crank open and a white-haired old woman wrapped up in a tartan coat steps off. It's where I intended to pick up a Victoria Line train north to the gym, but a better idea pops into my head. If anyone knows where Nathan has taken Pippa, it's his lying, scumbag brother. Time to pay Ryan another visit, and this time I'm not going to be fobbed off.

It's only a fifteen-minute walk from Hackney station to his flat at a hurried pace and by the time I arrive, I've worked myself into a fevered ill-temper, remembering how Ryan looked me in the eye the last time I was here and told me with utter conviction that he'd not seen Nathan in weeks.

I sprint up the steps to his ridiculously shiny black front door and hammer at the brass knocker.

Ryan answers with his phone clamped to his ear, chewing the end of a plastic ballpoint pen, and doesn't appear to recognise me at first, distracted by his call.

I wait patiently for him to finish and for the penny to drop. It gives me the chance to get a proper measure of the man, but there's not much I like. He has the swagger of a used-car salesman, scruffy stubble and shirtsleeves rolled up to his forearms, the cuffs hanging loose. Casually smart. The home workers' uniform since Covid. His piggy little eyes stare at the ground as he laughs and jokes with the caller on the line.

'Tony, mate, got to go. Someone at the door.'

He hangs up and finally looks into my face.

'Sorry about that —' he begins, before his dark eyes widen in surprise.

'Hello, Ryan.'

He attempts to shut the door in my face, but I'm too quick. I already have my foot inside and the door jams against it.

'What do you want?'

'You lied to me.'

The colour in his face drains away and he stares, blinking. 'I don't know what you're talking about.'

'Where is he?' I ask, enunciating slowly and clearly.

'Who?'

'Let's not play this game again. Where's Nathan? He's disappeared with Pippa. I want to know where they've gone.'

'No idea, mate.'

It's not so much his words that snap my patience as the snivelling, snide expression that creeps across his duplicitous face. I lunge at him and he falls into the hall where I pin him against the wall with my forearm across his throat, crushing his windpipe, our noses virtually touching, his fear as sour as vinegar.

There are many times when I've wished I wasn't as tall or as broad as I am and that I could shrink into the shadows without attracting attention or trouble. All those occasions when I've been out for a quiet drink and certain types of men, particularly when they've had a pint or six, see me as a challenge to their own masculinity and try to goad me into a fight. But this time, I'm glad my physique is so intimidating.

'Wrong answer. Where are they?'

'I haven't seen them, I promise.' His voice quivers.

'Don't lie to me!' I don't often find the need to raise my voice, but I can't help it with Ryan. There's just something so maddening about him. Spittle flies from my mouth and sprays his face.

Ryan grimaces and squirms, trying to break free. I press my arm harder, until his face turns purple and his eyes bulge.

'I... can't... breathe,' he gasps.

'If he's laid a finger on Pippa, I'll kill you both. Understand?'

I release the pressure on his neck a fraction and he sucks in a breath, his eyes watering. He coughs and a trail of spittle dribbles from the corner of his mouth.

'He's not going to hurt her. He loves her.'

'Is that right?'

'Yes! He worships the ground that woman walks on.'

'So where are they?'

'Honestly, mate, I don't know.'

'I'm not your mate and I've warned you already, stop lying to me.'

I lean into his throat to emphasise my point, enjoying the way his eyes almost pop out of their sockets.

'Alright,' he croaks.

'Alright, you're going to tell me everything you know?'

He nods, grasping my arm with his puny fingers, trying to pry them away from his neck.

'So start talking.'

'He's trying to prove himself to her. It's not a crime.'

'What do you mean? Prove himself how? Where's he taken her?'

'You know he proposed?'

'So?'

'And she turned him down in front of everyone? It was humiliating for him.'

I remember being surprised when Pippa told me he was so upset he stormed out of the restaurant like a petulant child. I couldn't believe the fragility of his ego, but good on Pippa for not being pressurised into doing something she didn't want to do.

'It still doesn't explain where they've gone. Keep talking.'

His Adam's apple bobs up and down against my arm as he struggles to swallow. 'He thought he'd lost her forever. He was devastated, and worried he wasn't good enough for her.'

'At least that's something we can agree on,' I growl.

Ryan scowls. 'He thought he could change her mind by showing her she was wrong about him.'

I shake my head. 'What do you mean?'

'The attack on Tower Bridge,' he says. 'It was a perfect opportunity for Nathan to prove to Pippa what kind of man he is, by helping all those people who'd been injured, and heading into danger without worrying about himself.'

I snort. 'Oh, yeah, a real superhero.'

Ryan casts his gaze sideways. 'Except, he froze. He said it was too horrific. He didn't know where to start.'

What a snowflake. 'So the only reason he abandoned Pippa was to act the hero? Except he didn't have the balls.'

'He's not proud of himself.'

Okay, so now it's all starting to make sense. 'And that's why he vanished?'

'He was embarrassed.'

'Yeah, I bet. What a deadbeat.' As I've always suspected, Pippa's better off without him. I've no idea what she saw in him in the first place. 'You still haven't answered my question. Where are they?'

'I'm trying to explain.'

I push my face up close to Ryan's, towering over him, using my size as a weapon. 'Oh, I get it alright. Your brother's a waste of space, but I don't care. All I care about is making sure he doesn't hurt Pippa. So for the final time, where are they?'

'I'm trying to tell you if you'd listen to me. When he realised there was nothing he could do for those people, he ran.'

'Like a true coward.'

'Whatever. You weren't there, big guy. Anyway, he turned up here, out of his mind and jabbering on about being caught up in the bombing and how he'd let Pippa down. To be honest, he wasn't making much sense. So, yes, I took him in, but he was in no fit state to go home.'

There's still a big missing piece of the jigsaw. 'And this van that he says turned up and all this nonsense about a conspiracy, what's all that about?'

I study Ryan's face, watching for any hint that he's lying to me again.

He takes a deep breath, his gaze fixed on the floor. 'We made that up.'

'Why?'

'We had to do something after Pippa spotted him in the pub. Talk about bad luck being in the same pub at the same time. I only took Nathan for a quick pint to cheer him up. I didn't even know she'd seen us until she came around here carping on about having checked the CCTV footage, which is when I knew we were screwed, because it was obvious Pippa wasn't going to let it go until she had some answers.'

'So you came up with this cock-and-bull story?'

Ryan nods. At least he has the decency to look ashamed. 'You don't understand how miserable he was. He thought he'd lost everything. But I saw it as an opportunity. If we could convince Pippa he'd been forced into hiding, rather than vanishing out of shame, he could come out of it looking like a hero after all.'

'And she'd jump back into his arms?'

'Something like that.'

'But he lied to her,' I point out. 'None of it is true.'

I can't believe they actually thought it was a good idea. It's so sick and twisted. Pippa deserves so much better.

I let Ryan go and step back, scratching my head. 'She was terrified. She thought someone had been in her flat. She even convinced herself she'd found a hidden camera in the smoke alarm. You know that when she finds out the truth, she's never going to forgive him.'

Ryan smirks as he runs a finger around his collar and rubs his neck. It's as much as I can do not to punch him.

'We didn't think she'd believe it, so we had to take steps to convince her,' he says.

'You?' I gasp. '*You* broke into her flat?'

'Actually, Nathan. He had a key and let himself in while I took Pippa out for a chat.'

'And the camera? The silent phone calls?'

Ryan nods. 'All Nathan. He even hacked her Instagram account.'

'You're a monster.'

Ryan frowns. 'I like to think I was helping the course of true love along its way.'

'Great. So now she thinks Nathan's Jason Bourne and they've gone to ground. I hope you're proud of yourself. Where are they, Ryan?'

'What? She's having the time of her life. Pippa thinks her boyfriend's a hero. It's like she's living in her own spy movie.'

'Except it's all lies.'

'Does it matter?'

'Of course it matters, you prick! Your brother's abducted her under false pretences.'

Ryan laughs an ugly laugh. 'Nobody's forced her to do anything. Let them sort it out for themselves.'

'Call Nathan. Tell him it's over and that he needs to bring Pippa home.'

'Why, are you jealous?'

'Fuck you, Ryan. Just do it.'

'They're supposed to be on the run, remember? He left his phone behind.'

'You must be able to get hold of him.'

'He's incommunicado. I did my bit. It's down to Nathan to seal the deal now.'

Seal the deal? What the hell? This is Pippa's life we're talking about. With a roar of anger, I throw myself at Ryan, snatch the collar of his shirt in my fist, and smash his head against the wall. He howls in pain, but I'm not finished with him. I spin him around and clench his head in the crook of my arm, squeezing tightly. He thrashes around in panic.

'Tell me where they've gone!' I scream. 'Where's Nathan taken her?'

Ryan fights back for a few seconds before his body goes limp. When I release his head, he falls to the floor, gasping. I roll him onto his back and raise my clenched fist. I might not be much of a street brawler, but right now, I'd happily break every bone in his face.

'Last chance.'

Ryan raises his arms to shield his face. 'Don't hit me, please,' he begs.

I feign a punch and he flinches. 'Talk!'

'I don't know for sure, I promise. He didn't tell me, but if I had to guess, he'll have gone to Norfolk. He loves it there. It's where we used to spend all our family holidays.'

'Where in Norfolk?'

'It could be anywhere. The Broads. The coast. We went to different places, but I'd stake my life that's where you'll find him. It's where he feels safe.'

I lower my arm and stand, peering down at the pathetic, snivelling scumbag at my feet.

'If you're lying to me, Ryan, I swear to god I'll be back. And next time it won't be pretty.'

Transcript from the podcast, Fallen Hero.
Interview with Ian Derbyshire, boat owner

I've lived in Blakeney all my life. It's a peaceful village. Most people come for the birds and the seals. A bit of tranquillity, although it gets too busy in the summer. We don't get much crime, which is why I was so surprised when I realised what had happened.

My first thought was that I must have forgotten to tie her up properly, but that's not like me. Me and Molly Mae *go back a long way and I'm always so careful. The only other explanation was that she'd been stolen. But who'd want to steal my old rowing boat when there's a dozen fancy yachts moored up at the quay? Bless her, I'm fond of her, but she's not much to look at.*

I figured it must have been kids. Maybe some drunken teenagers who'd taken her out on the river on the high tide. There'd been one due at around midnight, which was a bit of a worry because it's a dangerous stretch of water. You need to know what you're doing around the cuts and the currents. I've been doing it all my life and even I wouldn't want to do it in the dark. It's too dangerous, and the water's freezing at that time of year. If they'd fallen in, they wouldn't have stood a chance.

Though it wasn't the water that worried me most. It was the mud. The tide goes out so quickly, you see, and it can catch even the most experienced boatman by surprise. It's easy to get stranded, and if Molly Mae *had become trapped on the flats, and they'd hopped out thinking they could push her free, it would have been a disaster.*

The mud is like treacle. All gloopy and thick. It grabs your legs and it don't let go. It pulls you down and it holds you firm. You certainly wouldn't want to get caught in it while the tide's coming in, and it wouldn't be the first time there had been deaths on the flats. So you can see why that's what I was most afraid of.

Chapter 34

PIPPA
February 27, 2024

Every muscle in my body shivers uncontrollably as I hand Nathan my rucksack and he tosses it into the back of the boat as if it weighs no more than a bag of sugar. Freezing water laps over my trainers, soaking my socks and up my jeans to my knees, while my numb feet squelch in the soft mud. In the dark that envelopes us, unseen birds screech, whistle and warble with a haunting melancholy that cuts through the stillness of the night.

Nathan grips my arm and pulls me on board, his other hand clasping a torch whose beam bounces and jitters, illuminating flashes of ripples across the fast-flowing waters of the narrow river and the spiky tufts of grass growing haphazardly across the mudflats.

My feet suck out of the mud and I stumble into the vessel, falling onto a hard bench next to my bag. I wrap my arms around my body and brace myself against the cold as Nathan unties the mooring rope and pushes us off with a single wooden oar.

We've been hanging around the harbour for so long, the cold has seeped into my core and deep into my bones, settling like an unwanted visitor who's reluctant to leave. I can't imagine ever being warm again. Which is why, when Nathan announced he was going to steal a boat to reach the house, I didn't put up much of a fight, especially as the alternative was a three or four-hour hike along the beach. I just want to get inside and get warm. And besides, Nathan's promised he'll return the boat first thing before its owner even realises it's gone. He says we're borrowing it, not stealing it.

'How far is it?' I ask, teeth chattering.

Nathan settles on a bench facing me. He hands me the torch and instructs me to guide him in the right direction, although I have no idea which is the right way. I guess we just follow the river.

'Ten minutes. Maybe less,' he says. 'Keep us in the centre of the channel. Don't let me drift.' He dips the oars into the water and begins a lazy stroke, propelling us forwards. He makes it look effortless, like he's rowed since the day he was born.

We spent the afternoon and early evening keeping our heads down, killing time while we waited for dark to fall and the tide to rise. Nathan identified the boat earlier in the day. A nondescript wooden rowing boat moored on the muddy banks of the River Glaven. I liked her name, *Molly Mae*, like she was a real person helping us on our journey.

I've still no idea what to expect of the house Nathan's taking us to. All I know is that it's so remote we need a boat to get there. Ordinarily, I'd think it was romantic. The sort of weekend escape you'd see on Instagram with gorgeous young couples posing on the beach with flutes of champagne or staring wistfully from an open bedroom window as linen curtains billow in a warm breeze. But as I sit frozen, staring ahead through the darkness at the choppy, frigid waters, I have a horrible feeling it's not going to be anything like that.

But as long as it's warm. And there's a bed. And a bath with hot water...

Oh, how luxurious it would be to slip into the enticing embrace of a warm bath.

The river widens, but I struggle to hold the torch steady with my arm twitching and shaking, my body desperately trying to generate some heat.

'A little to the left,' I instruct.

Nathan adjusts our trajectory and glances over his shoulder, following the curve of a muddy bank to our right.

The plop of the oars dipping in and out of the water in the silence is mildly hypnotic, although we're far from alone. There are creatures all around. I can hear the occasional flap of wings, plaintive cries and splashes in the water, as if we're surrounded. Unwelcome intruders stealing our way into nature's dark lair.

Nathan checks our position several times before manoeuvring the boat towards a narrow inlet. With the light from the torch, I pick out a dark, rickety jetty, forlornly standing on tiptoes out of the mud. A long, craggy witch's finger beckoning us closer.

'Grab the mooring line,' Nathan says. 'Tie us up.'

I hunt in the bottom of the boat for the soggy, slimy rope and stand unsteadily as we drift close to the jetty, before stumbling ashore to tie off the mooring line.

Nathan checks my knot, nods his approval and retrieves our rucksacks while I shine the torch across the bleak landscape. I still can't see the house, but there's another distinctive sound now. The swell of the sea and the rush of waves on the shore. We must be close.

The house finally appears like a mirage as we march up a slippery track, a pimple on the horizon against a charcoal sky, sitting as if in exile at the end of the world like a forgotten relic, dark and crumbling. Everything about it looks wrong, from the single crooked chimney stack to its slanting walls and its tiny windows like dead eyes staring out across the flats.

'Is that it?' I ask, trying not to sound disappointed. Nathan's done his best and I don't want him to think I'm ungrateful.

'What do you think? Nobody will ever find us out here.'

I doubt anyone would even think to look. It's so remote, so foreboding, and as we draw closer, it appears virtually uninhabitable.

'Is it derelict?'

Nathan laughs. 'It's a holiday home.'

'Don't be ridiculous.'

'What? It is. For people who want to escape the rat run. Some people don't want luxury and full board when they go away. Some people are looking for a simpler way of life, where they can get back to nature.'

'You've actually paid for us to stay here?'

'Not exactly, but I figured it would be empty at this time of year. It's an old watch house. They built it as a lookout for smugglers in the eighteen hundreds. Me and Ryan used to come here exploring when we were kids. It's perfect, don't you think?'

I don't know what to say. It's so far from what I imagined, I'm lost for words. For a start, it's tiny. I doubt there's more than a single room on the ground floor. Maybe a solitary bedroom in the attic. And everything about it is weathered and decaying. The paintwork around the window frames and door is cracked and peeling, the walls disintegrating, eroded and scarred over the years by salt and sea air.

'It's... unique.'

'I knew you'd love it.' Nathan grins and plants a kiss on my forehead.

'It's only for a few days though, yeah? Until we can sort out a plan?'

'Let's see. I think we're going to have a great time. It's going to be an adventure. Just what we both need.' He takes the torch from me and swings it towards a small outbuilding. 'It is a little basic, though.'

My heart plummets. 'Is that an outside loo?' As if this could get any worse.

'It's part of its charm.'

'There is electricity though, right?'

Nathan shakes his head. 'It doesn't even have running water, although there is a rainwater butt if we need to wash.'

I stare at him in disbelief. 'I can't even have a bath?' What kind of hellhole is this?

'It's a good job we picked up plenty of drinking water.' He grins at me like it's a big joke.

I want to cry.

'Do you even have a key?' I nod at the painted wooden door at the top of a short flight of grey stone steps where someone has left a pile of painted stones and a small collection of shells. If it's intended to lend the house a charming holiday vibe, it doesn't work. It's just a bit creepy.

With a grunt, Nathan drives his shoulder against the door, splintering it open with an echoing crack.

'We don't need a key. Shall we make ourselves at home?'

I stare down the track towards the jetty and the boat we stole, but as tempting as it is to run away back to the village, the bitter wind driving off the sea dissuades me of the notion. The house at least provides some shelter, even if there is no electricity.

'We can light a fire, I presume?'

'Let's go and see.'

Inside, the house is dark and oppressive, the paint peeling from the walls, the stone floors cold and bare, although at least it's out of the wind, even if it's not exactly warm.

Nathan's torch casts long, eerie shadows as he goes from room to room, exploring a minuscule kitchen, a slightly larger bedroom with a single, narrow window and a pair of rickety camping beds, and a dining room with a fireplace and battered table and chairs. The wind rattles the glass in the windows, making them whistle with a haunting melody.

I tighten my grip on Nathan's elbow, staying close behind him as he wanders through the house, shadows dancing at the periphery of my vision like ghosts daring me to catch them.

'Not too shabby, is it?' Nathan's jaunty tone is at complete odds with the chill of fear lodged in my chest.

'You can't really expect us to stay here.'

'Why not? Look, there's some firewood. Why don't I light a fire and some candles? It'll feel cosier when it's warmed up.'

He points the torch at a tiled mantelpiece and a row of stubby white candles embedded into solidified pools of wax, and lights them with a match from a box left next to a pile of driftwood by the fireplace.

'There, you see? Better already.'

I drop my rucksack and rub the tops of my arms, staring at the shimmering candles as their light grows brighter and our shadows creep up the walls. Nathan grabs a handful of driftwood, tosses it into the fireplace and lights a fire using another match and some sheets of screwed-up newspaper that have been left with the wood pile.

As the wood crackles and pops under the flickering fingers of the flames, it's not long before the room begins to lose its chill. It's a far cry from my flat in Camden and all the comforts I've taken for granted all these years. My warm bed. Radiators in every room that heat up at the flick of a switch. A powerful shower. A bath.

Tears prick at my eyes as I slump down on my haunches, warming my hands. A log pops, making me jump. There's no way I'm staying here, even if we are being hunted. I'd rather take my chances back in London, with or without Nathan.

It's too late to find a hotel or a guesthouse, so for tonight we'll have to make do, but in the morning I'll tell Nathan I'm not staying and he can row us back to Blakeney.

One night. That's it. I'm not spending a second longer in this awful hovel than is absolutely necessary. And if Nathan doesn't like it, that's his problem. My mind's made up.

Chapter 35

PIPPA
February 28, 2024

As watery, grey light spills through the smeary bedroom window, I focus on a crack in the wall that spiders upwards, spreading like the dead branches of a diseased tree, and breathe in the taste of mildew and rotting wood. I must have slept a little, but not much. After I'd finally stopped shivering and shimmied into my sleeping bag on the narrow camp bed, still in my jeans and two jumpers, I lay for what felt like hours listening to the hiss of waves chasing the shingle up the beach, the wind whistling around the window frames, and Nathan's soft snoring as I tried to find a comfortable position.

One side of my body is almost entirely numb where I've been lying on the unforgiving canvas, while my nose and cheeks sting with cold. My eyes are gritty with tiredness, my shoulders ache from lugging my heavy rucksack halfway across the country, and every inch of my skin feels grubby. I have no idea of the time, but it's light outside, so I ought to get up. Although what's the point? There's nothing to do. I can't even have a shower to freshen up. As soon as Nathan's awake, I'll talk him into taking us back to Blakeney and we can make new plans. And if he wants to stay here, I'll make my own way back to London, but that's the last and only night I intend to spend under this roof.

I pull the sleeping bag around my shoulders, ignoring the pressure on my bladder, and bury down deeper inside, hunting out what little warmth I've generated during the night. I wiggle my frozen toes, trying to put some feeling back into them, but even with two pairs of socks on, they're like frozen rocks.

There's nothing about the house that remotely fits with the idealised image I'd formed in my head when Nathan first suggested we run away. It's grim and bleak. It doesn't even have running water, let alone electricity. The fire Nathan lit last night warmed the house briefly, but the heat has long since been chased off by a chill breeze that's insidiously creeping through every crack around the windows. There's absolutely nothing romantic about it.

Nathan's breath sucks in and out with a slow, steady rhythm, but when his sleeping bag rustles as he stretches and turns, I can't bring myself to face him to see if he's awake.

In the days after he went missing, I'd daydream about the moment we were reunited and how it would be. How his brush with death and the glimpse of a life without him might even bring us closer. I never imagined it would be like this, running in fear, and being forced to take refuge in a hellhole that doesn't even have basic amenities.

It's no wonder Nathan was so secretive about where we were going. If I'd have had even the slightest inkling that this was what he had planned when he talked about starting a new life away from London, free and unencumbered, I'd have run a mile. He must have realised, which is why he wouldn't tell me.

I don't care how much trouble we're in, I'd rather take my chances back at home than allow this house to become our prison. They can't prosecute Nathan for what he may or may not have seen. This isn't Communist China and they can't make him disappear or throw him in jail, especially if we have lawyers on our side. Sam will know what to do.

We'll tell her everything, starting with what Nathan thinks he saw on the bridge after the bombing, and explain how we've been harassed, terrorised and spied on. She can help us take the right legal steps to protect ourselves. It's crazy that I didn't speak to her before agreeing to come away, but Nathan can be so persuasive, especially after the shock of finding out that someone had broken into my flat, searched through my belongings and installed hidden cameras. I couldn't stay there and the idea of going on the run seemed so exciting.

But isn't that the story of my life? Always going along with what Nathan wants, trusting he knows best, rather than risking a confrontation or upsetting him. I've always thought compromise was the key to maintaining a healthy relationship. It's what all the experts say, isn't it? But compromise is a two-way street. Maybe I should have learnt to stand my ground and not always let Nathan get his own way. Maybe I shouldn't have been so quick to cancel plans to go out with friends when he said he'd be lonely on his own, or so readily make changes to my Instagram posts he insisted didn't fit with my brand or were giving the wrong advice, even when I disagreed.

How many times have I given in to him? That's not compromise. That's deference. Like when I suggested a long weekend in Rome not long after we started dating, and Nathan booked a hotel in Paris instead. And if we eat out, it's always at a restaurant he chooses. The only time I can ever remember telling him no was on Valentine's night when he proposed.

I used to believe I'd follow Nathan to the ends of the earth, and that because I love him, I'd do anything he asked, but have I been kidding myself? Sam's made it clear she doesn't like him. She's never shied away from telling me she thinks he's arrogant and controlling. I used to laugh it off and defend him, arguing it wasn't arrogance, but a confident charm. What if she's right? Have I been blinkered all this time?

I need to get back to London. Today. I'll tell Nathan as soon as he's awake that I want to go home.

The pressure on my bladder builds until it's uncomfortable and I have no choice other than to get up and brave the outside toilet, but unzipping my sleeping bag is another kind of torture. The flagstone floor is even colder than the frigid air, and as I wrestle with my coat, I start shivering again.

Outside, it's even worse. The wind has whipped into a squall and I'm almost knocked off my feet as I kick away a rock we used to wedge the door closed last night, and step outside.

I hurry in my socks into the crumbling brick outbuilding that houses the toilet, swallowing down the nausea at the stench of sewage. I do what I have to do as quickly as I can, and sprint back inside.

What I'd do for a hot shower, or even hot running water, right now. Every part of me is filthy. My hair desperately needs a wash, my clothes are sticking to my body and my teeth are furry. If my followers could see me now, they wouldn't recognise me.

It's strange to think that none of them, not a single one of my three-quarters of a million followers, has any idea of the hell I'm going through. I might not know any of them personally, but I draw strength from knowing they're there, rooting for me, their comments and messages giving me a sense of purpose and belonging. And yet I've had to turn my back on them all. Without my phone or my laptop, let alone a decent internet connection, I have no way of posting content or providing any updates on our situation. Not that Nathan would have let me do it when we're supposed to be in hiding. Of course, if I can't post content, I have no way of generating an income. Another reason I can't stay. But maybe it was part of his plan to make me financially dependent on him.

Everything about this ridiculous situation puts me in a bad mood. I'm cold, I'm tired, I'm scared and we're completely cut off from the rest of the world in this horrible house. It doesn't help that we've not had anything decent to eat for more than twenty-four hours and my blood sugar levels are low.

I stalk into the kitchen with its antiquated stand-alone cooker and wonky worktop under the window, hoping against the odds to at least locate a kettle and some tea. To my surprise, I find a dozen teabags in a ceramic pot and a chipped mug hanging from a hook under the worktop. I'd normally drink herbal tea. Chamomile, hibiscus or echinacea, which help to cleanse the body and soothe the mind, but beggars can't be choosers. Builders' tea will have to do, although I've no idea how long the bags have been in the pot.

There must be a kettle if there are teabags, but I can't find one. There's not even a saucepan. What kind of holiday home doesn't have any pots or pans or a kettle? It's surreal. I'll have to wait until we get back to Blakeney for a hot drink after all. Hopefully, Nathan will be awake soon and we can get moving. He's supposed to be taking the boat he stole back after all.

I creep into the bedroom hoping Nathan will be awake, but unbelievably he's still fast asleep, his face squashed against a patterned towel he's rolled up as a pillow. He looks so peaceful. Totally unburdened by worry. I'm tempted to shake him awake and tell him that if he won't take me back to the village, I'll row myself. And hitchhike to London, if I have to.

But is that such a good idea? Nathan's never in the best of moods if he's woken prematurely. No, this isn't about what Nathan wants anymore. It's about what I need. I step towards the bed, my footsteps cushioned by my socks and my stomach rumbling with hunger.

As I reach for his shoulder, intending to shake him awake, I almost trip over his rucksack that he's wedged under the bed. I never asked him if he brought any food, but there's a chance he's stowed some chocolate or an energy bar in one of the pockets.

I grab a strap and tug the bag free. God knows what he's got in there. It weighs a ton. Nathan stirs. He rolls over, smacking his lips, and returns to deep sleep.

I'm surprised his rucksack is buckled up with all the pockets zipped closed. My bag is leaning against the wall with clothes spilling out from every opening, but Nathan's always been tidier than me. He never leaves clothes lying around in a heap. He says he can't abide mess. On occasion, when he's stayed over, I've even caught him folding my dirty clothes into neat squares. He's such a neat freak.

I drag the bag into the kitchen, wincing as it grazes noisily across the flagstones, and close the door. I lean it against a bowed wall where the paint has flaked off in a patch that looks like a man howling in agony, his hands clutching his head in despair.

My fingers are so stiff with cold, I have to rub my hands together to get the blood flowing before unclipping the rucksack's top flap and loosening a drawstring.

Inside, it smells of Nathan, a musky scent tinged with stale sweat. I pull out a chunky black sweater, place it on the floor and rummage through T-shirts, several pairs of walking trousers, socks and boxer shorts that have all been folded and packed neatly. I push my hand down further, desperate to find some chocolate now the idea's in my head.

But it's not a chocolate bar my fingers wrap around. It's a hard, heavy, leather-sheathed object with a rubber handle. Curious, I pull it out and stare at it in shock.

Why does Nathan have a hunting knife? It's not a small knife either. It's easily the length of my forearm. Equally horrified and fascinated, I remove it from its sheath and stare at the razor-sharp steel blade with its vicious serrated edge.

Did he think he was going to be surviving off the land and hunting rabbits, like some second-rate Bear Grylls? It's laughable. There's no way Nathan could bring himself to kill a rabbit. He couldn't even dispatch a wasp that flew into his pint of beer in the pub garden last summer, hooking it out with a fork instead and coaxing it onto a leaf so it could dry its wings. He's a complete softy when it comes to animals.

Maybe he's brought it for another reason. Protection? A shiver spills down my spine. Surely he's not that stupid. If we get caught, he's not going to be able to fight his way free. He'll end up killing someone.

I slide the sheath back onto the knife, careful not to cut myself, and lay it on the floor alongside his jumper, before diving back into his bag, pushing my arm down deep to the bottom until I find a heavy lump of metal wrapped loosely in a cloth.

My heart skips a beat. I pull it out and fall back on my haunches, holding it in the palms of both hands, my mind in overdrive.

'Pippa? What are you doing?'

I let out an involuntary shriek of surprise. I didn't hear Nathan coming.

'I was looking for —' I glance at my hands, my cheeks burning. I've been caught red-handed.

He glowers at me, one hand on the doorframe, the other clenched in a tight fist. 'Is that my rucksack?'

'Nathan,' I mumble, my mouth dry. 'What the hell are you doing with a gun?'

Chapter 36

JAMES
February 28, 2024

'One of Pippa's followers has sent me a message,' Samantha says, her tone clipped and brisk. 'It sounds credible. I think it's worth checking out.'

I stare at the river through the window of the cheap bed and breakfast I booked into when I arrived in Norwich last night, gambling Ryan was right and that Nathan and Pippa are somewhere here in Norfolk.

'Okay, where?'

I hold my breath. Samantha has no idea that I've already left London. I didn't tell her because I didn't want her tagging along or talking me out of it.

'Great Yarmouth. She's convinced she saw Pippa on the pier.'

Bingo. I'll need to double check on a map, but I'm sure Great Yarmouth isn't far from Norwich. Maybe Ryan wasn't lying after all.

'I can probably be there within the hour.'

'An hour?'

'I'm already in Norwich. Ryan thought this was where they were headed. I couldn't sit around doing nothing.'

'Why didn't you tell me?' Samantha asks, the disappointment evident in her voice. Maybe she thought she would come with me, but I work alone. It's quicker and easier.

'Sorry. Do you have a name?'

Samantha hesitates for a beat, clearly cross with me. 'Lily-Ann. She works in the amusement arcade on the pier.'

'Tell her I'll meet her there at...' I glance at my watch, 'around ten-thirty.'

Great Yarmouth is closer to Norwich than I thought. A little over half an hour by car. I park on the seafront, next to a grand Victorian cinema with the faded charm of an old armchair that's seen better days, and zip my coat to my chin against the bitter wind racing off the sea.

The pier stretches towards the grey horizon but pulls up short before it reaches the sea, stunted, as if it's afraid of getting its feet wet. The entrance is a migraine of sound, colour and bright lights, a gaudy come-on to the tourists and holidaymakers hankering after nostalgic times of old, long before cheap flights and foreign package deals lured everyone away. A simpler time when a carousel ride and candy floss on a stick were the epitome of a good time. Now it all looks so sad and forlorn, particularly in mid-winter under black skies and with the grey sea lapping at its bandy, rusty legs.

I stride past a doughnut stand, the sickly sweet smell of fried batter swirling in the air, and in through a set of double doors chained open, following a neon sign for the amusement arcade.

It's staggeringly loud inside, my senses assaulted by a cacophony of noisy machines. Blips, beeps, warbles and shrills, accompanied by flashing red, white and blue lights, a sensory inducement to play. For a second, I'm transported back to my childhood, to sunny summer days in Margate. The games are all the same. The penny pushers. The fruit machines. The air hockey. The Space Invaders.

I glance around, looking for Lily-Ann. I'm early but I hope she's here already. A miserable-looking staff member in a red polo shirt that's too tight for her bulging waistline points me towards a booth at the back.

'Lily-Ann?' I ask the girl behind the glass.

She flicks a jet-black fringe out of her eyes and studies me with a lazy gaze as she chews on gum. My eye is drawn to the ring in her nose and the glimpse of an intricate blue and green tattoo that extends up her neck from under her collar.

'Yeah?' she says.

'I'm James. I'm helping Pippa Ravenscroft's family find her. You sent a message saying you'd seen her?'

'Yeah.'

'When?'

Lily-Ann shrugs. She reaches to scratch her neck, revealing a gaping hole under the arm of her top. 'Yesterday afternoon. She was in here playing on the slots.' She nods at the fruit machines where a dark-haired woman in a tracksuit top and baggy fleece trousers is plying a machine with pound coins.

'The slot machines? Are you sure?'

It doesn't sound like Pippa.

'Yeah, I recognised her right away. I'm a big fan.'

'Okay.' I'm reasonably sure Pippa's somewhere in Norfolk, so I'm prepared to suspend my disbelief for the moment. 'Was she alone?'

'Yeah. She's really nice. Have you met her?'

I smile. 'She's a good friend of mine.'

'Oh, right, cool.'

'Did you speak to her?'

'Yeah, she let me take a selfie with her.'

'Can I see?'

'Sure.' Lily-Ann dives under the counter and pulls out a phone. 'I thought she might be a bit, you know, about people bothering her, but she didn't mind at all.'

'Did she mention where she's staying? Is she spending time here in Great Yarmouth?'

'Nah, sorry. She didn't.'

I tap my fingers impatiently on the counter as Lily-Ann takes an age scrolling through the photos on her phone. How many pictures does she have on there?

'I've been following her for ages, like well before everyone else, since when she first started.'

'She's very popular.'

'I love her quotes. There was one I printed out and put on my wall in my bedroom so I can read it every morning. She said strength isn't just about muscles, it's about getting back up when you've been knocked down. How cool is that?'

'Do you have the photo?'

'Yeah, here.' She turns the phone around and holds it up to the glass.

It's a fuzzy picture of two women, clearly taken inside the arcade, next to the fruit machines. One of them is definitely Lily-Ann. There's no mistaking the jet-black hair and the nose ring. The woman with her, who has her arm around Lily-Ann and is holding up two fingers with her tongue poking out, looks a little like Pippa. At least if you squint. She has blonde hair that comes down to her shoulders, and an ugly-shaped nose and crooked eyes.

It's definitely not Pippa.

'Okay, thanks.' I force a smile. It's a dead end. Wasted time.

'Is she in trouble?'

'I don't know,' I say, my spirits deflating.

'I hope you find her.'

'Yeah, me too.' I turn and head back towards the car.

'And tell her I said hello, okay?'

Chapter 37

PIPPA
February 28, 2024

Nathan snatches the gun out of my hands. 'What the hell do you think you're doing?'

He reaches across me, grabs his rucksack and stuffs his jumper and the knife back inside. 'You ought to have more respect for my belongings.'

'You didn't answer my question. Why do you have a gun?'

He swings the rucksack onto his back as effortlessly as if it's filled with cotton wool. 'Why do you think?' he snaps. 'We don't know who's coming for us or when.'

'Is it... loaded?'

'No, I thought I'd wave it around a bit and hope it scares them off. Of course it's loaded.'

My hollowed-out stomach flips. I can't believe Nathan's brought a loaded gun. If it had gone off, one of us could have been injured. Or killed.

I haul myself unsteadily to my feet, my legs like putty. 'Let me see.'

'Why?'

'I want to see it.'

'I don't want you touching it again,' he says, unwrapping it from the cloth and presenting it to me to inspect in the palm of his hand. 'Happy now?'

What was he thinking? If we'd been caught and the police had found it on him, they'd have thrown the book at him for sure. This isn't the Wild West. You can't carry guns around without a licence in this country. I can't believe he could be so stupid.

'Where did you get it?'

'Does it matter?'

'Of course it matters. It's Ryan's, isn't it? It's the gun he was showing off at the party.'

'What party?'

'The party we went to at his flat last year.'

'I don't remember,' Nathan says, carefully rewrapping the cloth around the gun and shoving it into his rucksack under his clothes.

'Get rid of it.'

'What?'

'I want you to get rid of it. I don't want it in the house or anywhere near me.'

'Pippa, don't —'

'I said get rid of it, Nathan. I'm serious. I don't want anyone getting hurt.'

I don't know what's happened to him, but the Nathan I know would never have anything to do with guns or violence.

'And since when do you get to tell me what to do?' Nathan barks, his nostrils flaring with anger.

My breath stalls and my limbs turn to stone, the menace in his tone sending a cold rush through my veins.

'I'm sorry.' The apology tumbles from my mouth with a will of its own as I lower my gaze, unable to hold his eye. I hate that I keep saying sorry to him, but it's become a habit. My default to keep the peace. I don't want a gun, or a hunting knife for that matter, anywhere near me. No good can come of it. But there's no point making him angry. 'It's just that it makes me uncomfortable. And apart from anything else, it's illegal.'

Nathan snorts. 'Illegal? You want to talk about legality when I didn't do anything wrong? I was trying to help those people on the bridge and this is what happens? I've been forced out of my home. I don't know who I can trust anymore and I'm constantly looking over my shoulder thinking that at any moment I could be arrested and banged up. So I'm sorry if I wanted to take some precautions.' His eyes blaze. I've rarely seen him so worked up.

'Okay, I get it. I said I'm sorry.'

'You need to grow up, Pip, and start understanding this isn't a game. This is serious.'

'I know!'

'Do you?'

'Of course, but there's no need to yell at me. I'm not the enemy.'

'Then start acting like you're on my side,' he snarls.

'You know what? This is impossible. I can't do it anymore.' I drop my head in my hands and furiously scratch my itchy scalp. 'This isn't working. I want to go home.'

'What are you talking about?'

'This house. Us. Everything. I can't do it anymore.'

Nathan gives a slight, almost imperceptible shake of his head. 'Don't say that. Things will get better. I promise,' he says, his tone softening.

'How? We don't have any running water, let alone electricity. I'm cold, I'm tired and I'm scared. And to cap it all, I now find out you've had a gun hidden in your rucksack all this time.'

He nods like he understands. 'Okay,' he says. 'I'm sorry I shouted. I didn't mean to take it out on you, but honestly, my nerves are shot. You don't know what these last two weeks have been like.'

'Let's go home and get it sorted. I'll talk to Sam and we can —'

'No!'

'She'll know what to do.'

'I'm not going back, Pippa. It's too dangerous. You don't know what they're capable of.'

'Who?' I ask. 'Who exactly do you think is coming for you?'

'Them.' He waves a hand across the room. 'The security services. MI5. The police. I don't bloody know. And that's the scariest part.'

'I can't stay. Not living like this.'

'What do you mean?'

'Look at the place. It's freezing cold. It's draughty. We don't have any food or running water. How long do you think we can survive like this?'

'It's not that bad.'

'Nathan!'

'Oh, well, I'm sorry there isn't a four-poster bed and a spa, somewhere you can get your nails done and a turndown service at night, but it's the best I can do until I can work out something else.'

'And how long's that going to be?'

'As long as it fucking takes.'

'No.'

'What do you mean, no?'

'I'm not doing it. I'm not staying. This is... madness.'

'We're not going home. We can't.'

But my mind's made up. I'll go on my own if I have to. I want to go home to my flat. Sleep in my own bed. Soak in my own bath. Crash on the sofa in front of my TV.

'Either take me back to Blakeney or I'll row the bloody boat there myself.'

'Not happening.' He drops his rucksack, folds his arms with his shoulders pulled back, and shakes his head defiantly.

'Fine, I'll go on my own.'

I push past him and reach for the door.

'I said it's not happening,' he screams, shoving me against the wall with his shoulder, his other arm outstretched, slamming the kitchen door closed in my face.

'What are you doing?' I back away, wary. His eyes stare right through me, unfocused and glassy as if he's been transported to a faraway place.

'How many times do I have to tell you? We're not going anywhere,' he says through gritted teeth.

'You can't stop me leaving.'

Without breaking eye contact, he lowers himself to his haunches and rips open his rucksack. He reaches in and pulls out the gun, slowly and deliberately unwrapping its cloth covering and letting it slip to the floor.

I can't move. My chest tightens and it feels as if all the air has been sucked out of the room.

Nathan inches up to his full height and, in slow motion, raises the gun and levels it at my head. I catch a breath and hold it as I stare down the barrel with my insides turning to mush, shuffling backwards until I collide with the cooker and can't get any further away.

'It's not safe to go home,' Nathan says with a wistful sadness that raises goosebumps on my arms.

'Nathan...'

I can't tear my eyes from the black, ominous mouth of the gun's barrel. A dangerous, beady eye targeting my head. Is this how I'm going to die? Murdered by the man who's supposed to love me? Who professed to want to spend the rest of his life with me?

'Please,' I beg, finally finding my voice. 'Put the gun down.'

'How far do you think you'd get without me?' Nathan asks, cocking his head. 'You don't have your phone. You don't have any money. And you look a mess.' He glances up and down my body with a sneer of disgust.

He takes a step closer.

I have nowhere to go. No way to escape.

He grabs my face and grips my cheeks so tightly it hurts, lifting my chin and forcing me to look him in the eye.

'I love you, Pippa,' he says. 'More than you'll ever know.' If he didn't have a gun pointed at my chest, I could almost believe it. The cruelty and anger I saw in his eyes has vanished. In his own unique way, I think he believes every word. 'I'm doing this for us,' he says. 'You could at least pretend to be grateful.'

I wince as his grip tightens, his thumb and fingers digging into my jaw until my whole face aches. I can't speak even if I wanted to.

'You should be thanking me, not yelling at me like I'm dirt on your shoe.'

I try to apologise, to tell him I'm sorry for being so ungrateful, because I know it's what he wants to hear, but I still can't speak.

And then, as if someone's flicked a switch inside his head, his demeanour completely changes, like the old Nathan has returned. He releases my face and lowers the gun, letting it hang limply by his side.

When he leans forwards and plants a tender kiss on my forehead, my entire body knots. I stand, statue-like, with my heart thumping out of control in my chest.

'So that's settled then?' he says, raising his eyebrows as his hand caresses the back of my head. 'No more talk of leaving?'

I force myself to swallow, releasing the tightness in my throat. 'Sure,' I croak.

He glances at the mug I put on the counter. 'What about a nice cup of tea?'

I nod, fighting simmering tears. I don't want him to see me cry, or to show any weakness. I won't let him think he's won and I've lost. I have to make him think I'm being compliant and deferential, because I can see now with absolute clarity, it's the only way I stand any chance of getting out of here alive.

'A cup of tea would be lovely,' I say, forcing a smile.

Chapter 38

JAMES
February 28, 2024

My phone rings as I swing through the entrance to a marina at St Olaves, twenty minutes outside Great Yarmouth. It's supposed to be the gateway to the Broads, the vast network of navigable rivers and lakes popular with tourists and boating folk, if you believe the marketing hype. It seemed like as good a place as any to continue my hunt for Pippa and Nathan.

I hit the brakes too hard and skid to a halt in the gravel car park, drawing a disapproving look from a man in thigh-length waders, walking past.

It's Samantha. 'Any luck?' she asks.

I stare out across a sea of boats, many of them out of the water and propped up on stilts, crammed into every available space around the yard, their hulls flecked with peeling paint and masts punctuating the grey sky like needles trying to force rain from the clouds.

'It wasn't Pippa. She was mistaken.'

'Really?'

I don't care for Samantha's tone, as if she doesn't believe me. I explain about the selfie and that I didn't have the heart to tell her the woman in the picture wasn't who she thought she was.

'Where are you now?' Samantha asks.

I glance at a sign on a squat, single-storey building, its pastel paint tinged green with moss and algae. 'Willowbend Marina. Thought I'd ask around. You never know, someone might have seen them.'

'What, at a random marina? That's your plan?'

'Got any better ideas?' I ask, grinding my back teeth. It was definitely the right decision coming on my own. Samantha would have driven me to distraction if I'd brought her with me. 'I figured they might have hired a boat and tried hiding out on the broads.'

There are a hundred and twenty miles of waterways on the Broads. It would be the perfect place to hide. At least, it's what I would have done. They could have found a quiet inlet, dropped anchor, and no one would ever know they were there.

'Anything new your end?' I ask.

'Plenty of messages. Most of them useless. My favourite so far is a woman in New York who's convinced she's seen Pippa jogging around Central Park. And someone else who's certain she was driving the number twenty-three bus around Edinburgh.'

I groan. Do these people ever stop to think before hitting send? 'That's it?'

'No, actually, there is something that might be worth checking out.'

I instinctively duck as a mammoth seagull with a long, hook-like beak comes soaring towards my car, heading directly for the windscreen. At the last moment, it swoops onto the roof, landing with a loud thud.

'There's a woman who thinks she's seen Pippa with a man who could be Nathan, in Blakeney. Do you know it?'

'I've heard of it.'

'It's on the north Norfolk coast, about an hour's drive from where you are.'

The gull continues to pad noisily up and down my roof.

'Sounds promising.'

'The description of the man she was with sounds like a pretty close match to Nathan. It's the most promising lead we've got, unless you fancy driving to Manchester where someone claims to have seen them checking into a Travelodge off the A34 in Didsbury.'

I check the clock on the dashboard. If I left now, I could probably be in Blakeney by early afternoon.

'What's her name?'

'Shauna. She works in a food shack on the harbour.'

'Anything else?'

'The couple she saw were carrying big rucksacks, like they were travelling. And she said the woman she believes is Pippa was acting like she didn't want to be recognised.'

'That sounds hopeful.'

'Maybe.'

'You're not sure?'

Samantha sighs. 'I don't know. What the hell would they be doing in a place like Blakeney? There's nothing there. A few houses and some mudflats. That's it.'

'It sounds exactly like the kind of place I'd go if I wanted to disappear. I'll head there now. I'll call with an update as soon as I know more.'

I hang up, toss my phone on the passenger seat and pull away, kicking up gravel behind me.

In my rear-view mirror, I watch the seagull that landed on the roof take flight with an angry caw-caw and flap lazily off into the sky.

Chapter 39

PIPPA
February 28, 2024

Nathan unhooks a second mug from under the counter, sets it down and drops a teabag into it as if nothing has happened. As if moments before, he didn't have a gun pointed at my head, threatening me.

'I couldn't find a kettle,' I say, trying to keep my voice level and light. Letting him think I'm not shaken or cowed. 'Or any saucepans. I thought this was supposed to be a holiday home?'

Nathan frowns. 'Let me have a look.'

He disappears into the hall where I hear him rummaging around in a store cupboard. He returns a few moments later brandishing a scruffy kettle blackened with soot like it's a trophy. He fills it from a water bottle he plucks from his rucksack and puts it on the gas stove.

I stand well back, keeping my distance, watching him warily as he lights the gas with a match. As it hisses and crackles, I wonder how it's possible the house has a supply of gas but no electricity.

'Bottles,' Nathan says, as if reading my mind. 'I saw them stacked up outside last night.'

As we wait in silence for the water to boil, Nathan whistles a tune I don't recognise, as casual and as relaxed as you like. I ball my hands, digging my nails into my palms.

'We'll have to drink it black. Do you mind? I forgot to pick up any milk,' he says, glancing at me with an apologetic smile.

'It's fine.' My eye is drawn to the shape of the gun bulging at the base of his spine where he shoved it under his jumper, in his waistband of his jeans.

When the kettle boils, it whistles its own single-note tune. Nathan pours hot, steaming water into the mugs and suggests we sit in the attic room that we've not explored. The only way to get up there is by climbing a vertical ladder screwed to the wall in the bedroom, a task made infinitely more challenging while carrying a steaming mug of tea.

But the effort is worth it. A single window provides amazing views across the beach and the grey sea beyond, stretching towards the indistinct horizon where it's hard to tell where the sky and the water meet.

It's by far the smallest room in the house, which isn't saying much, with oppressive dark wood panelling that's been defaced by the graffiti messages of dozens of strangers.

I sit on a plump, pastel orange cushion with my tea between my feet, and fall into a hypnotic stupor listening to the hiss of the waves rolling up the pebble beach. It's so peaceful. So unspoilt. A world away from the bustle of my life in London and my flat in Camden. If I was here alone, it would be the perfect getaway.

The ladder rattles as Nathan ascends. His head pops through the hatch and my stomach tightens. He draws up a cushion beside me and sits with a groan.

'I forgot I packed these before I left.' He holds out an unopened packet of chocolate digestives. 'Peace offering?'

He pouts, sticking out his bottom lip, like a sulky child begging for forgiveness.

But I'm not ready to forgive him. I'm not sure I can ever forgive him.

'I'm sorry, Pip. I was well out of line.'

A seagull wheels past the window, screeching.

'Yes, you were.'

He runs a hand over his thick stubble and lets it roam over his eyes and through his hair. 'Can you forgive me?'

'You threatened to shoot me.'

His head slumps onto his chest. I take the packet of biscuits and peel it open. I'm starving, and even though it's not exactly a healthy breakfast, it's better than going hungry.

'I've been under a lot of stress,' he says. 'Not that it's any excuse. I shouldn't have taken it out on you. I love you. And it won't happen again. I promise.'

He rests his head on my shoulder, but I refuse to lean into him. He could apologise a million times and I'd never forgive him for pointing a gun at me. We're done. There's no coming back from something like that. 'I want you to get rid of it.'

'Oh, Pip, you know I can't.'

'You would if you loved me.'

'If you loved me, you wouldn't ask.'

'Nathan, I'm serious. I don't want that gun anywhere near me.'

He sits up straight and holds his hands up in submission. 'Okay, fine. If that's what you really want. It's gone. I'll lose it in the river later. Now, how's the tea?'

'It's fine.'

'It won't be like this forever, you know. It's only temporary, just while I sort out something better for us. We have our whole lives ahead of us. We can do anything we want. Go anywhere. You should be excited.'

'But you're always going to be running. Looking over your shoulder.'

Nathan chuckles. 'They'll lose interest eventually, especially if we keep our mouths shut and our heads down.'

'We? I don't have anything to hide.'

'All the time they're looking for me, you're not safe.'

'So you keep saying. And how long before they lose interest? A couple of weeks? A few months? Years? Decades? We don't even know what these people want.'

Nathan blows into his mug, slurps his tea and grimaces. 'I guess they want me to keep my mouth shut. It would be pretty damaging if anyone found out what I saw.'

'But you didn't really see anything, did you? That's what I can't get my head around.'

'I saw enough.'

'Some guys spilling out of a van and picking up one of the victims? So what?'

'I told you before. It obviously proves the government knew about the bomb and didn't do anything to stop it. My guess is the guy they picked up was either an informant or an undercover agent who'd infiltrated the gang of bombers. Either way, they can't risk that being made public. Can you imagine the outcry?'

Nathan's made his mind up, but I'm not sure it proves anything, let alone the kind of government collusion he thinks it does.

I finish my biscuit and lick my fingers clean, sipping my tea to wash it down. It's too strong. Too bitter. But at least it's hot and warms my fingers and my insides.

'So what did you see exactly?' I ask. 'What did these men who jumped out of the van look like?'

'I don't know, Pip. It all happened so fast.'

'Well, how were they dressed? In suits? Army fatigues?'

'No, more like special forces. All in black and wearing body armour and carrying guns. It was really scary.'

'Guns?'

'Yeah, you know, like assault rifles.'

'You never mentioned they had guns before.'

'Didn't I?' Nathan lifts his mug to his mouth, his gaze fixed on the window.

'What about the van? What was that like?'

'I can't remember.'

'You said it was dark-coloured before. So, like black?'

'Yeah, I think so. Honestly, Pip, it was all a blur.'

'Right.' I nod, trying to picture the scene and reconcile it with the hours and hours of CCTV footage I've been through on my computer. 'But it was definitely a black van?'

'Yeah, I think so. A black Transit with darkened windows.'

'You're sure?'

'Of course I'm sure. What is this, twenty questions?'

'Sorry.' There I go, apologising again. 'It's just that...'

If there had been a black van on the bridge in the immediate aftermath of the explosion, I would have spotted it, wouldn't I? I've seen footage from almost every conceivable angle while I was hunting for Nathan. A vehicle of any kind, speeding onto the bridge in the first few minutes after the blast, would have been captured on someone's phone or camera. And yet I've seen nothing like that in the hours of footage I've trawled through.

'It's just what?' Nathan asks. He stares at me as if he's challenging me to contradict him.

'Nothing,' I say, shaking my head. 'It doesn't matter.'

Chapter 40

Nathan behaves like a perfect gentleman for the rest of the morning, as if he knows he's overstepped a line. He's good-humoured and attentive and even cleans our dirty clothes in a bucket using a packet of old washing powder he finds in the cupboard in the hall and freezing water from the tank at the back of the house. He stands outside in the cold with his hands turning red, wrings our T-shirts, underwear and trousers out and hangs them on a line strung between two concrete posts, even though the air's so chill, I doubt any of it will dry.

When he sees me shivering, he lights another fire, and keeps peppering me with tender kisses and hugging me when I'm least expecting it. It's a trial to behave normally and not push him away, but it's what I have to do.

Whatever he saw on that bridge on the night he disappeared has profoundly affected him. I don't know whether it's the trauma of seeing people who'd been literally ripped apart and being overwhelmed by the scale and severity of their injuries, or if it's more to do with his paranoia since he witnessed what he claims is some kind of state conspiracy. Whatever it is, he's changed. I don't feel safe around him. It was a mistake to have trusted him when I agreed to come away and abandon my life in London, but how was I to know? And to think he brought a gun and was prepared to threaten me with it. That's not the Nathan I fell in love with.

I know he's scared, but it's no excuse for keeping me captive. It sounds melodramatic, but that's what it is, isn't it? I'm not allowed to leave, which makes me what, his hostage? I was stupid to have let him talk me into giving up my phone, and now I'm completely isolated, miles from anywhere. The only hope I have is to stay compliant and hope he eventually lets his guard down.

'I know I need to do better,' Nathan says, taking my hands as I sit warming myself in the dining room where the fire is blazing. 'I honestly don't know what came over me, but I promise I'm going to work on myself and it'll never happen again. Forgive me?'

He flutters his eyelashes like a showgirl teasing a crowd, and even though I'm still angry with him, it's hard not to smile.

'Do you ever think about that day we first met?' He falls to the floor and sits with his back to the fire.

'Sometimes.'

'Do you remember, you were in the gym, squatting, and I couldn't take my eyes off you? You were the most beautiful woman I'd ever seen.'

'Flattery will get you everywhere.'

'I'm serious, Pip. I knew straightaway you were the one.'

'Yeah, I must have looked like such a catch in my sweaty gym kit.'

'You could wear anything and still look incredible.'

'Right.'

'What? It's true. You made me the happiest man alive when you agreed to go on a date. I couldn't believe my luck. Even Ryan reckoned I was punching above my weight. But look at us now with our whole lives ahead of us. I'm never going to do anything to upset you ever again. You're my world. My everything. We're going to be so happy together. I know we are.'

He grins, showing off his immaculate white teeth.

I stare into the flames, watching them dance and shimmy around red-hot embers, smoke swirling like the light fingers of a thief hovering over a case of jewels, reminding myself I just have to bide my time and be ready to escape when the opportunity presents itself.

The sudden crack of a log splitting makes us both jump. A smouldering cinder leaps across the room and lands on the worn, patterned rug by Nathan's knee and immediately begins to smoke.

Nathan jumps up in a panic as a small flame sparks into life around the ember, a black hole widening in the fabric.

'Shit,' he hisses, flapping his arms.

'Get some water!'

He runs outside and comes back a moment later with a bucket as the room fills with choking smoke. He douses the flames, but leaves a dirty puddle in the middle of the room.

We stand shoulder-to-shoulder staring at the mess, a reminder that we need to be careful about the fire. If it had happened in the middle of the night, the smoke could have killed us while we slept.

I push the chairs and table to the back of the room and roll up the rug, intending to toss it outside, but Nathan takes it from me.

'I'll do it,' he says.

Is he ever going to let me lift a finger again? Not that I'm complaining. It was his decision to come here. Let him deal with the chores.

While he clears up the mess, I climb back up to the attic room, out of his way, where I can watch the sea and the birds. A brief tranquil retreat where I can be alone with my thoughts. But the peace doesn't last long. The ladder rattles and Nathan pokes his head through the hatch in the floor, grinning.

'Hungry?' he asks.

'Starving.' We finished the packet of biscuits between us with our tea and now my stomach's rumbling again. 'Do you want to go out and grab something? We could head back into Blakeney,' I suggest, sensing an opportunity to raise the alarm.

'It's okay, I'll go. I'll get some food to keep us going for a few days.'

'Don't you want me to come with you?'

'No, you stay here and keep your head down.'

'Are you sure?'

He hauls himself into the room and kneels at my side, taking my hands. 'Of course I'd prefer it if you came with me. I don't want to be apart from you for a single second, but it's such a small village. You know what people are like. They talk. And we can't take the risk that word gets out about us.'

I struggle to hide my disappointment. 'Okay,' I mumble.

'Oh, Pip, I'll be back before you know it. Are you worried about being left here on your own?'

I nod. 'Maybe a little.'

'No one's going to find you here. You're perfectly safe. And I'll be back in no time.'

I walk with him to the jetty with the wind tugging at my coat and stand braced against the gusts as he climbs into the stolen rowing boat and pushes himself off into the fast-moving current which appears to be on the turn and flowing out to sea, exposing a strip of thick, gloopy mud at the water's edge.

He blows me a theatrical kiss and I raise a hand to wave as he pulls away, watching as he battles with the wind and the choppy waters.

It's the first time I've been alone since we arrived at the house. Nathan's going to be gone for at least an hour. Maybe more. If ever there was a good opportunity to make a run for it, it's now. I could strike out along the beach and eventually I'm sure I'd come across a dog walker, a house or a road. Some sign of civilisation where I could ask for help. I could even be back in London by this evening. And by the time Nathan realises I've gone, I could be miles away. A nervous excitement bubbles in my gut as I turn back to the house, dipping my head against the strengthening wind whipping off the sea and bending the reeds.

But as I step inside and brush my hair out of my eyes, the warmth of the fire embracing me like a comfort blanket, my resolve weakens, the reality of what I'm planning sinking in. It's horrible weather outside. Bitterly cold and windy with threatening black clouds gathering, and I have no idea where I'd be going or how far I'd have to walk. The house is far from a palace, but at least there's a roof over my head. And my rucksack is so heavy, especially as I'd have to tramp across loose shingle.

Would it really be so bad if I stayed? Nathan should never have brought a gun, but I can understand why he felt the need. He's scared, and frightened people do stupid things. If I hadn't been poking around in his rucksack, I wouldn't even know he had it, but I put him in an impossible situation. I forced him to explain himself and made him feel like he'd done something wrong, even though his intentions were good. All he wanted was to protect us. He's made it clear how much he loves me. That he worships me. I'm sure he regrets threatening me, but we've both been stressed, hungry and tired. Neither of us is thinking straight and we've both done and said things we regret. He needs me. Whatever he's going through, whatever mental torture he's dealing with, I can't just abandon him. That would be cruel. He needs my help and my support. He needs my love. Running away would be the coward's option. And what do I always tell my followers?

True strength isn't about avoiding the storm. It's about learning to stand still in the rain.

What kind of role model would I be if I turned and ran at the first hint of trouble? I'm not a hostage here. I can walk out any time I like. Nathan's not going to stop me. He might try to talk me out of it, but I'd expect nothing less. We need to stick together. It's about time I stopped being so negative and started making the most of the situation. So the house is a little rickety. But it's dry and when the fire's going, it's warm enough. And its location is stunning, the landscape unspoiled and untamed. Wild and breathtaking. I love that the sky here seems to stretch on forever. I love the taste of salt in the air, the sense of freedom and of being so close to nature. I love the sounds of the birds and the smell of the sea. I bet in the summer, when the wind drops and the sun is out, it's idyllic. Nothing like you could ever find in London.

I can imagine creating some really inspirational posts here. Moody images of me staring out from the shore beneath the vast umbrella of the sky and dreamy instructional yoga videos shot on the beach. It's infuriating that I don't have my phone. I'd love to give my followers an update, but I know I can't. Even if I had the means, I can't reveal where we're hiding.

It's incredible how one event, completely out of my control, has changed my life forever. A single flap of a butterfly's wings that has brought a profound tornado of change. If Nathan and I hadn't gone for dinner on Valentine's, or eaten at a restaurant so close to Tower Bridge, or left early after Nathan proposed, none of this would be happening to us. Our lives would have carried on as normal, we wouldn't have been forced to abandon everything, and we wouldn't be in hiding.

I peel off my coat and settle in front of the fire, my mind made up. I'm going to stay and put in the effort to work it out with Nathan. I can't let our relationship become another victim of the bombing. Of course, it would be easy to walk away, but nothing of value ever came from taking the easy option.

When Nathan returns, we're going to talk. I'm going to tell him how frightened he made me feel when he pointed that gun at me, and I'm going to make him tell me how he's feeling and how he's processing the horrors of what he witnessed. I know he won't want to. He's a typical man, but if we're going to get through this and come out stronger, we have to. For the sake of our future together. I can only imagine what nightmares exist inside his head after what he saw that night.

He's not talked to me about any of it, but I can guess how harrowing it must have been. I've been through hours of footage from the scene, poring over it frame by frame when he disappeared. It was bad enough witnessing it second-hand through the lens of a camera, let alone being at the centre of it.

While we're at it, I want to pin him down on the claims he's made about this van and the armed men he supposedly saw, apparently dressed in body armour and carrying assault rifles, sent to rescue someone Nathan seems certain was an undercover agent, because it doesn't add up. He's painted such a vivid picture and yet I've found absolutely no evidence that it's true, despite going through all the available footage.

So the question is, did he imagine it? Or did he make it up? And if he made it up, why lie about something so serious?

Transcript from the podcast, Fallen Hero. Interview with Raj Mansoor, shopkeeper

I tried to make conversation with him, but he just grunted and shoved a note in my hand. A fifty! Not many people pay with cash these days and no one ever pays with a fifty-pound note. It's one of the reasons I remembered him, but also because he was acting so weirdly, like he didn't want anyone to see his face, which is why I thought at first he was a shoplifter.

I suppose what struck me most was that when he handed me the money, his hand was shaking so badly, and it was black with dirt, like he hadn't washed in a week. He kept checking over his shoulder while I was sorting out his change. He looked at me only briefly, but I got a clear view of his face.

For a split second, he stared right at me, and I don't want to sound dramatic about it, but there was something dangerous in his eyes which sent a chill down my back. I can't really explain it. But if he'd pulled out a gun or a knife and demanded that I hand over my takings, I wouldn't have been surprised. He had that look about him, do you know what I mean? Like he could kill you and feel absolutely no remorse.

Chapter 41

PIPPA
February 28, 2024

A row of candles on the windowsill flickers in a breeze that whistles through the cracks in the frame, while a smokey fire crackles and hisses in the hearth under our watchful gaze. It creates a warm and cosy atmosphere in the dining room, despite the brewing storm outside and the strong winds battering the house. Nathan surprised me with a ready-made veggie lasagne he picked up in Blakeney and has managed to heat it through in the gas oven. He's laid the table with cutlery, plates and glasses, and even created a centrepiece from wild grasses and seed heads from the beach. Who needs fancy restaurants and expensive champagne?

'Did you miss me?' Nathan leans across the table and pouts.

'You were only gone for an hour.'

'Nearly two, but it felt longer.' He takes my hand and draws circles on my skin with his finger.

'Maybe it's not so bad here. It would be amazing in the summer, when it's warm, and we could eat on the beach.'

Nathan frowns. 'I kind of like it like this, all cosy, with the wind howling outside.'

I bite my lower lip and chance my arm while he's in a good mood. 'We could always go home and come back in the summer.'

But it's immediately obvious I've said the wrong thing. Nathan sits up straight, stiffening as he lets go of my hand. 'What do you mean? You just said you liked it here.'

'I do! It's lovely. But don't you miss London?'

'Not a bit.'

'What about your friends? Your brother?'

'I have everything I need right here.'

'I know, but —'

'You know we can't go back, Pippa. It's too dangerous.'

'I miss my sister,' I say. Sam must be going out of her mind with worry by now. I wish Nathan had let me call or leave her a note.

Nathan smirks. 'Funny, you never had a good word to say about her before.'

'That's not true!' Sam can be a pain, but I couldn't bear the thought of never seeing her again.

'Whatever.'

I put my knife and fork together on my empty plate and take a deep breath. It's now or never while I have Nathan's full attention.

'You've never told me what happened that night, after you left me in the stairwell,' I say.

'You know what happened.'

'I know you went off to help, and I was cross that you'd abandoned me, but that's it. It must have been horrendous.'

Nathan rocks back in his chair and squeezes his eyes shut, his expression pained. 'I don't want to talk about it.'

But this is important. 'It was an incredibly brave thing to do, Nathan. I'm so proud of you.'

His eyes spring open. 'Are you?'

'Absolutely. You didn't need to put yourself in danger like that, but you did it anyway because there were people who needed you.'

'I did it because I wanted you to be proud of me. To see who I really am.'

'I already knew what kind of a man you are.' Or at least I thought I did. I run my finger over the faded, floral, creased tablecloth Nathan found folded up on a shelf. 'I can't imagine what you saw that night. If it had been me, I don't think I'd ever get over it.'

Nathan's eyes turn glassy as he stares at a point over my shoulder. He twitches and grimaces as if he's in pain. 'You don't want to know what I saw.'

I stand, walk behind him, and drape an arm affectionately around his shoulders. 'I'm worried you've been bottling it up. It's okay to talk about it, you know.'

'I don't need to.'

'Don't you think it might help?'

'Help with what? I'm fine.'

That's blatantly not true. His moods have become increasingly erratic and it doesn't take a genius to work out that it has to be connected to the psychological trauma.

'What about speaking to someone professional who could help you process what happened?' I say.

'A shrink?' He spits out the word like it's poison.

'A therapist. Someone who knows how to help. It can't do any harm, can it?'

Nathan stands suddenly and spins around, knocking me backwards, his face screwing up in anger. 'I don't need help.'

'Lots of people I know see therapists. It's nothing to be ashamed of.'

'I'm not ashamed, but that's not the point,' he yells. 'There are people looking for us. Dangerous people who could get us locked up for a long time, and you're worried about me seeing a shrink? I don't think you understand the seriousness of the situation.'

He stomps towards me, unblinking, a crazed look in his eye. I back away until I'm up against the wall.

'There's no one looking for us, is there?' I croak.

'What?' he snarls.

'There was no van, was there? No men in body armour. No guns. No conspiracy.'

He freezes on the spot, his gaze roaming across my face, his jaw locked with tension. 'Are you calling me a liar?'

'Of course not. I just want the truth.'

'Are you serious? You really think I made it up? How dare you, trying to tell me what I did or didn't see. Were you there? No.'

'Nathan, I'm —'

'And you're putting words in my mouth. I never said there was a conspiracy. I said it didn't feel right. Why do you always twist everything I say?'

I'm not making it up. He did say that. Or was it Ryan who told me? I don't know. I'm so confused.

'I thought that's what —'

'Do you think I brought us here for fun? Do you think I'd have walked away from my job and my family for nothing?' Nathan says, spittle flying from his mouth.

'Of course not, but you were under a lot of stress.'

'I didn't imagine it, Pippa.'

I should shut my mouth. There's no way to have a sensible conversation with him when he's like this, but I'm sick of the pretence. We're only here because of what Nathan imagines he saw. I need him to see that it's all in his head. That he needs help.

Nathan finally turns away from me and pads up and down the bare floorboards where the rug used to be before we accidentally set light to it.

'I thought you were dead.' My voice isn't much more than a whisper.

'What?'

'When you vanished, I thought you must be dead, so I spent hours going through every piece of footage that had been uploaded of the attack. But I never saw anything like what you described. I never saw a van and I didn't see any men with guns.'

Nathan spins around to face me again. 'You don't know what you're talking about.'

'There was no van, Nathan. No men,' I repeat.

'I know what I saw!'

'Do you think it's possible you imagined it? That your brain was so overwhelmed by what you'd seen that, I don't know, maybe your mind created a distraction?'

Nathan moves so quickly, I have no time to react. He grabs a chair with a roar of fury, raises it high above his head and smashes it on the table with a shattering crash, sending shards of plate, knives, forks and the centrepiece he arranged so beautifully flying.

I scream and slump to the ground, cowering with my arm across my face. It's my own fault. I poked a wasps' nest and now I'm about to get stung. I'm certain he's going to hit me.

But his tantrum is over almost as quickly as it started. Nathan storms out of the room while I curl up in a protective ball, trembling with fear.

Why couldn't I keep my big mouth shut?

He's never been like this before. It's a whole new side of him I've never seen, first threatening me with a gun and then this. As if I needed any further proof that he needs professional support and counselling.

But we're here on our own, miles from anywhere. There's no one to talk sense into him apart from me.

I take a moment to compose myself, steady my breath, and stand on shaking legs. There's blood on the back of my hand. It's only a small nick, presumably from a shard from one of the plates, but the way it's trickling down my wrist, it looks worse than it is.

'Nathan?'

I creep into the kitchen where he's pacing up and down with his hands on the back of his head, his face twisted in distress. When he sees me, all the tension in his body ebbs away and he crumples, his lip quivering.

'I'm so, so sorry. I don't know what came over me,' he cries.

'It's okay.' I put my arms around him and gently pull his head onto my shoulder.

He bursts into tears and sobs into my neck.

'Let's get you some help,' I say into his ear.

'No.'

'Alright, we can talk about it later.'

'I don't need help.'

We stand hugging each other silently for a few moments, rocking each other. When Nathan eventually stops sobbing, he lifts his head and looks me in the eye with the solemnity of a priest.

'I love you so much, Pip. I'd never do anything to hurt you. You know that, don't you?'

I shush him quiet. 'Of course.'

'Say it. Tell me you understand.'

'I know you'd never do anything to hurt me.' It's the biggest lie I've ever told him.

He smiles with relief. 'I mean it. If I didn't have you in my life, I don't know what I'd do. I couldn't carry on. I promise, I really am going to try harder.'

He takes hold of my face with both hands and kisses me, gently at first, but with increasing urgency. There's nothing romantic about it. I haven't cleaned my teeth properly in two days, but it's more than that. This morning, in almost the exact spot where we're standing now, he had a gun pointed at my head, threatening to shoot me, and only a few minutes ago he was smashing up furniture. He's not the man I fell in love with and unless he gets treatment, I can't see there's any future for us. I can't spend my life on tenterhooks, worrying about what he's going to do next.

When his hand slides under my jumper and kneads my breast, I stiffen with panic. Every atom in my body screams at me to tell him no, but I can't speak. Suddenly, I'm back in that shabby, airless caravan, pinned on the floor with Jago's beer-soured breath in my face, his hands all over me. No way to escape. No way to make him stop.

Powerless. Breathless. Terrified. Squeezing my eyes shut. Pressing my legs together.

My chest tightens. I'm trapped. Suffocating. I try to push Nathan away. 'No,' I gasp, finally finding my voice. 'I've not washed in days.'

'Come on,' he urges, grabbing my arm, his hot breath in my ear. 'I said I'm sorry.'

'Nathan, no.' I push him away and stumble backwards, pulling down my jumper, my hands clenching into fists.

His eyes blaze. 'Why do you always have to be such a tease?' he hisses. 'You keep saying you love me, but you have a funny way of showing it. I haven't seen you in weeks. I've missed you.'

'Maybe tomorrow.' It's the only thing I can think to say that might make him leave me alone, at least for the time being. 'Give me the chance to freshen up for you.' I force a smile, even as my stomach knots. 'Perhaps we could head back into Blakeney and find somewhere that has a shower?'

'I don't care. I love you as you are.'

'And I'm exhausted, Nathan. It's been such a tiring few days... I just can't.'

'Can't or won't?'

'Please.'

'Do you have any idea how hard I've been trying to keep us safe? To protect you and stop them destroying your life?'

'Of course. You've been amazing. It's not you. It's me.' It's such a cliché, but it's true.

'It's always you, isn't it, Pip? Every time I try to show you how much I care, you push me away. What am I supposed to think? Do you even love me any more?'

'Nathan —'

'Fine. Message received loud and clear. You've made your point, but don't worry, I won't bother trying again. I'm going to bed.'

He marches out of the kitchen, pausing only to blow out the church candles by the window, plunging the room into darkness, and slams the door behind him.

I take a deep breath and let it out slowly, counting to twenty. I hate the person Nathan's become, but it's not his fault or his choice. He's a victim and I shouldn't take it personally. But I have to do something or he's going to end up killing us both.

I straighten my jumper and pat down my hair, shivering as the window rattles in its frame and the wind whistles louder through every narrow gap it can find. Maybe in the morning, after a good night's sleep, he'll be more reasonable. Who knows, perhaps he'll come around to the idea that he's been emotionally damaged, and will be more open to accepting that he needs professional support. At least I've seeded the idea in his head.

When I've cleared up the mess in the dining room, swept up the broken plates and dropped them in the bin, extinguished the candles and spread out the dying embers in the fireplace to prevent another accident, I finally head for bed.

Nathan's curled up with his back to me, snoring lightly with a single candle flickering on the windowsill. I blow it out and quietly slip into my sleeping bag, pulling it up to my chin and trying to find a position on the creaking canvas camp bed that's vaguely comfortable, my heart beating too fast, adrenaline scorching my veins like acid.

I lie with my eyes open, staring at the outline of the wall for what seems like hours, my mind twisting the patchwork of peeling paint and exposed old plaster into a myriad of faces, animals and exotic flowers.

I have no idea how long it takes me to finally fall asleep, but when I wake, it's still dark.

And I can hear voices.

Chapter 42

How can there be voices coming from inside the house when there's only me and Nathan here? Then I hear it again. I'm wrong. It's not voices, but a single voice. A muted murmur, rising and falling with the cadence of a one-sided conversation.

I roll onto my back and try to pick out the words, to make sense of the sounds, but the voice is too faint, too indistinct, muffled by the crumbling walls of this creepy old house.

My heart canters in my chest like a herd of wild horses. Surely Nathan must have heard it too, but when I glance across the room through the gloom, his bed is empty, his sleeping bag puddled in a heap and half-hanging on the floor.

Is it Nathan's voice I can hear? I prop myself up on my elbows. Who's he talking to at this time of night? If I didn't know better, I'd have guessed he was speaking on the phone. But neither of us brought our mobiles. Nathan was insistent on it, terrified that we could be traced through the cell coverage and our movements tracked.

Although it's not possible to hear what he's saying, his voice is urgent. It's not exactly a full-on argument, but he's making a forceful point. Curious, I slip my legs out of my sleeping bag. The tiles are icy cold and the air frosts my breath, but I barely give it a fleeting thought as I pad quietly in my socks into the hall. Nathan's in the kitchen with the door shut, a flickering light glowing around the frame and spilling across the hall floor. I pull my hair back and press my ear to the door.

'But she won't let it go. What am I supposed to do?'

He falls silent for a few seconds as I imagine him listening to a voice in his ear.

'No, I don't. She's talking about going back to London. I'm really worried she knows I'm lying. Ryan, listen to me. It's not working.'

What the fuck?

Nathan's talking about me to his brother? My head spins. What's not working? And what's he lying about? The story he spun me about seeing armed men on the bridge on the night of the bombing? What else could it be?

And if he's lied about that, the only rational explanation is that he's covering up the truth about why he disappeared in the first place, and where he went for all that time while I was out of mind with worry.

Oh god, was he with another woman? Is that what happened? He left me for someone else?

And yet that doesn't make much sense either. If it were true, why would he go to all the trouble of making me leave London? As he said himself, he's given up his job and his family for us both to live in a crumbling, empty holiday home which has no running water or electricity. I can't square the circle.

After another pause, Nathan speaks again.

'Control the narrative? How?'

A brief silence.

'No, she found the gun. She tried to talk me into getting rid of it.'

I snatch a breath and hold it.

'Of course not. I'm not stupid. I'll use it if I need to.'

Blood pools in my feet, leaving my head floating, utterly blindsided. Surely I must have misheard or misunderstood. Nathan wouldn't really shoot me, would he?

I should have run when I had the chance. As soon as Nathan's back was turned, I should have listened to my gut, packed my bag and not looked back. I could have been back at home by now, this nightmare over. Instead, it's only just beginning. Nathan's treated me like an idiot. But worse, I've behaved like one, believing every word he told me like the gullible fool I am.

'I can hardly lock her in a room, can I? But if she goes back to London, how long do you think it'll take her to work out the truth? She's going to know I'm a fraud. And a coward. I'll lose her forever.'

I have a strange sense of sliding down the side of a mountain, plummeting towards an abyss. Has anything Nathan told me since he returned been true? Anger bubbles in my veins like hot lava. I hate that he's lied to me, but hate myself more because I've been taken in by the lies.

'Alright, thanks. I will. I'd better go,' Nathan says. 'Yeah, she's asleep in the next room. I'll talk to you in a day or two, let you know how it's going.'

I hurry back to the bedroom, creep into bed, zip my sleeping bag up to my chin and pretend to be asleep. The kitchen door clicks open and I catch the faint smell of candle smoke. The brave thing to do would be to confront Nathan and demand answers. I should tell him I know he's been lying to me and insist he take me back to London.

But first I need to think.

He's already threatened to shoot me once. If I call him out and he feels threatened, there's a danger he'll go through with it. He could make me vanish out here and no one would ever find out. I'd be better off going along with him until he leaves me another chance to escape.

Nathan shuffles into the room, his clothes rustling. Then silence. My breath is shallow and rapid. What's he doing? Watching me? Checking I'm asleep?

Time marches to a painfully slow beat in contrast to the rapid thread of my pulse and in that moment, sensing Nathan standing over me, my mind's made up. I have no choice but to play the dutiful girlfriend, pretending nothing's wrong. Let him think I believe his lies. And then I'll wait until he drops his guard and I'll be out of here faster than the beat of my heart.

At some point, he'll have to go out for groceries again, and clearly he doesn't want me with him, drawing attention. That's going to be my best chance. Maybe my only chance. But for it to work, I need him to believe I trust him.

Nathan's camp bed groans as he climbs onto it. He zips himself into his sleeping bag and rolls over with a sigh and a cough.

I listen to every little sound he makes. Every breath, every groan, every rustle. Sounds that set every nerve on fire and spark an urge to find that hunting knife in his rucksack and plunge it into his chest while he's sleeping.

Although, of course, I won't. I could never do anything like that, although as Nathan begins to snore, the air reverberating, it doesn't stop me imagining all the elaborate and inventive ways I could kill him in his sleep, if I wanted.

Chapter 43

PIPPA
February 29, 2024

My plan is simple. I'm going to be the most caring, obedient, loving partner Nathan could ever wish for, until I lull him into thinking I can be trusted and that he has me right where he wants me. At least until a chance presents itself for me to escape. I begin early, rising the next morning while Nathan is still asleep to make him a mug of tea he can enjoy in bed. I tiptoe into the kitchen, grab two mugs from under the counter, and I'm about to heat some water in the kettle on the stove when he appears unexpectedly at the door.

'You're up early,' he says.

I let out a cry of surprise and press my hand to my chest. 'The seagulls woke me,' I lie.

The truth is, I've been awake most of the night, thinking about the one-sided phone conversation I overheard, and worrying about what else Nathan has lied to me about. I even seriously thought about making a run for it in the small hours while Nathan was snoring, but talked myself out of it. It's going to be hard enough trying to find my way back to civilisation when I can see where I'm going, but almost impossible in the inky darkness of the night. It's too dangerous, especially with all the mudflats surrounding the house.

There are dark bags around Nathan's eyes, his hair is sticking up and he's badly in need of a shave. I'm not against a well-groomed stubble, but Nathan's beard is uneven and flecked with grey, which ages him desperately.

'I was going to bring you tea in bed.' I reward him with a bright smile.

'And what have I done to deserve that?' He grins, which is good. He's not suspicious, but why should he be?

'Do I need a reason to bring my wonderful boyfriend breakfast in bed?'

When he comes up behind me and wraps his arms around me, it takes all of my self-control not to squirm away.

After a few moments, hugging me so tightly he almost crushes the breath out of my body, he turns me around, takes me by the shoulders, and stares earnestly into my eyes. 'I want to talk to you about last night...' he says.

My heart flutters. I pull away and turn back to making the tea, distracting myself by carrying the kettle to the stove and lighting the gas with a match. It catches with a whoomph and a crackling hiss.

'I didn't hear anything,' I protest, my voice strained with tension.

'What?'

Shit. He's not talking about the call.

'Nothing. What were you going to say?'

'I was going to apologise for losing my temper. I was out of order.'

'Oh, right. That. It's fine. Forget about it.'

'I meant what I said. It'll never happen again.'

Which is exactly what he said the time before.

'It's okay, we're both tired and stressed out.'

'You forgive me, then?'

'Of course.'

'Friends again?'

He pulls me into another suffocating hug, his touch like being kissed by a decomposing corpse, but I sink into his body and let out a contented murmur. I deserve an Oscar.

'I must have been so good in a previous life to deserve someone like you,' he says.

He finally lets me go, leans against the wall and studies me, his sickly gaze prickling my skin.

'No, I'm the lucky one.' It's remarkable how easily the words trip off my tongue. How easy it is to summon a fake smile and make him believe what he wants to believe. As much as it pains me to be so fawning, so false, it's what I have to do.

'Did you give any more thought to what we talked about?' I ask lightly.

'What's that?'

'About going back to London and talking to a therapist?'

Nathan glowers at me, his mood instantly darkening. 'Not this again, Pippa. I don't need a therapist. Now stop going on about it, would you? Why do you always have to spoil things by nagging all the time?'

'I'm sorry. I didn't mean to nag. I thought we were being friends again?'

Why did I bring that up now? I shouldn't have said anything. He's never going to accept that he needs help. I should have known better, that I'm pushing my luck. Keep smiling. Keep playing nicely. Don't give him any excuse to hit me again.

'Let me make it absolutely clear. We're not going back to London and I don't need help, understood?' He speaks to me like I'm a misbehaving child.

'Okay.' I raise a hand in surrender. 'Forget I said anything.'

He mutters something I don't catch under his breath.

'Why don't we talk about the future? Where do you think we'll go?' I ask, hoping to shift to safer ground.

He gives a slight shake of his head. 'I don't know.'

'But we won't be staying here much longer, will we? A few more days? A week? I'm looking forward to starting our new life and the sooner the better.'

'We'll stay here until it's safe to move on,' Nathan snaps, his nostrils flaring. 'Now stop being so bloody ungrateful. At least we have a roof over our heads. You've done nothing but complain since we arrived. If you'd stop whining about it for a moment, you might actually find you like it here.'

'I do like it,' I say, hurriedly. 'Honestly, it's beautiful. I was just wondering, that's all. I didn't mean to make you cross.'

'We're not going anywhere.'

'But we're not going to stay here forever, are we?'

Nathan scowls, a darkness settling over his features, and I instantly regret my choice of words. All

I meant was that eventually he'd want us to find a place of our own where we could settle down. I need him to buy into the fantasy, to believe that we have a future together and that it's a dream I share.

'We'll stay for as long as I say,' he growls.

As he looms over me like a sparrowhawk about to wrap its kill under its wings, I shrink in fear and immediately hate myself for it. For not standing up to him and for letting him bully me.

'Fine. Whatever.'

'I thought you'd find it romantic. You're always saying we should get away and unplug, but you've done nothing but grumble since the moment we arrived. Stupid me for thinking it was somewhere we could reconnect and fall in love all over again.'

I can't remember saying anything about getting away to unplug. That's only ever something Nathan's suggested in the past, when he thought I was neglecting him. And as for being romantic, he could have at least found somewhere with electricity, clean running water and hot taps. If he'd been serious about reconnecting, he'd have taken me to a five-star hotel with a spa. Not a tumbledown shack with an outside toilet. And then maybe I wouldn't be plotting to leave him.

'Why do we need to fall in love again?' I ask. 'I've never stopped being in love with you.' My words taste as bitter as poison. I reach for his face and place a tender palm on his cheek.

To my surprise, he recoils from my touch.

'Your fingers are freezing.'

I snatch my hand back and pull it into my chest.

'*Do* you still love me?' he asks.

'Of course I do.'

I do still have feelings for him. You can't control your heart, no matter what your head is screaming. But if I can't trust him, how can I love him? Part of the attraction has always been that he's made me feel safe and protected, but in the last couple of weeks, everything's changed. The idea of being scared of him would have been ludicrous a couple of weeks ago, but now I fear living under the same roof, not knowing what he might do next.

'Not enough to marry me,' he says.

'That's not fair.'

He breathes out a hiss of discontent through his nose. 'You've no idea how much you embarrassed me that night. Most women would have been flattered that I'd gone to so much trouble. I bought you roses. I had champagne on ice. And the ring cost me a small fortune.'

But I'm not most women, and he should have known that I don't care about any of those material things, but he thinks that if he throws enough cash at it, he can get whatever he wants. I guess that's where we differ.

'I didn't mean to embarrass you.'

If anyone was embarrassed, it was me. What was he thinking, making a scene like that in a restaurant packed with people on Valentine's night without talking to me about what I wanted first? I could have died when he pulled out that ring and everyone turned to look at us.

'The whole restaurant was staring at me like I was an idiot. It was Valentine's Day, for fuck's sake, Pip. Way to kick a guy in the balls.'

'I said I'm sorry.'

But of course, I'm not. If I could turn back time and Nathan proposed again, I'd do the same in a heartbeat, especially knowing what I know now.

'That's it? You're sorry?'

'What do you want me to say?'

'I want you to be my wife, Pip. I want to grow old with you. I want you to have my babies and for us to never be apart.'

It's laughable that he thinks I'm going to agree to marry him and we're going to ride off happily into the sunset towards our perfect life together. What a joke. First, he vanishes off the face of the earth to do who knows what and with whom, then he drags me away from my home and my family on false pretences, and imprisons me in a house that's barely fit for human habitation. I would never marry him. I don't even want to be with him anymore.

'I want that too,' I say, although my smile falters.

By contrast, Nathan's face lights up like I've told him we've won the lottery. 'Really? That's wonderful.'

And in an instant, his mood switches again. He sweeps me up into his arms, showering my face with kisses, while every muscle in my body stiffens.

'Let's go back to London and make it official,' I suggest, a last-gasp attempt to bring him to his senses.

Nathan freezes. He puts me down and takes a step back, his face contorted into a mixture of puzzlement and disappointment.

'How many times, Pip? We're not going back to London,' he says, shaking his head.

'But we can't stay here if we're going to get married. The house doesn't even belong to us. Let's go home, tell everyone the good news, and start planning the wedding. I've always wanted a big church do. What about you?'

'I don't care about any of that. What's important is being together. We don't need a church or a white dress.'

'Okay, if that's what you want.' The words claw in my throat.

'As long as we have each other, that's all that matters.'

'Absolutely.'

I turn away, fearful the pained expression on my face is going to give me away.

'We should do it soon,' he says. 'What's the point hanging around?'

'Don't I get a ring, at least?' I laugh nervously. I don't want a ring. I don't want anything of Nathan's, but it might buy me some time.

He grins like a moron, then hurries out of the room and returns with the familiar red velvet box he produced at the restaurant on Valentine's night. He pops it open to reveal the diamond solitaire with a glistening rock bigger than the nail on my little finger. It's utterly hideous. Ostentatious beyond belief. I can't wear that. But how can I refuse?

Nathan takes my left hand and slips the ring onto my finger.

'There,' he says, with smug self-satisfaction. 'Now it's official.'

'It's... beautiful,' I croak, staring at it in horror.

He might as well have produced a red-hot branding iron and stamped his name across my arm for all it means to me.

'You like it?'

'I love it.'

This is madness. He's smothering the life out of me. I can't breathe.

'I knew you would, Mrs Pierce.'

The ring burns my finger, the urge to rip it off and throw it in Nathan's face all consuming. Even if I was serious about marrying him, what makes him think I'd take his name? His presumption is breathtaking.

'Did you pick up anything for breakfast?' I ask, desperate to change the subject.

'There's some bread and jam.' Nathan nods at a squashed loaf in a plastic wrapper I hadn't noticed on the shelf over the counter, and a jar of strawberry jam he's put on the windowsill. I can't eat processed bread. Does he have any idea of the chemicals they put in it?

The kettle whistles as it comes to the boil and with a trembling hand I finish making the tea.

'Maybe next time you could see if they have any Greek yoghurt and honey?' I ask.

'I was in a hurry,' Nathan huffs. 'You'll have to make do with bread.'

'It's fine. Honestly. It's only that carbs make me so bloated and I want to look my best for you.'

'Jeez, Pippa. Do you ever stop complaining?'

I bite my tongue to stop myself apologising. 'When do you think you might go shopping again?'

Nathan shrugs. 'I don't know. When we've run out of food.'

'Do we have anything to eat tonight?'

'Bread.'

I stare at him, not sure whether he's being serious or if he's trying to provoke me. 'Is that it?'

'We'll make do.'

'I'm hungry, Nathan. We need some fruit and vegetables. Something healthy. Do you want me to go? Give me some cash and I'll pop into Blakeney and do a proper shop.'

'You're going to row back to the village, are you?'

'I don't mind giving it a go. At least we wouldn't starve.'

Nathan slams his mug on the counter, sloshing tea all over his hand. 'Will you stop criticising everything I do? You can eat bread for one day. It's not going to kill you.'

'Come on, Nathan, be reasonable. I don't mind going. Or I could give you a list.'

'You're not going anywhere. And stop moaning about everything. You want to learn to be a bit more grateful for what you've got.'

'All I'm saying —'

But before I can finish my sentence, Nathan smacks me hard across the face with the back of his hand, sending me floundering across the kitchen. My mug flies out of my hand, across the room, and smashes against the wall while stars blink in my eyes and a sharp dagger of pain radiates through my cheek.

I touch my fingers to my skin and wince, feeling the wetness of blood.

I can't believe he's hit me.

'I don't want to hear another word,' Nathan shouts, waving a finger in my face, the veins on his neck throbbing. 'I'll decide when we need to go shopping. Until then, you'd be better off keeping your mouth shut.'

Chapter 44

JAMES
February 29, 2024

It's blatantly obvious there's no one in the shack, but I rattle the door anyway, more in frustration than hope. A solid padlock clunks against a metal ring and obstinately refuses to budge.

'Hello? Is there anyone in there?' I hammer with my fist, irritated it's taken me so long to get here.

I'd planned to arrive in Blakeney yesterday, but my whole day was thrown upside down by a puncture just north of Norwich. A nail embedded in the shoulder of the front off-side tyre, which I probably picked up at that boatyard. It should have been straightforward to fix. I always carry a spare in the boot, but when I took it out, I discovered the jack and wheel wrench were missing.

It took three hours for a roadside rescue van to arrive. A friendly mechanic fitted the spare, but told me I really ought to head back into Norwich to replace it in case it happened again. All the while, time was ticking.

He pointed me in the direction of the nearest garage, but of course they didn't have the right-sized tyre in stock and by the time they ordered one, fitted it and sent me on my way, it was late. I didn't reach Blakeney until gone six. So I booked myself into a comfortable hotel, more expensive than somewhere I'd normally stay, and was up by six, fuelled by a mug of strong, black coffee and a bucket-load of determination.

The woman who claims to have spotted Pippa and Nathan buying food on the quay remains the most credible sighting we've had since Samantha posted the appeal on Pippa's Instagram page and I'm keen to talk to her as soon as possible. I thought she'd be here first thing, but even though it's now gone eight, the whole harbour area is deserted, including the food shack.

There's nothing I can do but wait.

Two hours later, as I'm finishing my third coffee of the morning and devouring a crumbly, warm croissant from a delightful family-run bakery overlooking the quay, a petite young woman with long, dark hair that cascades down her back, finally arrives at the shack to open up. I'm so engrossed in my phone, checking the news, that I almost miss her.

A counter clatters open and the woman appears, framed through the open hatch, preparing for the day ahead. She's so busy, she doesn't notice when I approach and stand on a raised deck area waiting to catch her attention. She looks harassed. Maybe she overslept and is running late.

When she finally catches sight of me out of the corner of her eye, she doesn't stop, but continues to open plastic food tubs and butter slices of bread.

'Yes, love,' she says, swiping a loose strand of dark hair out of her eyes. 'What can I get you?'

'Shauna?'

She stops buttering, her knife in mid-air and a flicker of concern flitting behind her eyes. 'Who's asking?'

'I'm looking for Pippa Ravenscroft. I think you might have seen her?'

Shauna's eyes narrow as she sizes me up. I'd be suspicious too if a six-foot-four stranger with a beard so thick it covers most of his face approached me asking questions. I attempt a disarming smile, but it seems to do nothing to quell the woman's unease.

'You responded to the appeal on Instagram,' I add for clarity. 'I wondered if you could spare me a couple of minutes?'

'Oh, yeah, right. I'm supposed to be opening up. I should have been open half an hour ago.'

'It'll only take a minute or two.' After wasting the whole day yesterday, I don't want to have to come back later. The trail already feels as if it's going cold. 'I'm Pippa's friend, James. You might have information that could help us find her.'

'I can't tell you much.'

'Anything at all would be useful.'

Shauna lets out a weary sigh. 'Okay, but I can only spare a minute or two.' She sticks the knife into a tub of margarine, peels off a pair of blue surgical gloves and wipes her hands on her apron.

She grabs her coat from a hook at the back of the shack and we sit together on a wooden bench on the quay, overlooking wild, inhospitable mudflats, serenaded by the whoops and whistles of wading birds.

'I wasn't sure if it was her at first,' Shauna says. 'I thought she looked familiar, but she was acting all kind of nervous, keeping her head down and not really looking at me. But I kept sneaking glances at her, and that's when I realised it *was* Pippa. Although she's not like I imagined. She's much shorter in real life.'

'When was this?'

'A couple of days ago. She was with a bloke. Good looking in a kind of rugged way. He did all the talking. He ordered toasted halloumi sandwiches for them both and they sat over there to eat.' She points to a wooden picnic bench at the edge of the quay.

'And this man she was with, what did he look like?'

'Like I said, good looking. Fit. And he had these really dark, soulful eyes that looked deep into you. I thought about asking for a selfie. I'm a huge fan. But Pippa was wearing this kind of pissed-off look, like she didn't want to be noticed. It's weird. She's normally so smiley on Insta, but I don't know, she looked kind of miserable.'

'Did they mention where they were staying, by any chance?'

'Sorry, no.' Shauna zips up her coat. It's a damp, cold and grey morning with a biting wind. 'They both had big rucksacks, though, like they were hiking somewhere. So I don't know, maybe they were camping?'

I can't imagine Pippa sleeping under canvas and having to use communal showers, which is probably why I'd not thought about it before, but if they're staying in a tent, they could be hiding anywhere along the coast and I'm going to struggle to find them. Although, I think it's unlikely. The temperature's barely risen above freezing for the last few days and there's a bitter northerly wind running riot off the sea. Camping at this time of year, in this weather, would be wretched.

'You didn't manage to get a picture of them, then?' It sounds like it could be Pippa and Nathan, but photographic proof would settle any doubt. After all, the woman on the pier in Great Yarmouth was confident she'd seen Pippa, too.

Shauna shakes her head.

'Don't worry. I just need to be certain it was her.'

'It was. One hundred per cent, although she looked different.'

'How?'

'Tired. Her hair was a mess and she wasn't wearing any make-up, and she normally looks so elegant in all her photos and videos. Sorry I can't tell you any more, but I need to get back.' Shauna stands, stamps her feet, and rubs her hands together. 'I hope you find her.'

'Can I give you my number, in case you spot her again?'

Shauna shrugs, but takes my number before hurrying back to the food shack and disappearing inside.

She might be mistaken, of course, like the woman on the pier. It's easy to imagine you've seen someone you recognise from the TV or on social media, and be totally mistaken, but my gut feeling is that Pippa is close. But where? She and Nathan could be hiding out in a thousand different places, and if they are camping, I might never find them.

I still think it's more likely they've hired a cottage or booked a room in a guest house, and there can't be that many of them in a tiny place like Blakeney. So I pull out my phone and open a search engine, looking for hotels, holiday cottages, B&Bs and youth hostels in the area. Anywhere they could have found shelter and a bed. Then it's going to be a matter of putting in the hard miles, going door to door until I find them. After all, in a close-knit village like this, someone must know where I can find them.

Chapter 45

PIPPA
February 29, 2024

Nobody has ever hit me before, let alone a man who claims to love me. A man who moments earlier slipped an enormous diamond engagement ring on my finger and talked about how he couldn't wait to marry me. If I hadn't already made up my mind that it was over between us, this would have been it. There's no coming back from physical violence in a relationship.

I never thought in a million years I'd be that woman, that I'd ever let a man do that to me.

No, I mustn't think like that. I didn't *let* him do it. *He hit me.*

He lost control and he lashed out. He might be battling his own demons, but there's never any excuse. Ever.

It's unforgivable. As if I needed reminding, I need to get far away from him, and when I'm gone, I never want to see Nathan again.

Stunned, I touch my cheek with the tips of my fingers and inspect the smear of blood as vivid as the rage burning deep in my core. How could he do this to me after everything I've done for him? After all those hours I spent searching for him, never giving up hope that I'd find him alive? After giving up my life and my home to be with him?

Nathan stares at me with wild, dark eyes, his laboured breath slowly coming back under control. The urge to hit back, to face up to the bully and deal him a taste of his own medicine, is powerful, but although I'm strong and fit, I'm not as strong as Nathan. He could kill me with his bare hands if he wanted to, so what good will provoking him further do? Revenge will have to wait, but I'm not letting this lie. I'll never forgive him. He'll pay for it, one way or another.

'Oh god, Pippa, are you okay?' he asks, transforming before my eyes from a Hyde-like monster unable to control his temper to a simpering, anxious Jekyll. 'You really shouldn't wind me up like that. Look what you made me do.'

So it's my fault he hit me? My face happened to collide with his fist, did it?

'I didn't sleep too well last night,' I say, my voice shaky. 'I think I'll have a little lie down.'

'Let me help you.'

I don't want Nathan anywhere near me, but he insists on sliding a hand under my arm and walking me to the bedroom, even though the house is so small and the doors so narrow that it would be easier without him. Instead, we have to choreograph our movements, side-stepping and shuffling through the tight spaces as he holds me tightly. Under any other circumstances, it would be comical.

I climb into my sleeping bag and roll onto my side. Nathan sits on the edge of the camp bed and strokes my hair.

'How's your face?'

I stare at the wall and the patch of missing paint that looks like a troll, its face misshapen with spite.

'Maybe we could go for a walk along the beach later, while it's still dry. Would you like that? We could both do with some fresh air,' Nathan says.

'Okay.'

'Are you warm enough?'

'I'm fine.'

'You're shivering.'

'I'm fine.'

I pull my knees up to my chest and bury my frozen hands between my thighs. The sleeping bag at least offers some warmth, but it's so, so cold in the house.

'I'll light a fire. That'll cheer the place up.'

Nathan disappears out of the room, but my relief is short-lived. He's back a few moments later.

'We've gone through all the wood. I'm going to pop out and collect some more. Will you be okay on your own?'

I don't have the energy or the inclination to answer. I just want to be left alone.

'I won't be long. I'll be on the beach if you need me,' he says, as if sensing I need my own space.

A gust of wind sucks through the house as he opens the front door, and then he's gone. The house falls silent and I breathe in deeply through my nose and let it out slowly through my mouth.

I will not let Nathan define my story. I can get through this. I'm stronger than that. It's what I'd tell any of my followers if they were in the same situation. That I need to take one step at a time. That I'm a fighter. A survivor. And this is my moment to prove it. All I need to do is wait for Nathan to make a wrong step and I'll be gone.

I sit up too quickly, my head spinning, a throbbing pain behind my forehead now accompanying the ache around my cheek. What if I could find the phone Nathan was using last night? I could call for help. Sam would drop everything to come and get me, I'm sure, especially when I tell her what he's done. It turns out she was right about him all along. He is an arrogant prick.

I listen for Nathan but can't hear him, the wind whistling around the window frames drowning out everything apart from the crash of waves hitting the shore and the occasional seagull's cry. If he's collecting driftwood, he'll be at least ten minutes. Maybe longer, if I'm lucky.

The obvious place to look is in his rucksack. I doubt he's carrying the phone with him. At least, I hope he isn't. I pull the bag out from under his bed and search the outside pockets first. They're stuffed with socks and underwear. A penknife. A torch. A can of deodorant. A first aid kit and some protein bars. There's a bigger pocket in the top flap, which I unzip and shove my hand inside. I pull out a map. A notepad and pens. A blister pack of paracetamol and another of antihistamines. More socks. More underwear. But no phone.

With my heart beating double time, I open the bag's main compartment. The last time I went poking around, I found a knife and a gun. What else is he hiding from me in there?

I push my hand under a pile of his clothes and it doesn't take long to locate the phone. I pull it out with a triumphant grin, expecting it to be a cheap burner phone Nathan's brought for emergencies, but it's his iPhone. The one he always carries with him. Similar to mine, but with a less capable camera. The handset I thought he'd left at home when he said we couldn't bring our mobiles in case they were used to track us. More lies.

I power it on, but it seems to take forever to boot up. I peer out of the bedroom window, but the view is so restricted, I can't see Nathan. Only a strip of beach and the grey sea stretching out to an equally grey horizon.

When the phone's facial recognition software fails to recognise me, it prompts me to enter a passcode instead. I used to know it when Nathan and I didn't keep secrets from each other, but my head's spinning so fast I can't think of it now. Not an anniversary or his date of birth. Both are too obvious for Nathan. It was a random number. A pattern on the keyboard, I think.

Possibly the numbers around the outside of the keyboard?

1-3-9-7?

That was it. I'm sure of it.

My hand trembles as I punch in the sequence, but the phone vibrates with an error message and prompts me to try again.

This time I enter the sequence more carefully. It's still wrong.

How many attempts do I get before it locks me out? Three? Five? Ten?

Maybe it was the numbers on the keyboard going in an anticlockwise direction.

I try 1-7-9-3.

Nope.

What if Nathan's changed the code? I wouldn't put it past him, especially if he thought there was a danger I might find the phone. He'd want to make sure I couldn't call for help.

It looks like I'll have to go with the nuclear option. Even locked out, it'll allow me to make an emergency call. But before I can dial 999, the front door crashes open and another gust of wind chases into the house.

Nathan's back already.

Fuck.

I don't even have time to power the phone down before shoving it back into his rucksack, pushing it down deep. As I pull my hand out, it brushes against a heavy, metallic lump.

Nathan's gun.

The gun he promised he was going to throw in the river. I tease it out, unwrap it from the scrap of cloth, and stare at it in disbelief. It's heavy, cold and solid. Like death. I coil my finger through the trigger and grip it one-handed with a mixture of horror and excitement.

The thud of wood being dropped on the floor in the dining room carries through the house.

'Pippa?' Nathan calls.

In a panic, I slide the gun under my sleeping bag.

'How are you feel —' He appears in the doorway, his coat covered in crumbs of dead wood and thorns. His mouth drops open in surprise when he spots his open rucksack between my knees. 'What are you doing?'

'Nothing.'

He glares at me with the solemnity of a hanging judge.

'I thought I warned you about going through my things,' he says in a poisonous tone. He snatches the bag and shoves me onto my bed.

'I was looking for some painkillers. My head's killing me. It was quite a whack you gave me.' I tilt my head to show him the cut under the tender bruise that's swelling over my cheekbone.

A veil of guilt falls over his face, and he looks away, ashamed.

'I brought some paracetamol,' he says, pulling out a blister pack of pills and tossing them to me. 'That will have to do.'

I pop out two tablets and swallow them dry.

'Now you're up, why don't you come and sit with me while I light the fire?' He kicks his rucksack back under the bed and offers me his hand. 'It'll soon warm up.'

I'm torn. The last thing I want is to be in the same room as Nathan, but I'm frozen to the bone, the tips of my fingers, toes and the end of my nose numb. And anyway, until I can lay my hands on that phone again or find a way to escape this house, I still have to convince Nathan I'm compliant.

In the dining room, he pulls out a chair for me and then hunches down by the hearth to light a fire using dried seaweed and driftwood shavings since we don't have any newspaper left.

As it catches, a pall of black smoke billows and rises, rushing to escape up the chimney. If only it was that easy for me to escape. Nathan piles thick pieces of bleached, twisted driftwood onto the flames and soon has a raging fire burning. Slowly, the room warms up.

Nathan sits at my feet, stroking my calf while we stare into the flames, sitting in a tense, uncomfortable silence. If anyone happened to be looking in from outside, I'm sure we'd appear to be the perfect couple, but looks can be so deceptive.

I have to make Nathan believe I'm the model girlfriend. That he can trust me and that I still love him, although the thought of it twists in my stomach like an engorged tapeworm.

'I didn't mean to embarrass you at the restaurant.'

'I know.' Nathan chuckles. 'It's funny, really. Did you see the look on that waiter's face when he brought the roses and champagne? The poor guy didn't know what to do.'

'I was an idiot to turn you down.'

'Never mind. It turned out okay in the end. When do you fancy doing it?'

'What? Getting married?'

How about the first of never?

'There's bound to be some paperwork that needs sorting, and I need to find a register office, obviously, but I'm sure it can all be sorted fairly quickly. I don't see any reason to wait, do you?'

My throat tightens. I can't swallow. 'Why not? It's what we both want.'

Nathan sighs with contentment. 'I can't believe it's actually happening, that you're going to be my wife and we're going to start a new life together.'

The fire crackles and spits.

'We can think about starting a family,' he says, his fingers continuing to stroke my calf, seemingly oblivious to the tension in my leg.

'We'll need to find somewhere to live first. We can hardly bring children up here,' I say.

'Yeah, I know. We'll find somewhere, although I'd be happy in a hovel as long as we're together.' He lays his head in my lap and I run my fingers through his hair, contemplating how much pain I could inflict if I plucked out every strand one by one.

'I can't wait to tell Sam. She's going to be so excited.' I can't help myself. Nathan and my sister have never warmed to each other and I know I'm playing with fire bringing up her name.

Nathan jerks his head up. 'She's never liked me.'

'That's not true,' I lie.

'She hates me. She doesn't think I'm good enough for you.'

I've always defended Nathan to Sam. In my eyes, he could do no wrong. But where I saw confidence and charm, which is what I found attractive about him, she could only see arrogance and conceit. I thought he had my best interests at heart and that he'd walk across hot coals to protect me. Who doesn't want a man who'd do that for her? But Sam was right. He's manipulative and controlling. Vain and selfish. I can't believe it's taken all of this to lift the filter from my eyes. I guess I saw what I wanted to see.

'I'd love to call her and let her know the good news.' Will he bite, admit he brought his phone and let me use it to call her?

'It has to be our secret, Pip. We can't tell anyone.'

No, of course not. I'm not even surprised.

'She's my sister. Why can't we tell her?'

Nathan turns around and kneels in front of me. 'You know why.' He shakes his head as if I'm slow.

'She won't tell anyone. I'll swear her to secrecy.'

'No, Pip. It's too risky,' he says, his tone hardening.

'Okay.' Picking another fight probably isn't the best option right now.

'You understand, don't you? They're probably bugging your sister's phone anyway, and even if you made it a quick call, they'd be able to trace it and then they'd be swarming all over us. We'd stand no chance.'

'Yeah, it's okay. I get it.'

He's still hanging onto the fantasy that we're being hunted and our phones bugged, when we both know it's not true. Or maybe Nathan does still believe it. Maybe he's so traumatised that he can't see the truth.

Nathan takes my hands and wraps them in his own. 'I know it's hard, but we don't want to jeopardise everything, do we?'

'Absolutely not.' I have one more card to play to convince him of my loyalty and obedience, to give myself a chance to escape, but it's a high-risk strategy. 'Listen, I was thinking that maybe we could grab an early night tonight? I know you wanted to.'

'Seriously?' Nathan's eyes glisten with hope and desire.

'I suppose it's one way to keep warm.'

'If you're cold, we could always go to bed now.'

'No, let's wait. I want to freshen up first. Make myself nice for you.'

'Sure.' He stands and claps his hands together.

'What would make it special is if we could have a romantic meal first. Maybe even a glass of wine to put us in the mood?'

'We don't have any wine.' Nathan turns away to tend the fire, poking it with a spindly, warped and twisted branch.

'If you let me have some cash, I'll pop into Blakeney and pick up a bottle and some groceries.'

Nathan tosses the branch onto the fire and spins around.

'Do you think I'm stupid?' he spits.

'What do you mean? I don't mind going shopping.'

'I'm not letting you out of my sight, let alone on some spurious shopping trip on your own.'

'But we can't live on bread.'

'Back to the bread again. The same record playing over and over. Do you know how boring you're beginning to sound?' He leans over me and puts his face so close to mine, I can see the flecks of amber in his pupils. 'For someone so skinny,' he pokes me in the ribs, 'you bang on about food an awful lot.'

'Alright, forget it. I thought I'd cook us a nice meal to enjoy together, but if you're not bothered...'

'Don't you dare take that tone with me.'

'I'm trying to make the best of a bad situation, Nathan.'

'Here we go again. Always moaning. Always putting the blame on me. Yes, the house is a bit cold. Yes, the toilet's outside. Yes, we're scrimping on food for the time being. But it's not going to kill you. You really are a bit of a princess, aren't you?'

I jump up, shoving Nathan towards the fire. I've had enough of being spoken to like that. 'Fuck you,' I mutter under my breath.

'What did you say?' A vein in his neck pulses.

'Fuck. You!' I yell in his face.

I shouldn't have let him get under my skin, but I'm at the end of my rope. I can't do this anymore. I can't keep up the pretence and let him keep battering me down.

Nathan glares at me for a second or two, his eyes wild, roving over my face.

Why didn't I think to hide Nathan's gun down the back of my jeans? I'd love to see his face as I pulled it out and aimed it at his head. That would have evened up the score.

I don't even see his hand move. It's nothing more than a blur as he snatches a handful of my hair and forces my head down, bending me double.

'Ow, you're hurting me!'

'You need to watch your mouth, you ungrateful bitch,' he screams.

And then he slams my head on the table. Over and over and over again, until my vision blurs and my legs give way under my body.

Chapter 46

JAMES
February 29, 2024

The hotel bed is so soft, it's like collapsing into a cloud. I heel off my boots and wedge a firm pillow under my head, fighting the desire to close my eyes and drift off for a few minutes. I've been on my feet all day, calling at every hotel, B&B, guesthouse and hostel in a five-mile radius, but no one's seen Pippa. I'm beginning to wonder if the woman in the food shack was wrong and Pippa's not in Blakeney after all. It's possible I've been chasing my tail all day.

I promised to keep Samantha updated about progress, so tease my phone out of my pocket. I was hoping to have some positive news before I called.

'Have you found her?' she asks breathlessly.

'I've tried everywhere. Nothing.' Outside the window, storm clouds gather. I run a hand over my eyes and through my beard. My mouth's parched, my energy spent. I let out a long sigh. 'I'm doing my best, but I think they might have moved on.'

'Where?'

'If I knew that, I'd be halfway back to London with her by now.'

'They can't just disappear.'

'I take it there's nothing new your end?'

'Lots of messages of concern, but Blakeney's still the most credible sighting.' She lets a beat of silence hang for a moment, then says softly, 'You have to find her.'

'I will.'

'Promise me? I can't bear the thought of her with that man. What he might do to her.'

'I'm doing my best, but you know at some point, if we don't find her, we're going to have to admit defeat and call the police. They need me back at the gym.'

'Pippa needs you.'

A splatter of rain scratches at the window like pebbles being dropped on a metal tray.

'I have other commitments, Samantha. Kids who rely on me. When I don't show, they think it's because I don't care.'

'James, please,' she pleads. 'I'm terrified something's going to happen to her if we don't find her soon. It's been three days now. Have you tried the pubs? They're always a good source of information.'

'Yes, of course I have.' Does she think I'm stupid?

'What about cafes? Restaurants?'

'I'm going to go now, Samantha. I'll call you as soon as I hear anything.'

I hang up and squeeze the bridge of my nose.

Is this really the best use of my time? I should be back in London where I'm needed, where I'm making a difference. I can't help but feel that I've been drawn into something that really isn't any of my business. Of course, I'm worried about Pippa, but she's a grown woman and what she decides to do with her life is nothing to do with me. Nathan's lied to her. He's misled and deceived her in an elaborate fantasy that he's concocted with his brother, but it's not as if he's abducted her. She left of her own free will. The way Nathan's behaved is contemptible, but Pippa's not a child. Eventually, she'll work it out for herself. After all, the truth always comes out in the end. And she can decide whether or not to walk away.

I understand Samantha's concerns, but there's a limit to what I can do. It's not my job or my place to rescue Pippa from her idiot boyfriend. Maybe if Samantha was that concerned she should be here, knocking on doors instead of giving me grief from her Hampstead mansion, talking to me like I'm her personal private detective.

I've done what I can. More than could be expected. Tomorrow, I'll head back. If I leave early, I can be in London first thing. At a push, I might even make it back in time for the kids' morning run. I can't keep relying on Clayton to cover for me. It's not fair to anyone. And it's only a matter of time before questions are asked about what I'm doing chasing shadows in Norfolk.

My eyes flutter closed and the heavy blanket of sleep descends over my body, coaxed by the beat of the rain battering the window. Just a quick nap to restore my batteries and then I'll grab something to eat.

I've no idea how long I've been asleep when my phone rings on my chest and jerks me awake.

'James? It's Shauna.'

My mind, groggy with sleep, struggles to connect the dots. Shauna?

'From Harbour Bites. You talked to me earlier about Pippa?'

'Yeah, hey. How are you?'

'Sorry it's so late, but I've only just seen the text.'

She sounds a little drunk, her words slurring into each other.

'What text?'

'From my friend, Ange.'

I sit up. It's dark outside, but the light from the bedside lamp reflecting in the window makes it almost impossible to see out. 'Is this about Pippa?'

'Yeah, Ange reckons she's seen her, too.'

Suddenly, I'm wide awake. 'Where?'

'The thing is, Ange takes her dog for a walk along the beach every day. She's had him for thirteen years, which is a pretty long time for a dog, don't you think? He's only a little terrier. Terry the terrier, she calls him, which I think is pretty lame.'

'Shauna, listen to me. Has your friend seen Pippa or not?'

'That's what I'm trying to tell you, but you keep interrupting.'

'I'm sorry. Go on.'

'Anyway, Ange takes Terry for a walk twice a day, every day, along the beach. They walk for miles but Ange says it's the one thing that keeps her sane. She goes come rain or shine. Never misses a day.'

I sigh to myself, but let her ramble on. Hopefully, she'll get to the point sooner or later.

'The thing is, she texted me earlier to say she was out walking past the old house by the Marrams —'

'The Marrams? What's that?'

'I don't know. It's just what we call that area. It's on the other side of the river, by the sea.'

'That's where she saw Pippa?'

'She thinks she might be staying at that house. There was a bloke there with her. Sounds like the same bloke I saw her with at the Bites.'

'What house? A house on the beach?' I scramble around by the side of the bed for a pad of paper and pen.

'Yeah, that's it. It's usually empty, especially at this time of year, but Ange says there was smoke coming out of the chimney, so she went to take a look. That's when she saw her. She's a massive fan like me, but wasn't sure if it was her at first. She only came out of the house for like a minute to use the loo, and went back inside again, so she couldn't be certain. But I said I expect it was her because I'd seen her too, at the shack. And then I remembered you were looking for her, so I thought I'd better let you know.'

I fish around the floor for my boots while Shauna's talking, my excitement mounting. It's the first sighting of Pippa since she was seen at the food shack on the quay two days ago.

'When was this?'

'This afternoon.'

'That's brilliant. And this house on the beach, it's easy to find, is it?'

'You can't miss it. Everyone around here knows it.'

I dump the call and navigate to a mapping app on my phone, switching to satellite mode and zooming in on Blakeney, looking for this abandoned house where Pippa is supposedly staying. It doesn't take long to find it.

The Old Lifeboat House.

It seems to be a holiday home and it's exactly how Shauna described it, perched on the flats on the other side of the river, isolated between the village and the sea on an arm of land that creates a natural harbour. It looks like a giant tractor without wheels, clad in sky-blue corrugated iron, with white windows and trim. It even has an original wooden ramp that I guess was used for launching the lifeboats. It's the perfect bolt-hole for Nathan and Pippa. It's no wonder I couldn't find them.

I grab my coat from the back of a chair and shoot out of the door.

Maybe today won't be a wasted day after all.

Chapter 47

PIPPA
February 29, 2024

It's taking Nathan longer than usual to fall asleep. He keeps tossing and turning, the camp bed creaking, while I remain curled up with my back to him. My stomach's rumbling and my body is hollow with hunger. All I've eaten today are four slices of bread with jam. On top of that, my head is still throbbing, the ache only partially dulled by the painkillers I swallowed earlier. It feels like the inside of a church bell after a morning of ringing practice, and I have a tender, egg-shaped lump on my forehead where Nathan slammed it against the table in his rage.

I understand now, clearer than ever, that if I don't get out of this house, Nathan's going to kill me. He's lost his mind, he's out of control and I don't have the physical strength to stop him hurting me. I wasn't going to risk sneaking out while he was sleeping, the danger's too great, but he's left me no choice. I can't spend another day under the same roof as him. I'm going home. And I'm leaving tonight.

It's not an ideal night for it. The weather is conspiring against me, but what's a small storm when your life's on the line? As if to make the point, a fresh splatter of wind and rain attacks the windowpane, rattling it in its frame, but it's so dark outside, the skies heavy with thick cloud, I can hardly even make out the peeling paint on the walls a few inches in front of my face, let alone the rain on the window.

Time ticks painfully slowly, every grunt, moan and snuffle coming from the other side of the room making me hate Nathan more and more. But each time I summon the courage to make my move, he rolls over, muttering to himself in his sleep, and I catch my breath. I have one shot at escaping, but if he catches me, I can't bear to think about what he'll do.

I have no idea what time it is when I finally pluck up the courage to slip out of my sleeping bag. Over the last few days, without my phone or a watch, I've become reliant on the rise and fall of the sun to keep track of time. I guess it's gone midnight. Probably more like one in the morning, which means that if I leave now, I should get a five or six hour head start before Nathan wakes and discovers I've gone.

I've practised opening and closing my sleeping bag zip as noiselessly as possible, but no matter how slowly I move my fingers, it's as loud as a chainsaw in the silence of the bedroom.

Nathan continues to purr softly in his sleep as I slip my legs out of bed and onto the cold, hard floor. The flimsy camp bed creaks as I stand and I wince. My pulse chases around my veins like it's being pursued by the devil. Who knew getting out of bed could be so noisy?

Nathan's breath catches. He stops breathing for a second. Then he snorts, smacks his lips, and begins to snore again.

I snake my hand under the fleece jacket I've been using for a pillow and wrap my fingers around Nathan's gun. It fits surprisingly well in my palm. It's heavy, but not unwieldy. Quite the opposite. It's solid and dependable. Reassuring.

Nathan rolls over. I can't believe how restless he is tonight. Maybe it's his conscience catching up with him and he's reliving the moment he smashed my head repeatedly against the table.

Bastard.

I raise the gun and aim towards the vague lump I can just about make out on his side of the room. It would be so easy. A gentle squeeze of the trigger. A flash of light. A deafening explosion. And I'd be free.

What am I thinking? I can't shoot him. I shudder at the thought of taking a life. All that blood. I might hate him, but I could never bring myself to kill him, no matter what he's done. I can't believe the thought even entered my head. The gun's for insurance. I've no intention of using it.

I lower it, slip it into the waistband of my jeans and sweep my hand across the floor, feeling for my shoes, then shuffle towards the door with them in one hand, somehow managing to avoid bumping into the bed with my knees.

With the care of a brain surgeon, I ease open the door. I'm about to step into the hall, taking my first steps to freedom, when the weight of the darkness hits me. It's so black, so utterly disorientating, I might as well be blind. I can't see a thing. I can hear the crash of waves on the beach beneath the roar of the wind battering the house and the clatter of rain against the windows. I can smell stale woodsmoke and I can taste the fibrous spores of mould growing in the dark corners. But I can't see my own hands in front of my face. Or my feet. Or the floor. I tiptoe in what I think is roughly the direction of the front door, relying on memory, until my fingers brush the solidity of a wall where I expected there to be only air.

How the hell am I going to make it to the rowing boat and safely back to Blakeney if I can't see? It's far too dangerous. Too easy to take a wrong step and I could end up sinking into sucking mud or be swept out to sea.

I need a torch. There was one in Nathan's rucksack, but I'd rather not risk rummaging around under his bed while he's asleep. He's bound to hear me.

But what choice do I have? I can't operate blind.

With a silent sigh, I lay my shoes down and head back into the bedroom with delicate shuffling steps, running my hand along my bed as a guide.

For the first time in my life, I'm grateful for Nathan's snoring. I crouch down and flail blindly until I find his bag, haul it out from under his bed and search through the pockets. The torch is a penlight, only about as wide as my little finger, but it sits perfectly in the front pocket of my jeans.

I don't bother pushing the rucksack back under the bed. What's the point? As soon as Nathan wakes up, he's bound to discover I'm gone anyway.

Outside, the wind and rain hits me with a full frontal assault, my coat and hair flapping wildly. I do my best to wedge the front door closed with the rocks we found on the beach, but in such strong winds, it's almost impossible and I'm forced to leave it partially open, letting in chill gusts which I can only pray don't wake Nathan.

I couldn't have picked a worse night. The wind is so strong it almost lifts me clean off my feet. Hardly ideal conditions to take a boat onto the river, but my options are limited. The only alternative is a long hike along the beach, but without a map and with so many perilous mudflats to negotiate, it could be just as dangerous, and much slower than taking the boat.

With my hair whipping into my eyes, I flick on the torch and point the pathetically weak beam towards the path that leads to the jetty. It looks different in the dark, the torch picking out clumps of grass and tangled bushes I hadn't even noticed in the daylight. Fortunately, the path is unmistakable, meandering through the vegetation and winding away from the house.

Ignoring the bitter cut of the freezing, salty air, I zip my coat up to my chin, put my head down and march off, stumbling over the uneven pebbles where the beach meets the land. I keep my eyes ahead and force myself on with a single-minded determination, picturing Nathan appearing in the doorway and hunting me down.

I push the thought away. There's only one thing I need to worry about and that's reaching that boat. Several times, I stumble, almost turning my ankle. If I sprain an ankle out here, I'll never make it. And then what?

When the jetty eventually appears ahead, my heart soars. Even making it this far feels like a triumph.

The boat's pointing downstream and tied to the jetty by a thick rope. Although the water's moving fast, rushing in on what looks like an incoming tide, the boat remains rigidly fixed in place. When I peer over the edge of the jetty, it becomes obvious why. The boat has sunk deep into a bank of thick mud. A wave of panic hits me like a tidal wave. If I can't float the boat, I'm stuck here. Or I'll have to attempt to hike out after all.

The light of the torch catches the surface of the muddy water being pushed up the tributary at surprising speed, like someone at the other end has turned on a tap. It's flowing around the hull of the boat, seeping over the mud and swirling around the jetty legs. Eventually, the boat is bound to float. But how long will that take? I don't have all night.

I cast a nervous glance back towards the house, fully expecting Nathan to be running towards me in a furious rage. But the path is deserted and I can't even see the house, hidden in the dark behind a gentle rise.

I'm going to take a chance. The water's flowing steadily and the mud bank rapidly disappearing. I tug at the mooring rope, which comes undone with a sharp tug, toss it into the boat and climb aboard, gripping the torch between my teeth.

Remembering how Nathan rowed backwards, I sit in the bow on the hard, wooden seat, lift the oars and rest them on my lap. If I had one superpower right now, it would be to speed up time, but for the moment the boat remains firmly stuck in the mud. I glance over the side, but it's worse than watching a kettle boil. The water is inching up the side of the boat so slowly, it hardly seems to be moving at all.

While I wait, I take the time to orientate myself, working out how I'm going to navigate back to the village. First, I need to get back into the main river and take a left. At least the incoming tide should be in my favour. My biggest concern is being swept out to sea, especially as the squall is unabating. The wind whistles through the undergrowth with an eerie howl and the rain soaks through my coat and hair. My hands are already numb and my nose is running.

Finally, the boat lurches to one side, tipping me off balance, before righting itself again. It starts to bob and rock and my spirits rise. It's being lifted out of the mud and at any moment I'm going to be free. I ready myself and clip the oars into the horseshoe-shaped mountings, just as I've seen Nathan do.

At last, I allow myself to believe. Nathan can't stop me now.

I cast a tentative glance back along the track. At first, I think my imagination must be taunting me as I squint into the darkness towards a dancing prick of white light. A super-bright firefly jiggling its way towards me. What is it? An optical illusion? A reflection?

Water laps against the wooden hull, the gentle rocking becoming stronger.

And then I make out a figure, racing towards me, running to the jetty, and too late I understand that the prick of light is coming from the torch on Nathan's phone, held out in front of him as he scrambles down the slippery track.

'Pippa!' His scream pierces the howling wind and turns my blood to ice. 'What are you doing? Where the hell do you think you're going?'

Chapter 48

JAMES
February 29, 2024

I've hit a problem. The house where Pippa and Nathan are holed up is on the other side of the River Glaven. I need a boat, but where am I going to find one at almost midnight?

There is no shortage of boats to hire if you want to go seal-watching, according to a quick search on my phone, but how am I going to find someone to take me in the middle of the night? And if I leave it until the morning, it might be too late. The chances of raising anyone at this time of night are slim, but I have to try.

Most of the numbers go straight to voicemail or direct me to booking websites, but eventually I get lucky and one of the mobile numbers is picked up by a gruff, sleepy-sounding man.

'I need a boat. Tonight. Can you help me?'

There's a long pause where I imagine the man's checking his watch or a clock on the wall. He must think I'm insane, but to my amazement, he doesn't hang up.

'Tonight?'

'It's an emergency. I can pay you.'

'This a wind-up?'

'No, I'm deadly serious. I need to find my friend. I'm worried she might be in trouble.'

'What kind of trouble?'

'She's with a guy. It's kind of... complicated. They're staying at the Old Lifeboat House. Do you know it?'

The boatman leaves another long pause, like he's weighing up whether it's going to be worth his while. 'It's going to cost you,' he says.

'I don't care what it costs, but I have to get there as soon as possible.' After all, it's not me who's going to be paying. 'Can you help?'

'Weather's not looking great.'

'Yes, I know. And I wouldn't be phoning at this time of night if I thought there was any other way, but she's my friend and I'm really worried she's in danger.'

'Ex-girlfriend, is it?'

'What? No, nothing like that. Can you help me or not?'

'Alright. Meet me at the quay in fifteen minutes,' he says.

Chapter 49

PIPPA
March 1, 2024

Nathan blinks the rain out of his eyes. His hair's matted to his head and in the light of my torch, he looks haunted and pale. He stares at me as if he can't believe what he's seeing, that I would dare to run away.

'I'm done, Nathan. I'm going home.'

'What are you talking about? You're not going anywhere.'

He takes tentative steps along the slippery jetty, its wooden slats wet and slick.

'That's close enough.' I drop one of the oars and hold up my hand.

Nathan winces as if I've stabbed him through the heart, but he doesn't stop. He keeps drawing closer.

'Come back to the house. You'll catch the death of cold out here.'

'No.'

'Pippa, don't be difficult. Look at you, you're drenched.'

'I don't care.'

He reaches out a hand, fingers splayed. It would be so easy to take it, follow him to the house and slip back into the life Nathan wants me to lead. To play the role of the subservient girlfriend. I loved him once. And for all his faults, for everything he's put me through, a part of me still does.

As much as I hate myself for it, I'm still hooked on the dream of a cottage in the Cotswolds with roses growing around the door, surrounded by our children, laughing and playing, the house full of happiness and joy. An idyllic Hallmark movie life where everything is perfect. Where we grow old together, welcome grandchildren into our family, and never want for anything.

But it's an illusion. An intangible aspiration. And I'm nobody's doormat.

My temple throbs with a sudden stab of pain as if my body's reminding me how, only a few hours ago, Nathan physically attacked me. I'm not a victim. Or anyone's punchbag. And I'd rather lead my life alone than in fear and violence.

'Pippa,' he growls. 'I'm not going to tell you again.'

'Get away from me.'

I snatch up an oar and frantically attempt to push the boat away from the jetty. But it's still stuck. Buried too deeply in the clawing mud.

'Why are you being like this?'

'You need help, Nathan. You're not well.'

He glowers at me for a second or two, and I'm convinced he's going to fly into another rage and drag me back to the house by my hair. But instead, he laughs.

'Help? That's a bit rich coming from you, isn't it? The woman who's been hiding behind a social media persona for the last five years because she's too scared to face the real world. And now look at you, running away like a scared little girl because you can't handle the truth.'

'The truth? What truth?'

'I saved you, and this is my thanks?'

'Saved me? What are you talking about? You didn't save me. Whatever you think's going on, it's all in your head.' I tap my temple with my fingers. 'None of it's real. There is no big conspiracy, is there? No one is hunting us. There are no government agents lurking in the shadows, trying to silence us. There was no van. No men in dark suits, carrying guns. There never was a cover-up.'

'How do you know? You weren't there.'

A sudden gust of wind hits the side of the boat, making it lurch, needles of rain stinging my face. Nathan is almost lifted off his feet but catches his balance and stands with his fists clenched at his side.

'You said we had to leave our phones behind.' I nod at the mobile he's clutching. 'You said if we brought them, they'd be able to track us.'

Nathan glances at the phone as if he'd forgotten he was holding it.

'I heard you talking to your brother last night.' I watch his reaction closely, but he's always been able to maintain an impenetrable poker face.

'Don't think so. It must have been your imagination.'

'Nathan! Give me some credit.'

He grins with an evil twinkle in his eye. 'Okay, fine. You got me. I'm sorry.'

'Say it?'

'What?'

'I want to hear you say that everything you've told me is a lie.'

'Pippa —'

'Say it!'

He throws his arms up like a petulant child having a tantrum. 'Fine. It's all been a lie.'

His confession sucks the breath from my lungs as surely as if he'd punched me in the stomach. My whole body deflates and my shoulders slump.

Everything has been a lie.

'Why?' I gasp.

'Don't be so naïve. You know why.'

I shake my head, my mind racing with snippets of memories. The bomb. The chaos. The worry and anxiety of Nathan going missing. The joy when I found him again and the fear when he told me why he'd gone into hiding. Where did the truth end and the lies begin?

'Do I really have to spell it out?' he asks.

I wipe an arm across my face, clearing the rain out of my eyes and a dewdrop from the end of my nose. 'I thought you were having a breakdown.'

He laughs again. 'So you keep saying. Honestly, Pippa. Therapy? You do have some strange ideas.'

'There's nothing wrong with asking for help.'

'I don't need help.'

I shiver, my teeth chattering and my arms and legs jerking involuntarily. I take a sideways glance at the water levels still rising, but not quickly enough.

'So why bring me here? Why tell me a pack of lies? To scare me?'

'I was frightened of losing you, okay?' he snaps. 'You made a fool of me when I asked you to marry me and I was terrified you wanted us to break up. You're all I've ever wanted, Pippa. I couldn't stand the thought of not being with you.'

Am I supposed to be flattered?

'And when that bomb went off, I saw an opportunity to make you proud of me. I don't know,' he lowers his gaze and stares into the water, 'I guess I thought if I could prove to you that I was worthy, you'd change your mind.'

'I *was* proud of you, but what you did that night didn't change how I felt about you. I already loved you.'

'Loved? Past tense?'

Everything is slotting into place, with one big, black hole left to fill in.

'But if you wanted to prove yourself to me, why did you disappear? It doesn't make sense.'

His head snaps up and he fixes me with a hard stare, every muscle in his face taut. 'Because I couldn't do it, okay?'

'Couldn't do what?'

'You should have seen it, Pip. It was awful. There were bodies everywhere. People in pools of their own blood. Clothing, ripped off people's bodies, lying in the road. I saw a severed leg, the foot still in its shoe. One guy who was missing half his face. It was... stomach-churning. And the noise. Everyone was screaming. I couldn't stand it.' Nathan clutches his hands to his ears and screws up his face. 'I still hear it every time I try to sleep.'

I heard it, too. The haunting, unearthly howls that drilled into my brain and have stayed there, dormant, until they return to me when I least expect it, triggered by the most innocuous things. The squawk of a seagull. The screech of car brakes. A baby's hungry cries.

'I really wanted to help,' he continues. 'I wanted to be that guy everyone talks about who saves people's lives but won't accept any praise. But most of all, I wanted you to see what you were missing. But the thing is, Pip... I couldn't do it. I didn't know where to start. It was too... horrific.'

'What are you talking about? You said you were —'

'I said, I couldn't do it. I didn't know where to start. Do you know how shameful that is to admit? But you still don't get it, do you? How could I face you after that and tell you what really happened?'

I had no idea. 'So where did you go?' I ask, shaking my head, trying to process his confession.

He shrugs. 'I sat for a while. I was numb and hated myself for not doing anything. And then the ambulances arrived and there was no need for me anymore. But what was I supposed to tell you? That I was nothing but a failure and a coward?'

I don't know what to say. 'At least you tried.' It's a meaningless platitude, but what else can I tell him? It's the thought that counts? There's no way of denying what happened that night. He wasn't a hero. He did nothing. But it doesn't make him a coward. It makes him human.

'I let people around me die. How could I look you in the eye after that?'

'If you'd been honest with me, it wouldn't have changed anything. I would have understood, but instead you abandoned me and let me think you were dead.'

'I didn't know what else to do. And if I hated myself, how could I expect you to love me? Thank god for Ryan. At least he was there for me. He didn't judge me.'

'You never gave me the chance.' If only Nathan had come back to me and we'd been able to talk, things might have turned out so differently.

'I'm telling you now.'

'It's too late, Nathan.'

'Don't say that.'

'You didn't need to lie to me.' A tear rolls down my cheek.

He shrugs. 'You were never supposed to find out.'

'Whose idea was it? Ryan's? Did he come up with the story about the conspiracy?'

Nathan sucks in his bottom lip and nods. 'I never really thought you'd believe it.'

I snicker. 'Yeah, well, that's me, isn't it? Mug written across my forehead.'

'I'd have done anything to get you back, Pip. I couldn't bear the thought of losing you. Ryan said this was the best way.'

'By lying to me? Are you kidding? You put the fear of god into me and persuaded me to abandon everything. You made me so scared I was even prepared to hide out in a cold, draughty house in the middle of nowhere with you. All because of a lie. Are you out of your mind?'

'Why do you always have to be so negative? I did it for us. So we could be together and start over. You should be grateful.'

'You're insane. There is no *us*. There was no *us* from the moment you lied to me and hit me for the first time,' I hiss.

'You're not still going on about that, are you? I said I'm sorry.'

I glower at him through the mist of rain driving sideways. 'You never used to be like this. This isn't you. What the hell happened?'

'Come back to the house. Let's talk about it. We can fix this,' Nathan says, as if he can wave a magic wand and make everything right.

'It's over. I'm going home.'

'Pippa,' he growls. 'Don't be difficult.'

He lunges for the boat, batting away the oar and reaching for my arm. My terrified scream is lost in the wind.

'Get off me!'

The sleeve of my wet coat slips through his fingers and he loses his grip. We both fall backwards and I land in a puddle of bilge water in the space between the hard bench and the bow of the boat.

Panic sharpens my thoughts and spikes my adrenaline. I can't let him stop me. I won't.

I scramble to sit upright with my free hand snaking into the waistband of my jeans and around the handle of Nathan's gun. I rip it out and aim it at his stunned face, illuminated by the fading beam of the penlight torch.

'Get away from me! Or help me god, I'll blow your brains out.'

Chapter 50

JAMES
March 1, 2024

The skipper checks his boat over with painfully slow and methodical care, examining the fuel and oil levels, and looking for leaks. I wish he'd hurry, but he won't be rushed, checking and double-checking every detail as we're rocked by the wind. Rain runs in thick streams off the wheelhouse roof and splashes onto the deck. He tosses me a life jacket and insists that I wear it while he fusses over the radio and navigation systems and assesses the weather conditions.

'Not the best night to be heading out,' he says.

'I know, but it's an emergency.'

He raises a wild, grey eyebrow from under the peak of his woollen cap.

'Woman trouble, is it?'

'It's not like that.'

'If you say so.'

'How long will it take?' I ask, making a point of checking my watch.

'I'll get you there in no time. Don't worry.'

Finally, he starts the engines, unties the lines and switches on a powerful spotlight mounted on the wheelhouse roof to light our way. He pushes a throttle forwards and we pull away, cruising desperately slowly along the narrow river, flanked on both sides by mudflats and the occasional pleasure craft moored to small wooden jetties.

'Can you go any quicker?'

'Not through here. There's a five-knot speed limit.'

I nod and keep my mouth shut. At least we're moving at last, although the visibility is appalling. A single wiper struggles to keep the wheelhouse window clear as rain batters us head on.

'Who's this friend of yours?' the skipper asks.

I could do without the inquisition, but the man's just trying to make conversation and I have dragged him out in the middle of the night when most sensible people should be tucked up in their beds.

'Her name's Pippa. She's an old friend who's made some bad choices. She's with a guy I don't think has her best interests at heart.'

'Sounds complicated.'

'Yeah, it is.'

'And how's this guy going to take it when you go rushing in there to save her?'

It's a good point. I've not really thought through how Nathan might react when I confront him or even if Pippa's likely to be grateful to see me, especially if Nathan's brainwashed her. 'I'm not sure.'

'Sounds like you've got a thing for this girl.'

My cheeks flush, but hopefully in the darkness of the wheelhouse, he doesn't notice. 'She's a good friend. She deserves better, that's all.'

'Let's hope she sees it like that.'

Eventually, the river meets a wider channel and the skipper swings the wheel hard to the left, navigating around a series of buoys bobbing like headbangers on the surface of the turbulent water.

'Problem is,' he says, 'it won't be high tide for nearly another hour, but I'll get you as close as I can to the beach. Might get your feet a bit wet, though.'

Wet feet are the least of my worries. I stare past the wiper, which screeches every time it swipes across the glass, into the dark, rough water. I've come this far, and if it means saving Pippa from that lunatic boyfriend, it'll be worth getting cold, wet feet.

'Will you wait? I shouldn't be long.'

'You're paying. Just watch out for the mud. Head towards the beach and you'll be fine, but if you stray towards the flats, you'll be in trouble. The mud around here is like sinking sand. It'll drag you down and never let go. A couple of young lads who lost their way died out here a few years ago. Stuck up to their waists and couldn't move. And when the tide came in...' The skipper draws a thumb across his throat and croaks, rolling his eyes into the back of his head.

'Thanks for the warning.'

'There she is. The Old Lifeboat House.' He points through the window to a vague shape in the distance.

He cuts the engines to a dull hum and the rear of the boat drifts sideways. 'It's about as close as I can get you, I'm afraid.'

I take a deep breath and hop over the side, landing in the water up to my waist with a splash. The cold takes my breath away, instantly numbing my feet and legs, while the wind and rain assault my face. I hope Pippa appreciates this.

With my head down against the squalling gusts, I wade towards the beach, helpfully illuminated by the boat's spotlight. All I need to do is keep my head down and follow the light.

The water gets shallower and shallower until I finally burst out onto the soft sand and follow a well-trodden path. Ahead, the building I'm aiming for becomes clearer and I finally recognise its curved, bright blue corrugated roof.

It's hard to believe that Samantha's plan of mobilising Pippa's followers to find her has worked so well. The only question is whether Pippa will be pleased to see me or furious I've tracked her down.

The house is in darkness. I circle it, looking for a door and find it at the top of a set of wooden steps. I run a hand over my beard and pull back my shoulders. If Nathan answers, I want to be ready for him and any trouble he might cause. I lift my fist and bang. Six sharp thuds that would wake the dead.

I count the time in seconds in my head, waiting for the sound of movement inside.

I'm about to knock again when a light comes on.

A lock clicks, the door opens a fraction, and the face of a worried-looking old man stares out at me.

'Hello?'

I blink through the rain running off my forehead, confused.

'I'm looking for Pippa.'

'Who?'

'Pippa Ravenscroft.'

Another voice calls out from inside the house. 'Roger, who is it?'

'A man. I think he's lost.'

Shit.

'She's with a guy. Nathan. Have you seen them?'

The man looks at me blankly. 'I think you have the wrong house.'

Chapter 51

PIPPA
March 1, 2024

The boat wobbles perilously under my feet as I stand. My arm is trembling so violently with the cold, it's almost impossible to keep the gun levelled at Nathan's head, the beam from the torch in my other hand bobbing and weaving over his face and shoulders, lighting him up and then plunging him back into shadow.

He holds up a hand to protect his eyes and frowns. 'Pippa, what are you doing?' He sounds disappointed.

'I'm not afraid to use it.'

I curl my finger around the trigger and apply light pressure. I don't want to shoot Nathan, but I will if I have to. He's not going to stop me leaving, and I'm not going to let him hurt me ever again.

'Go back to the house.'

'Don't be stupid, Pippa. I'm not going to leave you here to drown. Do you even know the way back to the village?'

'I'll work it out.'

'In this weather? Good luck.'

'I mean it, Nathan. Back off. I'm leaving and you're not going to stop me.'

'Don't be ridiculous. Give me your hand.' He reaches towards the boat. 'Come back and we can talk about it.'

'I want you to turn around and walk away.'

He stands up straight, cocks his head and slicks his wet hair off his forehead. 'I don't think so.'

'Last chance.'

'Or what?'

'I'll shoot.'

I lower the gun and angle it towards his legs. Maybe the threat of a bullet in his knees might focus his mind as neither of us really believes I'd shoot to kill him.

'Go on then.'

'I'm serious.'

'Prove it.' He throws his head back and laughs. 'You don't have what it takes. Always so strong and independent until it actually comes to doing something that matters. You're all talk, Pip. But this is the real world. There are no filters or like buttons. This is hard, cold reality. So what are you going to do?'

My finger tightens on the trigger as rage boils in my chest. Even now, as I'm looking down the barrel of a gun pointed right at him, he's belittling me. Poking fun at my expense. I've had enough.

'Do it. Pull the trigger if you think you're woman enough.'

His smirk, that curl of his lips, the crinkle around his eyes, mocking me, says everything. He thinks he's won, that he's still holding all the cards, and I'm nothing but a puppet to be manipulated for his needs.

I think about all the times he's made me doubt myself, when I've deferred to him and let him win. All the times he's lied to me. And he still has the gall to stand there mocking me, trying to bend me to his will. He thinks the woman with the nerve to stand up to him was dead and buried a long time ago. That smirk of his, that evil curl of his lip, isn't just a weapon. It's the final straw.

I squeeze my eyes shut and pull the trigger.

He's pushed me to the brink.

I don't care if I kill him. I'll deal with the consequences later. I just want him out of my life forever.

But instead of an ear-splitting blast, all that happens is a dull click.

I peel open my eyes and stare at Nathan, who's standing on the end of the jetty with his arms folded and his lips quirked in amusement.

I pull the trigger again.

And again.

Another dull click, followed by another. And another.

I scream in frustration. I never even thought to check the gun was loaded. I wouldn't know how. I just assumed...

'You didn't really think I'd be able to lay my hands on a real gun, did you?' Nathan says.

'It's a replica?'

I lower the gun and cast my gaze over it, not sure what to think. Whether he's lying to me again.

'Looks authentic though, doesn't it? But you don't even need a licence for it.'

My throat constricts as I try to swallow a ball of panic.

The gun's useless to me. I drop it and it clatters into the bottom of the boat, vanishing into the darkness.

'Careful! Ryan will kill me if I don't get it back to him in one piece.'

'Fuck you, Nathan!'

'Language, Pippa. Now, are you coming back to the house or do I have to drag you?'

'Stay away from me. Don't touch me.'

I step backwards, but there's nowhere to go, my legs pressing against the gunwale with nothing but mud and the rushing tide beyond it.

Nathan reaches into the pocket of his coat and pulls out the hunting knife. Why didn't I think to grab that instead of the gun? At least I know it's not a replica.

He removes it from its sheath and holds it up. It glistens menacingly in the light of the torch.

'Please, Nathan,' I beg. 'Let me go. I won't tell anyone you're here, if that's what you're worried about.'

'I don't care who knows. Tell all your followers for all it matters. The only thing I care about is that we're together. Forever.'

'I can't,' I whimper.

'You said you loved me. And I love you. We're meant to be together. Let's get married, Pippa.'

'What? Are you out of your mind?'

He scowls. 'Don't talk to me like that.'

I yank the diamond ring off my finger and throw it at him. Remarkably, he plucks it out of the air, catching it in one hand.

'You're crazy. I don't know what happened on that bridge that night, but something in you changed. You've lost your mind.'

He shakes his head, globules of water flying from his hair. 'No, I just realised how much of a fool I'd be if I let you go. Imagine the life we could have. The family we'll create. It's going to be amazing.'

'Never going to happen. I'm sorry, Nathan, but you're deluded. I don't want you and I don't need you. And if you truly loved me, you'd let me go.'

He winces. 'After everything I've done for you? You ungrateful cow.'

'Everything you've done for me? Are you kidding? Everything I've achieved, I've done on my own, while you've been hanging on my coat-tails, jealous of my success.'

'Jealous? Of what, exactly? Of you prostituting yourself on Instagram, pretending you're the patron saint of women with all that sickly motivational crap. Give me a break.'

'Admit it. You hate that I'm more successful than you. That I have hundreds of thousands of followers who are fanatical about what I do, while you can't even pass the basic police entry test.'

'Shut up!'

'It's true, isn't it? I mean, who the hell fails an aptitude test for the police? You'd have to be pretty messed up.'

'I'm warning you.'

'Yeah? What are you going to do? Stab me?'

'Don't test me.'

I suck in a deep breath through my nose.

True strength isn't about never being afraid to act. It's about being afraid and acting anyway.

Without taking my eyes off Nathan, I step over the wooden seat, sit, and pick up the oars. The boat is virtually afloat. With one final effort, I should be able to free it from the mud.

'I'm leaving now,' I say, as calmly as my racing heart will allow. 'Please, don't try to stop me.'

'Don't you dare!'

I dig an oar into the mud and lean on it with all my strength. The boat inches towards the deeper water, and my heart skips.

'Pippa!'

'Goodbye, Nathan.'

His scream is otherworldly, like nothing I've ever heard before. A raw, guttural sound dredged up from a dark, primitive place that echoes across the mudflats and bounces off the emptiness like a wounded animal's cry. Desperation? Or the fear that he's lost control?

He leaps off the end of the jetty with arms flailing, but loses his footing as he launches himself towards me. His upper body overtakes his legs and he lands half on and half off the boat, his face contorted with anguish. The knife flies from his hand and clatters into the hull with the replica gun, lost. It should make us even, but I'm no match for Nathan. He's far stronger than me. I don't stand a chance.

I snap one of the oars out of its mount and swing it with every ounce of strength left in my arms. At the precise moment the oar strikes the side of Nathan's head, another gust of wind catches the hull, rocking the boat on its side.

Nathan yells in pain and slips off, clawing desperately for a grip, but the rain has made everything greasy and wet. He slides feet first into the river, up to his knees, his eyes widening with the shock of falling into the freezing water.

Finally freed from the mud, the boat drifts off, away from the jetty and Nathan, and spins slowly around on the current.

I shove the torch in my mouth and fumble with the oars, trying to fix them back into their mountings and gain some control before I'm beached on the opposite bank.

'Pippa, for god's sake, help me,' Nathan screams.

I shine the torch over my shoulder towards the jetty. Nathan hasn't moved. He's standing where he fell in, although the water is now up to his waist and rising.

I don't understand. How can the water be so high already? The tide isn't rising that quickly.

But then it strikes me. It's not the water rising. It's Nathan sinking. He's landed in the sucking mud and is being dragged down. Even as I watch, horrified, the water reaches his chest.

'Pippa!' he screams with a fearful, crackling panic.

'I'm coming! Hang on!'

I've never rowed in my life and it's not as easy as Nathan made it look. I can't co-ordinate my strokes like he did, the oars dipping into the water either too deeply or not deeply enough and not at all synchronised. All I manage to do is spin the boat around, while strong currents carry me further towards the wider channel where the river runs out to the sea. No matter how frantically I try, the further I drift from Nathan.

I shine the torch towards him, but he's so far away, the weak beam struggles now to illuminate his face, which is about the only part of him still above the water. He's holding his chin up, his arms splashing furiously as if he can doggy-paddle his way out of trouble.

Another gust hits the boat side on, spinning me around and I lose sight of him once more.

If I don't reach him, he's going to drown. And as much as I hate him right now, I don't wish him dead. Not like this. It's a horrible way to go.

With the torch gripped between my teeth and a fresh assault of heavy rain lashing the boat, I snatch up the oars and put every ounce of strength I can muster into fighting the current and the wind.

Every muscle in my arms and chest screams in agony as I battle to gain control of the boat, but it's hopeless. I'm being pulled further and further away.

'Nathan!'

I can't hear him anymore. He's gone deathly quiet.

Oh god.

I search frantically with the torch, pointing it towards the jetty which hangs out over the water, resolute against the cruel weather.

Nathan was standing right in front of it a moment ago. But now I can't see him.

'Where are you?' I yell again.

He has to be here somewhere. Maybe he's managed to swim away. In which case, he'll be in the water. Or climbing up the bank.

I sweep the torch across the surface of the river, scanning for any movement. Then across the mudflats with an intensifying panic.

'Nathan!'

But there's no sign of him.

He's gone.

Trapped by the mud and drowned on the rising tide.

And there was nothing I could do to save him.

Chapter 52

JAMES
March 1, 2024

The only thing worse than the embarrassment of dragging an elderly couple out of their beds in the middle of the night is confessing to the skipper of the boat that I had completely the wrong house.

I don't know how. Shauna was adamant her friend had seen Pippa with Nathan at the property. I guess, like the woman on the pier who was convinced she'd seen Pippa playing on the slot machines, she was mistaken. It shouldn't be a surprise. People make terrible eyewitnesses.

The skipper drags me shivering out of the water and onto the boat. He drapes a blanket around my shoulders and hands me hot tea in a tin mug that he pours from a Thermos flask.

'How did it go? Find her?' he asks.

'Not exactly. Unreliable intel.' It's as much as I can bring myself to admit.

Thankfully, he doesn't demand to know why I've disturbed his night for a pointless trip out in a storm. Instead, he quietly fires up the engines, swings the boat around and points it back towards the village, while I huddle on the floor in the corner of the wheelhouse, trying to keep warm, the vibrations of the old vessel rattling through my bones. At least he's getting paid well. We agreed on double what he'd usually charge for a seal-watching trip because of the short notice and inconvenience.

I'll call Samantha in the morning and tell her I'm coming home. I've wasted too much time already. Neglected my job. The kids at the gym need me more than Pippa. If she's in trouble, she's going to have to help herself. This isn't my problem to solve.

I draw my knees up to my chest and finish the last mouthful of tea, shivering in my wet clothes that cling to my body like a frigid second skin. I need a hot shower before I freeze to death.

But after only a few minutes, and with no warning, the skipper cuts the engines to a gentle idle.

What now?

When I glance up, he's standing on the tips of his toes, leaning over the wheel and peering through the rain-splattered windscreen.

'Did you hear that?' he asks.

'What?' I cock my ear as the boat drifts sideways, caught by the current and the howling wind. 'I can't hear anything.'

'There! You must have heard that?'

The sound is so faint that if he hadn't pointed it out, I'd have thought I imagined it. It could be an animal crying out in alarm or pain. Or someone calling for help. It's hard to be sure. It seems unlikely to be a shout for help out here on the river at this time of night, but it's spooked the skipper, and you'd think he'd be familiar with all the usual sounds around the creek.

I jump up, catch my balance and stare through the glass as the skipper reaches above his head for a handle and angles the spotlight mounted on the roof to sweep the choppy waters and the scrubby mudflats, unsure what we're looking for.

He's tense and alert, his head swinging left and right as he surveys the bleak scene.

He spots it first. A small rowing boat being tossed about on the water by the squall a little way off in the distance. Inside, a solitary figure waves at us.

The skipper throttles the engine and grips the wheel with one hand. As we draw closer, the figure continues to stand and wave, occasionally stumbling as the boat pitches and rolls.

'Pippa?' I gasp.

The skipper flashes me a sideways glance. 'That your friend?'

'Yeah, I think so.'

What the hell is she doing out on the river in this weather? It's lucky we spotted her.

The skipper expertly draws alongside the vessel, cuts the throttle, and runs to the stern. I follow close on his heels and between us, we haul a bedraggled Pippa on board and guide her into the shelter of the wheelhouse.

She collapses in a wet puddle, shaken and dazed, while the skipper rushes off to tie the rowing boat to his craft.

'What are you doing out here?' I ask, dropping my damp blanket over her. She must be frozen.

Her head jolts up and she stares into my face, her expression a picture of confusion.

'James?' she asks, frowning. Her hair's flattened to her head and she looks painfully thin and frail.

'I've been looking for you all over.'

She attempts to scramble to her feet, but her legs buckle. I grab her arm to steady her. 'Nathan!' she shouts, craning over the gunwale.

'Is he out on the water too?' I ask, confused.

She points into the darkness. 'He fell in.'

'Where?' I scan the narrow tributary, looking for a flash of clothing. A body floating in the water.

'By the jetty. He was trapped and the water kept rising.' She's babbling, frantic.

I hold her by the shoulders and force her to look me in the eye. 'I don't understand. Trapped where?'

'In the mud,' she cries. 'He fell in the mud and couldn't get out.' I can't tell whether it's rain or tears on her cheeks.

With the wooden rowing boat secured, the skipper hurries back to the wheelhouse, shooting me a worried look, his words of warning about the dangers of the mud fresh in my mind.

'Don't worry, we'll find him,' I assure her, even though the chances are slim.

The skipper manoeuvres our boat further into the narrow channel, the mud banks coming perilously close to either side. The engine chugs slowly, the vessel bobbing and rolling on the waves.

'I can't get too far up here,' he says, the frustration apparent in his tone. 'Not without getting grounded.'

There's no sign of Nathan anywhere.

Pippa tugs at my arm. 'You have to find him,' she pleads.

The skipper calls the police on his mobile, but any hopes of locating Nathan alive are vanishing fast. Even if by some miracle he's freed himself from the mud, there's no way he could survive the freezing temperatures in the water. Even if he'd dragged himself to the shore, he has next to no chance of surviving.

The skipper grabs my arm and pulls me to one side, out of Pippa's earshot.

'I think we're looking at a body recovery job now,' he says. 'Let's get your friend back onto dry land before she catches hypothermia.'

I nod. I hate to abandon anyone in trouble, but it's highly likely Nathan's beyond saving, and Pippa's wellbeing has to be our priority.

She screams and yells when I tell her we've decided to head back.

'We can't leave him.'

'There's nothing we can do for him. I'm sorry.'

After a few minutes, she calms down and drops to the floor. That's when I notice the ugly bruise above her eye, swollen and purple.

'Did you hit your head?' I ask.

She touches it and winces, but doesn't offer an explanation.

'We need to get you checked over.'

'I just want to go home,' she grumbles.

I sit next to her and put my arm around her shoulders. 'We've been worried about you.'

'How did you find me?'

I explain how Samantha appealed to her followers for help and how Shauna from the food truck on the quay recognised her when she served her a few days ago.

'I knew I was getting close, but I couldn't find you.'

When Pippa tells me about the ramshackle house on the beach with no running water or electricity, my mistake makes sense. I was looking at the wrong house. I hadn't even realised there was another property further along the beach. It was a stupid and costly mistake.

Pippa explains that she ran off in the night when Nathan's mood became increasingly erratic and he'd started to physically abuse her. I guess that explains the bruising.

'He brought a gun,' she whispers, staring into the distance, her eyes glassy. 'I stole it and I was going to shoot him.'

'A gun?' My body stiffens. What was Nathan doing with a gun?

'It wasn't real. It's probably still in the bottom of the boat where I dropped it.'

I make a mental note to retrieve it the moment we get back onto dry land. I'd hate for it to end up in the wrong hands.

'He lied to me,' Pippa says. 'And I trusted him. But none of it was true. There was no conspiracy. How could I have been so stupid?'

'You weren't to know.'

She turns her face to mine. 'You don't sound surprised.'

'Ryan told me everything.'

She nods as if it all makes perfect sense.

'And you came to look for me,' she says. A statement, not a question.

'I promised your sister I'd find you.'

'Thank you.' She reaches up and kisses me on the cheek.

Transcript from the podcast, Fallen Hero.
Pippa Ravenscroft, podcast host

Hello, and welcome to my brand-new podcast, Fallen Hero. My name is Pippa Ravenscroft, and this is my true story.

What you're about to hear over the coming episodes is a story of manipulation and control, lies and deceit, conspiracy theories and betrayal. But most of all, it's a story of survival and overcoming the odds. It's about stepping out of the shadows of fear and control and into the light of self-trust and courage. It's about vulnerability and being able to admit you're scared, but brave enough to take the next step. It's about embracing who you really are, even when the odds are stacked against you.

I thought long and hard about whether I should, or even wanted to, record this series. I wasn't sure I was emotionally ready to reveal the whole unedited, shocking truth or even whether I should change the names of those people involved. But in the end, I decided I owed it to myself, and that if even one person listens and finds their inner strength from what I went through, then it would be worth doing.

If you've been following me on social media for a while, you might think you already know my story. That you know me. But you don't. You only know the persona and the perfect life I wanted you to see and believe. This podcast is about pulling back the veil and giving you an unfiltered, unsanitised insight into the real me.

During this series, you'll hear from a number of people who were directly and indirectly involved in what unfolded earlier this year. You'll hear from members of my own family and some key witnesses who became unwittingly drawn into this crazy story.

The only person you won't hear from is my friend, James. He's too modest to admit it, but if it hadn't been for his determination to find me when I went missing, I might not be here today. James didn't want to take part and it's only right that I respect his wishes. He has, however, allowed me to use his name - and you can decide for yourselves whether he's the real hero of this story or not.

So how did it all start? To answer that, we need to roll back the clock to Valentine's Day. It was the day my boyfriend, Nathan, a fit, healthy, charming fitness fanatic, like me, vanished without a trace. It was the day my life changed forever.

Chapter 53

PIPPA
March 2, 2024

A detective with his shirtsleeves rolled up to his elbows and a tattoo on his right forearm that's too faded to read, pushes the gun and the knife, sealed inside two plastic evidence bags, across the table towards me. He raises an eyebrow, creating deep creases in his forehead. He has one of those monotonous voices that lacks pitch and variation.

'We found these in the bottom of the boat you stole,' he says. A female detective, who looks like she crawled out of bed the wrong side, sits beside him, scowling at me.

At least they're not counter-terrorism officers. Nathan's death is being investigated by the local force in Norfolk and I'm here at the police station in Norwich as a witness, they assured me. Not as any kind of suspect.

I can't look at the weapons. The gun's a potent reminder that I would have shot Nathan if it had been real.

'The gun's a replica.'

'Where did you get it?'

'I found it in Nathan's rucksack.'

'How did it end up in the boat with the hunting knife?'

They've already recovered Nathan's body. It was exactly where I told them they'd find it, his legs embedded in the mud, his lungs filled with water. But it's all they'll tell me for now. I've explained in detail what happened, how Nathan tricked me into coming to Norfolk and how he isolated me and refused to let me leave when I discovered he'd been lying to me.

'I took the gun, but Nathan dropped the knife when he tried to jump onboard.'

The detective asking the questions looks puzzled. 'Did he tell you why he brought the weapons with him? Or what he planned to do with them?'

'No. I guess it was all part of the act to make me believe his lies.'

'That he was on the run?'

I nod.

'You must have been pretty angry with him for everything he'd put you through? For lying to you. For the physical abuse.'

My fingers fly to the bruise on my forehead, which is still tender and has turned an angry shade of purple, and I focus on a spot on the wall behind the detective's head. What is that? A scuff mark? Or maybe it's where the paint's peeled.

'I guess.'

'Enough to want him dead?'

Sam's head jerks up, her pen poised in mid-air. 'Really, detective?' Her tone is so withering, the detective seems to shrink. 'If you have an allegation to make against my client, I suggest you arrest her and read her her rights.'

The detective blows out his cheeks and shakes his head. 'No, no. Just curious, that's all.'

'Let me remind you that Ms Ravenscroft is the victim in this whole sorry story, and she's here in a voluntary capacity. She has been cooperative throughout this interview and has given a full and frank account of the events that led up to Mr Pierce's unfortunate death.'

The detective continues to stare at me, ignoring my sister, but I can see from the sweat on his brow that she's getting under his skin.

'Tell me again how Nathan ended up in the water,' he says, resting one hand on top of the other.

I wish he'd take that gun off the table. I know it's not real, but I didn't know that when I stole it. When I aimed at Nathan and pulled the trigger. What if it had been real? What if it had been loaded? Would I have killed him?

'He fell in when he tried to stop me leaving.'

Sam resumes taking notes on a pad of lined A4 paper.

'He fell in?'

'He slipped on the jetty as he jumped.'

'And how far was the boat from the jetty at the time?'

'A metre. Maybe two.'

'So not far?'

'No.'

'He was a fit, athletic man, wasn't he? I can't imagine a jump of that distance would have caused him any problems.'

I'm about to agree with him, but Samantha holds a hand up. 'Is that a question, detective? My client has already told you that Mr Pierce slipped. It's not her place to answer what Mr Pierce was or wasn't physically capable of.'

The detective grinds his teeth. 'So you're maintaining that Nathan's death was a tragic accident?'

'Yes.'

'Albeit it a fortunate one, given the circumstances?'

'My client isn't here to speculate,' Sam says, causing the detective to sigh. 'Nor is she a suspect, is she?'

'Not at this stage, no.'

'That's right, because the postmortem revealed Mr Pierce died from drowning and he had no marks on his body that would suggest it was anything other than an accident? Am I right?'

I've only seen this side of my sister once before, the last time she rode to my rescue, when I found myself on the wrong side of a police interrogation after the Tower Bridge bombing. As much as I hate to admit it, she's good. I'm glad she's on my side.

'That's correct.'

Sam sits up straight and pops the cap back on her ballpoint pen. 'So, unless you have any further sensible questions, I think we're done here.'

I glance at Sam and back at the detective, uncertain whether I can leave. I'm not under arrest, but does that mean I can go?

'There is just the small matter of the theft of the rowing boat,' the detective says.

'Which was stolen by Mr Pierce,' Sam points out.

'With Ms Ravenscroft as an accessory.'

'Seriously? You want to charge her with that? Try it,' Sam snarls.

'But I was going to say, on this occasion, I don't think it would be in the public interest to prosecute.'

'Good decision. Come on, Pippa, we're leaving.'

Transcript from the podcast, Fallen Hero.
Interview with Ryan Pierce, Nathan's brother

Nathan was a mess and he was acting so weirdly that I thought at first he was drunk. His eyes were glazed and he was mumbling all kinds of stuff I couldn't make sense of, but I took him inside, sat him down, and slowly worked out what had happened.

It was late, but I was up anyway like a lot of people, glued to the news. He told me he'd been on the bridge when the bomb went off and that he and Pippa were lucky not to have been injured.

He was shaking like a leaf, his face white, and I think he might even have been crying, although he wouldn't thank me for telling you that. At first, he didn't want to talk about it, but we sat and had a drink and eventually he opened up.

He told me his first instinct, after making sure Pippa was safe, was to help. It was obvious a lot of people had been injured, but at that point he didn't realise how bad it was. I've heard people say he was just trying to play the hero, but they're wrong. I think he genuinely wanted to do the right thing. Okay, maybe there was a bit of bravado and he wanted to prove himself to Pippa, but there was also this sense he had of doing his duty. It was instinctive. I like to think I'd have done the same if I'd been in his shoes.

He was trained in first aid, but he wasn't prepared for how bad it was. The way he described it was like walking onto a battlefield. There were so many people injured, some really badly, like with arms and legs missing and stuff. The kind of things nobody ever wants to see. It definitely scarred him. I mean, it would, wouldn't it?

It was far worse than anything he could have imagined, and he was paralysed with shock. It's one thing to resuscitate a plastic dummy in a training room in Lambeth, but a whole different ballgame when real people are suffering in front of your eyes, isn't it? It's not uncommon. Lots of people in difficult situations react the same way. I've since done some research into it and found out there's even a medical name for it. They call it Acute Stress Reaction or ASR. It's literally when the body shuts down in the face of extreme stress. He was certainly still traumatised when he turned up at my flat, and definitely not thinking straight.

It's easy to say he should have gone back for Pippa, but he was in a lot of distress, and to be honest, he was embarrassed. There he was, this strapping, fit guy, and he froze. He couldn't help anyone, let alone himself. What you have to understand is that when he proposed and Pippa turned him down, it was a big blow to his ego. Then, when he was presented with this opportunity to redeem himself and to prove his worth to her, he blew it. That's not my words. That's how he said he felt. A spineless coward. He couldn't face her, so he came to me instead.

I tried to persuade him to contact Pippa and let her know he was safe. I knew she'd be worried, but he was absolutely adamant that he didn't want her to know what had happened. Did I do the right thing? I don't know. Probably in retrospect I made the wrong decision, but Nathan's my brother and I thought I was looking out for him.

I've had to deal with some pretty nasty accusations since it all came out in the news, but I don't think I did anything wrong. My only concern at the time was helping Nathan get his head straight. Like I said, he was a total mess. If I'm honest, I didn't really think about what Pippa must have been going through or that she'd be out of her mind with worry, thinking the worst and that Nathan was dead. At least not until she showed up on my doorstep asking awkward questions. I didn't plan on lying to her, but I panicked and it snowballed from there.

I had no idea she'd spot us in the pub. I mean, what are the chances? There must be thousands of pubs in London, but she happened to be in the same one at the same time. You couldn't make it up. I keep thinking how things would have turned out so differently if I'd not dragged Nathan out that night, but he'd been stuck in my flat for days. I thought a couple of pints and a change of scenery would cheer him up. But his head wasn't in it. We couldn't have been there much more than half an hour before Nathan begged me to take him home. He wasn't in the mood.

It was after that when it occurred to me how we could turn the situation around. It was obvious Nathan was missing Pippa terribly, and when she came knocking at my door, I had to think on my feet. We needed to come up with a believable reason why Nathan disappeared after the bombing, and the idea that he'd witnessed some kind of government cover-up just popped into my head. I know it's far-fetched, but what do they say? If you're going to tell a lie, might as well make it a big one.

I didn't really think it would work. I mean, Pippa's not stupid or gullible, but Nathan loved the idea, so we worked on the details and put it into action. I never thought any harm would come of it.

I just wanted Nathan to be happy and for him to find a way back to Pippa.

I thought I was doing a good thing. I'm just sorry that I got it so wrong. I had no idea how fragile Nathan's mental health had become and when I heard what he'd done to Pippa and how badly he treated her, I was genuinely shocked. And yeah, I guess I do feel partly responsible. All I can hope for now is that in time Pippa can forgive me.

Chapter 54

PIPPA
March 20, 2024

It's weird living with my sister again. I've moved in on a semi-permanent basis. At least until I get back on my feet. After Norfolk, I tried returning to my flat in Camden, but there were too many ghosts. I was jumping at every sound. At every voice in the street. Even at my own shadow. Sam wanted me to move in with her from the day she brought me home from Norwich, after the police confirmed they wouldn't be taking any further action against me, but I was reluctant at first. I thought I could pick up my life where I'd left it, but that was never going to happen. Life wasn't the same after Nathan's death.

I gave notice to my landlord, packed up my belongings and loaded them into the back of Sam and Alex's Range Rover without so much as a look back. That flat is a part of my past now and the bad memories it holds have no place in my future.

It's only been a few weeks, but Sam and I haven't been as close in a long time. Not since we were children. Maybe because for the first time, we've made the effort to talk honestly and openly about what happened with Nathan, and more importantly, the past. She was horrified when I finally told her I'd been assaulted by Jago, and disappointed that I'd never felt able to confide in her. But I've never told anyone. Not Sam. Not my parents. Not my friends. It was my dark secret, one I thought would eventually shrivel up and disappear if I kept it hidden away. The only other person who knew was my brother, Daniel.

Although there's going to be an inquest into how Nathan died, his cause of death has been confirmed as drowning. The inquest will inevitably mean dredging everything up and I'll probably have to give evidence in court. I don't want to, but I doubt I'll have any choice. For now, I'm concentrating on rebuilding my life.

I spent a long time going through all the messages from my followers on my social media channels in response to Sam's appeal for help to find me. The outpouring of sympathy from people I've never met was beyond moving. It was humbling. I personally replied to every single one, thanking them for their kindness. It was the least I could do. I'll always be thankful to every one of them, but especially to the young woman in the food shack in Blakeney who recognised me and took the time to let Sam and James know. I'm so incredibly grateful to Shauna for her kindness. Who knows, one day I might even go back and thank her personally, although I can't face returning to the village yet.

It was also an opportunity to revisit all the old content I'd posted under the *PippaRavenscrofthealth* banner. All the videos and inspirational quotes, all the carefully curated and filtered photos, studying the caricature I'd created and didn't recognise. None of it was me. At least, not the real me. It was a mask. A costume I wore, not intending to deceive, but unintentionally as a protective shield. It was an easy decision to delete all those accounts and with a few swipes, the old Pippa Ravenscroft was gone.

It's not that I want to erase history, but it's time for a truer version of me. Although Sam's said she won't be charging me rent and I don't need to work if I don't want to, I've started a job with a charity which works to end domestic violence against women and girls, and I'm thinking about starting a podcast to tell my story. I'm not committed to the idea yet, but

I thought it might be useful to help process everything, and maybe what I've been through might help someone who finds themselves in a similar situation or struggling to cope in a controlling and abusive relationship.

Because that's what it was. I can see it clearly now, like a fog over a beautiful mountain valley has lifted. Nathan was never in love with me. He was too invested in himself and what he wanted. I think he was only interested in marrying me because he feared that otherwise he might lose me.

I didn't go to his funeral. It didn't seem right, and I didn't want to attract attention. It was a time for his family. For the people who really did love him, with all his faults. I mourned him alone, in my own way, and on the day of his funeral I left flowers by the canal, close to where we met on our second date. I never wanted him to die, but if he'd lived, I wonder how free of him I would ever have been.

'Pippa, there's someone here to see you,' Sam calls up the stairs.

I roll off the bed and flatten my hair. I'm not expecting anyone. Most people don't even know I've moved in with my sister. Curious, I step onto the landing and peer over the banister, but whoever's at the door is standing out of view.

I creep down the stairs to find Sam grinning, and Daniel standing sheepishly by the door.

'Hello, Pippa.'

'What are you doing here?'

I glance at Sam, not sure what's going on. She hasn't seen or spoken to Daniel in years. Or if she has, she's not told me. They fell out when it became apparent Daniel's addictions were out of control. First there was the drinking. And then the drugs. She didn't want him anywhere near her kids, which I can understand. So why the sudden change of heart?

'It's okay, I'm clean.'

I've heard that before, although he looks better than when I last saw him. He's shaved, for a start, and the black, bruised rings around his eyes have gone. There's still a lingering smell of tobacco smoke on his clothes and his breath, like he's had a sneaky cigarette before coming inside, but he doesn't appear to be drunk, hungover or high.

'Daniel reached out to me when he heard you'd been in trouble,' Sam says. 'We had a good chat about everything and cleared the air. I promised if he cleaned himself up, he could come and visit.'

'A chat about *everything*?'

Daniel nods, shuffling his feet on the doormat. 'I'm glad you finally told her about... him.'

He still can't bring himself to say Jago's name.

Daniel's kept my secret for all these years and never told a soul. Not even Sam. That's loyalty for you. The kind of devoted allegiance that only blood ties know.

'I'm your sister. You didn't need to keep secrets from me,' Sam says.

She still doesn't understand. I was fifteen. I thought it was my fault for putting myself in a situation where he was able to take advantage. I'm pretty sure Daniel has always blamed himself. He left me alone with Jago, but what happened is no more his fault than it is mine. There was only one person to blame, and I hope he's dead.

'I heard what happened,' Daniel says. 'Are you okay?'

I nod. I'm not fifteen anymore. I don't need protecting. I'm a strong, independent woman. I'm a survivor.

'I've asked Daniel to stay for dinner,' Sam says. 'That okay with you?'

'Sure.'

She turns for the kitchen and the source of mouth-watering cooking aromas, where dishes clatter noisily and Alex is humming along to a song playing on their smart speaker.

I give Daniel a tight smile. I could never have imagined when this madness began that it would end with the three of us sitting down civilly for dinner. Mum and Dad would be shocked. Or maybe proud.

'Great timing, Daniel. I'm about to carve,' Alex hollers from the kitchen.

He's cooking roast pork, even though it's mid-week. Like I said to Sam, he's definitely a keeper, even if he is ridiculously posh.

'I never liked Nathan anyway,' Daniel says, putting an arm around my shoulders and planting a tender kiss on the top of my head. 'He wasn't good enough for you.'

No, he wasn't, but I still miss him. Not the Nathan who lied to me and almost killed me, but the Nathan I used to know. The Nathan who used to train at the gym with me, go with me on long walks in the country, and who loved to regale me with tall tales of his travels abroad, although I suspect now, much of that was made up to impress me. He was never perfect, but what happened to him on that bridge on Valentine's night changed him beyond all recognition. One more victim of the terrorist's bomb.

Daniel breaks away as Alex appears at the door with his hand outstretched, welcoming my brother like they're the best of friends.

My phone buzzes in my back pocket. I hover in the hall to check it while Daniel heads into the kitchen. It's a text message from James.

> **How are things?**

> **Great. We're about to sit down to dinner with Daniel, would you believe?**

James replies with a shocked-face emoji.

I've not seen much of him since we returned to London. He's been busy at the gym and I've been caught up with Sam and moving house. It's a shame. I'd like to thank him properly for everything he did to find me.

My fingers hover over the keypad. Would it be presumptuous to ask if he'd like to go for a drink? I don't want him getting the wrong idea. Reading into it. Twisting my words. I'm not ready for anything like that. Not for a long time yet. I've been burnt once. I'm not jumping straight back into the fire.

> **We should catch up soon**, I type.

> **That would be nice. X**

And that's how we leave it. With a vague promise and our renewed friendship intact.

Chapter 55

JAMES
March 25, 2024

Around twenty kids are here for the early run, a staggering turnout for a Monday morning. Even more surprising, Clayton, who only a few weeks ago was struggling to keep up with the bigger kids, is surging ahead, chin up, arms pumping.

'Good lad, Clayton. Keep going.'

As he approaches the final straight, closing in on the finish line outside the gym, his legs tie up and he's overtaken by two fifteen-year-olds who are barely out of breath, but it doesn't wipe the smile off his face. He grins from ear to ear and collapses on the ground, chest heaving.

'Did you see me?' he asks.

'I did. What a difference a few weeks can make.'

'I've been practising,' he says, swelling with pride. He's a whole different kid from the cocky loner who was picked up by police carrying a cache of heroin, cannabis and Valium a few months ago.

'And more importantly, you never threw in the towel. Well done. Now go and get changed. Don't be late for school.'

Clayton hauls himself up and staggers inside, following the rest of the group, all of them breathing hard, all wearing big smiles.

Carl intercepts me as I shepherd the stragglers towards the changing rooms.

'You've got a visitor.' He jerks a thumb over his shoulder towards the office. 'I'll leave you two to it.'

I put my head around the door, wiping sweat off my face with a towel.

The man in a tailored suit sitting in the worn leather swivel chair at the desk has his hands resting on top of his crossed knee. He glances up and twists his lips into a practised smile, his cold, grey eyes boring into me like lasers.

'How was your run?' he asks, lifting his head back as if to loosen the tightness of his stiff collar.

I check no one is hanging around eavesdropping outside and push the door closed.

'A little chilly.'

George Marley has never visited the gym before, and his presence immediately puts me on guard. He uncrosses his legs and unbuttons his suit jacket, letting it fall open to reveal a crisp, white, immaculately ironed shirt and black silk tie. He could be a city banker or a fund manager. He smells of money, privilege and an Etonian education. Not the sort of visitor we're used to receiving.

'I have good news. I thought you'd like to hear it in person.'

I mop my forehead with the towel and toss it onto a chair in the corner. 'What kind of good news?'

'Your funding for the next three years has been approved.'

I nod, grateful. 'Good.'

'You're doing a terrific job, James. Keep it up.'

He sniffs and looks around the office with a sneer, at the framed black-and-white photos of the heroes who fought in the ring during the gym's heyday. The newspaper cuttings and certificates hanging on the walls. At the piles of paper and the ancient computer with its clunky keyboard and cathode-ray monitor.

'I must say, it certainly looks authentic,' he says.

'Authentic, sir?'

'The boxing club. It looks the part.'

'Gym, sir. We don't call it a boxing club these days.'

'Quite right.'

Aside from the astronomical rent the council charges, it costs a fortune just to heat the place. The building is so draughty and badly insulated that the ancient central heating system, a relic from the last century, struggles, especially in the depths of winter. Without investment, the gym couldn't survive. Although without Marley, we wouldn't exist at all. He was the mastermind behind our creation, and a dozen other community gyms like it across the country.

'Anything new on the horizon I should know about?' he asks, his expression blank. Trying to read his face is like studying a closed book, but that's spies and spooks for you. It's how they're trained. Schooled in giving nothing away.

'Nothing significant, sir. A few murmurings about a new gang muscling into Finsbury Park and ruffling some feathers. Probably nothing to be concerned about at this stage, but I'll keep my ear to the ground.' I wonder how often the daily briefings I send to headquarters are actually read. 'A few of our kids have been approached with *opportunities* and there have been whispers there could be connections to Laheeb al-Haqq, but it's unconfirmed at this stage.'

The arch of Marley's left eyebrow is so subtle it would be easy to miss.

Laheeb al-Haqq, a Shia militant extremist organisation, was proscribed by the UK government seven years ago, and although its reach into Britain has so far been limited, it's been responsible for a number of terror-related attacks in Bahrain and Saudi Arabia and actively promotes violence against both the British and American governments on social media. If there was concrete evidence it had any real influence inside the UK, it would be cause for concern.

It's why MI5 funds us. We're an early warning system, our eyes and ears attuned to what's going on in the dark underbelly of the capital's streets, while trying to prevent vulnerable young people from being radicalised and exploited. Sadly, there's nothing unusual about criminal gangs trying to muscle their way into London's lucrative drugs markets. More often than not, they follow the same approach. Recruit some local kids as mules and dealers, flood the market and expand quickly. It's more a policing issue than a threat to national security, but occasionally the gangs are linked to terrorist groups, and that's where we come in. It's our job to identify those links.

Marley steeples his fingers over his mouth and nods. 'And the girl? That's all gone quiet now, has it?'

So that's the real reason he's here. Why else would he risk getting his expensive suit dirty when he could have picked up the phone to tell me about the funding extension? He's still worried about Pippa.

'I'm confident she knows nothing, sir. It was a misunderstanding.'

'Confident or certain?'

'Certain.'

'How can you be sure?'

'I've spent some time with Ms Ravenscroft. I promise, she has no idea.'

If only Pippa knew the trouble she stirred up in the corridors of MI5 and the counter-terrorism office by being in the wrong place at the wrong time. She became an official person of interest when she first spoke to the police after the bombing, and the investigating officers from counter-terrorism flagged their concerns about her in the confusion of those first few hours after the attack. Although it was known that a *Patriots of the Isles* cell was responsible for the bombing, the manner of the attack suggested the bomber might have had unknown accomplices. Everyone was a suspect, but because Pippa had been caught filming on the bridge, apparently documenting the aftermath of the bombing, and then reported Nathan missing, it was a massive red flag. Could she and Nathan have been working together with the bomber? A decision was taken to put surveillance on Pippa and because of my past relationship with her, I was given the task of finding out what she knew.

I never had any doubts she was entirely innocent, until Nathan reappeared, claiming he'd witnessed some kind of cover-up on the bridge which had forced him into hiding. As dubious as it sounded, it was another red flag, especially because of Xavier Huxley.

Huxley was one of ours. He was on the bridge in a surveillance role when the bomb went off. He was killed outright, but his name never appeared in the official roll of casualties, for obvious reasons. If it had been made public that we'd known about the bomb but failed to stop it going off, it would have been a national scandal. So it was covered up. Xavier Huxley was the sixteenth unnamed victim of the Tower Bridge bombing, but even his own family doesn't know the truth about his death.

We'd known about the bomb plot for a while and had been actively monitoring a *Patriots of the Isles* cell planning the attack. A well-placed source had even given a date and location of when it was going to happen. February the twenty-first, near the Houses of Parliament, a whole week later than the Tower Bridge attack. We knew the identity of the bomber and everything about Jack Reeves. We knew about the van hidden in a lock-up in Lewisham. And we knew there was going to be what we thought was a dummy run on Valentine's night. What we didn't know was that a bomb had already been installed and activated inside the van and that there was no dummy run, which is why we were watching but never attempted to intercept Reeves.

We were spectacularly wrong-footed. It quickly became obvious that our source had deliberately fed us erroneous information about the date of the attack, which we were too readily prepared to accept without any corroborating evidence. It was a monumental intelligence failure, which, if it had been made public, would have been hugely damaging to the organisation's reputation. If Pippa or Nathan had any inkling of the truth and there was any danger they would reveal it, they had to be stopped.

'Do I need to remind you of the seriousness of the situation?' Marley says, picking a fleck of lint off his trouser leg.

'Of course not, but I'm certain Ms Ravenscroft knows nothing. She was deceived by her boyfriend who'd concocted an elaborate story simply to impress her when he thought he was on the verge of losing her. It was the ramblings of a desperate man. Nothing more. Nothing less. She fully accepts there never was any conspiracy, and in fact, she's pretty embarrassed that she was taken in by Nathan Pierce so easily.'

'Okay,' Marley says finally. He stands and buttons up his jacket. 'Continue to monitor her for the time being though, just in case.'

'Of course, sir.'

'Right, carry on. I'll see myself out.' He crosses the room in three easy strides and marches out.

A few seconds later, Carl sticks his head around the door. 'What did he want?'

'They've renewed our funding for another three years.'

'Okay, that's good.' Carl shrugs. 'Marley came all the way down here to tell you that?'

'They're still running around covering their arses, terrified the truth about Tower Bridge is going to leak. He wants me to keep monitoring Pippa.'

Carl grins. I know what he's thinking, but there can't be anything between me and Pippa. It wouldn't be ethical. And imagine if she found out why I reached out to her again after the bombing. She'd never forgive me.

'What are you going to do?' he asks.

'Maybe I'll see if she fancies going out for a drink sometime.'

Acknowledgements

Every author who sets their stories in a contemporary, modern context faces the same dilemma. Do we use real life settings for added realism or imaginary ones for artistic licence?

Both have their merits and their pitfalls. Using real life locations can often be helpful when writing scenes and imagining how the action plays out.

On the other hand, it can also be straitjacketing, restricting the plot in ways which are unhelpful.

My books often have a mix of both for this reason. So while Pippa has a flat in Camden in London and Nathan lives in an apartment in Clapham, their residencies exist solely in my head – well, and yours now!

Obviously, Tower Bridge is real and I've attempted to present that setting as realistically as possible.

The house where Nathan takes Pippa in Norfolk also has a grounding in reality too – but you'll excuse me again for taking some dramatic licence.

It's based on The Watch House in Blakeney, which is owned by The National Trust and maintained by The Blakeney Watch House Trust. In fact, you can even stay there – and although facilities are basic, maybe not as basic or as horrifying as presented in The Night He Disappeared.

If you'd like to find out more, look up a fascinating blog post from Norfolk photographer, Chris Taylor, who filmed his experience staying there recently – and from where I drew much inspiration, so thank you to him.

Also check out the Blakeney Lifeboat Station which makes a brief appearance towards the end of the book and where James mistakenly believes Nathan is holding Pippa. It's a beautiful and stark old building.

As always, a special thanks to my wife and number one supporter, Amanda, for her detailed eye editing the novel for me and her unwavering cheeriness through my grumpy periods when the plot and characters weren't working out right.

It's taken longer than I anticipated to write The Night He Disappeared, but I believe it's all the better for it and has quickly become my favourite of my recent novels.

I hope you enjoyed it to. And if you want to find out more about my thrillers and my writing, please take a look at my website ajwillsauthor.com

If you'd like to keep up to date with all my writing news, please consider joining my weekly newsletter. I'll even send you a free e-book! You can find more details at bit.ly/hislostwife or scan the QR code below.

Or follow me on Facebook - @AuthorAJWills join me on Instagram at @ajwills_author or find me on Goodreads @ A.J.Wills

I look forward to seeing you there,

Adrian.

Also By AJ Wills

The Stranger at the Door
While Gwyneth Kerrison lies in a coma, the victim of a hit-and-run, her husband, Harvey, spends every waking hour at her bedside praying for her swift recovery. That is until his daily routine at the hospital is disrupted by a stranger who claims to be Gwyneth's long-lost mother, Freya.

The Boy in the Woods
Would you lie for your son to save your family? When Sabine witnesses a boy who looks a lot like her son, Leo, attacking a young girl in the woods, she's torn between reporting it to the police and holding her silence. But surely, lightning can't strike twice?

The Phantom Child
Is Karina's young son, Jacob, really missing? Or did he never really exist ?
It was supposed to be much-needed summer break but when her son goes missing and her husband denies they've ever had children, Karina's world slowly starts to fall apart.

The House Guest
Marcella Middleton has set her sights on Carmel Van Der Proust's fabulous life. But Carmel is concealing a gruesome secret from the past and Marcella isn't the only one with a hidden agenda.

The Lottery Winners
Winning the lottery should have been the best thing that ever happened to Callum and Jade, but when they decide to help a desperate stranger they soon find themselves running for their lives.

The Warning

When Megan discovers a text message on a phone hidden in the loft of her new house with a chilling warning about her husband, she's forced to confront some dark truths about their relationship...

The Secrets We Keep

When a young girl vanishes on her way home from school, a suspicious media suspects her parents know more than they're letting on.

Nothing Left To Lose

A letter arrives in a plain white envelope. Inside is a single sheet of paper with a chilling message. Someone knows the secret Abi, and her husband, Henry, are hiding. And now they want them dead.

His Wife's Sister

Mara was only eleven when she went missing from a tent in her parents' garden nineteen years ago. Now she's been found wandering alone and confused in woodland.

She Knows
After Sky finds a lost diary on the beach, she becomes caught up in something far bigger than she could ever have imagined - and accused of a murder she has no memory of committing...

The Intruder
Jez thought he'd finally found happiness when he met Alice. But when Alice goes missing with her young daughter and the police accuse him of their murders, his life is shattered.

Printed in Dunstable, United Kingdom